GRAVEYARD TO HELL

THE GRAVE

Miller is new to the graveya
when the driven and the desperate come out to play. Tonight
Ben Garvald is out of prison. After nine years inside, he's
back in the old neighbourhood. Back to his remarried
ex-wife. Back for revenge.

BROUGHT IN DEAD

Then, after a fatal night out, a girl's body is pulled from an
isolated stretch of river. The last person to see her alive had
enemies on both sides of the fence. Miller wants justice.
But so does her father – with or without the law on his
side.

HELL IS ALWAYS TODAY

And the Rainlover, whose victims are always women.
Always at night when the streets are wet. He could be any
one of a thousand men. Hounded by the public and the
press, Miller needs to find him before he strikes again. It's
time to throw out the rule book in the line of duty.

Also by Jack Higgins

JACK HIGGINS

Graveyard to Hell

THE NICK MILLER TRILOGY

The Graveyard Shift

•

Brought in Dead

•

Hell is Always Today

WITH AN INTRODUCTION BY
MIKE RIPLEY

HarperCollinsPublishers

HarperCollins*Publishers*
1 London Bridge Street, London SE1 9GF

www.harpercollins.co.uk

HarperCollins*Publishers*
1st Floor, Watermarque Building, Ringsend Road
Dublin 4, Ireland

This paperback edition 2022
1

Published in one volume by HarperCollins*Publishers* 2021

First published in Great Britain by John Long Ltd 1965, 1967, 1968

A catalogue record for this book is available from the British Library.

ISBN 978-0-00-848361-6

Typeset in Meridien by
Palimpsest Book Production Ltd, Falkirk, Stirlingshire
Printed and bound in the UK using 100% renewable
electricity at CPI Group (UK) Ltd

MIX
Paper from
responsible sources
FSC www.fsc.org   FSC® C007454

INTRODUCTION

The name Jack Higgins will be eternally associated with the 1975 bestselling novel (and film) *The Eagle Has Landed*. But spectacularly successful as it was, it was anything but an overnight sensation, as Jack Higgins had already earned his spurs as an author guaranteed to provide action-packed, fast-paced thrillers.

Before that famous eagle landed, Jack Higgins had written – under several pen-names – 35 novels, and has written 37 more since then, proving beyond doubt his legendary status as a born story-teller.

His career as a novelist began in 1959 when, as a 29-year-old teacher with a growing family to support, he sold his first book, *Sad Wind from the Sea*, a treasure-hunt adventure set in Macao and China, for the princely advance of £75. He never looked back and regularly produced two books a year, often set in exotic locations, always providing red-blooded – though far from perfect – heroes and suitably nasty villains, with the action always moving at a furious pace. He used the pen-names Martin Fallon, James Graham and Hugh Marlowe, as well as his given name, Harry Patterson. In an early novel (*Cry of the Hunter*) he was suitably self-depreciating when the main character is revealed to be a writer and admits: 'I write thrillers under two different names . . . All they do successfully is pay the bills and keep me in whisky.'

From similar modest beginnings, Jack Higgins' fan base grew inexorably during the 1960s, a golden decade for British authors of adventure thrillers, with novels by Alistair MacLean, Hammond Innes and Desmond Bagley regularly topping the international bestseller lists. Jack Higgins was soon to join their company. As it was also a decade when relatively few readers had travelled abroad unless in the armed forces, adventure stories set in locations such as China, Albania, Tibet, the Greek islands, Greenland, the Bahamas and the Brazilian jungle provided an additional touch of the foreign and dangerously exotic. He also offered a variety of settings, from wartime Egypt, Portugal, Austria and the Channel Islands, to Prohibition America, Mexico in the 1920s, Ireland in the nineteenth century and, treading where few other thriller writers dared to tread, contemporary Northern Ireland with its legacy of sectarian violence.

Higgins' books were populated by a rich cast of colourful characters, some heroes but more often anti-heroes, at least to begin with, who were no strangers to violence and could handle themselves in a rough house, and were skilled at handling weapons, fast boats, aeroplanes and scuba-diving equipment. They may have dabbled in gun-running or smuggling, be washed-up pilots or whiskey-priests, ex-IRA gunmen, former soldiers or sailors down on their luck seeking one last chance of a quick fortune or a last shot at redemption. Whatever their background and their motives, they would come good and do the right thing in the end, usually revealing a rather romantic sensitivity along the way – especially when there was a damsel in distress.

Yet for thriller readers, and cinemagoers, the dominant flavour of the 1960s was the spy story, from the fantastical escapades of James Bond and his many imitators to the more downbeat and cynical accounts of spies and spying as documented by John Le Carré and Len Deighton, and on television by James Mitchell's *Callan*.

Jack Higgins was not slow to recognize the trend, and in 1962 – the year *Dr No* hit the cinemas and *The Ipcress File* the bookshops – he launched the career of the half-English, half-French secret agent Paul Chavasse in *The Testament of Caspar Schultz*. A much-underrated recruit to the Sixties' panoply of fictional spies, Chavasse's first published assignment saw him on the trail of a Nazi war criminal, one of the most popular thriller plotlines, not just then but for many years after.

For whatever reason, Higgins did not extend the fictional life of his secret agent beyond 1969, by which time he had also turned his restless pen to the crime thriller, with a new hero, and his first protagonist to be a serving British policeman – Detective Sergeant Nick Miller.

Not that the three novels in the Nick Miller trilogy, published between 1965 and 1968, were the sole focus of Higgins' creative energy. Far from it, as in the same period he produced seven other novels of secret agents, rogue gunmen and high adventure under his various pen-names, a quite remarkable achievement for an author who had not yet given up 'the day job'. (It was around this time that he ran into a friend he had not seen for a while who greeted Higgins with: 'Are you working – or just doing the books?')

What drew Jack Higgins to the crime novel in the mid-Sixties? Secret agents and tales of high adventure in dangerous foreign parts dominated popular fiction, and he had proved his worth in both those fields. The crime novel was something different to the thriller, often referred to as a 'detective story' or a 'whodunit', where part of the pleasure for the reader was to guess who the murderer was (there was usually a murder) before the fictional detective did. In the thriller, of course, it was not what had happened *before* that propelled the story but what was going to happen *next* – how was the hero going to triumph or, indeed, survive?

Unlike the devil-may-care adventurers who populated

thrillers, policemen were restrained by law and legal procedure as to what they could do when confronted with the villain of the piece. In Britain, the police were not usually armed, although well-publicised criminal gangs of the period certainly were and were not afraid to use violence in robberies or in territorial disputes with rival gangs; plus there was a growing drugs problem.

How did *fictional* British policemen deal with all this? The answer is probably not very well. Those future 'queens of crime' P.D. James and Ruth Rendell were only just starting out and the British crime novel was going through a rather lethargic period, certainly compared to the boom in British thrillers. If anything, American crime novels were now more popular than the domestic product, especially those featuring the resourceful private eye acting independently of the police, a figure notably absent (apart from a very few examples) in British crime-writing.

On television, the British police were depicted with either a warm glow of nostalgia, as in the evergreen *Dixon of Dock Green,* or with stiff-upper-lip reverence for British values of decency and fair play as personified by Commander George Gideon in *Gideon's Way* or Detective Superintendent Lockhart in *No Hiding Place*. True, there was an inclusion of harsh realism in new Sixties' shows such as *Z-Cars* but the violent action, guns and car chases of *The Sweeney* were still a decade away.

If anything, Jack Higgins was ahead of the curve with his Nick Miller trilogy, for here was a hero who could have stepped straight out of the pages of one of his thrillers. All crime novels had to be exciting in some way, if only in the competition between detective and reader to discover 'whodunit'; but Jack Higgins wrote them as *thrillers*, packing them with incident, violence and action that could only be sorted out by a resourceful, supremely confident detective unafraid to follow his hunches.

Not that he neglected the traditional elements of the crime novel in these books. The setting – a modern urban landscape where it seems to rain constantly, with a harsh underbelly of seedy bars and gambling clubs populated by drug addicts and prostitutes – was a world away from the traditional country house murder mystery, but Higgins still played by the rules of the game, and in both *The Graveyard Shift* and *Hell is Always Today* there are fairly laid clues early on as to the identity of the main villain. (And it should be noted that *Hell is Always Today* features a serial killer who predates both the real Yorkshire Ripper and the fictional Hannibal Lecter.)

By contrast, *Brought in Dead*, the second book in the trilogy, is more of an all-action revenge thriller in which the identity of the villain is never really in doubt. The suspense Higgins generates comes from whether Miller can – or should – prevent a private, very personal, vendetta in a gripping shoot-out in the countryside.

Nick Miller may not be a typical British policeman, but he was certainly a typical Jack Higgins hero. At the age of 26 and with a law degree, he is young for a Detective Sergeant, having been, as we would say today, 'fast-tracked' through the recruitment process, and has already collected six official commendations. This naturally causes resentment among his fellow officers who have 'come up through the ranks' and possibly explains why Miller draws so many night ('graveyard') shifts.

Not that this seems to worry Nick Miller unduly, as he is certainly not a man to skulk in the shadows. He drives the latest souped-up Mini-Cooper and, thanks to a family business, not only has financial security but also access to an E-type Jaguar. He has his own fashion sense, favouring Chelsea boots, a hand-stitched dark blue Swedish trenchcoat and a German army style 'rain cap' (well, it was the Sixties); and as an accomplished pianist, he is not afraid to duet with the resident jazz pianist in one of the many nightclubs he has to visit.

Naturally, when it comes to the rough stuff Miller can take care of himself: he has a brown belt in judo and is something of a dab-hand at karate, an almost compulsory skill for the heroes of thriller fiction at the time, notable examples being Adam Hall's Quiller, James Munro's John Craig and Andrew York's 'Eliminator' Jonas Wilde, not forgetting Cathy Gale and Emma Peel from *The Avengers*.

The Nick Miller trilogy is, of course, of its time, but no less interesting for that, depicting a gritty world of dank canals, coal fires, gas lamps, Bobbies on the beat, telephone boxes, Sunday sports papers and stocking-tops. It was a world where the 'officer class' could, and sometimes did, get away with murder and where, lower down the social scale, simply seeking to change a £10 note was regarded as highly suspicious and probably an arrestable offence.

Yet the stories in *Graveyard to Hell* were not written as social commentary – though the author was one of the earliest sociology graduates in the country – they were written as thrillers, and Jack Higgins thrillers at that, which guaranteed rapid, no-frills action and excitement.

Even if they were a departure from the tales of high adventure in exotic foreign lands for which he was already well-known (and which he was to continue writing with great success), all the familiar Jack Higgins trade-marks are present and correct: the underlying romantic tendencies in even the toughest characters, the adoration of 'the old country' of Ireland and the former criminal seeking redemption, personified no better than by 'Gunner' Doyle in *Hell is Always Today*.

If early fans of the Nick Miller books yearned for a longer series, they were to be frustrated. Higgins moved on to write more character-driven – though no less exciting – thrillers such as the highly-rated *A Game for Heroes* and *A Prayer for the Dying* before the gigantic success of *The Eagle Has Landed* and a clutch of bestsellers with Second World War themes: *To Catch a King*, *Storm Warning* and *The Valhalla Exchange*. He also showed that he could strike a topical nerve, controversially so, as with his spy novel *Exocet*, which appeared in 1983 in the wake of the Falklands War.

Apart from global fame and sales of his books now being measured in hundreds of millions, that eagle which landed in 1975 left another legacy in the shape of rogue Irish gunman Liam Devlin, a hugely memorable character. After four novels putting Devlin centre-stage, Higgins created a younger, contemporary version in Sean Dillon and those fans who prefer their heroes to feature in a long-running series of adventures certainly got their wish, with Dillon appearing in more than twenty bestselling novels.

Today, Sean Dillon and Liam Devlin are undoubtedly Jack Higgins' best known characters. Nick Miller may be a new name to many of his readers, despite his inception more than fifty years ago, but if they are fans of Jack Higgins, they will not be disappointed.

MIKE RIPLEY
April 2021

Mike Ripley is the author of Kiss Kiss, Bang Bang, *a history of the British thriller from* Casino Royale *to* The Eagle Has Landed, *which won the 2018 H.R.F. Keating Award for non-fiction.*

CONTENTS

When the times change, all men change with them. So many of both the friends and critics of the police talk as if police constables were not men.

—WITNESS, ROYAL COMMISSION ON POLICE POWERS

To the ordinary soldier, the battle is his own small part of the front.

—GENERAL GRANT

NAME: MILLER Nicholas Charles   NUMBER 982
ADDRESS: 'Four Winds,' Fairview Avenue
DATE OF BIRTH: 27th July, 1939
AGE ON JOINING DEPARTMENT: 21
OCCUPATION ON JOINING DEPARTMENT: Student
EDUCATION: Foundation Scholar at Archbishop Holden's
        Grammar School
    Open Exhibition to London University 1956
    London School of Economics
EDUCATIONAL ATTAINMENT: Bachelor of Law with Second Class
        Honours, University of London, 1959
SERVICE RECORD: Joined Department, 1/2/60
    Passed out District Training centre, 1/5/60
    Certified as passing probationary year satisfactorily, 1/2/61
    Appointed to Central Division, 3/3/61
    Appointed Detective Constable and transferred to 'E' Div. on
        2/1/63 (See File National Bank Ltd., 21/12/62)
    Need to sit promotion exam waived by Watch Committee
        and put forward for place at Bramshill, 2/12/63 (See File Dale-
        Emmett Ltd., 3/10/63)
    Completed Special Course Bramshill with Distinction and
        promoted sub-stantive Detective Sergeant, Central Division,
        effective 1/1/65
COMMENDATIONS: 1/8/60 See File 2/B/321/Jones R.
    5/3/61 See File 2/C/143/Rogers R. T.
    4/10/61 See File 8/D/129/Messrs. Longley Ltd.
    5/6/62 See File 9/E/725/Ali Hamid
    21/12/62 See File 11/D/832/National Bank Ltd.
    3/10/63 See File 13/C/172/Dale-Emmett Ltd.
CONFIDENTIAL ASSESSMENT: A highly intelligent officer with a
genuine capacity for police work who possesses potential leadership
qualities of a high order. Greatest fault, a tendency to work on his own.
Tends to unorthodoxy in methods. It should be noted that this officer
is a judo brown belt and an exponent of the art of karate, a Japanese
mode of self-defence by which it is possible to kill an opponent with the
bare hands. The undesirability of using such methods in the execution
of his duty has been pointed out to this officer.

BOOK ONE

THE GRAVEYARD SHIFT

As always – for Amy

1

Fog drifted up from the Thames, pushed by an early morning wind, yellow and menacing, wrapping the city in its yellow shroud, and when the duty officer at Wandsworth opened the judas gate and motioned the half dozen waiting men through, they stepped into an alien world.

Ben Garvald was last in line, a big, dangerous-looking man, massive shoulders swelling under the cheap raincoat. He hesitated, pulling up his collar, and the duty officer gave him a quick push.

'Don't want to leave us, eh?'

Garvald turned and looked at him calmly.

'What do you think, you pig?'

The officer took an involuntary step back and flushed. 'I think you always did have too much bloody lip, Garvald. Now get moving.'

Garvald stepped outside and the gate clicked into place with a finality that was strangely comforting. He started to walk down towards the main road, passing a line of parked cars and the man behind the wheel of the old blue van on the end turned to his companion and nodded.

Garvald paused on the corner, watching the early morning traffic move in a slow line through the fog, judged his moment and crossed quickly to the small café on the other side.

Two of the others were there before him, standing at the

counter while a washed-out blonde with sleep in her eyes stood at the urn and made fresh tea in a metal pot.

Garvald sat on a stool and waited, looking out through the window. After a while, the blue van cut across the line of traffic through the fog and pulled in at the kerb. Two men got out and entered the café. One of them was small and badly in need of a shave. The other was at least six feet tall with a hard, rawboned face and big hands.

He leaned against the counter and when the girl turned to Garvald from serving the others, cut in quickly in a soft Irish voice:

'Two teas, me dear.'

He challenged Garvald to say something, a slight, mocking smile on his mouth, arrogantly sure of himself. The big man refused to be drawn and looked into the fog again as rain spattered against the window.

The Irishman paid for his teas and joined his companion at a corner table and the small man glanced furtively across at Garvald.

'What do you think, Terry?'

'Maybe he was hot stuff about a thousand years ago, but they've squeezed him dry in there.' The Irishman grinned. 'This is going to be the softest touch we've had in a long, long time.'

The girl behind the counter yawned as she filled a cup for Garvald and watched him out of the corner of her eye. She was used to men like him. Almost every morning someone crossed the road from the place opposite and they all had the same look. But there was something different about this one. Something she couldn't quite put her finger on.

She pushed the cup of tea across and brushed the long hair back from her face. 'Anything else?'

'What have you got?'

His eyes were as grey as woodsmoke on an autumn day

and there was strength there, a restless, animal force that was almost physical and she was aware of her body reacting to it.

'At this time in the morning? You're all the same, you men.'

'What do you expect? It's been a long time.'

He pushed a coin across the counter. 'Give me a packet of fags. Not tipped. I want to taste them.'

He lit a cigarette and offered the girl one, the two men in the corner watching him in the mirror. Garvald ignored them and gave her a light.

'Been up there long, then?' she said, blowing out smoke expertly.

'Long enough.' He looked out of the window. 'I expect I'll find a few changes.'

'Everything's changed these days,' she agreed.

Garvald grinned and when he reached out, running his fingers through her hair, she was suddenly breathless. 'Some things stay the same.'

And then she was afraid and her mouth turned dry and she seemed utterly helpless, caught in some inexorable current. He leaned across the counter quickly and kissed her full on the mouth.

'See you some time.'

He slid off the stool and with incredible speed for such a big man, was out through the door and moving away.

The two men in the corner went after him fast, but when they reached the pavement, he had already disappeared into the fog. The Irishman ran forward, and a moment later caught sight of Garvald walking briskly along. He turned a corner into a narrow side street and the Irishman grinned and nudged the small man with his elbow.

'He's really asking for it, this one.'

They turned the corner and walked along the uneven pavement between decaying Victorian houses fringed with iron railings. The Irishman paused, pulling the other man to a halt, and listened, but the only sound was the roar of the early morning traffic from the main road, strangely muted by the fog.

A frown creased his face and he took an anxious step forward. Behind him, Garvald moved up the steps from the area in which he had been waiting, swung the small man round and raised a knee into his groin.

He sagged to the pavement with a gasp of agony and the Irishman turned round. Garvald stood on the other side of the writhing body, hands in the pockets of his raincoat, a slight smile on his face.

'Looking for somebody?'

The Irishman moved in fast, great hands reaching out to destroy, but they only fastened on thin air and his feet were kicked expertly from beneath him.

He thudded against the wet flagstones and scrambled to his feet cursing. In the same moment, Garvald seized his right wrist with both hands, twisting it round and up, locking the man's shoulder as in a vice.

The Irishman gave a cry of agony as the muscle started to tear. Still keeping that terrible hold in position, Garvald ran him head-first into the railings.

The small man was being sick into the gutter and now he got to his feet and leaned against the railings, an expression of horror on his face. Garvald stepped over the Irishman and moved a little closer and the small man felt such fear as he had never known before move inside him.

'For Christ's sake, no! Leave me alone!' he gabbled.

'That's better,' Garvald said. 'That's a lot better. Who sicked you on to me?'

'A bloke called Rosco – Sam Rosco. He and Terry did some bird together at the Ville a couple of years back. He wrote to Terry last week from this dump up North where he lives. Said you were bad news. That nobody wanted you back.'

'And you were supposed to convince me?' Garvald said pleasantly. 'How much was it worth to pass the message along?'

The small man moistened his lips. 'A century – between us,' he added hastily.

Garvald dropped to one knee beside the Irishman and turned him over, whistling a strangely sad little tune in a minor key as he searched him. He located a wallet and took out a wad of five-pound notes.

'This it?'

'That's right. Terry hadn't divvied-up yet.'

Garvald counted the money quickly, then slipped it into his inside breast pocket. 'Now that's what I call a very satisfying morning's work.'

The small man crouched beside the Irishman. He touched his face gingerly and recoiled in alarm. 'Holy Mother, you've smashed his jaw.'

'You'd better find him a doctor then, hadn't you?' Garvald said and turned away.

He vanished into the fog and the sound of his whistling hung on the air for a moment, then faded eerily. The small man stayed there, crouched beside the Irishman, the rain soaking through the shoulders of his cheap coat.

It was the tune – that damned tune.

He couldn't seem to get the sound of it out of his head and for some reason he could never satisfactorily explain afterwards, he started to cry, helplessly like a small child.

2

And then there was the night with a cold east wind that swept in all the way from the North Sea like a knife in the back, probing the alleys of the northern city, whistling along

the narrow canyons that divided the towering blocks of
flats that were the new housing developments. And when
the rain came, it was the cold, stinging rain of winter that
rattled the windows like lead shot.

Jean Fleming sat on a hard wooden chair in the main
C.I.D. office at Police Headquarters and waited. It was a little
after nine and the place seemed strangely deserted, shadows
crowding in from the corners, falling across the long, narrow
desks, filling her with a vague, irrational unease.

Through the frosted glass door of the room on her left,
she was aware of movement and the low murmur of voices.
After a while, the door opened and a heavily built, greying
man in his early forties beckoned to her.

'Superintendent Grant will see you now, Miss Fleming.'

She got to her feet and went in quickly. The room was
half in shadow, the only light a green shaded lamp on the
desk. It was simply furnished with several filing cabinets
and a map of the city on the wall, divisional boundaries
marked in red.

Grant was past feeling tired in any conscious sense, but
a persistent ache behind one eye and a slight involuntary
shiver, which he found quite impossible to control, seemed
to indicate that he was under attack from the Asian flu that
had already placed something like a fifth of the entire force
on the sick list.

He opened a drawer, took three aspirin tablets from a
bottle and washed them down with a glass of water. As he
reached for a cigarette, he glanced across at the girl on the
other side of the desk.

Twenty-seven or -eight and Irish-looking, dark hair
razor-cut to the skull in a way he didn't really approve, but
it certainly gave her something. The heavy sheepskin coat
had cost anything up to forty pounds and the knee-length
boots were real leather.

She sat down in the chair Brady brought forward and

crossed her legs, giving Grant the first lift he'd had that night. She arranged her skirt carefully and smiled.

'You don't remember me, Mr Grant?'

'Should I?'

He frowned. Fleming – Jean Fleming. He shook his head and his ugly face split into a smile of quite devastating charm that was one of his most useful assets. 'I must be getting old.'

'I'm Bella Garvald's sister.'

As if she had said some magic word, it all dropped neatly into place. Ben Garvald and the Steel Amalgamated hoist. Eight no, nine years ago. His first big case as a Chief Inspector. His mind jumped back to the house in Khyber Street, to Bella Garvald and her young sister.

'You've changed,' he said. 'As I remember, you were still at the Grammar School waiting to go to college. What was it you wanted to be – a school-teacher?'

'I am,' she said.

'Here in the city?'

She nodded. 'Oakdene Preparatory.'

'Miss Van Heflin's old school? That was on my first beat when I was a young copper. Is she still active? She must be at least seventy.'

'She retired two years ago,' Jean Fleming said. 'It's mine now.'

She was unable to keep a slight edge of pride from her voice and her northern accent became more pronounced.

'A long way from Khyber Street,' Grant said. 'And how's Bella?'

'She divorced Ben not long after he went to prison. Married again last year.'

'I remember now. Harry Faulkner. She did all right for herself there.'

'That's right,' Jean Fleming said calmly. 'And I don't want anything to spoil it for her.'

'Such as?'

'Ben,' she said. 'He was released yesterday.'

'You're sure?'

'With all his remission it would have been last year, but he lost time for breaking from a working party at Dartmoor some years ago.'

Grant blew smoke up to the ceiling. 'You think he'll make trouble?'

'He was difficult about the divorce. That's why he tried to break out when he did. Told Bella he'd never let her go to anyone else.'

'Did she ever visit him again?'

Jean Fleming shook her head. 'There wasn't any point. I went to see him last year when she and Harry got together. I told Ben that she was remarrying, that there was no point in ever trying to contact her again.'

'What was his reaction?'

'He was furious. Wanted to know who it was, but I refused to tell him. He swore he'd run her down when he got out.'

'Does Faulkner know about all this?'

She nodded. 'Yes, but he doesn't seem particularly bothered. He thinks Ben will never dare show his face here again.'

'He's probably right.'

She shook her head. 'Bella got a letter a few days ago. More a note, really. It just said, *See you soon – Ben*.'

'Has she shown it to her husband?'

Jean Fleming shook her head. 'I know this sounds silly, but it's his birthday and they're throwing a party tonight. An all-night affair. Dancing, cabaret, the lot. I'm looking in myself when I leave here. Bella's put a lot into it. She wouldn't like Ben to spoil things.'

'I see,' Grant said. 'So what do you want us to do? He's served his time. As long as he keeps his nose clean he's a free agent.'

'You could have a word with him,' she said. 'Tell him to stay away. Surely that isn't asking too much?'

Grant swung round in his chair, got to his feet and crossed to the window. He looked down at the lights of the city in the rain below.

'Look at it,' he said, turning to Jean Fleming. 'Seventy square miles of streets, half a million people and eight hundred and twenty-one coppers and that includes the ones who sit behind a desk. By any reasonable standard we need another two hundred and fifty right now.'

'Why can't you get them?'

'You'd be surprised how few men want to spend the rest of their lives working a three-shift system that only gives them one weekend in seven at home with their families. And then the money isn't exactly marvellous, not when you consider what you have to do to earn it. If you don't believe me, try standing outside the Exchange around eleven o'clock on a Saturday night when the pubs are turning out. A good copper earns his week's money in an hour down there.'

'Which is a roundabout way of telling me that you can't help.'

'I've got fifty-two detectives under me. At the present time eighteen have got flu and the rest are working an eighty-hour week. You may have noticed how quiet things are around here. That's because Detective Constable Brady and I are the only people in the office at the moment. At the best of times we only run a token squad during the ten till six shift. Tonight, you could say things are thinner than usual.'

'But there must be someone available.'

He laughed harshly and returned to his desk. 'There usually is.'

She got to her feet. 'It'll be all right, then? You'll see to it?'

'We'll check around,' Grant said. 'It shouldn't be too difficult to find him if he's in town. I can't promise much, but we'll do what we can.'

She fumbled in her bag and took out a card. 'I'll be at Bella's place in St Martin's Wood for an hour or two. After that, I'll be at home. I'm living in Miss Van Heflin's old flat at the school. The number's there.'

She turned to the door. As Brady moved to open it for her, Grant said, 'One thing I don't understand. Why you? Why not Bella?'

Jean Fleming turned slowly. 'You don't remember her very well, do you? She was never much of a one for positive action about anything. If it was left to her she'd just pretend Ben Garvald didn't exist and hope for the best. But this time, that's not good enough, because if anything, I stand to lose even more than she does. A scandal could ruin me, Mr Grant, destroy everything I've worked for. We've come a long way from Khyber Street, you said that yourself. Too far to be dragged back now.'

When she turned and went through the main office, she found that she was trembling. She didn't bother with the lift, but hurried down the three flights of marble stairs to the ground floor and out through the revolving door into the portico at the front of the Town Hall.

She leaned against one of the great stone pillars that towered into the night above her and a gust of wind kicked rain into her face in an oddly menacing manner, ice-cold, like the fear that rose inside her.

'Damn you, Ben Garvald! Damn you to hell!' she said fiercely and plunged down the steps.

'Quite a girl,' Brady said.

Grant nodded. 'And then some. She couldn't be anything else to survive a place like Khyber Street.'

'Do you think there's anything in it, sir?'

'Could be. They didn't come much tougher than Ben Garvald in his day. I don't think nine years of Parkhurst and the Moor will have improved him any.'

'I never knew him personally,' Brady said. 'I was pounding a beat in "C" Division in those days. Had he many friends?'

'Not really. He was always something of a lone wolf. Most people were afraid of him if anything.'

'A real tearaway?'

Grant shook his head. 'That was never Garvald's style. Controlled force – violence when necessary, that was his motto. He was a commando in Korea. Invalided out in '51 with a leg wound. Left him with a slight limp.'

'Sounds a real hard case. Shall I get his papers?'

'First we need someone to handle him.' Grant pulled a file forward, opened it quickly and ran his fingers down a list. 'Graham's still on that rape case at Moorend. Varley went to a factory break-in Maske Lane way an hour ago. Gregory, sick. Lawrence, sick. Forbes, gone to Manchester as a witness in that fraud case coming up tomorrow.'

'What about Garner?'

'Still helping out in "C" Division. They haven't got a plain clothes man capable of standing on his own two feet out there at the moment.'

'And every man a backlog of thirty or more cases at least to work through,' Brady said.

Grant got to his feet, walked to the window and stared down into the rain. 'I wonder what the bloody civilians would say if they knew that tonight we've only got five out in the whole of Central Division.'

Brady coughed. 'There's always Miller, sir.'

'Miller?' Grant said blankly.

'Detective Sergeant Miller, sir,' Brady stressed the title slightly. 'I heard he finished the course at Bramshill last week.'

There was nothing obvious in his tone and yet Grant

knew what was implied. Under the new regulations any constable who successfully completed the one year Special Course at the Police College at Bramshill House had to be promoted substantive sergeant immediately on returning to his force, a source of much bitterness to long-serving police officers who had either come up the hard way or were still awaiting promotion.

'I was forgetting him. He's the bloke with the law degree, isn't he?' Grant said, not because he needed the information, but mainly to see what the other man's reaction would be.

'So they tell me,' Brady replied, a knife edge to his voice that carried with it all the long-serving officer's contempt for the 'book man'.

'I've only met him once. That was when I was on the interviewing panel that considered his application for Bramshill. His record seemed pretty good. Three years on the pavement in Central Division so he must have seen life. As I remember, he was first on the spot after the Leadenhall Street bank raid. It was after that the old man decided to transfer him to the C.I.D. He did a year in "E" Division with Charlie Parker. Charlie thinks he's got just about everything a good copper needs these days.'

'Including a brother with enough money to see him all right for fancy cars,' Brady said. 'He turned up for parade once in an E-type Jag. Did you know about that?'

Grant nodded. 'I also heard he took Big Billy McGuire into the gym and gave him the hiding of his life after Billy had let the air out of the tyres on the same car. They tell me that Billy says he can use himself and that's praise from a master.'

'Fancy tricks, big words,' Brady said contemptuously. 'Can he catch thieves, that's the point.'

'Charlie Parker seems to think so. He wanted him back in "E" Division.'

Brady frowned quickly. 'Where's he going, then?'

'He's joining us,' Grant said. 'The old man gave me the word this afternoon.'

Brady took a deep breath and swallowed back his anger. 'Roses all the way for some people. It took me nineteen years, and at that I'm still a constable.'

'That's life, Jack,' Grant said calmly. 'Miller's supposed to be on leave till Monday.'

'Can I roust him out?'

'I don't see why not. If he's coming to work for us, he might as well get started. His phone number's on the file. Tell him to report in straight away. No excuses.'

A slight, acid smile burned the edges of Brady's mouth and he turned away with his small triumph. As the door closed, Grant lit another cigarette and walked to the window.

A good man, Jack Brady. Solid, dependable. Give him an order and he'd follow it to the letter which was why he was still a Detective Constable, would be till the day he retired.

But Miller was something different. Miller and his kind were what they needed – needed desperately if they were ever to cope with a situation that got more out of hand month by month.

He went back to his chair, stubbed out his cigarette and started to work his way through the mountain of paperwork that littered his desk.

3

The houses in Fairview Avenue were typical of the wealthy town dweller. Large without being mansions, each standing remotely in a sea of green lawn. The knowledge that Nick Miller lived in one of these did nothing to improve Jack Brady's temper.

Four Winds was at the end, a late-Victorian town house

in grey stone with a half-moon drive and double entrance. Brady drove in, parked his old Ford at the door, got out and rang the bell.

After a while, the door was opened by a slim, greying man of about his own age. He had sharp, decisive features and wore heavy rimmed library spectacles that gave him a deceptively scholarly air.

'Yes, what is it?' He sounded impatient and Brady noticed that he was holding a hand of cards against his right thigh.

'I'm from the Police Department. I've been trying to get hold of Detective Sergeant Miller, but I can't seem to get any reply. Is your phone out of order?'

The other man shook his head. 'Nick has his own flat over the garage block at the back and a separate phone goes with it. As far as I know, he should be in. I'm his brother – Phil Miller. You want him for something?'

'You could say that.'

'I thought he was on leave till next Monday?'

'So did he. Can I go round?'

'Help yourself. You can't miss it. The fire escape by the main garage door will take you straight up.'

Brady left him there, went back down the steps and followed the gravel drive round the side of the house to a rear courtyard illuminated by a period gas lamp bracketed to the wall above the back door.

The sliding doors of the garage were partially open and he went in and switched on the light. There were three cars parked side by side. A Zodiac, the famous E-type Jaguar and a green Mini-Cooper.

The anger which suddenly boiled inside him was something he found impossible to control. He switched off the light quickly, went out and climbed the iron fire escape to the landing above.

*

Nick Miller came awake to the sharp, insistent buzzing of the door bell. For a little while he lay there staring up at the ceiling, trying to collect his thoughts, then he threw back the blankets and swung his legs to the floor. He got to his feet, padded into the living-room, switching on a table lamp as he passed, and opened the front door.

Brady took in the black silk pyjamas with the Russian neck and gold buttons, the monogram on the pocket and then his eyes moved up to the face. It was handsome, even aristocratic with sharply pointed chin, high cheekbones and eyes so dark that all light died in them.

At any other time, those eyes would have given him pause, but the frustration and anger boiling inside had taken the sharp edge from his judgement.

'You're Miller?' he said incredulously.

'That's right.'

'Detective Constable Brady. You certainly took your own sweet time answering.' Brady brushed past him. 'Is it the butler's night off or something?'

Nick shut the door and moved towards the fireplace. He opened a silver box that stood on a side table, selected a cigarette and lit it from a Queen Anne table-lighter.

'If you could get to the point,' he said patiently. 'I'd been hoping for an early night.'

'You've had that for a start. Superintendent Grant wants you down at Headquarters. Seems he has a use for your valuable services.' Brady walked across to the telephone which was off the hook and replaced it. 'No wonder I couldn't get a bloody answer.' He swung round angrily. 'I've been trying to ring you for the past half hour.'

'You're breaking my heart.' Miller ran a hand over his chin. 'Anyway, no sense in you hanging around. I'll see you down there. I'll use my own car.'

'Which one, the Rolls?' As Nick moved past him, Brady grabbed his arm. 'The old man said on the double.'

'Then he'll have to wait,' Nick said calmly. 'I'm going to have a shower then a shave, because I need them. You can tell him I'll be there in half an hour.'

With surprising ease he pulled himself free and turned away again and all Brady's anger and frustration flooded out of him in a torrent of rage. He pulled Nick round and gave him a violent shove.

'Just who in the hell do you think you are? You jump up out of nowhere after only five years in the force with your bloody degree and your fancy cars, write your way through an examination and they make you a sergeant. Christ, in that rig-out you look more like a third-rate whore-master.'

He looked around the luxuriously furnished room, at the thick carpets, the coloured sheepskin rugs and expensive furniture and thought of his own small semi-detached house. A police dwelling on one of the less desirable slum clearance estates on the other side of the river where men like himself and their families lived in a state of perpetual siege.

The irrational anger which he was by now quite unable to control, bubbled out of him. 'And look at this place. More like the waiting room of one of those Gascoigne Square knocking shops.'

'You would know, presumably?' Nick said.

His face had gone very white; had changed completely. The skin was clear and bloodless, the crisp hair in a point to the forehead, the eyes staring through Brady like glass.

They should have warned him, but Brady was long since past the point where reason had any say in the matter. He reached out, grabbing at the black tunic, the silk ripping in his hands and then pain coursed through him like liquid fire and he staggered, a cry rising in his throat as he swung on his right arm, quite helpless.

The pressure was released and he sagged to one knee,

and almost at once the pain left him. He got to his feet, dazed, rubbing his right arm in an attempt to restore some feeling to numbed muscle and nerve and looked into the dark, devil's face. Nick smiled gently.

'You need brains for everything, even the heavy stuff, these days. You made a mistake, Dad. You weren't the first and you won't be the last, but don't speak to me like that again. Next time I'll throw you down the fire escape. Now get out – and that's an order, *Detective Constable Brady*!'

Brady turned, wordless, and stumbled to the door. It closed behind him and Nick stood there listening to the sound of the feet descending the iron fire escape. He sighed heavily, and went into the bathroom.

He stripped the torn tunic from his body and stood looking into the mirror for a while, waiting for the coolness to thaw inside him. After a moment or two he laughed shakily, opened the glass fronted door of the shower cubicle and turned it on.

When he stepped out five minutes later and reached for a towel, he found his brother leaning in the door holding the torn tunic.

'What happened?'

'A difference of opinion, that's all. Brady's the sort who's been around for a long time. He finds it difficult to get used to someone like me jumping the queue.'

Phil Miller tossed the tunic into a corner and swore softly. 'Why go on, Nick? I could use you in the business right now. We're developing all the time, you know that. Why waste yourself?'

Nick moved past him into the bedroom, opened the sliding door of the wardrobe which occupied one side of the room and took down a dark blue worsted suit and freshly laundered white linen shirt. He laid them across the bed and started to dress.

'I happen to like what I'm doing, Phil, and all the Bradys

in the Force won't make me change my mind. I'm in and I'm in to stay. The sooner they accept that, the better it will be for all of us.'

Phil shrugged and sat on the edge of the bed, watching him. 'I wonder what the old lady would say if she was still alive. All her plans, all her hopes and you end up a copper.'

Nick grinned at him in the mirror as he quickly knotted a dark blue knitted tie in heavy silk. 'She'd enjoy the joke, Phil. Probably is doing right now.'

'I thought you were supposed to be on leave till Monday?'

Nick shrugged. 'Something must have come up. I was talking to Charlie Parker from "E" Division this afternoon. He was telling me recruiting's hit an all-time low. We're better than two hundred men under establishment. On top of that, God knows how many are on their backs with this Asian flu that's going around.'

'So they need Nick Miller. But why now? What kind of a time is this for a man to be going to work?'

Nick took a dark blue Swedish raincoat from the wardrobe. 'We do it all the time, Phil. You should know that by now. Ten p.m. till six in the morning. The Graveyard Shift.' He grinned as he belted the coat around his waist. 'What would you do if someone turned over one of the shops right now?'

His brother raised a hand defensively and got to his feet. 'All right, you've made your point. So the great Nick Miller goes out into the night to defend society. Watch yourself, that's all I ask. Anything can happen these days.'

'And usually does.' Nick grinned. 'Don't worry, Phil, I can look after myself.'

'See you do. I don't want any phone calls around four in the morning asking me to come down to the Infirmary. Ruth and the kids would take it pretty hard. For some strange reason they seem to think a lot of you.'

'All we need now are violins.' Nick adjusted the peak of

the dark blue semi-military rain cap over one eye and turned. 'Will I do?'

'You'll do all right,' Phil said. 'I'm not sure what for, but you'll do.'

Nick grinned and punched him in the shoulder. 'With any kind of luck I might manage breakfast with you.'

He moved to the door and as he opened it, Phil called sharply, 'Nick!'

'What is it?'

Phil sighed heavily and something seemed to go out of him. 'Nothing. Nothing at all. Just watch it, that's all.'

'I always do.'

He turned and went out into the night, clattering down the fire escape to the cobbled yard, a strange restless excitement surging up inside him at the prospect of being back on the job after a year of space.

Phil stood in the centre of the living-room, a slight frown on his face, and beneath him from the garage came a sudden surge of power as an engine roared into life. As he opened the door, the little Mini-Cooper moved across the yard into the drive and disappeared round the corner of the house.

He stood there in the rain at the top of the iron stairway listening to the sound of it fade into the distance on the run down the hill towards the city. And when the silence came, he was afraid. For the first time since he was a little boy he was really and truly afraid.

4

The wind howled fiercely around the corner of the Town Hall and hail rattled the windows of the Information Room.

'God help any poor lad walking the pavement on a night

like this,' Grant said as the Duty Inspector turned from the telephone.

'It keeps the other lot indoors as well, sir,' the Inspector pointed out. 'One good thing about this flu. It's no respecter of persons. There are just as many villains on their backs tonight as our lads. I can tell that by the 999 calls. Only five so far. We're usually good for thirty at least by this time.'

'A good thing, too, with only four mobiles out to cover the city.' Grant looked down at the great map in the well below with the green and red lights flashing. It was just after ten and he sighed. 'Anyway, don't start counting your chickens. The boozers aren't out yet. We might see some fun then.'

He went into the corridor and met Brady on his way up from the basement where the teleprinter was housed. 'Anything from C.R.O.?'

'They confirm he was released yesterday morning. That's all.'

'What about Miller?'

'No sign of him yet.'

They moved into the main C.I.D. office and Grant snorted. 'Taking his bloody time, I must say. You'd better get all the relevant stuff out of the file ready for him then, Jack. We've wasted enough time already.'

'I'll be in Records if you want me,' Brady said and moved out.

Grant paused to light a cigarette and went into his office. Nick was standing by the window looking out into the night. He turned quickly and smiled.

'Good evening, sir.'

Grant took in the highly polished Chelsea boots, the hand-stitched raincoat, the white collar and last of all, the continental raincap.

He took a deep breath. 'What in the hell is that thing on your head?'

Nick took it off with a slight smile. 'This, sir? It's what the Germans call a *Schildtmütze*. Everyone will be wearing them soon.'

'God save us from that,' Grant said, sitting behind his desk.

'Something wrong, sir?'

'Oh, no, if you want to go around looking like one of those burks who stands behind the good-looking bird in the adverts in the women's magazines, good luck to you.'

'As a matter of fact, that's exactly how I do want to look, sir,' Nick replied calmly.

Grant glanced up sharply, suddenly conscious that he was being taken by this supremely confident young man and discovering at the same moment – and this was the most surprising thing of all – that he didn't really mind.

He started to smile and Nick smiled right back at him.

'All right, damn you, one point each. Now sit down and let's get started.'

Nick unbuttoned his coat, sat in the chair opposite and lit a cigarette as Grant continued. 'Brady's getting you all the files you'll need for background on this one, but these are the main facts. Nine years ago, Ben Garvald, one of our better known citizens, went down the steps for a ten stretch. He was released from Wandsworth yesterday morning.'

'And you're expecting him back?'

'His wife is, his ex-wife I should say. That's Bella Garvald. She divorced Ben and married Harry Faulkner five years ago.'

'Harry Faulkner the bookie?'

'Never let him hear you call him that, son. Turf Accountant sounds better. He hasn't soiled his hands with a ready money bet in years. Got his fingers in all sorts of pies these days. Even runs his own football pool.'

'That isn't all he runs,' Nick said. 'From what I remember when I was on the pavement in Central Division, he owned half the cat houses in Gascoigne Square.'

Grant shook his head quickly. 'Try proving it, and in any case, that isn't what we're interested in tonight. It's Ben Garvald we're after.'

'He's in town?'

'That's what I want you to find out and in a hurry. Apparently he made the usual threats to his wife when the divorce went through. She's afraid he's going to show up and spoil her rich full life. Especially tonight. She's throwing a big party for Harry at their place in St Martin's Wood. It's his birthday.'

'How touching,' Nick said. 'She's made an official complaint?'

'Her sister has. That's a Jean Fleming. She's a teacher. Runs her own prep school in Oakdene on the York Road near the city boundary.'

Nick had pulled Grant's desk pad forward and was making rapid notes and now he looked up sharply, a frown on his face. 'Fleming – Jean and Bella Fleming. I wonder if they could be the same?'

'They were both raised in Khyber Street, that's on the south side of the river.'

'That's it,' Nick said. 'My mother kept a shop on the Hull Road just around the corner from Khyber Street. I lived there till I was ten, then we moved to a bigger place in Brentwood.'

'You remember them?'

'I couldn't forget Bella. She was the best known tart in the district. Half the population did nothing else except wait for her to walk by. One of life's great experiences. I was too young, I didn't know what was happening to me. I do now.'

'And never been the same since,' Grant said. 'What about Jean?'

Nick shrugged. 'Just a scrawny kid about my own age. I don't think we ever did more than pass the time of day. They didn't use our shop. My old lady wouldn't give credit.'

The door opened and Brady came in, a pile of files under his arm. He ignored Nick and said to Grant, 'Where do you want these?'

'In the outer office.' Grant looked enquiringly at Nick. 'Need any help? You haven't got much time.'

'Up to you,' Nick said, ignoring Brady.

'All right, Jack can give you a hand for half an hour. If you want any advice, just come in.'

He pulled a file forward and Nick got to his feet and walked into the outer office. As he took off his raincoat and hung it on a stand, Brady dropped the files on one of the desks.

'What do you want me to do?' he said woodenly.

'That depends,' Nick said. 'What have you got there?'

'Garvald's personal file and the files on everyone else who was close to him.'

'Fine,' Nick said. 'I'll take Garvald myself. You start making abstracts of the others.'

Brady didn't argue. He left Garvald's file on the desk, picked up the rest, and went to his own desk in the corner by the window and started to work immediately.

Nick opened Garvald's file and examined the ID card. The face which stared out at him was tough, even ruthless, but there was strength there and intelligence, even a suggestion of humour in the slight quirk at one side of the mouth.

As usual, the card carried the briefest of details and referred only to the offence and charges for which Garvald had last been sent down, namely factory breaking and the stealing of £15,817, the property of Steel Amalgamated Ltd. of Sheffield.

The story contained in the confidential file attached was even more interesting.

Ben Garvald had served for two years in the Marine Commando during the war, being demobilized in 1946.

Three months later he was sentenced to one year's imprison-
ment for conspiracy to steal.

A charge of conspiracy to rob the mails had been dropped
for lack of evidence in 1949, and in 1950 he had been
recalled from the reserve to fight in Korea. A bullet in the
leg had brought him home in the early part of 1951 with
a permanent limp and a $33\frac{1}{3}$ per cent disability pension.

Between then and his final conviction in June 1956, he
had been questioned by the police on no less than twenty-
seven occasions in connection with indictable offences.

The door to Grant's office opened and he came out, a
cigarette dangling between his lips. 'Got a light?' Nick struck
a match and the Superintendent sat on the edge of the
desk. 'How are you getting on?'

'Quite a character,' Nick said. 'From the looks of this,
they've tried to hang about every charge in the book on
him at one time or another.'

'Except for living on immoral earnings and that sort of
thing, you're probably right,' Grant said. 'A funny bloke,
Ben Garvald. Every villain in town was frightened to death
of him and yet where women were concerned, he was like
someone out of one of those books they like reading. He
treated Bella like a princess.'

'Which would explain why he was so cut up when she
decided to divorce him. I've just got to the entry on his last
job, the one he got sent down for.'

'I can save you some time there,' Grant said. 'I handled
it myself at this end. Garvald and three associates lifted over
fifteen thousand quid from the Steel Amalgamated works
in Birmingham. Wages for the following day. The daft
beggars never learn and I don't mean Garvald and his pals.
Anyway, they didn't hit the nightwatchman hard enough,
he raised the alarm and Birmingham police sewed the city
up tight.'

'Too late?'

'Not quite. There were two cars. One of them crashed and went up like a torch taking a well-known peterman called Jack Charlton and his driver up with it.'

'And Garvald?'

'He and the other bloke crashed a road block and got clean away. We lifted Garvald next day and the night-watchman picked him out at an identity parade with no trouble at all.'

'And the money?'

'Garvald said it was in the other car.'

'A likely story.'

'Strangely enough I was inclined to believe him. We certainly found traces of some of it in the ashes. That's as far as we got anyway and we didn't get the other man.'

'So Garvald kept his mouth shut?'

'True to the code. Went down the steps like a man.'

'The bloke who was with him in the car that night, did you have any fancy ideas at the time?'

'Plenty and they all came down to Fred Manton.'

'Manton?' Nick frowned. 'Doesn't he run that place in Gascoigne Square – The Flamingo Club?'

Grant nodded. 'He and Garvald were partners in a small club on the other side of the river at the time of the robbery. Trouble was, too many customers came forward to swear that Fred Manton had been in the club all night and one or two of them were pretty respectable citizens.'

'Has Manton got any form?'

Brady crossed the office and placed a foolscap sheet in front of him. 'There's an abstract of his file.'

Nick examined it quickly. *Frederick Manton, 44, club owner, Gascoigne Square, Manningham. Four previous convictions including thirty months for conspiracy to steal; larceny; loitering with intent. On eighteen occasions the police had thought he might be able to help them with their enquiries, but Manton had always managed to walk right down the Town Hall steps again.*

'Let's suppose you were right about Manton after all,' he said to Grant. 'And that the cash from the Steel Amalgamated job didn't go up in smoke. A place like the Flamingo must have cost a lot to get started. It would be understandable if Garvald turned up and wanted a slice of the cake.'

'Ingenious, but there's only one fault.' Grant got to his feet and moved towards his office. 'Harry Faulkner owns the Flamingo Club. Fred Manton's just hired help as far as he's concerned and don't try to drag Harry Faulkner into this. His cars are worth fifteen grand alone.'

The door closed behind him and Nick looked up at Brady. 'What about the rest?'

'There are nine here, all people he was pretty thick with,' Brady said. 'Five of them are in one nick or another. Four are still around. They're on top.'

He dropped the abstracts on Nick's desk, walked to Grant's door, opened it and leaned inside. 'All right if I take my break now?'

Grant glanced at his watch. 'Fine, Jack, see you back here about midnight.'

Brady closed the door, took his raincoat from the stand, and pulled it on as he went out into the corridor. He stood at the wire grill of the lift shaft impatiently pressing the button.

If Ben Garvald *was* in town, there was one place he was bound to go, one person he was certain to visit. That much was obvious to anyone with any experience and if he was there, he – Jack Brady – would have him back at Headquarters within an hour at the outside while that clever sod Miller walked the pavements looking for him. It would be interesting to see what Grant had to say then. When he got into the lift, he was trembling with excitement.

5

Round about the time Jean Fleming was having her interview with Grant, Garvald was dropping off a truck at a bus stop on the North Circular Ring Road that linked the city with the A1. Ten minutes later, he boarded the first bus to come along and left it half a mile from the city centre, going the rest of the way on foot.

The journey from London could have taken no more than a comfortable four hours in a Pullman car, but that would have been too conspicuous an entrance into the city under the circumstances.

There were people to see, things to be done, accounts to be settled – notably Sammy Rosco's – but first he needed a base from which to operate.

He found what he was looking for without too much trouble, a third-rate hotel in a back street near the centre of town. When he went in, a woman in a blue nylon overall was sitting behind the reception desk reading a magazine. She could have been anywhere between twenty-five and thirty with dark curling hair and bold black eyes.

Garvald rested an elbow on the desk. 'And who might you be?'

She closed the magazine, a spark of interest in her eyes and responded to his mood. 'A poor Irish girl trying to make an honest living in a hard land.'

'God save the good work,' Garvald said. 'You can give me a room for a start. A room with a bath.'

'All our rooms have a bath,' she said calmly. 'There's one at the end of the corridor on each floor.'

She took a key down from the board, lifted the flap of the reception desk and led the way up the stairs.

The room was no better and no worse than he had expected with the usual heavy Victorian furniture and a

worn carpet. A modern washbasin with tiled splashback
had been fitted in one corner. He dropped his holdall on a
chair, walked to the window and looked down into the
street as the woman turned back the bedspread.

'Will that be all?' she said.

Garvald turned. 'Any chance of a drink?'

'We aren't licensed. There's a pub down the street.'

He shook his head. 'Not to worry. I could do with an
early night, anyway.'

She dropped the key on the dressing-table.

'Anything you want, just ring. I'm on call all night.'

Garvald grinned. 'The thought of that's more than flesh
and blood can stand.'

She smiled right back at him and the door closed behind
her. Garvald's grin disappeared and he lit a cigarette, sat on
the edge of the bed and leafed through the phone book.
There was no entry for Sammy Rosco and he sat there for
a while, a slight frown on his face, trying to think of someone
he could trust. Someone from the old days who might still
be around.

He discarded the names as they came to him one by one,
and was left finally with only Chuck Lazer, the quiet
American who'd been resident pianist at the old One-Spot
when Garvald and Fred Manton had run it together.

But Chuck would never have stayed on, couldn't have.
He'd have gone back to the States years before, so much
was obvious and yet, when Garvald looked in the phone
book again, the name jumped out at him. Chuck Lazer – 15
Baron's Court.

He reached for the telephone, hesitated, then changed
his mind. This was something that would be handled better
in person. He pulled on his hat and left, locking the door
behind him.

At the head of the stairs he hesitated, then moved along
the corridor and tried a door at the end. It opened on to a

narrow flight of dark stairs and he went down quickly, a stale smell of cooking rising to meet him through the darkness. At the bottom, he found himself in a dimly lit passage facing a door. He opened it and stepped into the alley at the side of the hotel.

To save time he took a taxi from a rank in City Square. Lazer's address was not far from the University, a district of tall, decaying Victorian houses which had, in the main, been converted into cheap boarding houses or flats.

Garvald followed a narrow path through an overgrown garden and mounted several steps to a large porch. He could hear laughter from somewhere inside and music as he examined the name cards beneath the row of bell pushes.

Chuck Lazer had Flat 5 on the third floor and Garvald opened the door and moved into the hall. As he closed it behind him, a door on his right opened, music and laughter flooding out and a young man with tousled hair and a fringe of beard emerged, carrying a crate of empty bottles.

Garvald paused at the bottom of the stairs. 'Chuck Lazer wouldn't happen to be in there, would he?'

'Good God, no,' the young man said. 'Booze and bints, that's all we go in for, old man. Not Chuck's style at all. You'll probably find him in his pit.'

He disappeared along the corridor and Garvald mounted the stairs quickly, a slight frown on his face, wondering what all that was supposed to mean.

It was strangely remote from things up there on the third floor and the music sounded faint and unreal, like something from another world. Garvald checked the card on the door, listened for a moment, then knocked. There was no reply and when he reached for the handle, the door opened to his touch.

The stench was overpowering, a compound of stale sweat, urine and cooking odours mixed with some other indefinable essence that for the moment escaped him.

He switched on the light and looked around the cluttered, filthy room to the narrow bed against the far wall and the half naked man who sprawled on it face down. Garvald opened a window wide, drawing the damp, foggy air deep into his lungs, then lit a cigarette and turned to the bed again.

On top of a small bedside locker were littered the gear which told the story. A hypodermic with several needles, most of them dirty and blunted. Heroin and cocaine bottles, both empty, a cup still half-full of water, a small glass bottle, its base discoloured from the match flame and a litter of burned-out matches.

The bare arm hanging over the side of the bed was dotted with needle marks, some of them scabbed over where infection had set in. Garvald took a deep breath and turned Lazer on his back.

The American's face was fleshless, gaunt from malnutrition, a dark beard giving him the appearance of an emaciated saint. He stirred once and Garvald slapped him across the face. The eyelids fluttered in an uncontrollable muscular spasm, then opened, the dark eyes staring blindly into an eternity of hell.

'Chuck, it's me,' Garvald said. 'Ben Garvald.'

Lazer stared blankly at him and Garvald placed his cigarette between the man's lips. Lazer inhaled deeply and started to cough in great, wrenching spasms that seemed to tear at his entire body. When he finally managed to stop, he was shivering uncontrollably and his nose was running.

Garvald threw a blanket over his shoulders. 'It's me, Chuck, Ben Garvald,' he said again.

'I read you, loud and clear, Dad. Loud and clear.' Lazer started to shiver again and pulled the blanket up around his neck. 'Christ, I need a fix. Oh, sweet Jesus, I need a fix.' He took a great shuddering breath as if making a real effort to get control and looked up at Garvald. 'Long time no see, Ben.'

'Thanks for all the letters.'

'There was never anything worth saying.'

'Oh, I don't know. What about Bella?'

'A harlot, Benny boy. A lovely whore, dancing with tinkling cymbals to the tune of whoever tossed the largest gold piece.'

'They tell me she got married again.'

'The pot of gold, Benny boy. The end of the rainbow. Didn't you know?'

'Who's the lucky man?'

'Harry Faulkner.'

'Harry Faulkner?' Ben frowned. 'He must be pushing sixty.'

'And then some, but he's a big man these days, Ben. A big man. He has a finger in just about anything that pays off and he isn't too particular. He and Bella live in a replica of Haroun al Raschid's palace out at St Martin's Wood in the gin and tonic belt.'

'Is Fred Manton still around?'

'Sure, he works for Harry these days. Runs a club called the Flamingo in Gascoigne Square. I play the piano for him whenever I remember.' He moaned suddenly and again his body was racked by uncontrollable shivering. 'Christ, but I need that fix.' He struggled for breath, his teeth chattering. 'What time is it?'

'About ten fifteen.'

Lazer's face tightened visibly. 'Too late for evening surgery. That means I can't get a prescription till the morning.'

'You're a registered addict?'

Lazer nodded. 'The only reason I didn't go back to the States years ago. Over there, they'd sling me in the can. Here, at least they allow me to exist, courtesy of the Health Service.'

'How long have you been on this stuff?' Garvald said, picking up the empty heroin bottle.

Lazer bared his teeth in a ghastly grin. 'Too long to be able to get through the night without a fix, Benny boy.'

'You know where you can get one?'

'Sure, outside the all-night chemist's in City Square. Plenty of junkies getting their evening surgery prescriptions filled, but it could take money. Something I'm fresh out of.'

Garvald took a wallet from his breast pocket and counted ten one-pound notes out carefully on top of the bedside locker.

'Enough?'

'Plenty.' Lazer's eyes were suddenly full of light and he reached for the notes.

Garvald covered them with one large hand. 'Sammy Rosco, Chuck. Where would I find him?'

'Sammy?' Lazer looked surprised. 'He works for Manton around the clubs.'

'The Flamingo?'

'With his mug?' Lazer shook his head. 'Fred manages one or two other places for Faulkner, dives mostly. Bad booze and worse women. You know the sort of thing. Sammy goes where they need him most. Barman and chucker-out, that's his style. I think he's at Club Eleven this week.'

'He and Wilma still together?'

'He couldn't manage without her. Mind you, things haven't been the same since the Act pushed 'em all in off the streets. She mostly works from the house now.' He frowned desperately, trying to remember. 'Carver Street. Yes, that's right – Carver Street. I don't know the number, but it's about half-way along, next door to a shop with its window boarded up. The whole street's due down soon.'

Garvald gathered the notes in one quick movement and pushed them into Lazer's open hand, closing the fingers tightly. 'Good man, Chuck, I'll see you.'

'At whose funeral?'

Ben Garvald turned in the doorway and smiled briefly.

'I haven't quite made my mind up yet. When I do, I'll let you know. You'd make a good mute.'

The door closed behind him. For a little while Lazer crouched there on the bed, the blanket wrapped tightly around him, the money clutched in his right hand and then, in one quick, positive movement that started off a chain action, he jumped up and started to get dressed.

6

Carver Street was a row of crumbling terrace houses near the river in a slum area which, as Chuck Lazer had said, was due for demolition.

Garvald found the shop with the boarded window about half-way along. The house next to it looked as if it might fall down at any moment and he followed a narrow tunnelled passage that brought him into a backyard littered with empty tins and refuse of every description.

He stumbled up four steps and knocked at the door. After a while, footsteps approached, it opened a few inches and a woman's voice said, 'Who is it?'

'I'm looking for Sam,' Garvald said. 'Sammy Rosco. I'm an old friend of his.'

'He isn't in.'

The slight German accent that had been one of her great attractions when he first knew her was still marked, and he moved closer to the door.

'It's Ben, Wilma. Ben Garvald.'

There was a sudden, sharp intake of breath, a slight pause and then the chain rattled and the door opened. As he stepped into the dark corridor, a hand reached for his face and arms pulled him close.

'Ben, *liebling*. I can't believe it. Is it really you?'

She drew him along the dark corridor and into a room at the far end. It was reasonably clean and comfortable with a carpet on the floor and a double bed against the far wall.

She turned to face him, a large heavily built woman running dangerously to seed, make-up too heavy, the flesh under the chin sagging. Only the incredible straw-coloured hair was as he remembered it and he smiled.

She coloured and her head went back. 'So, I look older. It's been a long time.'

'You've still got the most beautiful hair I've ever seen.'

Something glowed deep in her eyes, and for a moment she was once again the young, slender German girl that Sammy Rosco had brought home after the war. She moved close to Garvald, her arms sliding up around his neck, and kissed him firmly on the mouth.

'Always, you were worth all of them put together.'

Garvald held her close for a moment, savouring with a conscious pleasure the feel of a woman's body against his own, the first in a long time, then he pushed her firmly away.

'Business, Wilma, business. Is there a drink in the house?'

'The day there isn't will be the day.'

She moved to a cupboard, took out a bottle of gin and two glasses and Garvald sat in a chair at the table. He looked around the room. 'Still on the game?'

She shrugged as she sat in the opposite chair. 'What else can I do?'

'Ever thought of going home?'

'To Bavaria?' She got to her feet, went to a corner by the window, lifted the carpet and produced a white envelope. She opened it and took out a passport which she threw on the table. 'I keep it well out of Sammy's sight. Last time I tried to use it, he beat me up so bad, I was in hospital for a week.'

'You didn't prefer charges?'

'Do me a favour.' She shrugged. 'Since then, I haven't been able to scrape more than a fiver together at any one time. He sees to that. Waits in the kitchen for the clients to go, then he's straight in for the cash.'

Garvald picked up the passport and opened it. 'It's still valid, I see?'

'So what? It's about as much good as a ticket to the moon.' She swallowed her gin and refilled the glass. 'What brought you back, Ben? There's nothing for you here. I suppose you know Bella married again.'

'So I'm told. Where's Sammy now?'

'The Grosvenor Taps, that's a boozer at the end of the street.'

'Expecting him back?'

She glanced at the clock and nodded. 'They've been closed about five minutes. He usually looks in before going on to work.'

'And where would that be?'

She shrugged. 'Various places. This week he's at Club Eleven, that's a clip joint about half a mile from here that Fred Manton runs for Faulkner.'

'Who's in charge?'

'Molly Ryan.'

'Girls, too, eh?'

Wilma shrugged. 'You know what these places are like. Anything goes. Do you want Sammy for something special?'

Garvald lit another cigarette and blew smoke up at the shaded lamp. 'When I came out of Wandsworth yesterday morning, a couple of hard cases tried to take me, Wilma. They made a bad mistake.' He grinned coldly. 'So did Sammy.'

The outside door crashed open and steps sounded along the corridor. A moment later, Sammy Rosco lurched into the room. He was a squat ox of a man with arms that hung down to his knees. His face was sullen and bloated with whisky and he stood there, swaying, a nasty gleam in his eye.

'What's going on here, then?'

'Someone to see you, Sammy dear,' Wilma said, a deep, ripe pleasure in her voice. 'An old friend.'

Garvald turned his head and smiled gently. 'Now then, Sammy, you old bastard.'

His face was very calm, but the grey eyes, changing constantly like windswept smoke on an autumn day, told Rosco everything he needed to know. He swung round, lurching for the door, but Garvald was even quicker. His hand fastened on Rosco's collar and with a tremendous heave, he sent him crashing across the room.

Rosco came up from the floor in a rush, and Garvald coolly measured the distance and booted him in the stomach. Rosco keeled over with a sigh, falling across the bed, writhing in agony.

Wilma sat watching, no pity in her eyes, and Garvald emptied the gin bottle into his glass, sat down and waited. After a while, Rosco turned, his face the colour of paper.

'Feeling better, Sammy?'

'You get stuffed, you bastard,' Rosco managed to squeeze out.

'That's better,' Garvald said. 'That's a lot better. Now why did you sic those two tearaways on to me yesterday morning?'

'I don't know what in the hell you're talking about.'

In one quick movement, Garvald seized the empty gin bottle by the neck and smashed it across the edge of the table. He leaned forward and held the jagged, vicious weapon under Rosco's chin.

'Maybe you've forgotten, Sammy, but I never liked playing games.'

Sweat sprang to Rosco's brow in great heavy drops and his eyes widened visibly. 'It was Fred, Ben. Fred Manton.

He told me to line it up for him. Said he didn't want you back.'

Garvald frowned and all light died in his eyes. 'Why, Sammy? Why would Manton do a thing like that? It doesn't make sense.'

He pushed the bottle forward viciously and Sammy screamed. 'That's all I know. I swear it, Ben.'

Garvald tossed the bottle into the fireplace with a quick gesture, then hauled Rosco to his feet. He opened the man's coat, pulled the wallet from the inside pocket and opened it quickly. There was fifty pounds in five-pound notes, all new. He counted them quickly, then gave Rosco a contemptuous shove towards the door.

'Start running and don't come back.'

Rosco turned in the doorway, opening his mouth to say something, then obviously thought better of it. He stumbled along the corridor in the darkness and, a moment later, the back door banged behind him.

Garvald tossed the fifty pounds on to the table. 'More than enough to get you back home there, Wilma. Unless things have changed since I was around, there are still night expresses to London.'

She flung herself into his arms, straining against him and when she looked up, tears shone brightly in her eyes, smudging the mascara.

'I'll never forget you, Ben Garvald. Never.'

He kissed her once, gave her a quick squeeze and was gone. She stood there listening to him pass through the tunnel at the side of the house, his footsteps fading along the hollow pavement.

She gazed around the room, filled with a sudden hatred of this place, of Sammy Rosco and the wasted years and what they had done to her. Very quickly, she started to pack.

It was almost midnight when she was ready. She pulled

on her raincoat, picked up the suitcase, looked round the room briefly for the last time and walked out along the dark passage.

As she reached the door, someone knocked.

Oh, God, no. Oh, dear God, no. The cry rose in her throat and she turned and stumbled back along the dark passage to the room and behind her, the door opened.

She fell on her knees at the fireplace, her fingers scrabbling desperately in the broken glass. They fastened upon a large piece, curved like a dagger and as sharp. She arched her throat striking upwards and was aware of pain, pain like fire that flowed through the arm so that she dropped the glass with a scream. A hand pulled her to her feet, swung her round and sent her staggering across the room to fall across the bed.

She raised an arm to protect her face from the blow that always followed and then lowered it with a tiny whimper because it wasn't Sammy Rosco who stood by the table looking down at her. This was a much younger man, someone she'd never seen before in an expensive blue raincoat with strange, dark eyes that seemed to look right through her.

7

Charles Edward Lazer, 45, musician, 15 Baron's Court. American citizen. Joined RAF October 1939, demobilized June 1946. Rank, F/Lieutenant Navigator. Record – Excellent. Awarded DFC in May 1944. Four previous convictions including conspiracy to steal, suspected person, larceny and illegal possession of drugs. Not deported because of excellent war record and fact of all offences being concerned with subject's addiction to drugs.

Nick went through the facts again in his mind as he

waited outside the door in the dimly lit passage. There was no reply to his knock, and when he tried the handle the door opened to his touch.

The window was open, the curtains lifting in the wind, and rain drifted through in a fine spray. Nick looked briefly around the dirty, untidy room, his nostrils flaring at the stench of the unwashed bedding, then he turned, left the room and went downstairs.

The noise from the flat on the ground floor was tremendous, a steady, pulsating beat vibrating through the night as a blues and rhythm group really started to move. Nick knocked on the door a couple of times without getting a reply, opened it and looked inside.

There must have been at least thirty or forty people packed into the room, mainly students from the look of them, eating, drinking, dancing to the three-man group in the corner. In one case even making love on the floor behind the old-fashioned sofa.

A young man with tangled hair and a fringe beard was moving through the crowd, refilling glasses from a large enamel jug. As he turned from one group, he caught sight of Nick and came across.

'Sorry, old man, no gate-crashers. Strictly private this time.'

Nick produced his warrant card and the other's face dropped. 'Now what, for Christ's sake?'

He opened the door and Nick followed him out into the corridor, closing the door behind him, effectively cutting off most of the din.

'No trouble,' he said. 'I'm just trying to trace a bloke who lives upstairs – Chuck Lazer. He wouldn't be inside by any chance?'

The young man grinned, took a cigarette from behind his ear and stuck it in the corner of his mouth. 'Chuck? I should say not! Moves in his own narrow circle, God help him.'

'Is he still on junk?' Nick said.

'As far as I know, but he's a registered user now.' The young man frowned suddenly. 'Look, what *is* all this?'

'Nothing to get worked up about, I'm not trying to hang anything on him. I want his help with a routine enquiry, that's all.'

'That's what you lot always say.'

Nick shrugged. 'Suit yourself.'

He turned towards the door and the young man said quickly: 'Oh, what the hell. He overslept, missed the evening surgery. Someone came looking for him about half an hour ago.'

'What kind of someone?'

'Big man, dirty raincoat, Irish looking.' The young man grinned suddenly. 'That cap's the coolest thing I've seen in years. Where can I get one?'

'Any good men's shop in Hamburg. Did they leave together?'

The young man shook his head. 'Lazer went out about ten minutes ago. I was having five minutes with one of the birds up at the end of the passage when he came down.'

'Was he in a hurry?'

'They always are when they need a fix. I'd say he was on his way round to see his quack about a prescription.'

'And who would that be?'

'Dr Das, just round the corner in Baron's Square. He's about the only one in town who'll take junkies on his list. Say, are you really a copper?'

'As ever was.'

'Crazy!' the young man said, frank admiration in his eyes. 'If I join will they guarantee me a uniform like that?'

'I'll mention it to the Chief Constable in the morning. We'll be in touch.'

'You do that, man.'

He opened the door and returned to his party as Nick

went down the steps into the rain. There was a touch of fog in the air, heavy and acrid, catching at the back of the throat, and he climbed behind the wheel of the Mini-Cooper and drove around the corner to Baron's Square.

Dr Das lived at number twenty and a brass plate on the door disclosed the surprising fact, considering the district and circumstances, that he was not only an MD but also a Fellow of the Royal College of Physicians.

Nick rang the bell and after a while heard footsteps approaching. The door was opened by a tall, cadaverous Indian with high cheekbones and serene brown eyes.

'Dr Das?'

'That is correct. What can I do for you?'

'Detective Sergeant Miller, C.I.D. I'm trying to trace a patient of yours, a Mr Lazer. I've just missed him at his home and one of his neighbours thought he might have intended calling on you.'

'Come in, please, Sergeant.'

Nick followed him along the passage and the Indian opened a door at the far end and led the way in. A cheerful fire burned in a polished grate, there was a desk in one corner and the walls were lined with books.

Dr Das took a cheroot from a sandalwood box on the mantelpiece, lit it with a splinter from the fire and turned with a smile. 'You will excuse me not offering you one of these, Sergeant, but the supply is limited and I can only obtain them with great difficulty. You'll find cigarettes on the desk behind you.'

Nick helped himself and the Indian stood with his back to the fire, his face perfectly calm. 'Mr Lazer is in trouble?'

Nick shook his head. 'No question of that at all. It's just that I'm trying to trace someone rather urgently and I think Lazer might be able to help me. I understand he's a drug addict and registered with you.'

'That is perfectly correct,' Das said. 'Mr Lazer has been

a patient of mine for two years or more now. I take a particular interest in people in his unfortunate condition. Very few doctors do, I might add.'

'How advanced is Lazer?'

Das shrugged. 'His daily intake is of the order of seven grains of heroin and six grains of cocaine a day. When you appreciate that the normal dose to relieve pain is one-twelfth of a grain of heroin, this indicates the extent of the problem.'

'Can't anything be done?'

'For most patients, I'm afraid not. I have patients who've been "dried-out," as they call it, as many as sixteen or seventeen times. They regress with astonishing ease. The trouble is that most of them have quite crippling personality defects which explains their initial need for drugs, of course.'

'I find that hard to accept where Lazer's concerned,' Nick said. 'I've seen his record. He did rather well with the RAF during the war.'

'Charles Lazer is a particularly tragic case. He first took heroin and cocaine at a party something like three years ago. Apparently he was quite drunk at the time and didn't know what he was doing.'

'And after that he was hooked?'

'I'm afraid so. He's dried-out on two occasions, once for almost five months before regression set in and believe me, that's really quite remarkable.'

'So there's still hope for him?'

Dr Das smiled slightly. 'You seem to have a personal interest here.'

Nick shrugged. 'I've seen his record, I like the sound of him – it's as simple as that. He fought a good war, Dr Das. I'm still old-fashioned enough to think that should count for something. Isn't there anything you can do for him – anything concrete?'

The Indian nodded. 'There is a new method which a colleague of mine in London has enjoyed remarkable success with during the past year. It involves the use of apomorphine and the actual withdrawal of drugs from the patient over a period of some months.'

'And it really works?'

'With co-operation from the patient. Apomorphine is morphine minus a molecule of water. Injected into the patient, it cuts his craving for the drug and prevents the withdrawal symptoms usually associated with any attempt to cut down the daily intake. These can be extremely unpleasant.'

'Have you mentioned this to Lazer yet?'

'I was going to tonight, but he didn't turn up for evening surgery.'

'Isn't it possible that he would come outside surgery hours if his need was urgent enough?'

Das shook his head. 'He'd be wasting his time. My first rule is that I never give prescriptions for drugs outside surgery hours. This may seem harsh to you, but I assure you that firmness and an insistence on some sort of discipline are absolutely essential in handling this type of patient.'

'So Lazer would have to wait till morning surgery and get through the night the best way he could?'

'Highly unlikely.' Das shook his head. 'Unless I'm very much mistaken, he'll make straight for the all-night chemist's in City Square. There are certain to be one or two addicts having their prescriptions for the following day filled and they all know each other in a town of this size. Lazer will borrow or buy a few pills to tide him over till morning.'

'You think I'll find him there?'

'I'm certain of it.'

'I'd better be moving then. I don't want to miss him.'

'I should warn you of one thing,' the Indian said as they moved back along the corridor to the front door. 'After Lazer's first injection, you will notice something of a change in him. Sometimes the subject becomes paranoic with a particular fear where the police are concerned. More often than not, his tongue will simply run away from him or he'll have temporary aural or visual hallucinations. All quite harmless, but disturbing if you aren't used to this sort of thing.'

'I'll bear that in mind.' Nick held out his hand.

'Any time I can help, Sergeant.' The Indian's grip was surprisingly strong. 'Don't hesitate to call.'

The door closed behind him and Nick went down the steps, got into the car quickly and drove away through the heavy rain.

8

Chuck Lazer held on grimly as the beetles started to crawl across his flesh with infinite slowness, setting up a muscular reaction he found impossible to control. He stepped out of the entrance of the all-night chemist's and turned his face to the night sky, the stinging lances of rain giving him some kind of temporary relief.

Behind him, a small wizened man in an old beret and raincoat moved out, unwrapping the package he held in his hands.

Lazer turned quickly. 'Hurry it up, Darko, for Christ's sake. I can't take much more of this.'

The little man opened a pillbox and shook some heroin tablets into Lazer's palm. 'Don't forget where they came from,' he said. 'I'll be in the Red Lizard for coffee around eleven in the morning. You can pay me back then.'

He moved away quickly and Lazer walked to the kerb. At the same moment, a green Mini-Cooper pulled in beside him. The door swung open and a young man in a spectacular blue raincoat got out.

'Detective Sergeant Miller, Central C.I.D., Lazer. I'd like a word with you. Where can we talk?'

Lazer took in the coat, the strange dark eyes, the military style cap and laughed wildly. 'General, you could be Alexander the Great and Napoleon rolled into one for all I care. Right now, you'll have to take your place in the queue.'

He dodged across the road between two cars, reached the centre island and disappeared down the steps of the public lavatory. Nick judged his moment and went after him.

At the bottom of the steps, the attendant's little office was dark and empty and when he turned the corner into the vast tiled lavatory, he found it deserted except for Lazer who was feverishly wrestling with the handle of one of the stalls at the far end.

As Nick reached him, the American got the door open and lurched inside. He pulled down the seat, ignoring Nick and dropped to one knee, taking several items from his pocket and laying them out.

He took off his raincoat and jacket, pulled back his sleeve and knotted a brown lace around his upper arm in a rough tourniquet to make the veins stand out. He filled a small bottle with water from the pan, dropped in a couple of tablets, struck a match feverishly and held it underneath.

He turned his head, teeth bared in a savage grin, all the agony of existence at this level spilling from his eyes. 'It's a great life if you don't weaken, General.'

He reached for another match, knocked the box to the floor, spilling its contents, and moaned like an animal. Nick took a lighter from his pocket, flicked it into life and held it out without speaking.

Lazer held the flame under the bottle for another couple of minutes and then dropped it quickly and filled his hypodermic.

Four years as a policeman in one of the largest industrial

cities in the North of England had hardened Nick Miller to most things, but when that filthy, blunted needle went into Lazer, it went into him also. Blood spurted, Lazer loosened his crude tourniquet and his head went back, eyes closed.

He stayed that way for only a second or two and then his whole body was convulsed. He grabbed at the wall with an exclamation and lurched into Nick who crouched in front of him.

The American stayed that way for a while, head down and then he looked up slowly and managed a ghastly smile. 'The moment of truth, General. Now what was it you wanted?'

9

The club was just around the corner in a side street, the sort of place that had mushroomed by the dozen during the past few years, and Nick remembered it well from his days on the pavement in Central Division.

The big West Indian on the door grinned as they came down the narrow stairs. 'Hi, there, Chuck! How's every little thing? You going to play for us tonight?'

'No can do, Charlie,' Lazer said as he scrawled his name in the book. 'I got a gig someplace later on when I can remember where it is.'

The Negro turned to Nick and immediately something moved in his eyes. Nick held up a hand quickly. 'Strictly pleasure, Charlie. How's business?'

'Fine, Mr Miller. Just fine. Ain't seen you around. I heard you'd left the Force.'

'Just a nasty rumour, Charlie. I'm a sergeant with the Crime Squad now. You'll be seeing a lot of me.'

Charlie grinned, exposing his excellent teeth. 'Not if I can help it, I won't.'

There were no more than half a dozen people in the main bar, all coloured. Lazer raised a hand to the barman and sat down at a mini piano on a dais against the wall. Nick lit a cigarette, pulled forward a chair and sat beside him.

The American's hands crawled across the keys, searching for something in a minor key, finding it after a moment or two, a pulsating, off-beat rhythm that had something of the night and the city mixed in with it.

Nick waited his chance, then moved in with the right hand, blending in expertly. The American turned and grinned his appreciation.

'You've bin there, General. You've bin there.'

They finished with a complex run of chords that had the other people in the bar applauding. The American's eyes glittered excitedly and his face was flushed. When the barman brought two whiskies on a tray with the compliments of the house, he swallowed one down quickly and laughed.

'You've got a soul, General, a golden, shining soul. I can see it drifting around you in a cloud of glory. You're Tatum and Garner rolled into one. If Brubeck heard you, he'd turn his face to the wall and weep tears of pure joy, General. Tears of pure joy.'

'Garvald,' Nick said. 'Ben Garvald.'

Lazer faltered, the spate of words drying momentarily. 'Ben?' he said. 'My old buddy Ben? Sure, I know Ben. He was around my place earlier tonight.' He paused, a worried frown on his face. 'Or was it tonight? Maybe it was some other time.'

'What did he want?' Nick said patiently.

'What did he want? What did old Ben want?' Lazer's mood changed suddenly. He reached for Nick's glass, emptied it, then started to play a Bach prelude with exquisite skill. 'Well, I'll tell you, General. Old Ben wanted to

know about his wife, what her new name was and where
she lived.'

'And that's all?'

'Then he wanted to know where he could find Sammy.'

'Sammy?'

'Sammy Rosco. He's the strong-arm man at Club Eleven.
Lives in Carver Street.'

'Why did Garvald want to see him?'

Lazer changed to a Strauss waltz. 'He didn't mean him
any good, General, that's for sure. The Angel of Death
walked at his side. The Lord have mercy on the soul of
Samuel Rosco, miserable sinner.' He laughed wildly. 'Heh,
you know what that creep did, General? Sicked a couple
of cheap punks on to Ben in the fog outside Wandsworth.
Did *he* make a mistake.'

He was at the high point of his ecstasy, knowing and yet
not knowing what he was saying and Nick pushed his
advantage.

'What did he want Bella for, Chuck? Was he angry with
her?'

'With Bella? Why should he be angry?' The waltz changed
into a slow, dragging blues that brought a Negro couple in
the corner to their feet to dance. 'He loved that woman,
General. He loved her and she threw him overboard and
married another man.'

'So maybe he wants to even the score a little.'

'You mean cut her up or something?' The fingers faltered,
the melody drifted into silence. 'General, you don't know
Ben Garvald. You sure as hell don't know Ben Garvald.'
He leaned forward and laid a hand on Nick's shoulder.
'Where women are concerned, he's the softest touch in
town.'

'You've made your point.' Nick started to his feet.

Lazer held on tight. 'Why all the interest? You think he's
going to have a go at Bella?'

'She does.'

'She's made an official complaint?'

'Something like that.'

'The lousy bitch. After all he did for her. Nine stinking years, then she divorces him and marries an old man with a bag of gold.'

'Life can be hell,' Nick said.

He moved away quickly, aware of Lazer's quick cry, went straight up the stairs without looking back and went along the alley into City Square. Carver Street and Sammy Rosco were obviously next on the agenda and he got behind the wheel of the Mini-Cooper and moved away quickly. Behind him in the entrance to the alley, Lazer paused, a hand raised in a futile gesture as Miller drove off. A match flared in a doorway beside him and Ben Garvald moved out, lighting a cigarette.

'Who's your friend, Chuck?'

Lazer swung round in surprise. Already, the initial jolt of the drug was wearing thin and he was dropping fast towards a level more consistent with normal behaviour.

'Where in the hell did you spring from?'

'I wanted to see you again. Remembered what you said about the all-night chemist's in City Square. You and the character in the blue coat and fancy cap were standing at the kerb when I came round the corner. Who is he?'

'A copper, Ben. Detective Sergeant.' Lazer searched his memory. 'Miller. That's it – Miller.'

'You're joking,' Garvald said. 'I've never seen a peeler that looked like him before. What did he want?'

'You, Ben,' Lazer said. 'He wanted to know if I knew where you were.'

'Did he say why?'

Lazer tried again. 'Bella, that's it, Bella. She doesn't want you around.'

'She's got her nerve,' Garvald said. 'What did you tell this peeler, then?'

And Lazer, his mind chilling as the ecstasy ebbed away, couldn't remember. Garvald saw the situation for what it was and nodded quickly.

'Forget it, Chuck. It doesn't matter. I'm clean as a whistle and those sods up there at the Town Hall know it. In any case, I've more important things to think about. Where would I find Fred Manton round about now?'

'The Flamingo for sure.'

'Can you get me in the back way? I'd like to give him a surprise.'

'Nothing simpler,' Lazer said. 'He has a private service stair with a door to the alley at the side. You wait there and I can go in the front way and open it for you.'

'Then let's get moving, I'm running out of time,' Garvald said and somewhere in the distance, muffled by the rain and fog, the Town Hall clock sounded the first stroke of midnight.

10

At forty-five, Jack Brady had been a policeman for nearly a quarter of a century. Twenty-five years of working a three-shift system, of being disliked by his neighbours, of being able to spend only one weekend in seven at home with his family and the consequent effect upon his relationship with his son and daughter.

He was not a clever man, but he was patient and possessed the kind of intelligence that can slowly but surely cut through to the heart of things and this, coupled with an extensive knowledge of human nature gained from a thousand long hard Saturday nights on the town and numerous times like them, made him a good policeman.

He had no conscious thought, or even desire, to help society. Society consisted of the civilians who sometimes got mixed up in the constant state of guerrilla warfare that existed between the police and the criminal and, if anything, he preferred the criminal. At least you knew where you were with him.

But he was no sentimentalist. A villain was a villain and there was no such thing as a good thief. One corruption was all corruption. He'd read that somewhere and as he walked through the streets, head down against the rain, he remembered it and thought of Ben Garvald.

From the way he had discussed the case with Grant, Miller had seemed to take a fancy to Garvald. If that was his attitude, then the sooner he fell flat on his face and got the boot, the better. A copper's job was to catch thieves and all the education in the world couldn't teach a man to do that – only experience.

Brady sighed morosely and paused to light a cigarette. The strange thing was that now that his initial anger had evaporated, he found to his surprise that he had been more impressed with Miller than he had thought possible. On the other hand, that was no reason for not teaching him a lesson. It would sharpen the lad up for next time.

Gascoigne Square was a quiet backwater no more than a quarter of a mile from the Town Hall. Its gracious Georgian town houses were still in excellent condition and occupied mainly as offices by solicitors and other professional men, but one or two of the larger houses had proved ideal for conversion into the kind of night club-cum-gaming houses that had mushroomed all over the country since the change in the law.

And some of them also provided for more elemental needs. Brady smiled sardonically as he passed Club Eleven and a taxi unloaded half a dozen middle-aged businessmen who jostled each other excitedly as they went up the steps to the narrow entrance.

They'd get everything they needed in that hole. Molly Ryan would see to that and one or two of them might even pick up a little more than they'd bargained for. But that was life and you took a chance with each new day that dawned.

The Flamingo certainly had more class, but still looked a little out of character in the old Square with its striped awning and garish neon lighting. A few yards from the entrance, a small wizened man in tweed cap and army greatcoat sat on an orange box, a pile of Sunday newspapers spread out beside him.

The old man knew Brady and Brady knew the old man, but no sign of recognition passed between them. The policeman mounted the steps to the entrance and passed through the glass door that a commissionaire in red uniform held open for him.

A dark haired Italian in a white dinner jacket moved forward at once, an expression of consternation on his face. He tried to conceal it with a brave smile, but failed miserably.

'Mr Brady. What a pleasure. There is something I can do for you?'

Brady stood there, hands in the pockets of his cheap raincoat, ignoring the man, distaste on his face as he took in the thick carpets, the cream and gold décor and the cloakroom girl in her fishnet stockings.

'I want Manton. Where is he?'

'Is there perhaps something wrong, Mr Brady?'

'There will be if you don't get Manton down here fast.'

A party of three or four people, newly arrived, glanced at him curiously and the Italian stepped to a door marked *Private* and opened it.

'I believe Mr Manton is at the bar. If you'll wait in here, I'll go and see.'

Brady moved inside and the door closed behind him. The office was little more than a cubbyhole, with a desk and a green filing cabinet taking up most of the space. There was a half-completed staff duty list on the blotting pad and he turned it round and examined it idly, noting a familiar name here and there.

The door clicked open behind him and closed again. When Brady turned, Fred Manton was leaning against the door, lighting a cigarette. He was a tall, lean man with good shoulders that showed to advantage in the well-cut dinner jacket. The blue eyes and clipped moustache gave him a faintly military air which went down well with the customers, many of whom nicknamed him the Major and imagined him the product of one of the better public schools.

Nothing could have been further from the truth as Brady knew well and he dropped the duty list on the blotter and looked Manton up and down, contempt and open dislike on his face.

Manton went behind the desk, opened a drawer. He held up the duty list. 'Some people might say you'd been sticking your nose into things that didn't concern you.'

'You're breaking my heart,' Brady said. 'Garvald – Ben Garvald. Where is he?'

Manton seemed genuinely surprised. 'You must be getting old. Last I heard he was in Wandsworth. I thought everybody knew that.'

'He was released yesterday. But you wouldn't know about that, would you?'

Manton shrugged. 'I haven't seen Ben in nine years, not since the day he went down the steps for the Steel Amalgamated job in Birmingham or aren't you familiar with that one?'

'In detail,' Brady said. 'Garvald's wheelman got clear away after that little tickle. We never did manage to run him down.'

'Well, don't look at me,' Manton said. 'I was at home that night.'

'Who said so, your mother?' Brady sneered.

Manton crushed his cigarette in the ashtray very deliberately and reached for the telephone. 'I don't know what you're trying to pull, but I'm getting my lawyer in before I say another word.'

As he lifted the receiver, Brady pulled it from his hand and replaced it in its cradle. 'All right, Manton, let's stop playing games. I want Garvald. Where is he?'

'How should I know, for Christ's sake. This is the last place he'll show, believe me.'

'When we pulled him in for the Steel Amalgamated job, you and he were partners in a club on the other side of the river.'

'That's right. The old One-Spot. So what?'

'Maybe Garvald thinks you still owe him something or did you pay him off while he was inside?'

'Pay him off?' Manton started to laugh. 'What with – washers? After they pulled Ben in, your boys cracked down on the One-Spot so hard we went bust inside a month. I owed money from here to London. So did Ben if it comes to that, but he wasn't around when the bailiffs arrived. I was.'

There was a bitterness in his voice that gave the whole sorry story the stamp of truth and Brady, facing the fact that his hunch had been wrong, swallowed his disappointment and made one last try.

'You've got a place of your own upstairs haven't you? I'd like to have a look round.'

'Got a warrant?'

'What do you think?'

Manton shrugged. 'It doesn't matter. Look all you want. If you find Ben, let me know. I could put him to work for two years and he'd still owe me money.'

'My heart bleeds for you,' Brady said and he opened the door.

Manton smiled, teeth gleaming beneath the clipped moustache. 'Come to think of it, I could do with another man on the door in the spring, Brady. How long before you retire?'

Brady's hand tightened on the door handle, the knuckles whitening as the anger churned up into his throat in a tight ball that threatened to choke him.

He took a deep breath and when he spoke, his voice was remarkably controlled. 'Now that was a stupid remark for a smart boy like you to make, Manton. Really stupid.'

And Manton knew it. As his smile evaporated, Brady grinned gently, closed the door and walked across the thick carpet to the entrance.

The rain, which had drifted on the wind for most of the evening, was falling heavily now and he paused beside the old newspaper man who was swathing himself in a groundsheet. Brady picked up a newspaper and opened it at the sports page.

'Ben Garvald, Micky. Remember him?'

The old man's voice was hoarse and broken, roughened by disease and bad liquor over the years. 'Couldn't forget one like him, Mr Brady.'

'Has he gone in the Flamingo tonight?'

The old man ignored him, pretending to search for change in one of his pockets. 'Not a chance. There's always Manton's private entrance, mind you, beside the staff door in the alley. There's a stair straight up to his flat.'

'Good man, Micky.'

Brady dropped a couple of half crowns into the old man's palm, received a copper or two in change for appearances' sake and moved away. At the corner of the alley which cut along the side of the Flamingo, he paused and glanced back. There was no sign of the commissionaire at the entrance and he moved into the narrow opening quickly.

There was a row of overflowing dustbins, and an old gas

lamp bracketed to a wall illuminated two doors. One was marked *Private – Staff Only*. The other carried no sign and when he tried the handle, it was locked.

At the other end of the alley, he could see the main road and the sound of the late night traffic was muted and strange as if it came from another place. He checked his watch. It was a little after eleven and he didn't have to return to the office till midnight. He went back along the alley towards the square, found a doorway, moved into the shadows and waited.

It was bitterly cold and time passed slowly. He leaned in the corner, hands thrust deep into his pockets, and time crawled, minute by slow minute, and no one came. He was wrong, that was the truth of it. *You must be getting old.* Manton had said that and maybe it was true. Was this all he had to show for twenty-five years?

A strange nostalgia gripped him. If only he could start again, go back to the beginning, how different everything would be. As if from a great distance, he seemed to hear voices. He took a deep breath and came back to reality with a start, realizing to his annoyance, that he had almost fallen asleep.

A man had moved from the shadows and stood beside the staff entrance lighting a cigarette. Brady recognized Chuck Lazer at once, and also remembered that the American was employed as a pianist at the club.

As the staff door closed on Lazer, Brady leaned back again, shivering as a cold wind moved along the alley, lifting the skirts of his raincoat. He was wasting his time, that much was obvious.

He lifted his wrist to examine the luminous dial of his watch and saw to his astonishment that it was ten minutes past twelve and at that moment the door to Manton's private staircase opened and someone whistled softly. Ben Garvald moved out of the shadows farther along the alley, paused under the lamp and vanished inside.

Trapped by his own astonishment, Brady stayed there in the shadow for a moment, then pulling himself together, he went forward, a cold finger of excitement making his stomach hollow.

The door to Fred Manton's private staircase was still immovable, but the staff entrance opened to his touch and he hurried inside.

11

When Lazer opened the private door and Garvald entered, he found himself in a small square hall at the bottom of a flight of carpeted stairs. Lazer went first. At the top, he opened a door cautiously and peered into a narrow corridor.

'What have we got here?' Garvald demanded softly.

'Manton's private suite. His office is at the far end. He's in there now, I've just been speaking to him. He wants me to take a couple of boys from the band and go up to Bella's place to make with the mood music. Big party night.'

'Anything special?'

'Harry's birthday.'

'She *must* be getting sentimental in her old age,' Garvald said. 'Don't tell her you've seen me. I'd like it to be a surprise.'

'My pleasure.' Lazer grinned widely. 'Maybe you'll be up there later on?'

'Depends on how the cards fall. I'm staying at the Regent Hotel in Gloyne Street. If anything comes up, you can get in touch with me there.'

'Will do.' They moved along the corridor and the American opened a green baize door on the left. 'This way to hell,' he said as music and laughter drifted up. 'Don't do anything I would.'

Garvald went along the corridor and paused outside the door at the far end. For a moment he hesitated, waiting for some sound through the half-open transom. He was conscious of a movement behind him and turned quickly.

A tall, broad shouldered man was standing watching him. He had long dark hair swept back over each ear, curling slightly at the nape of the neck and one good eye regarded Garvald unwinkingly. The other was coated with an obscene patina of cream and silver.

'What's a game, Jack?' he demanded in a harsh voice.

Garvald looked him up and down calmly, turned without a word and opened the door. The room into which he entered was decorated in cream and gold and a fire flickered in a Queen Anne fireplace. Manton was sitting behind a walnut desk, papers spread before him. He glanced up with a start.

For several moments he and Garvald looked steadily at each other and then Manton sighed. 'I hoped you wouldn't do this, Ben.'

'Come back?' Garvald shrugged, opened a silver box on the desk and helped himself to a cigarette. 'A man needs his friends after what I've been through, Fred. Where else would I go?'

The man with the wall-eye spoke from the doorway. 'He couldn't have got in through the club or the kitchen, Mr Manton, they'd have buzzed through. That means the side door. Shall I check him for a key?'

'You do and I'll break your arm,' Garvald said genially.

Wall-eye took a sudden step forward, his face dark, and Manton held up a hand. 'Leave it, Donner. He'd put you in hospital for a month and I need you around. Go back downstairs.'

Donner stood there for a moment, his single eye glaring ferociously at Garvald, then he turned on his heel and the door slammed behind him.

Manton went to a wall cabinet, opened it and took out a bottle of whisky and two glasses. He filled them both and toasted Garvald silently.

'How *did* you get in, Ben?'

'Now I ask you,' Garvald said. 'When did I ever need a key to open a door?'

Manton chuckled. 'That's true enough, God knows. You were the best door and window man in the business in the old days.'

He moved back to the desk and lit a cigarette, taking his time over it. 'Why did you come back, Ben? There's nothing for you here.'

'Then why were you so anxious to keep me out? Sicking those two tearaways on to me in the fog outside Wandsworth yesterday was a mistake. Nothing on earth could have kept me away after that.'

'Things have changed,' Manton said. 'It isn't like the old days any more. The kind of money people throw around now, you can make more out of a good legitimate club than we ever did from the rackets. With the form you have behind you, Ben, you'd be bad for business. It's as simple as that.'

'They tell me you work for wages now, I never thought I'd see the day.'

'If you know that, then you know who I work for,' Manton said calmly. 'Harry Faulkner – and he treats me just fine. I get a good basic plus a slice of the cake twice a year. More than we ever dreamed of making at the old One-Spot.'

'When you were in partnership with me.'

Manton put down his glass and said deliberately: 'Let's get one thing straight, Ben. After the coppers picked you up for that Steel Amalgamated job, they shut the One-Spot up tight. It took me two years of working for Faulkner to pay off the debts. I don't owe you a thing.'

Garvald grinned. 'I didn't say you did.'

Manton was unable to control his surprise. He stood behind the desk frowning suspiciously, and then, as if coming to a sudden decision, sat down, took out a bunch of keys and unlocked a drawer. 'Oh, what the hell. So I owe you a favour.' He produced a couple of packets of notes and threw them on to the blotter. 'There's five hundred there, Ben, that's all I can manage.'

Garvald looked down at the money, a strange smile on his face, then he moved to the cabinet and poured himself another whisky. When he turned, his face was without expression.

'No thanks, Fred.'

Manton jumped up angrily. 'Then what do you want? Is it Bella?'

'She *is* my wife, Fred.'

'Don't you mean *was?*' Manton chuckled sourly. 'That kind of talk's going to get you nowhere. Bother her and Harry Faulkner will have you cut down to size so fast you won't know what hit you.'

Garvald smiled. 'And you telling me everything was so legitimate these days.'

Manton frowned, a puzzled expression in his eyes. 'No, it isn't Bella, is it? It's the cash – the cash from that Steel Amalgamated job.'

'Which went up like a torch with Jacky Charlton.'

'Or did it?' Manton said softly. 'Maybe you'd already divvied up?'

'An interesting thought, you must agree.'

There was a rush of footsteps in the corridor, the door was thrown open and Donner came in. He leaned on the desk, ignoring Garvald. 'There's a load of trouble on its way. That blasted copper, Brady.'

'What's he want?'

'Our friend here. Jango's stalling him at the bottom of the stairs, but I wouldn't give him long.'

Manton looked at Garvald angrily. 'What in the hell have you been up to?'

The big Irishman was already on his way to the door. 'Search me, but I've got other fish to fry. Give him my respects, Fred. I'll see myself out.'

As he disappeared along the corridor, Donner moved to go after him, but Manton caught him by the sleeve. 'Let him go. He hasn't been here, understand?'

He sat down behind his desk and lit a cigarette. A moment later, he heard voices in the corridor and Brady burst into the room, brushing aside a small, black-bearded man in a dinner jacket, whose black hair was close-cropped to his skull.

He stood at the side of Manton's desk, his face swollen with passion, and spoke with a heavy Greek accent. 'He came in through the staff entrance like a crazy man, boss,' he said, one hand weaving an intricate pattern in front of Manton's face. 'When I tried to stop him coming up, he nearly broke my arm.'

'Never mind this little squirt,' Brady said harshly. 'I want Ben Garvald. Where is he?'

Manton managed a frown with little difficulty. 'Ben Garvald? You must be out of your tiny mind.'

Brady went round the desk in a rush and jerked Manton to his feet, one massive hand crushing the silken lapels of the expensive dinner jacket. 'Don't give me that kind of crap, Manton. I was outside in the alley. Someone let him in through your private door.'

For a second only, Manton lost control. He glanced at Donner with a frown and Brady laughed harshly. 'I read you like a book, you pig. Now where is he?'

Manton pulled himself free and backed away. 'I don't know what all this is about, but I'd like to see your warrant. If you haven't got one you'd better get to hell out of here before I call in some real law.'

'You don't frighten me,' Brady said contemptuously.

'Maybe not,' Manton told him, 'but Harry Faulkner will.'

But Brady had already passed over into that area where action is in command of reason. At the best of times, caution had never been one of his virtues.

He glared at Manton, his eyes bloodshot. 'Ben Garvald's here, I saw him come in and, by God, I'm going to find him.'

He swung round, shoved Jango to one side with a careless sweep of his arm and went into the corridor. He opened the first door on the left, switched on the light and found himself in the bathroom.

When he turned to walk out, the three men were standing in the corridor watching him. There was a slight, polite smile on Manton's face. 'Find anything?'

'Maybe he thinks we flushed Garvald away,' Donner said.

Brady ignored both remarks and opened the next door.

'The sitting room,' Manton said helpfully. 'My bedroom next to it.'

Brady checked both of them without success and as he came out of the bedroom, noticed that a door at the other end of the corridor was standing slightly ajar. He moved to it quickly, pulled it open and looked down the stairs to Manton's private entrance.

He turned, his face suffused with passion. 'So that's it.'

'For Christ's sake, boss, how long is this farce running for?' Donner said, turning to Manton. 'Can't you give him a couple of fivers or something? Maybe that's all he came for in the first place.'

A growl of anger erupted from Brady's throat and he grabbed at Donner's shoulder, pulling him round. All Donner's pent-up rage and frustration surged out of him like a dam bursting.

'You keep your bloody paws off me,' he said viciously. He turned, catching the punch that Brady flung at him on his left shoulder and, at the same moment, moved in close, raising a knee into the unprotected groin. As Brady doubled over, the knee swung into his face, lifting him back. For a moment, the big policeman poised there in the doorway, clawing at the wall for support and then he went backwards into the dark well of the staircase.

12

As the three men stood in shocked silence, crowding the doorway, there was a slight creak behind them and Ben Garvald emerged from the linen cupboard.

'You're getting careless in your old age, Fred.' He shook his head. 'Remember the eleventh commandment? Never do a copper for it shall be returned unto you an hundred-fold.'

He brushed past them and went down the stairs. Brady was lying on his back at the bottom, legs sprawled in an unnatural position on the stairs, head and shoulders jammed against the wall. Blood matted his hair, trickling down into his eyes and his head moved slightly.

Garvald turned and looked up at Manton who had paused six or seven steps from the bottom. 'He doesn't look too good, Fred. I wish you joy.'

He opened the door and went out in one quick motion. As it closed, Manton pulled Jango down beside him. 'Get after him. Lose him and I'll have your ears.'

The door opened and closed behind the Cypriot and Manton dropped to one knee beside Brady. The policeman opened his eyes and glared up at him. There was a strange, choking sound in his throat, blood trickled from his nostrils and his head lolled to one side.

'My God, he's croaked,' Donner said in a whisper.

Manton got to his feet. 'What a bloody mess.'

'It was an accident,' Donner said desperately. 'He swung at me first. You saw.'

'I can just see a judge and jury taking my word for that,' Manton said bitterly. 'Be your age, Donner. You've killed a copper and that's a topping job.'

Donner pointed a shaking finger at him. 'If I go, you go. We're in this together, make no mistake about that.'

'You don't need to rub it in,' Manton said. 'Even if those swine up at the Town Hall couldn't find any evidence to implicate me, they'd invent some.'

'Then we've got to get rid of him,' Donner said. 'That stands to reason. What about dumping him in the canal off Grainger's Wharf? That's not far away.'

'That would make it look more like murder than ever,' Manton said. 'It's got to be cleverer than that. An accident, that's what we want. A convenient accident. Hit and run, perhaps.'

Donner nodded eagerly. 'That's not bad. That's not bad at all.'

'Especially if we used someone else's car and dumped it later. There's one thing, though. Who else saw him come in?'

'Only Jango,' Donner said. 'Luckily it was the staff break before the main floor show. They were all in the kitchen. He kept Brady talking at the bottom of the stairs and buzzed for me.' He hesitated. 'There's always Garvald.'

'We'll see to him later. First, we've got to get rid of our friend here. We'll take him up the alley between us to Stank's Yard, then you go and pick up a car and don't waste any time.'

The alley was deserted and they moved through the darkness, Brady's limp body a dead weight between them. Stank's Yard was at the far end near the main road and the door to it from the alley was never kept locked.

It was a dark well of a place between tall warehouses due for demolition. Much used by scrap merchants, it was choked with the accumulated junk of the years. Wide gates giving access to a narrow lane leading into the main road stood permanently open.

Manton leaned against the wall, trying to shelter from the driving rain, a cigarette cupped in one hand. Strangely enough, he wasn't afraid. Excited, if anything. In a strange way it was as if he were living again for the first time in years and he grinned ruefully. Now that would have given Ben Garvald a laugh if you like.

Someone entered the alley behind him from the main road and moved quickly along the uneven flagstones, footsteps echoing between the high brick walls. Manton stood back and waited. A moment later, Jango passed the doorway, his face clear in the dim light of the gas lamp which hung at the entrance to the alley.

Manton called softly to him and Jango turned and came hurrying back. He peered cautiously through the darkness. 'What's going on?'

'Brady died on us. We've got to get rid of him. I'm waiting for Donner to show up with a car.'

The Cypriot's breath whistled between his teeth. 'That isn't so good, Mr Manton. I'm not so sure I like to be mixed up in a killing.'

'You're in it up to your neck whether you like it or not,' Manton told him brutally. 'Unless you'd like me to remind someone about all that killing you did for EOKA. Now cut out the double talk and tell me about Garvald.'

'He's staying at a place called the Regent Hotel in Gloyne Street. It's no more than five minutes' walk from here. A fleapit. They don't even have a night porter on duty, just a chambermaid.'

'Did you speak to her?'

'Sure.' Jango chuckled and his eyes gleamed through the

darkness. 'She's a whore, Mr Manton. I know that place. They only keep her on to oblige the customers. A pound in the top of her stocking and she'll give you fifty-seven varieties.'

'How interesting,' Manton said softly. 'And just how far would she be willing to go for twenty quid?'

'I shudder all over to think of it,' Jango said simply.

The sudden roar of an engine echoed within the narrow walls and twin headlamps picked them out of the darkness as a vehicle moved in through the main gates.

It was a blue Thames van and as they went forward Donner got out of the driving seat. 'Best I could do. Get him in the back and let's get out of here.'

There was still light traffic about, but the lateness of the hour and the heavy, constant rain had by now almost cleared the streets as Donner drove out of the yard and turned into the main road.

'Don't waste time on anything fancy,' Manton told him. 'Any of these side streets will do.'

'Maybe it's not so good to make it so near the club,' Jango said.

'Use your brains,' Manton told him. 'He works Central Division, doesn't he, and he was seen to call at the club earlier on. It's got to be round here.'

Donner swung the wheel, crossing the dual carriageway, and turned into a narrow street that swung in a curve between tall warehouses towards the river. By now, it was raining even harder and the unheated cab was bitterly cold.

'This should do it,' Donner said and he braked in the middle of the deserted street so that the Thames skidded on the wet asphalt.

Manton opened the door and jumped out. The street had started to curve and at this point they were out of sight of the main road and the warehouses, lifting into the night on either side, were dark and still.

'Keep the engine running,' he told Donner. 'Jango and I can handle this.'

He moved to the rear of the van, opened the doors and pulled Brady out by the ankles. The Cypriot took him by the shoulders and together they carried him round to the front of the van, and propped the body upright against the bonnet.

They stood back and allowed Brady to slide to the ground, the blood that had soaked his face and shirt leaving its traces on the bonnet of the van. Manton raised his foot and smashed the nearside headlamp, glass splintering in a shower that cascaded over Brady's crumpled body.

'That should do it,' he said and clambered into the van, pushing Jango in ahead of him.

'Maybe I should run over him or something,' Donner said. 'Just to make it look good.'

As Manton hesitated, for the suggestion had its merits, the light from a car's headlamps splayed against the curved wall of a warehouse in front of them.

'Get moving,' he said hoarsely.

Donner slammed the van into reverse and the rear wheels bounced over the kerb as he swung the wheel. They shot forward, one wheel bumping over Brady's right foot, and drove away quickly as a small saloon car came round the curve behind them.

'I don't want it any closer than that,' Donner said as they crossed the dual carriageway into another side street.

'What do we do now?'

'You can drop Jango and me on the next corner,' Manton said. 'Then turn into Canal Street and run this thing off Grainger's Wharf. We don't want to make it too easy for them. We'll see you back at the club and make it fast. There's Garvald to take care of, remember.'

'Now that I look forward to,' Donner said. 'I really do.'

*

The man at the wheel of the saloon car was past his prime and the girl in the passenger seat was certainly not his wife, an added complication. He looked across in fascinated horror at the body which sprawled in the middle of the road and glanced nervously at the shadows crowding from the warehouse walls.

'The rotten swine,' the girl said. 'Didn't even stop.'

Her companion nodded, opened the door and walked across to Brady. When he came back he looked sick.

'Blood all over his face, I think he's dead.'

'Then we'd better get out of here,' the girl said briskly.

He turned, horror in his eyes. 'We can't just leave him here.'

'Why not?' she said brutally. 'We certainly can't do him any good. If it makes you feel any better, we can stop at the first call box. Dial 999, but don't give your name.' He sat there staring at her and she shrugged. 'Of course, if you want to see your name in the paper . . .

It was all he needed. He switched on the motor and drove away quickly, leaving the horror behind him under the dim light of the old-fashioned gas lamp.

After a while, the body stirred and a strange, inhuman sob lifted in the throat. Jack Brady rolled on to his face and tried to push himself up, but the arm was broken and he slumped forward, his blood washing across the asphalt, waiting for them to come as he knew they would, hanging on to that final hidden reserve that is in all men and which refused to allow him to die.

The bell of the approaching patrol car, a cry in the night, was warm and comforting and it was only when he heard it that he let go and slid into darkness again.

Ben Garvald lay on the bed smoking a cigarette and stared up at the ceiling. He'd had a lot of practice over the years, but this was different. Here, he could walk out any time he felt like it.

He wondered what Manton was doing about the copper and a grin touched the corners of his mouth. Now there was a problem, but on the other hand, no skin off his nose. He checked his watch. It was 1 a.m. and he frowned, trying to plan ahead.

If it was the sort of party he imagined it would be, it could run till morning. Certainly there was no point in trying to contact Bella before four or five by which time most of her guests would probably either be flat on their backs or in no fit state to know what was going on. He smiled, trying to imagine the look on her face when she first saw him.

There was a light knock on the door, it opened and the Irish girl came in with a cup and saucer in one hand. 'I made some tea.'

'I'll remember you in my prayers.'

She gave him the tea and laughed as she looked down at him. 'That'll be the day.'

She went to the window and stood looking into the street. When he had finished his tea, she came back and sat on the edge of the bed.

'Mind if I have a cigarette?'

'Help yourself.'

She took one and he produced his lighter. When she leaned forward, the nylon overall opened to the waist. She was wearing a slip, no brassière and her breasts were white and firm. She held his wrist tightly as she lit her cigarette, looking straight into his eyes. Garvald slid his left hand inside the neck of the overall and cupped it over a breast, the nipple hardening immediately against his palm.

'Aren't you the one?' she said softly.

He dropped the lighter, took the cigarette from her mouth and crushed it into the ashtray on the bedside table. 'It's been a long time,' he said. 'A hell of a long time. I'm warning you.'

Her arms went around his neck and he slid the overall down over her shoulders as their mouths came together. He was trembling, just like a kid having it for the first time, which was strange, and the light in the room seemed to grow dimmer.

She tumbled on to her back, her limbs asprawl, pulling him down into her softness, but his body seemed to have turned to water. For some reason he was on the floor and she was sitting on the edge of the bed staring down at him, the overall rucked up around her thighs, and her legs were the longest and most beautiful things he had ever seen.

Across the bed, the door opened and Donner came in. He was laughing but there was also something else in his face and when his mouth opened no sound seemed to come out. He moved round the end of the bed and Garvald tried to haul himself up, but it was too late. A boot swung into his side and the girl's cry was the last thing he heard as he plunged into the dark.

13

Nick lit a cigarette and sat on the edge of the table and watched her. After a while, Wilma emptied her glass with a shudder. She looked up at him, eyes wide and staring, the mascara smudged by her tears.

'I must look like hell. Could I have another?'

'It's your gin.'

He reached for the bottle and half filled her glass. 'Things must be pretty bad when you try to go out like that.'

She took the gin down in one quick swallow, made a face and reached for the bottle again. 'I thought you were my husband.'

'You must think the world of him.'

'I wouldn't cut him down if he was hanging.' She laughed harshly. 'I'll tell you about my husband, mister. I'll tell you all there is to know about Sammy Rosco. He's from under a stone. When he picked me off a Hamburg street in 1945 and married me, I thought it was a miracle. In those days I still prayed. I was only fifteen, but I lied about my age.'

'What happened?'

'We came home when he got demobbed. Home to this place.' She looked around her, an expression of loathing on her face.

'The honeymoon lasted for as long as it took him to run through his gratuity, then he brought the first man home.'

'And he's lived off you ever since?'

'Something like that. Come one, come all, drunk or sober, black or white, I was never known to refuse. Sammy saw to that. The first time I tried, he knocked me senseless. Roses all the way.'

'Ever tried moving out?'

'You could say that.' She emptied her glass and ran a hand over her eyes. 'Look, I've got a train to catch. I don't know who gave you my address, but I'm not playing those kind of games any more.'

'I didn't come for that.'

She hadn't eaten since lunch and the gin had gone straight to her head so that when she looked up at him, she had to concentrate hard, a frown on her face.

'Who are you?' And then in alarm, 'You aren't a friend of Sammy's, are you?'

'Not from the sound of him,' Nick said and took a chance. 'Nick Miller's the name. I'm a pal of Ben Garvald's.'

'You're a friend of Ben's?' She peered up at him in bewilderment. 'Come to think of it, I have seen you somewhere before,' and for some unaccountable reason she shivered.

'You couldn't have,' Nick told her. 'I'm new in town.

Ben and I did some bird together at Parkhurst. I was released last October.'

'You've just missed him,' she said. 'He was here a little while ago.'

'I was supposed to meet him outside Wandsworth yesterday, but something came up. I hear there was trouble.'

'They were waiting for him in the fog,' she said, staring into her empty glass.

Nick filled it again quickly. 'Who was, Wilma?'

'Oh, some rat or other that Sammy knew on the inside.' She started to laugh and drank some more of the gin. 'My God, he couldn't have told them much about Ben.'

'He's a hard man all right.'

'He can take 'em all.' She stared dreamily into space. 'But when it comes to women.' She shook her head drunkenly, slow tears oozing down her cheeks and reached for her handbag. 'See this?' She waved the fifty pounds in Nick's face. 'That's Ben for you. I'm going home, do you understand? I'm going home.'

'What about Sammy?'

She laughed contemptuously. 'Ben gave him the hiding of his life, then tossed him out on his ear.'

'Good for Ben.' Nick walked to the fireplace and kept his back to her.

'One thing I don't understand. Why would Sammy want to have Ben worked over when he came out of Wandsworth yesterday? It doesn't make any kind of sense.'

'You don't think he was working for himself, do you?' She stopped abruptly, as she caught sight of his face in the mirror over the fireplace.

'Go on, Wilma,' Nick said turning. 'Who was he working for?'

A sudden realization came to her that something was wrong and she shook her head vigorously and got to her feet.

'I don't know, I don't remember. I've got to get out of here. I've a train to catch.'

She reached for her case, but Nick beat her to it. 'Was it Fred Manton?'

She stared up at him, sobering rapidly, a dawning comprehension in her eyes. 'You aren't any friend of Ben's.'

She came closer, peering up into his face and Nick nodded slowly. 'Right every time, Wilma. I'm the law.'

There was real horror in her eyes now and she sobered completely, grabbing for the case and trying to push past him. 'I've done nothing wrong. You can't hold me here. I've got a train to catch.'

Nick shoved her back with all his force. 'Where did Ben go, Wilma? Tell me that and I'll run you to the station myself.'

For a moment she seemed to have lost the power of speech and then she pointed a shaking finger at him and the words came tumbling out.

'I know now why I was afraid of you, where I've seen you before. When I was a kid in Hamburg during the war, I had a cousin just like you, same white face, same eyes that looked through you like glass. He was in the Gestapo. When the end came, a mob hung him from a lamp post at the end of our street.'

'Ben,' Nick said. 'Where is he, Wilma? I only want a chat with him. He's done nothing wrong, yet.'

'You could put a white-hot poker on my feet and I wouldn't tell you. He's the only man ever treated me like a human being in my life.'

Nick shrugged. 'That's too bad. That means I'll have to take you in for questioning. You'll miss your train.'

Her face went very white, the mouth slack and she stared stupidly at him. 'But if I miss my train, Sammy will catch up with me again. He'll bring me back.'

Her head moved slowly from side to side and Nick said

patiently, 'All you have to do is tell me where Ben was going when he left here.'

The strange thing was that she genuinely didn't know and yet an inner pride, a strength she had never realized she possessed before, refused to allow her to betray the man who had helped her.

She swallowed the tears and her chin tilted. 'All right, so we go to the station.'

Nick sighed heavily and nodded. 'That's right, Wilma. The railway station. Come on. I'll give you a lift in my car.'

She stared at him incredulously, then snatched up her case and pushed round him. 'I'd rather ride with the devil.'

He followed her along the dark passage, down the steps into the yard and reached for her shoulder as she turned into the street beside his car.

'Don't be a fool, Wilma. I can have you there in a couple of minutes. There's a train at twelve twenty. We'll just make it.'

'Take your hands off me.' She pulled away. 'From now on, I walk alone.' Her face was yellow in the lamplight and full of hate as she gazed up at him. 'English police, Gestapo, what's the difference? You don't give a damn who gets hurt as long as you find out what you want to know. I hope Ben Garvald cracks your skull.'

She spat on the pavement at his feet, turned and walked away, the case banging against her leg, her high heels clicking on the hollow pavement, fading into the night. Nick stood there gazing into the darkness. After a while, he got back into the Mini-Cooper and drove away.

He ran from the car and mounted the steps to the plain white door that was the entrance to Club Eleven, head down against the driving rain. He pressed the bell and looked along the wet pavement to the Flamingo, a bright splash of light in the darkness. That could come later. For the moment, there was nothing he wanted so much as a few quiet words with Sammy Rosco.

The door opened and he moved in past a uniformed commissionaire and found himself standing in a tiny, thickly carpeted foyer. A young girl in black stockings and not much else, took his coat and a white-haired military-looking type came forward and smiled charmingly.

'Membership card, sir?'

'I haven't got one, but I'd like to see Miss Ryan. Tell her it's Nick Miller.'

'A personal friend, sir?'

'I think you could say that. We've even pounded the same beat together.' The man frowned and Nick produced his warrant card and dropped it on to the reception desk. 'Give her this with my compliments.'

The man's face fell, but he picked up the telephone and pressed a button. After a few moments' muttered conversation he replaced the receiver. When he turned, the smile was back and pasted firmly into place.

'Miss Ryan will be with you in just a moment, Mr Miller. Perhaps you would care to wait at the bar? The floor show is just beginning.'

'I'll find my own way,' Nick said.

He went through a door at the end of the passage and found himself standing at the top of a short flight of steps which dropped into a crowded dining-room. Above the tables was a raised catwalk and scantily dressed show girls were engaged in a dance routine.

The tables were crowded and the customers were exclusively men, most of them being entertained by the hostesses Club Eleven supplied in such profusion.

Nick ordered a drink and stood at the end of the crowded bar. After a while, there was a drum roll and a fat and balding comedian came skipping along the catwalk, a mike in one hand.

His patter was the usual mixture of crude filth and innu-
endo, but mixed in with it was a genuine acid wit, mostly
directed at the customers themselves, a fact none of them
seemed to grasp.

Finally the comedian stood to one side and took up his
ancillary role as compère of the big event of the evening
and the one for which, to judge from the applause, most
of the customers had been waiting.

It was the usual sort of thing. Famous beauties through
the ages. Each time the comedian announced a name, a
curtain rose at the back of the room disclosing a nude
tableau and various fleshy young women depicting Helen
of Troy, Eve in the Garden and so on.

At various times, the girls paraded along the catwalk,
displaying their ample charms in a manner the Lord
Chamberlain would have found very difficult to accept. All
the time, the comedian kept up a line of patter that verged
on the obscene.

There was sweat on the faces at the tables in the half
light beneath the catwalk, lust and desire and grasping hands
that reached up to touch the legs of the girls parading above.

Finally, there was a sudden gasp as a completely naked
coloured girl appeared from behind the curtains and started
a slow, careful promenade that reduced the room to silence
and awe. She half turned, the room was plunged into darkness and a light bulb flashed between her ample buttocks.

'Ten thousand volts,' the comedian cried and as the lights
came on again, the room rocked with laughter.

Nick turned to reach for his drink and found Molly
standing a few feet away looking at him. She was somewhere in her late twenties, a striking redhead in a green
dress that showed off to advantage a figure that was still
worth looking at. There was strength in her face, a touch
of arrogance, but when she looked at Nick and smiled, there
was nothing but warmth there.

'It's been a long time, Nick.'

'Too long.' He took her hands and held them tightly for a moment. 'I've been away for a year – on a course.'

'So I heard. Detective Sergeant now they tell me.'

'That's right. With Central Division. Let me buy you a drink.'

She shook her head. 'Not here. This is strictly for the mugs and that goes for the kind of booze we sell them too. Let's go up to my office.'

She threaded her way between the tables, dropping a word here and there, mounted a few steps beside the stage and went through a door marked *Private*. Inside, they passed what were obviously the girls' dressing-rooms, and finally came to another door which opened into a small and rather severely furnished room with filing cabinets, a desk and several telephones.

Molly opened a cabinet, took out a bottle of whisky and filled a glass. She handed it to him with a slight smile. 'Irish, pot distilled. I remember what you like.'

'Aren't you having one?'

'Straight poison. I'll never have another drink as long as I live.' She grinned. 'Besides, it slows you down.'

He looked around the room curiously and shook his head. 'Somehow this doesn't seem you.'

'This is my office,' she said calmly and sat down in the chair behind the desk. 'Strictly business. Isn't that what you're here for?'

'You must read me like a book.'

'I should be able to. I've known you long enough.' She chuckled. 'Remember when we first met? You were a young probationer pounding a pavement and I was a probationer of another sort.'

'Two o'clock in the morning and raining cats and dogs.'

'And we'd both had enough, so I took you back to my place.' She laughed. 'You thought I was the original scarlet woman.'

He shook his head. 'Never that, Molly. Never that.'

She lit a cigarette and leaned back in her chair. 'What do you want, Nick?'

'Ben Garvald for a start. Have you seen him tonight?'

She seemed genuinely amazed. 'Have I seen Ben? As far as I know, he's still doing time.'

'Not any more. Got out yesterday. The word is he's back and looking for Bella.'

Molly laughed harshly. 'Then I hope he finds her.'

'You don't like her much?'

'She isn't fit to clean his shoes. In my book, he's the tops. Oh, he's hard – hard as steel, but where women are concerned . . .

She sighed, her face softening, and Nick said: 'So you're on his side?'

'I should say so. When I first came over from Ireland, I was a green kid of eighteen. Didn't know the form. Before I knew where I was, the wrong mob had me under their thumb and I was being squeezed dry. Ben Garvald got me out of that, free, gratis and for nothing. That's his one weakness – he can't resist helping a woman in trouble.'

'All right,' Nick said. 'So you haven't seen him tonight?'

'All it happens, I haven't. Has Bella made a complaint?'

'Something like that.'

'The cow. I know where I'd like to see her.'

Nick decided to try another line. 'Is Sammy Rosco here by any chance?'

She nodded. 'He's on duty upstairs. Don't tell me you're looking for him as well?'

'Just a couple of questions. Routine mainly. Can we go up?'

She shrugged. 'I don't see why not.'

They left the office, moved along the passage and paused outside a door which carried the legend *Health Club Section – Members Only.*

'A new name for it,' Nick said, but she ignored the remark, opened the door and led the way in.

They moved along a quiet corridor, passed through a swing door and entered a long tiled room thick with steam. A fat and rather ugly middle-aged man came towards them, swathed in Turkish towels, a young woman in a white nylon smock helping him along. They moved into a cubicle and she pulled the curtain.

The room was lined with such cubicles and one of them didn't have its curtain properly drawn. As Nick passed, he glanced in and saw another fat and ageing specimen lying on a couch while a young woman massaged him. She seemed to find a pair of black knickers sufficient garment in the great heat.

As Molly held open the door at the end for him, she smiled. 'Strictly legal, Nick. They've all got diplomas from an institute of physical culture and massage I know in London.'

'Some institute.'

The room into which they entered was white tiled with a shower stall in one corner and a padded table in the centre. Sammy Rosco was sitting on a chair in the corner reading a magazine. He wore a white singlet and slacks.

'Very ornamental,' Nick said. 'What's he supposed to be?'

Rosco looked up with a frown, then threw down the magazine and got to his feet. 'Who's the funny man, Molly?'

Nick turned to her quickly. 'You can leave us now.'

'Heh, wait a minute,' she said in surprise.

'I said leave us.' His voice was hard and with the cutting edge of a razor. She turned and went out almost immediately, her face red, and Nick produced his warrant card. 'I haven't got much time, so let's have some straight answers, Rosco. You hired two men to attack Ben Garvald outside Wandsworth yesterday morning. Why?'

Rosco looked over his shoulder like a hunted animal. 'I don't know what you're talking about.'

'Don't waste my time,' Nick said wearily. 'I've seen your wife. She told me what happened at your place earlier and what Ben Garvald did to you.' He poked a finger at the livid bruise on the other man's left cheek. 'He must be quite a puncher.'

'That lousy rotten bitch. Just wait till I get my hands on her. I'll make her wish she'd never been born.'

'You'll have to wait a long time,' Nick said. 'She caught a London train about ten minutes ago. I put her on it myself.' He smiled softly. 'She's gone home, Sammy.'

Rosco shook his head in bewilderment. 'She couldn't. She didn't have the cash.'

'Garvald saw to that. Good of him, wasn't it?'

With a cry of anger and frustration, Rosco swung a tremendous punch, that Nick found no difficulty whatever in avoiding. Remembering Wilma, he moved in fast, his left sank in well below the belt, and his right swung to meet the descending face, splintering teeth. Rosco staggered back, cannoned into the padded table and slid to the tiled floor.

He lay there moaning, blood trickling into his white singlet and Nick crouched beside him. 'That was from Wilma, Sammy. And don't let's have any of that assault by a police officer crap. It wouldn't get you anywhere, believe me. Not with the kind of form you've got behind you.'

As he got to his feet, the door opened and Molly came in. 'He slipped and fell,' Nick said. 'Better see if there's a doctor in the house.'

She looked straight at him, her eyes hard. 'Don't come back, Nick. Never again as a friend. I like to know where I stand.'

'What's this?' he said. 'The Berlin Wall? Me on one side, you on the other?'

'Something like that.'

'Suit yourself. See you sometime.'

He brushed past her and went out through the steam,

past the cubicles and into the corridor beyond, his feet sinking into the thick carpet. Strangely enough, he felt no regret. In fact, already his mind was on his next move.

It was curiosity more than anything else that took him up the steps of the Flamingo. Manton would certainly deny having had any part in the attack on Garvald outside Wandsworth. Would probably deny having seen Garvald even if he had. Still, it might be worth having a look at him.

Manton was in the bedroom of his private suite, hurriedly changing out of his wet clothes, when the phone rang. He listened to what the man on the door had to say and nodded.

'Put him in the front office. I'll be five minutes.'

He dressed quickly in a clean white shirt and dark lounge suit, his mind racing. Detective Sergeant Miller? A new boy. Certainly no one he'd ever heard of round Central Division. But what did he want, that was the thing? The one comforting thought he carried with him when he left the room was that it couldn't have anything to do with Brady – there simply hadn't been enough time.

Nick was examining a framed historical map of the North of England on the wall when Manton came in and he turned and smiled pleasantly.

'Mr Manton – sorry to trouble you, sir. My name's Miller. Detective Sergeant, Central Division. I'm trying to locate an old acquaintance of yours, Ben Garvald. I've reason to believe he arrived in town today and I thought he might have contacted you.'

Manton decided to play the honest but puzzled businessman. 'Everybody wants Ben Garvald. What is all this, Sergeant? As I told Mr Brady earlier I didn't even know Ben was out.'

Nick frowned. 'Jack Brady's been here?'

'About an hour or so ago.' Manton hesitated. 'I hope I haven't said anything out of turn, but he came in through the front door just like you. Everybody saw him.'

'That's all right, Mr Manton,' Nick said. 'A misunderstanding, that's all. So you can't help me with Ben?'

'As I told Brady, I didn't even know he was out.'

'Fair enough. I won't trouble you any more then.' Nick moved to the door, hesitated and turned. 'Just one more thing. Does Sammy Rosco work for you?'

Manton frowned. 'That's right, just along the street from here. Why, what's Sammy been up to?'

'Nothing really,' Nick said pleasantly. 'But I'd get rid of him if I were you.'

'Why should I do that?'

'He tells lies, Mr Manton, mainly about you.'

Nick smiled and the door closed behind him. Manton stood there behind the desk for a moment, eyes narrowed, and then he picked up the telephone and dialled a number.

14

Harry Faulkner's house was in St Martin's Wood, an exclusive residential area not far from Nick's own home. It was a late Victorian mansion set back from the road in a couple of acres of ground. The whole place was a blaze of lights and there were so many cars in the drive he found difficulty in parking.

He mounted the wide steps to the porch and rang the front door bell, but there was no reply. After a while, he tried the ornate bronze handle. The door opened to his touch and he went inside.

The house seemed to be full of people. The hall was

crowded with them and couples sat all the way up the stairs, most of them with glasses in their hands.

And every bed occupied, he thought to himself wryly.

He took off his cap and coat, left them on a walking stick rack in the porch and pushed his way through the crowd towards the sound of a driving piano with rhythm and bass accompaniment that was somehow familiar.

He found himself in the entrance to a long, narrow room flanked by French windows to the terrace outside.

It had a beautifully polished parquet floor, obviously specially laid for dancing and was as crowded as the hall outside.

Chuck Lazer sat at a baby grand in a corner opposite the bar at the far end. Nick was just about to push his way towards him, when he felt a tap on the shoulder and turned quickly.

A tall, heavily built man in his thirties faced him, a polite smile on his face. He wore a dinner jacket that had been cut by someone who knew what he was doing, but the slightly crooked line of the nose and the hard eyes made Nick immediately wary.

'I saw you come in, sir. Is there something I can do for you?'

'And who might you be?'

'Craig, sir. Mr Faulkner's manservant.'

Nick almost laughed out loud. 'I'd like to see Mrs Faulkner. Do you know where she is?'

'She's rather busy right now, sir. Was it something important?'

Nick took out his warrant card. 'I think you'll find she'll come running when you tell her who it is.'

The smile disappeared, the eyes seemed harder than ever. 'If you'd come this way.'

Nick followed him through the crowd along the hall. Craig paused outside a door, took a key from his pocket and opened it. 'Mr Faulkner's study, Sergeant. If you'll wait in here, I'll fetch Mrs Faulkner. I believe she's in the kitchen checking on the supper.'

It was a pleasant room, lined with books from floor to ceiling. There was a magnificent walnut desk near the Adam fireplace and a small bar in one corner, carefully designed to stay in character. From the heavy velvet curtains, to the Persian carpet on the floor, everything was perfect. Too perfect. It was as if someone had called in a firm of interior decorators and ordered a gentleman's study as per the catalogue.

He helped himself to a cigarette from a box containing Turkish and Virginian, another anachronism, and moved across to the shelves. From their general appearance, the books had come with the study in some kind of package deal. He took one down, examined it and smiled. Even the pages hadn't been cut. As he replaced it, the door opened and Bella came in.

It was quite incredible. She didn't look a day older, no different from the healthy young animal he'd worshipped as a kid, hanging around on the corner of Khyber Street to see her go by.

The clothes were more expensive, of course. The red dress had obviously cost Faulkner a packet, the diamond brooch on one shoulder looked real.

But these were inessentials. The hair was still as dark, the eyes bright, mouth full and generous and when she moved to meet him, the old indefinable something was still there. A complete, deep sensuality that would still move men when her hair was grey.

'Miller?' she said. 'Nick Miller? Don't I know you?'

'A long time ago,' he said. 'Around the corner from your old house in Khyber Street. My mother kept a shop.'

Her smile was like a bubble breaking through to the surface. 'Now I remember. You're Phil Miller's kid brother.

I met him at a party the other week. He told me all about you.'

'I'm surprised he mentioned me in company.'

She took a cigarette from the box and he gave her a light. 'So you're a Detective Sergeant now?' She shook her head. 'And everywhere I go I see another of those television shops of Phil's. It doesn't make sense. Why aren't you working with him?'

'Phil has a flair for making money.' Nick smiled. 'I run to darker talents. In any case, I'm a sleeping partner.'

'Isn't that illegal or something? For a policeman, I mean?'

'We don't mention that.' He threw his cigarette into the fire. 'I've been trying to run Ben to earth for the past two or three hours without success. He's here in town, but that's as far as I've got.'

'Ben?' she said warily, her smile vanishing. 'What are you talking about?'

'Your sister made a complaint earlier this evening. Said you'd had a message from Ben saying he'd look you up. She asked us to run him down. Warn him not to bother you.'

'Why can't she mind her own damned business?' Bella said angrily.

'I didn't see her personally,' Nick said. 'But from all accounts, she was worried about you. About what might happen if Ben showed up.'

'Worried about herself and that precious school of hers more likely,' Bella flashed back at him, lapsing momentarily into the harsher accent of her youth and then she seemed to pull up short. 'No, that isn't really fair. She does worry about me – always has.' She smiled and shook her head. 'Daft, when you think about it. She's five years younger than me, but she started to do the thinking for both of us a long time ago.'

'Can I see the letter?'

'I've got it in a drawer in the bedroom. I'll only be a second.'

She crossed to the only other door in the room, opened it and went in. Nick could see a luxuriously furnished bedroom in red and gold with a reproduction four-poster bed. She opened a drawer in a dressing-table and came back carrying the letter. It was a small sheet of official prison notepaper, folded to envelope size and dated a couple of days previously. It was brief and to the point. *See you soon – Ben.* Even the prison officer who censored mail could have taken no exception to such an innocent sounding message.

'When did you get this?'

'The day before yesterday.'

'And you haven't shown it to your husband?'

'With his temper?' She shook her head and tapped her fingers impatiently on the edge of the desk. 'What would be the point? It might never happen. If he does show up, it'll be more for old times' sake than anything else. Ben would never do anything to hurt me.'

'Then what are you worrying about?'

She laughed. 'It seems to be Jean who's doing all the worrying. Maybe you'd better have a chat with her.'

'I'd like that.'

'I'll see if I can find her. She may still be in the kitchen. She was giving me a hand with the supper arrangements. You can't trust these catering people out of your sight.'

The door closed behind her and Nick moved across to the fireplace. He was standing with one foot on the polished brass fender, gazing into the flames and thinking about Ben Garvald, when the door opened again.

Some things can happen in life which have such a devastating effect that, after them, nothing can ever be quite the same again. Nick Miller was caught in such a timeless moment when he turned to find Jean Fleming standing just inside the door.

She wore high-heeled shoes, dark stockings, a simple dress of black silk which was barely knee-length and left her arms bare. There was about her a tremendous quality of repose, of detachment, as she stood there looking across at him.

It was as if in some strange way she was waiting for something. It was not that she was beautiful. The dark hair, razor-cut to the skull, gave her a rather boyish appearance and the sallow, Irish peasant face indicated strength more than any other quality, yet never before in his life had he felt such an immediate and over-riding attraction to another human being.

'We've met before,' she said.

He nodded. 'A long time ago.'

She moved towards him and when he took her hands, she was trembling slightly. 'What are you thinking?'

'That I'd like to take you away now – this minute – to some quiet place where no one could touch us.'

'Is there such a place?'

'Only in dreams.'

She laughed shakily, pulled her hands free and took a cigarette from the box on the table. He gave her a light and she smiled.

'I think you must have been about nine years old when I first fell in love with you.'

'Is that a fact now?'

'Oh, yes.' She nodded seriously. 'I used to hang around your mother's shop on the off-chance that you might come out.'

'I always thought you hated me.'

'Not you – Bella. Everything male in the district from the kids upwards thought she was the last word. I never minded till you joined in.'

'It would seem I've got quite a lot to make up for,' he said calmly and when she turned to look up at him steadily, her eyes were sea-green, so deep a man could drown in them.

She took a deep breath, as if pulling herself back sharply to reality. 'Bella said you wanted a word with me about Ben.'

'That's right. She didn't seem very pleased about you coming to see us.'

'Bella's been putting off what she should do today till tomorrow, ever since I've been old enough to understand her,' Jean Fleming said. 'If it was left to her, she'd pretend Ben didn't exist and never had. That's no good. No good at all.'

'I've done a little checking with some of his old friends,' Nick said. 'He's definitely in town.'

Her head came up sharply. 'You've no idea where he is now?'

'None at all. I thought he might come here.'

'Oh, God. I hope not.'

She walked away from him, obviously in deep distress, and Nick frowned. 'What can he do? Kick up a fuss, be a little unpleasant, that's all. Anything more and we run him in.'

'That's what Harry said.'

She reached out momentarily, almost as if she would recover the words and Nick said: 'So you told him about the letter?'

She nodded. 'Bella didn't want to, so I went to him behind her back. She still isn't aware that Harry knows. That's why I wasn't completely honest with Superintendent Grant. I thought that if Ben turned up in town and the police had a word with him, that would be enough.'

'What did Faulkner say when you told him?'

'He laughed about it. Said he could have Ben taken care of any time he wanted. He also said I was more worried about myself than Bella in this business.'

'And are you?'

'I suppose I am if I am honest. If Ben turned up here now, created a scene and had to be arrested, the scandal would brush off Bella within a week at the most. It could ruin me.'

'The school, you mean?'

She nodded. 'I can just see the newspaper reports. A headmistress with a brother-in-law released from prison after a ten-year sentence for armed robbery. They'd have a field day.'

'It means a lot to you, doesn't it?'

'Oakdene?' She laughed. 'It isn't even mine. Not completely, anyway. When Miss Van Heflin had to retire unexpectedly and offered to sell me the school, I didn't have the necessary capital.'

'Wouldn't Faulkner help?'

A muscle tightened in her right cheek. 'That kind of assistance, I don't need. Not from him. Miss Van Heflin suggested I should pay her a percentage of the annual profit for an agreed period.'

'And it's worked out all right?'

'Another five years and it's all mine.'

There was real pride in her face and he grinned. 'A long way from Khyber Street.'

'That's what Superintendent Grant said.' She smiled. 'A long way for both of us.'

He took her hands and held them tightly. 'I'd like to see more of you, Jean. A lot more.'

She moved into his arms and touched him gently on the face. 'I don't think you could get rid of me if you wanted to, now.'

They stayed there for a moment and then she pulled gently away. 'I'd like to have a few words with Bella, then you could take me home. I didn't bring my car. Or are you staying?'

He shook his head. 'I don't think so. I'd like to see Chuck Lazer before I go, though. Do you know him?'

'He used to play at Ben's club in the old days. He's the best there is. I'll look for you in there after I've seen Bella.'

She turned to the door and he caught her hand. 'I wouldn't like to be responsible for what might happen if I do see you home.'

Her face was very calm, the eyes fathomless. 'Then I'll be responsible.'

The door closed behind her softly. For a long time, he stood looking after her and then he started to move. Life could certainly be complicated and that was the understatement of the evening for a start.

When he went into the Long Room, Chuck Lazer was really high, way out on the edge of a cloud in a cool and quiet place where no one could touch him. After a while, he came back to earth slowly, his fingers crawling down the keyboard in a series of intricate chords and opened his eyes.

No one was listening and half the couples on the floor kept on dancing as though the music was still playing. As Lazer recognized him, Nick grinned sympathetically.

'You were on your own, man. Nobody heard.'

'Depends on your point of view, General. They were all out there with me, alive or dead, makes no difference. Fats and Bix, Jack Teagarden, Charlie Parker, Goodman, Billie Holliday. Anyone there ever was or ever will be.'

Nick offered him a cigarette, gave him a light. 'How about a drink?'

The American shook his head, ran the back of a hand across his forehead to wipe away the sweat. 'I need more than any drink, General, for what ails me.'

'I was speaking to your doctor earlier tonight,' Nick said carefully. 'He seems to think there's some hope for you.'

'Don't they always?'

'A new treatment,' Nick said. 'Not really new, but it's been tried successfully.'

'What's it involve. Withdrawal?'

'With the assistance of a drug called apomorphine. Prevents withdrawal symptoms and cuts out the craving for the usual stuff.'

'Sounds too good to be true.'

'How did you get hooked in the first place?'

Lazer shrugged. 'The wrong kind of party, too much booze. Someone gave me a shot for a giggle after I passed out. That's all it took.'

Nick's hand balled up into a fist on top of the piano, the knuckles gleaming whitely, and Lazer grinned. 'I know, General, that's just how I felt.' He got to his feet abruptly. 'Sit in for me a couple of minutes, will you? I need a fix.'

He pushed his way through the crowd to a door in the corner by the bar. Nick sat down, nodded to the bass man and drummer and moved straight into a solid, pushing arrangement of 'St Louis Blues'. He was into the third chorus when Lazer returned. Nick started to slow, but the American shook his head, sat on the edge of the stool beside him and joined in.

The volume increased gradually with the tempo, Lazer gauging the length of each break expertly, Nick responding in the bass. Quite suddenly, there was something there, something different that had the couples on the floor turning in surprise to move towards the piano, crowding in, drawn by something that was real, that was as elemental as life itself.

Without changing the tempo, Lazer moved into 'How High the Moon' and Nick, challenged by the brilliant phrasing, countered with a rhythm pattern that had the American crying out in delight, head thrown back.

His hands found a richer theme and Nick balanced with an intricate series of chords, dissolving into an eight-bar break that left his arms aching. He started to slow and Lazer followed him, down to the valley after the mountaintop, the quiet places where they finally faded in a minor key.

People were applauding all around and Lazer grinned, his eyes shining feverishly. 'You've been there, General. You've been there.'

Jean pushed through the crowd, her face glowing with surprise, and reached out to take his hand as he got to his feet. 'One of my minor vices,' Nick said with a grin. 'Are you ready to go?'

There was a slight tap on his shoulder and he turned to find Craig standing there, a polite, remote smile on the craggy face.

'Mr Faulkner's compliments, sir. If you'd be kind enough to follow me, I'll take you to him. He'd like a few words before you leave.'

15

Although Nick had never met Harry Faulkner personally, he had seen him at a distance on many occasions and knew that his brother met him now and then at clubs of the sort frequented by the wealthier businessmen of the town.

Respectable businessman with wide interests, philanthropist, sportsman, chairman of several charities. That was the image he liked to cultivate. Harry Faulkner had come a long way from the riverside slum where he'd first seen the light of day and he wore his possessions for all to see, like the fresh gardenia in his buttonhole daily, his house in St Martin's Wood, his cars, his beautiful young wife.

And he had won all these things, his position in society, by breaking the law or, at least, by using it for his own ends. All his life he had worked on the fringe of the underworld, using his brains to make others do the things he wouldn't do himself, always careful so that whatever happened, whatever went wrong, nothing could touch Harry Faulkner.

He was sitting at the desk in his study when Nick was shown in, a stockily built man of middle height who carried his sixty years lightly. Even the iron grey hair somehow gave an impression of force and vitality.

Craig withdrew and Faulkner got to his feet and came round the desk, hand outstretched, a pleasant smile on his face. 'So you're Nick. I've heard a lot about you. Play golf at the club with your brother regularly.'

'Is that so?' Nick said.

'How about a drink? Whisky all right?'

'Irish if you have it.'

He sat on the edge of the desk as Faulkner went behind the bar. He was wearing one of the most beautiful dinner jackets Nick had ever seen, superbly cut and somehow right up to date without being too far out. His pleated shirt front gleamed in the firelight, the cufflinks had just the right touch of ostenation.

There wasn't a hair out of place as he busied himself with the drinks, looking like something in an advertisement for good whisky in one of the better magazines. He was too perfect. It was as if someone had given him a list containing all the characteristics of a gentleman and he had ticked them off one by one.

He handed Nick one of the glasses and sat down behind the desk again. The whiskey was Jameson's and Nick savoured the inimitable flavour with conscious pleasure.

'Excellent,' he said.

'Glad you like it.' Faulkner carefully fitted a cigarette into a silver holder and leaned back in his chair. 'I've just had a little chat with Bella about this whole business. It's a pity that damned sister-in-law of mine can't keep her nose out of other people's affairs.'

'She seems to think it *is* her affair.'

'She would,' Faulkner said. 'All she can think of is that precious school of hers.'

'So you're not worried about Ben Garvald turning up here and causing any trouble?'

'He wouldn't be such a mug,' Faulkner said crisply, his accent slipping a little. 'I can look after my own. If Garvald doesn't know that by now, then it's time he learned.'

'An interesting point.' Nick swallowed a little more of his Jameson's. 'Someone tried to teach Ben a lesson outside Wandsworth when he was released yesterday morning. From what I hear, they came badly unstuck.'

'These things happen all the time,' Faulkner said blandly. 'All you need's a little bit of fog and every tearaway in town turns out to see what he can pick up.'

'Strange you should say that,' Nick said. 'Although we didn't have any fog up here, it was quite thick around Wandsworth yesterday morning.'

Faulkner had stopped smiling. 'What's that supposed to mean?'

'It means that a lump of dung called Sammy Rosco arranged the hit outside Wandsworth. He made a mistake. So did Fred Manton.'

Faulkner's face was quite expressionless. 'And what's Manton got to do with this?'

'That's the interesting part. From what I can make out, he was acting as middleman for a friend. Now I wonder who that could be?'

When Faulkner answered, his accent had slipped right back to the canal docks and his eyes sparkled viciously. 'If you've got anything to say, spit it out and be sure you can make it stick because I'll take you all the way.'

Nick swallowed the rest of his Jameson's, walked to the bar and helped himself to another. 'All right, it goes something like this. When Bella got that note from Ben the other day, she didn't want to tell you because she's the kind who thinks that if you close your eyes to a situation and pretend it's not there, maybe it'll go away. But her sister's built differently. She decided, on balance, that it would be better if you were told.'

'So?'

'You had a word with Manton, told him to arrange a reception for Ben when he got out of Wandsworth. The only kind of reception you thought he'd understand.' Nick grinned. 'You made a bad error there.'

'Finished?' Faulkner asked.

'I wonder what he wants with Bella?' Nick said. 'Maybe he'd like her back. She might even go with him. From what I hear, they used to be pretty thick in the old days.'

Faulkner's anger overflowed like hot lava and he jabbed viciously at a button on the desk. 'Who in the hell do you think you're talking to?'

'Big Harry Faulkner, the punter's friend,' Nick said. 'Businessman philanthropist, a dream at the orphans' Christmas party every year. Also thief, whoremaster and pimp.' He emptied his glass and put it down on top of the bar. 'Tell me something, Faulkner. I know those Gascoigne Street brothels of yours can supply any kind of female anyone ever wanted, but is it true you run a special line in the male variety as well?'

The door opened and Craig entered. He moved to the desk and Faulkner, his face ashen, raised a trembling hand. 'Throw him out.'

Craig turned slowly to face Nick, his fingers opening and closing. 'You know, I didn't like the look of you from the moment you walked in.'

He seemed very sure of himself. When he was about three feet away, he swung a tremendous punch that carried everything he had.

Nick moved in close, catching the blow with a karate block delivered with his left hand and kicked the big man viciously on the shin, lifting his right knee into the unprotected face as Craig doubled over.

He lay on his back moaning, a hand to his mouth, blood trickling between his fingers. 'Get up, Craig! Get up!' Faulkner ordered.

'I don't think he's going to be quite that stupid.' Nick walked across to the door. He turned with it half open, the dark eyes sending a cold shiver through Faulkner. 'There's more to this than shows on the surface, Faulkner. Much more. I'll be back when I find out what it is.'

Jean was standing at the entrance to the Long Room, a light evening coat over one arm, a jewelled bag swinging from the other. 'What did Harry want?'

'Nothing special. Ready to go?'

Before she could answer, Chuck Lazer pushed through the crowd. 'Leaving, General?'

Nick nodded. 'It's been sweet, but we've got to go.'

'Mind if I string along? I've had enough of this wake.'

Nick turned to Jean with a grin. 'A chaperon. That just about settles everything.'

'I wouldn't be too sure,' she said as he held her coat for her and, when they moved towards the door, they were laughing.

Faulkner moved round the desk and kicked Craig in the side. 'Go on, get out!'

Craig scrambled away from him, dodging another blow, got to his feet and wrenched open the door. As it closed behind him, Faulkner went to the bar and poured himself another whisky. He emptied the glass in two swallows, coughing as the liquor burned its way into his stomach.

For some strange reason, Miller reminded him of his teacher at Dock Road Elementary, old Walter Street who'd had a hard war in the trenches in the first lot and walked with a limp.

He remembered the first time he'd met Street after leaving school. He was nineteen, already living on the earnings of three women, dressed up to the nines in the best money could buy. He'd been a mug, really, trying to come the big man and old Walter in his shabby trenchcoat had looked at him as if he were a lump of dung he'd be glad to scrape off his shoe.

He hurled the glass into the fireplace, moved across to the bedroom and opened the door. Bella was standing in front of the mirror by the bed, pulling the red dress over her head. The flame coloured slip she was wearing had lifted over her rounded haunches and white flesh gleamed at the top of a dark stocking.

'What are you doing?' he demanded hoarsely.

'Ringing the changes. I'm wearing the black one next. Give me a hand, will you? This damned zip has broken.'

He stood beside her, reaching to pull the dress over her head, conscious of the warmth, the sweetness. He slid his hands under the armpits, cupping the full breasts, pulling her hard against him.

'For God's sake, Harry,' she said impatiently. 'There are a hundred and twenty people out there.'

As she turned, all the rage, all the anger and frustration boiled over and he slapped her across the face. 'Don't tell me what to do!' he shouted. 'I'm Harry Faulkner, understand? And you're my wife and you'll do whatever I say!'

She started to back away, fear on her face, and the sight of it made the blood race through his veins like fire. He grabbed for the neck of the slip, ripping it from top to bottom and she staggered, falling back across the bed.

He flung himself on her, hands sliding across her breasts, mouth reaching for hers and as always, she responded, running her fingers through his hair, kissing him passionately.

And it was no good. It was just like all the other times. The strength, the emotion, drained out of him and he pushed

himself up and looked down at her, a dazed expression in
his eyes. When he turned to the mirror, an old man stared
out at him.

'Can I get dressed now?' she said calmly.

He walked to the door like a dead man, opened it and
turned, moistening dry lips. 'I'm sorry, Bella. I don't know
what got into me.'

'That's all right, Harry.'

She stood looking at him, magnificent, the torn slip
hanging around her waist, but there was only pity in her
eyes and that was not what he wanted. He closed the door,
went to his desk and pressed the buzzer. There was still a
power he could command, a certain kind of power. That
was better than nothing.

After a while, the door opened and Craig came in, his
lips bruised and swelling. 'Yes, Mr Faulkner?'

'Has Miller left?'

'About five minutes ago. It looked to me as if he was
taking your sister-in-law home.'

'Just her type.' Faulkner ground his cigarette viciously
into the ashtray. 'It's time he was cut down to size, Craig
– and I mean cut. Are you with me?'

'Perfectly,' Craig said, his face wooden. 'I'll see to it, Mr
Faulkner.'

'I wouldn't waste any time if I were you. He mightn't
be at the schoolhouse long.'

'Fifteen minutes is all it takes, Mr Faulkner.'

Craig withdrew and Faulkner went to the bar and poured
himself a large tonic water. He drank it slowly, savouring
the freshness, and after a while the bedroom door opened
and Bella appeared.

She looked quite beautiful, her face freshly made up, a
three-quarter length dress of black lace moulding her
magnificent body.

'Ready, Harry?' she said brightly.

He took both her hands and shook his head. 'My God, but I'm proud of you, Bella. You're the most beautiful damned thing in there tonight.'

She kissed his cheek affectionately and took his arm. When they opened the door to return to the party, they were smiling.

16

The flat overlooked the school yard and when Nick drew the curtain and peered into the night, rain hammered relentlessly into the asphalt and fog crowded the spiked railings, yellow in the glow of the street lamps.

'How many kids have you got?' he called.

Jean Fleming answered from the bedroom. 'One hundred and fifty-three. I could double it with no trouble, but you can't get the staff these days.'

As he turned, he caught a glimpse of her through the half open door beside the bed, her supple body outlined boldly under the nylon slip as she unfastened her stockings.

He watched as she continued to undress, curiously detached about the whole thing, not even conscious of the overwhelming physical attraction he had experienced earlier.

The secret graces of a woman's body. Something utterly fundamental to life itself, something of the quiet places where a man could find peace. *Was this what he wanted?*

He turned and looked down into the rain again, and from the music room below the sound of Chuck Lazer's playing rose into the night. He was working his way through all the standards, Berlin, Cole Porter, Rogers and Hart. The kind of stuff nobody seemed to be writing any more. A hint of summer that had gone and memories only now.

Jean came into the room wearing a pair of dark trews and a quilted jacket, her face wiped clean of make-up so that she seemed startlingly young and innocent.

'What would you like – coffee or tea?'

'Tea if that's all right with you, then I must be going.'

Her smile was replaced by a slight frown. 'Must you?'

He nodded. 'I'm still on duty.'

She went into the kitchen and filled the kettle and he leaned in the doorway watching her. She prepared a tray, spooned tea into an old brown pot, then sat on a stool, hugging her knees, waiting for the kettle to boil.

They had lost something, some essential contact they had found earlier, and Nick searched quickly for the right note.

'It's much larger than I expected.'

'The school?' She nodded. 'At first there was just this old house and then Miss Van Heflin had extensions made. We have additional classrooms at the rear now. You can only see them properly in daylight.'

'How long have you been here?'

'Five years. Ever since I qualified. When Ben was arrested, I didn't think I'd be able to continue my training. The Principal of the teaching college where I was supposed to be going wrote to say he couldn't offer me a place after all.'

'What did you do?'

'At first I cried, then I got mad.' She smiled. 'Funny how a kick in the teeth brings out the best in you. Somehow a teaching college wasn't good enough after that so I decided to go to University. Bella couldn't help. She had enough on her plate, but I managed to get a small grant from the local authority. I made it up by working in the vacations. One year I even took a job as a barmaid in the evenings.'

'That must have been tough.'

'It wasn't as bad as it sounds. When I got my degree, I came here to work for Miss Van Heflin. She was marvellous.'

'Things always seem to come out right in the end if you live right.'

As the kettle boiled, she moved to the stove and started to fill the teapot. 'What about you?'

'Nothing as complicated. Phil was keen on me going to University and the way the business expanded, I certainly never had to worry about money. I went to the London School of Economics and read law.'

'And then found you didn't want to become a lawyer?'

'Something like that.'

'But why the police?'

'Why not?'

'You know what I mean.'

'Perfectly. I get it from Phil at least twice a day. Labourers in uniform, a working man's profession. Big men, small brains. Isn't that how it runs?'

'I didn't say that.'

'No one ever does, but that's roughly what they mean.'

He was suddenly angry. He walked back into the other room, opened the window and leaned into the rain. She followed him in, placed the tray on the table and moved to his side.

'I'm sorry, Nick. Truly I am.'

He grinned tightly. 'People are funny. A solicitor misappropriates a client's funds, a schoolmaster criminally assaults a child; they get what they deserve. No more, no less. But no one would dream of attacking either of their professions as a whole. That kind of reasoning never applies where the police are concerned.'

'I said I was sorry.'

'When the chips are down, people always are. When they need help, they can't reach a telephone fast enough.'

She placed a hand on his sleeve and when she spoke, her voice was strangely subdued. 'It means a lot to you, doesn't it?'

He looked down at her, no expression in those strange dark eyes, but there was a harsh finality in his voice. 'I wouldn't be anything else. Not now or ever, Jean.'

And then she smiled and her hand reached up to touch his face in a gesture that meant more than any kiss. 'That's all right then, isn't it? Come and have your tea.'

They sat by the fire in companionable silence and Nick drank his tea and watched her. She closed her eyes and rested her head against the back of the chair looking strangely defenceless.

'Tell me something,' he said. 'About Ben – are you worried? Really worried, I mean?'

She opened her eyes and it was there, no need for her to try to put it into words. 'All my life I wanted to get out of Khyber Street. And I managed it, Nick. I'm where I want to be in a calmer, more ordered world. And now Ben has to come back to spoil it all.' The knuckles of her hands gleamed whitely as her fingers interlaced. 'God, how I hate him.'

Nick leaned forward, a slight frown on his face. 'You really mean that, don't you?'

'I've always hated him.' She got to her feet and walked to the window. 'I was fourteen when he married Bella and from the day she brought him back to live with us, my life became a sort of nightmare.' She turned suddenly. 'No, that isn't quite true. It's just that whenever I turned, he seemed to be there watching me. When I was dressing or undressing. I'd find him in the doorway, that smile on his face.'

She shuddered visibly and Nick's throat went dry. 'Go on.'

'There isn't anything else. Not what you mean, anyway. He was too clever for that. But there were other things.' She stared into the past. 'He was so damned strong. When he put those great hands of his on me there was nothing I could do – nothing.'

'Didn't you ever try speaking to Bella?'

'I threatened to do just that, but he only laughed. Said she wouldn't have believed a word and he was right.'

Nick got to his feet and took her in his arms gently. When he pulled her close, she started to tremble. 'That was a long time ago. Long gone. Ben Garvald will never trouble you again, I promise you that.'

She stared up into his face and then her hands slid around his neck, pulling down his head, her mouth opening beneath his. As the blood surged in his temples, Nick slid his hands over her buttocks, holding her fiercely against him.

Through the turbulence he was aware that she was repeating his name over and over again and he closed his eyes and hung on, waiting for the roaring to diminish. After a while, he opened them again and smiled down at her.

'I wonder what the Sunday supplements would make of this? I can see the headlines now. Case of the Amorous Detective.'

She smiled up at him, her eyes bright. 'To hell with the Sunday supplements.'

'I know,' he said. 'But I've still got to go.'

She sighed deeply and pushed herself away from him. 'Any chance of your coming back?'

'I'm afraid not. I'll give you a ring tomorrow. Maybe we could have dinner.'

'I'd better give you my number.'

'Isn't it in the book?'

'Only the school office, not the flat.' She smiled. 'A trick of the trade. If it was, I'd have half a dozen parents phoning through every evening. I'd never know a moment's peace.'

She rummaged in a drawer, found a folded piece of notepaper, and quickly scribbled her name and telephone number on it. She folded it again, slipped it into his inside pocket and smiled up at him.

'No excuses now.'

'None at all.'

'Especially if you have this.' She took a Yale key on a ring from her pocket and held it up. 'If you *can* get back before breakfast, let yourself in.'

'Won't you be in bed?'

'I should imagine so.'

She smiled delightfully and he pulled her close and kissed her again. 'Now let's get out of here before I'm completely corrupted.'

Chuck was still sitting at the upright piano in the corner of the music room playing by the light of the street lamp that drifted in through the window.

'End of score,' Nick called softly from the doorway.

Chuck ended on a fast run of intricate chords, swung round and stood up. 'I'm with you, General. Where to now?'

'I want to check in at Headquarters,' Nick said. 'I can drop you off at your place if you like.'

They moved into the small porch a few yards from the side gate in the railings. The rain still hammered down through the fog and Jean shivered.

'Rather you than me.'

He grinned down at her. 'Pity the poor copper. I'll see you.'

They walked across the yard, opened the side gate and moved along the narrow pavement. The street was little more than an alley and bordered on the other side by a high stone wall.

The Mini-Cooper was parked under an old-fashioned gas lamp and Nick took the keys from his pocket as he stepped off the pavement to reach the off-side. From the lighted porch, Jean called his name urgently.

As he started to turn, a fist lifted into his face and some inexplicable reflex caused him to duck so that the blow glanced from his cheek. He was aware of sharp pain as a metal ring sliced his skin like a razor and then his hand swung expertly as he turned, catching his assailant across the side of the neck.

The man staggered back towards the outer darkness beyond the light thrown out by the gas lamp and Nick was aware of others. Three, perhaps four, he couldn't be sure because they came out of the fog with a sudden rush like a rugby forward line.

One of them held an iron bar in both hands. As he came within striking distance it swung up and down, the man grunting with the effort. Nick ducked and the bar thudded across the roof of the car. He lifted his foot savagely into the man's crutch, the bar rang against the cobbles and the man collapsed with a choking cry.

There was no time for words. Two more came boring in, one of them wielding a bone-handled razor, the blade gleaming dully in the rain. Nick reached for the wrist, turning his head to avoid a blow from the other and was aware of Jean Fleming's face beyond the man's shoulder, contorted with anger, teeth bared.

She hooked her fingers into long, greasy hair, dragging the man's head back and Nick concentrated on the other. He swung in, pushing the razor away from him and applied a wrist lock. The man screamed, dropping the razor, and Nick delivered an elbow strike at close quarters that produced a cry of agony.

The man fell backwards, got to his feet and stumbled away. Nick turned and found Lazer rolling in the flooded gutter, grappling with a man in an old trenchcoat. Jean was against the wall, struggling furiously.

Nick moved in fast, grabbed the man by the collar with both hands and sent him staggering into the fog. At the same moment, Lazer's assailant rolled on top, got to his feet and went after his comrades fast.

There was silence. Only the rain hissing down, Jean

struggling to catch her breath, a slight moan from the one who had carried the iron bar.

Lazer, sitting in the gutter, got to his feet with a queer, choking laugh. 'What brought that little lot on?'

'I think I must have hurt somebody's feelings.' Nick turned to Jean. 'You all right?'

She laughed shakily. 'You're damned right I am. What on earth was it all about?'

'I don't know, Jean.' He shook his head. 'There's more to this whole business than meets the eye. Much more.'

There was a slight noise behind them and as he swung round, the man who was lying face down on the pavement beside the car, reached for the iron bar and started to his feet. Lazer moved across quickly, pulled it easily from his grasp and slammed the man hard against the car.

'Another move like that and I'll bend this across your skull.'

The man hung there, hands clawing across the roof for support, head down and Nick took Jean by the arm and led her to the gate. 'Mix yourself a stiff drink, you've earned it. Then go to bed.'

She looked up at him anxiously, her face pale in the lamplight. 'What about you?'

'I'll take this character down to Central with me, not that I expect to get very much out of him. On the other hand we should be able to put him away for a couple of years, which is something.'

'Can you get back later on?'

'I'll try, I really will.' He took her hand and held it tightly for a moment. 'You looked good in there.'

'The Khyber Street brand goes clear to the bone,' she said. 'You can never quite get rid of it.' She took a handkerchief from her pocket and reached up to dab the blood on his right cheek. 'That's a nasty cut. It needs looking at.'

He caught her wrist gently, pulled her close in his arms

and kissed her and it was like nothing he had ever experienced before, touching something deep inside him, fierce yet gentle.

She stared up at him, an expression of wonder in her eyes, and then she smiled and it was as if a lamp had been turned on inside. She reached up and touched his face once, then ran through the rain across the yard to the porch.

17

The pale green walls of the Interrogation Room seemed to swim out of the shadows caused by the strong central light hanging above the table at which sat Charles Edward Foster, head in hands, his entire body one great ache.

Nick stood at the window and looked into the deserted rainswept street outside. His cheek throbbed painfully and he gingerly prodded the broad strip of sticking plaster with a finger end.

It was a little after two-fifteen. He yawned, took out a crumpled packet of cigarettes and extracted the last one. He was in the act of lighting it when the Duty Inspector entered.

'I've filled in the charge sheet for you.'

'I'll remember you in my will.'

'I think your next move should be to the Infirmary. That's a nasty cut you've got there. Probably needs a stitch or two.'

Foster raised his head. 'Never mind that bastard. What about me? I need a doctor if anyone does after what he did. Just wait till my solicitor gets here.'

'And just what did he do to you, Charlie?' Superintendent Grant said from the doorway.

Foster contrived an expression that was a mixture of

innocent mystification and hurt dignity. 'Kicked me in the crutch, he did, Mr Grant. You've got a right one here, I can tell you.'

The Inspector handed the charge sheet to Grant without a word.

'Presumably this little lot has got nothing to do with the case at all?'

Grant walked across to a side table on which were laid neatly the iron bar, bone-handled razor and length of bicycle chain which had been left on the scene of battle by Foster's friends.

Foster lapsed into sullen silence and Grant looked enquiringly at Nick. 'All right, are you?'

'He needs a few stitches in that face, if you ask me, sir,' the Duty Inspector put in.

Grant nodded. 'Have somebody take this cowboy downstairs will you, Jack? I'll have a word with him later.'

The Inspector nodded, took Foster by the arm and led him out. Grant sat on the edge of the table and lit his pipe.

'You've heard about Brady?'

'When I brought Foster in. What happened exactly?'

'Looks like a hit and run. We had an anonymous 999 call, but that doesn't mean anything. Probably some good citizen who didn't want to dirty his hands by getting mixed up in police business.' He sighed. 'What a night. A factory break-in at Maske Lane that'll push the crime figures up by £7,000 at least. God knows how many smash and grabs in the fog, three robberies with assault, obviously the same artist, and one attempted rape. On top of that, this Brady business.'

'How is he?'

'There's the preliminary report if you're interested.'

'It doesn't look too good, does it?' Nick said, handing the casualty report back to Grant.

'They turned out a consultant and I had a word with him

after his examination. Apparently the skull fracture's the only really serious part. The rest is just trimmings. As things are at the moment, he doesn't see why Jack shouldn't pull through.' He sighed and applied another match to his pipe. 'I'd like to know what he was doing in Canal Street, though.'

Nick crushed his cigarette into the ashtray. 'Did you know that after leaving here, he went looking for Ben Garvald?'

Grant stared at him blankly, a look of genuine amazement on his face. 'What in the hell are you talking about? Ben Garvald is your pigeon.'

'Which didn't stop Brady visiting the Flamingo before me to ask Fred Manton if Garvald had been around.'

'You're sure about this?'

'Manton told me himself.' Nick shrugged. 'I can't see any reason for him to lie.'

Grant frowned heavily, his teeth clamped hard on the stem of his pipe. 'I wonder what Jack was playing at?'

'I think it's simple enough,' Nick said. 'He finds me pretty hard to take. Perhaps he thought he'd be proving something if he got to Garvald first.'

Grant sighed heavily. 'You could be right. In any case, we won't know anything for sure until he regains consciousness.'

'What about the car that hit him?'

'A needle in a haystack on a night like this, but we'll find it, never fear.' Grant applied yet another match to the bowl of his pipe. 'You'd better fill me in on what you've been up to. You've certainly stamped good and hard on somebody's toes when they go to the expense of putting Charlie Foster and his gallant band on to you.'

Nick filled in the details quickly, leaving nothing out. When he was finished, Grant sat there, a frown on his weatherbeaten face.

'What do you think?' Nick asked after a while.

'I think it stinks,' Grant said, 'to high heaven. When you get cautious birds like Fred Manton and Harry Faulkner allowing themselves to be dragged down, there must be a reason.' He stood up abruptly. 'Find Ben Garvald, Miller. He's the key.'

Nick picked up his cap and coat from a chair and grinned tightly. 'It's a great life if you don't weaken.'

'Not at half past bloody two in the morning with the sodding Asian flu seeping into your bones it isn't,' Grant said. 'I'll have Aspro coming out of my ears if I take any more. Keep in touch. I'll be at that factory in Maske Lane if you need me.'

He walked away along the corridor to his office and Nick pulled on his coat and cap and went downstairs to the main entrance. Chuck Lazer leaned in a corner, eyes closed.

Nick nodded to the desk sergeant and touched Lazer on the shoulder. 'Let's go, America.'

He moved out through the glass doors and paused at the top of the main steps beside a tall pillar, pulling up his collar against the rain.

'What happens now?' Lazer demanded as he joined him.

Nick grinned. 'For you, bed. I'll drop you off at your place. I'm still on duty till six and a lot later than that if I don't find Garvald.'

'It's that important, is it?'

Chuck Lazer hesitated. 'Look, you meant what you said earlier, didn't you? About only wanting a chat with Ben? I mean, he hasn't done anything, has he?'

'Not that I know of, but he could certainly clear a few things up for us,' Nick frowned. 'Don't tell me you know where he is?'

Lazer made his decision and sighed. 'He said something about the Regent Hotel, General. It's not far from City Square. That doesn't mean he'll be in, mind you.'

'Maybe not, but it's something to go on,' Nick said and together they hurried down the steps to the Mini-Cooper.

*

When they went into the foyer of the Regent Hotel, it was deserted. Nick rang the bell and after a while, the door to the office opened and the Irish girl came out, sleep in her eyes. She straightened the skirt of her nylon overall and yawned.

'What can I do for you?'

'Police,' Nick said. 'I'm looking for a man called Garvald – Ben Garvald. I understand he's staying here. Probably booked in this evening.'

Something moved in her eyes, but it was quickly gone and she managed a puzzled frown. 'There's been some mistake. We don't have any Mr Garvald staying here.'

'He could be using another name. A big, tough-looking Irishman. Aged about forty.'

'No. We've nobody like that.' She shook her head positively. 'As a matter of fact, we've only had two new guests in the last three days and they were a couple of Indian gentlemen.'

'Can I see the register?'

She produced it from beneath the counter without a flicker and he opened it. The last signatures half-way down a page were two days old – the Indians she had mentioned. If the book was any guide, she was certainly telling the truth.

'Satisfied, Sergeant?' she said brightly.

Nick smiled and closed the register. 'Sorry you've been troubled. Must be some other hotel.'

Lazer had said nothing throughout the interview, but when they got outside into the street, he grabbed Nick by the sleeve. 'The Regent Hotel, Gloyne Street. That's what the man said, General.'

'I know, I know,' Nick said. 'She's lying. It stuck out a mile. Give it a couple of minutes and we'll go back in.'

He lit a cigarette and stood there on the bottom step just inside the porch, staring into the rain, feeling suddenly tired.

He hadn't got his second wind yet, that was the trouble. He flicked the cigarette through the darkness in a gleaming curve, nodded to Lazer and pushed the glass door open softly.

The foyer was deserted again, but the office door stood ajar. He moved forward quietly and gently raised the flap of the reception desk.

The Irish girl was standing at the office desk, a handbag open in front of her. She took a wad of notes from it quickly, put one foot on a chair, slid back her skirt and pushed the notes into her stocking top.

Lazer clapped his hands together gently. 'Now that's what I really call a show.'

The Irish girl swung round, straightening her skirt, alarm on her face. For a moment, she seemed shaken and uncertain and then obviously decided to brazen it out.

'Hey, is that nice, sneaking up on a girl like that?'

'Oh, we didn't think you'd mind.' Nick took her hands. 'What's your name, sweetheart?'

'Aren't you the one?' As he pushed her back against the desk, she put her arms around his neck. 'And what would the Chief Constable say to this, I wonder?'

'He likes us to have our fun. After all, that's what keeps us going.'

He leaned down to kiss her and at the same moment, slid his right hand quickly up a warm leg. She started to struggle, but he found what he was looking for and grinned as he held up the wad of notes.

'Give me that, damn you,' she said, striking out at him, trying to grab his hand. 'What in the hell do you think you're playing at?'

He shoved her away and counted the money quickly. 'Twenty quid and all in oncers.' He shook his head. 'You've never had this much together at any one time in your life before.'

'You give me my money,' she spat, tears of rage in her eyes.

He flung it in her face and as she staggered back with a cry, grabbed her by the shoulders and shook her viciously. 'Ten seconds, that's all I'm going to give you. Garvald was here, wasn't he?'

She cracked wide open, terror in her eyes, arms up before her face to block the blow she expected to follow. 'Don't hit me for God's sake. I'll tell you! I'll tell you!'

Nick stood back and waited and after a moment or two, the words came tumbling out. 'He came in this evening, about nine o'clock. He didn't sign the book because I forgot to ask him to.'

'Did he go out?'

'Not as far as I know. He was in at one o'clock when the men came for him.'

'Who were they?' She hesitated and he took a quick step towards her, his voice grating. 'I said who were they?'

'One of them was a bloke I met at a party a few weeks ago. A Greek or a Cypriot or something. They called him Jango. I don't know who the other was. He had a wall eye, that's all I can tell you.'

'Max Donner,' Lazer put in quickly. 'He and Jango are a couple of heavies. Manton keeps them around to handle the rough stuff.'

Nick nodded and turned back to the girl. 'So they gave you twenty quid. What for?'

'I had to take Mr Garvald a cup of tea. Jango put something in it. Knock-out drops I suppose. I think they were afraid of him.'

'And it worked?'

She nodded. 'They took him away in a car. I don't know where to.'

Nick turned to Lazer and the American shrugged. 'Maybe the Flamingo?'

'I shouldn't think it's very likely,' Nick said. 'But we can try.'

They turned to the door and the Irish girl grabbed his sleeve. 'I didn't mean any harm. They said they were friends of his, that they were just playing a joke on him.'

'Do I look as if I came over on a banana boat?' Nick tapped her gently on the side of the face with his open hand. 'You've got twenty quid and there's a boat train leaving for Liverpool around 6 a.m. Be on it.'

He turned and walked out leaving her standing in the middle of the room. She stood there gazing at the open doorway for a while, a dazed expression on her face, then got down on her hands and knees wearily and started to pick up the money.

There was plenty of activity outside the Flamingo, mainly cars driving away, and Nick stood in a doorway opposite the Mini-Cooper and smoked a cigarette as he waited for Chuck Lazer.

The plot was thickening with a vengeance, so much was evident, but the reasons were still far from clear. One thing was certain. Whoever wanted Ben Garvald out of the way, must have a pretty good reason.

The American came round the corner from the alley and joined him in the doorway. 'No sign of them. Manton isn't there either.'

'You're sure?'

'Absolutely. I even went upstairs and searched his private apartment. Let myself out of the side door.' He shrugged. 'Maybe he's in the river already – Ben, I mean.'

'Is there anywhere else they could take him? Somewhere secluded or out of the way, perhaps.'

Lazer frowned and then suddenly his face lit up. 'Why didn't I think of it before? There's an old Georgian house on the edge of town near Ryescroft. They call it The Grange locally. Stands on its own in a couple of acres.'

'Is it Manton's?'

Lazer shook his head. 'Another of Faulkner's buys. He's going to turn it into a swish country club, but Manton's in charge out there. At the moment, there's only a caretaker. Weird old boy called Bluey Squires. Used to be on the door at the Flamingo till he broke a leg.'

Ryescroft. That was half a mile beyond the city boundary which strictly speaking brought it within the jurisdiction of the county constabulary. Nick considered that along with several other important facts and made his decision.

'Let's get moving,' he said and went down the steps to the Mini-Cooper.

18

The Grange was the sort of place that had been built in grey Yorkshire stone on the high tide of Victorian prosperity by some self-made megalomaniac. Vast Gothic chimneys lifted into the night from the pointed roof and the grounds were surrounded by a ten-foot wall.

Nick parked in a narrow lane some thirty or forty yards from the main gate, opened a door and got out. 'It looks like a bad set for *Wuthering Heights*.'

Lazer slid behind the wheel and grinned. 'Wish me luck, General. Maybe they'll give me a medal or something.'

'Play it by ear,' Nick told him. 'If Manton *is* there, you know what to say. I'll wait for you here.'

The American slammed the door and drove away rapidly. The iron gates stood open and he followed the drive between a double line of poplar trees leading up to the great dark pile of the house. No light showed anywhere and he took a narrower path that went round the side to a cobbled yard.

Light streamed from a rear window, falling across

Manton's Jaguar, and Lazer switched off the engine. As the
sound died into the night, a dog started to bark inside the
house, hollow and menacing, touching something elemental
inside him so that he shivered.

As he got out of the Mini-Cooper, the house door opened,
a shaft of light picking him from the night.

'Who is it?' a hoarse voice croaked.

'It's Chuck Lazer, Bluey,' the American replied. 'I've been
looking for Fred. Thought he might be here.'

Squires was sixty and looked older. Tousled grey hair fell
across a broad forehead and he was badly in need of a
shave. He carried a shotgun under his left arm and his right
hand was clamped firmly around the collar of a magnificent
black and silver Alsatian who strained eagerly towards Lazer,
the growl rising from deep inside his throat like a volcano
about to erupt.

'He's pretty busy,' Squires said. 'Is it important?'

'You're telling me it is,' Lazer moved forward. 'Are
Donner and Jango here?'

The old man glared at him suspiciously. 'You want to
know a hell of a lot, don't you?'

'What's all the mystery? I've been here before, haven't
I?'

'All right, all right,' the old man said. 'I suppose you'd
better come in.'

They entered what had obviously been the main kitchen
of the house in its great days, a large, stone-flagged room
with a black kitchen range and stove running along one
side. It was dirty and untidy, the table in the centre cluttered
with unwashed dishes, a couple of empty milk bottles, half
a loaf of bread and several opened cans of food. The narrow
bed in the corner was unmade.

Squires gave the Alsatian an order and it crouched in
front of the fire, staring unwinkingly at the American. 'You
wait here. I'll get Manton.'

He leaned the shotgun against the wall and went out. Lazer sat on the edge of the table. After a while, the door opened again and Manton entered, Donner behind him.

Manton had an overcoat hanging from his shoulders against the cold and he was frowning. 'I thought you were supposed to be playing at Faulkner's party?'

'I left,' Lazer said simply. 'Some lousy copper turned up asking about Ben Garvald. C.I.D. sergeant called Miller.'

'Ben Garvald?' Manton said. 'But he's still inside.'

'Not any more he isn't. They released him yesterday. According to this guy Miller, he's right here in town.'

'What do they want him for?'

'A routine enquiry, that's what the man said, but I figured you should know, Fred. You and Ben having been so close in the old days. Maybe this copper will be calling on you next.'

'You did right, Chuck. Thanks a lot.' Manton hesitated. 'This bloke Miller – did he mention my name?'

Lazer shook his head. 'He went off in one hell of a rush. Seems some detective or other was on the receiving end in a hit and run earlier tonight. He's in the Infirmary now hanging on by a thread.'

There was a stifled exclamation from Donner in the doorway and the skin seemed to stretch a little more tightly across Manton's face. He managed a ghastly smile.

'Sorting that little lot should keep them out of mischief till the morning. Thanks for the good word, Chuck. You did right to come.'

'That's all right then.' Lazer got to his feet. 'I'll be making tracks. It's time for some shut-eye.' He moved to the door, opened it and turned with a grin. 'See you at the club tomorrow.'

The door closed behind him and a small trapped wind raced round the room, looking for a way out and died in a corner. It was Donner who broke the silence first.

'If Brady pulls through and talks . . .

'Fifteen years each,' Manton said in a whisper. 'There isn't a judge in the country would give less.'

'We could be in Liverpool by morning,' Donner said. 'A quick passage to Spain and no questions asked. I know the right people.'

'That kind of thing costs money.'

'Plenty in the safe at the club. Seven maybe eight grand.'

'Faulkner's, not mine.'

'We could go a long way.'

Manton made his decision and nodded. 'There's just one thing. What if the coppers are on to us already? They could be hanging around the club right now waiting for us to show.'

'That's an easy one.' Donner shrugged, his face quite calm. 'Send Jango. He'll find out for us.'

'But will he go?'

'I don't see why not.' Donner grinned. 'Especially if you don't tell him the score.'

Manton started to chuckle and shook his head. 'You're a hard bastard, Donner.'

'It's the only way,' Donner replied. 'What about Garvald?'

'No point in hanging on to him any longer. He should still be out cold. We'll take him with us and dump him on the side of the road going over the moors.'

Squires limped into the kitchen from the passage. 'Jango's gone to check on the bloke upstairs, Mr Manton. How long is he going to be with us?'

Before Manton could reply, there was a high-pitched cry from somewhere deep inside the house and he swung round quickly. 'That sounded like Jango!'

Without a word, Donner snatched up the shotgun and ran along the dark passage.

Ben Garvald drifted up from a wall of darkness and opened his eyes. The room was festooned with cobwebs – giant grey cobwebs that undulated slowly.

He closed his eyes and breathed deeply, fighting the panic which rose inside him. When he opened them again, the cobwebs had almost disappeared.

He was lying on a narrow bed against one wall of a small room. A shaded light hung down from the ceiling and curtains were drawn across the window.

He swung his legs to the floor and sat on the edge of the bed for a while before trying to stand. There was a bad taste in his mouth and his tongue was dry and swollen. Whatever had gone into that tea had been good – damned good.

He got to his feet and staggered across the room, steadied himself against the wall, turned and moved back to the bed. After a while, the cobwebs disappeared completely and everything clicked back into place.

His room at the hotel, the Irish girl with her cup of tea, he remembered that. And then Donner had arrived, which could only mean one thing. The copper who'd gone down the stairs at the club had snuffed it.

An interesting situation. He got to his feet again and checked the door. It was securely fastened, a mortice dead-lock from the look of things, and there was no transom. He crossed to the window and drew back the curtains. The sash lifted easily and he looked out.

He was on the top floor and the gardens lay forty feet below in the darkness. The nearest window was a good ten feet away to the left and impossible to reach.

He closed the window, moved back to the bed to consider the situation and a key rattled in the lock. For a moment he hesitated, then quickly got back on the bed and closed his eyes.

The door opened and someone walked across. Garvald waited and as a hand gripped his shirt front to shake him gently, opened his eyes and looked into the startled face of Jango. The Cypriot managed one cry of alarm before Garvald's right fist sank into his stomach. Jango keeled over, gasping for air, and Garvald got to his feet and moved out of the room quickly, closing the door behind him.

He descended a flight of stairs to the next landing and Donner's voice drifted up from the hall below. 'Jango! Jango, what's going on!'

Garvald opened the nearest door, stepped into the darkness of the room beyond and waited. There was a step on the bare floorboards and Donner moved into view, the shotgun held at waist level. Garvald moved out into the corridor, the edge of his hand swinging down with numbing force against Donner's right arm. Donner grunted and dropped the shotgun.

'Watch it, Manton, Garvald's on the loose!' Donner called and threw himself at the big man, the fingers of his left hand hooking for the eyes.

From the hall below came a terrifying banshee howl as Squires released the Alsatian. Donner and Garvald swayed together for a moment and then the dog erupted into the corridor, skidding on its haunches.

With a tremendous heave, Garvald sent Donner staggering along the corridor towards the stairhead. He dropped to one knee, picked up the shotgun and thumbed back the hammer. The dog was already half-way along the corridor when he started to swing the barrel. It leapt forward and he fired, the blast catching it in mid-air.

The Alsatian gave a sort of strangled whimper and fell against the wall where it lay on the floor, kicking feebly. There was a hoarse cry of anger and Squires appeared at the other end of the passage to join Donner, Manton at his shoulder. As all three started forward, Garvald threw the shotgun at them, turned and ran back along the corridor.

A narrow service staircase dropped into darkness and he thundered down it and found himself in a stone-flagged passage at the bottom. He wrenched open the door at the far end and ran into the courtyard.

The light from the kitchen window falling across the cobbles showed him the ten-foot wall on the far side and a narrow door. He wrestled ineffectually for a moment with its rusted bolts, then turned to the place where the stable joined the wall. With the aid of a drainpipe, and using the sill of the stable window as a middle step, he pulled himself on to the sloping roof. He swung across the wall, hung by his hands for a moment and dropped into wet grass.

He got to one knee and an arm slid around his throat, a hand applied pressure savagely. As he moved, the pressure increased, completely cutting off the supply of air to his lungs.

A match flared and Chuck Lazer said: 'Lay off, General. It's Ben.'

Nick released his grip. Garvald stayed on one knee for a moment, shaking his head, a hand at his throat, then he got to his feet. 'Where's your car?'

'At the end of the lane.'

'Then let's get moving.'

Nick grabbed his arm. 'Not so fast, Garvald. We heard what sounded like a shotgun blast inside there a minute or so ago.'

'You're damned right you did. The old sod they have running this dump put his Alsatian on me. I had to finish it off. You going to arrest me for that?'

'Could be. Depends on how you answer my questions. Let's get moving.'

They hurried back along the lane to the main road. The Mini-Cooper was parked under some trees, lights out, and Nick opened the door. 'Get in the back.'

Garvald obeyed without hesitation, his mind working furiously. He had already wasted a great deal of time and things seemed to be getting completely out of hand. Far better to pick up what he had come for and get out of town fast. But first he had to get rid of Miller and from the look of him that wouldn't be easy.

'How did you know where I was?'

The American turned in his seat to face him. 'I remembered you saying you had a room at the Regent Hotel. The Irish bird who does the night shift there filled us in on the rest with a little persuasion.'

'I'd like to fill her in, the bitch.' Garvald lit a cigarette and leaned back. 'What's all this then, Chuck? You playing at being an aide to the C.I.D. or something?'

'For God's sake, Ben. I was trying to help you.'

'Sounds pretty thin to me.' Garvald turned to Nick. 'Why the witch hunt? I'm clean as a whistle. Only got into town a few hours ago.'

'When I started looking for you earlier tonight, Garvald, it was only to warn you to stay away from Bella.'

'So she's behind it?' Garvald chuckled. 'She's safe enough, copper. I wouldn't touch her with a ten-foot pole.'

'Then you came back for the money,' Nick said calmly. 'Your share of the take from that Steel Amalgamated job. The best part of eight thousand quid. Nothing else fits.'

Garvald, searching desperately for a way out, played a hunch. 'How's Brady?'

'For Christ's sake, Ben, what do you know about Brady?' Chuck Lazer cried.

Nick cut in, his voice cold and hard. 'What about Brady, Garvald?'

'One of your blokes, isn't he?' Garvald said. 'Turned up at the Flamingo earlier looking for me. There was some kind of a row and Donner knocked him down the stairs of Manton's private entrance.'

'He was found lying in a street near the river,' Nick said. 'Looked like a hit and run.'

'Now I call that neat.' Garvald smiled softly. 'That would

be Manton's idea. Takes a fine, twisted mind like his to think up a touch like that.'

'You're sure about this?'

'I saw it happen, I was hiding in a linen cupboard in the same corridor.' Garvald laughed harshly. 'Why in the hell do you think Manton and his boys picked me up at the Regent? They killed a copper and I was the only witness. I can imagine what they intended to do with me.'

'The irony is that Brady isn't dead,' Nick said. 'He's still unconscious, but they think he stands a fair chance of pulling through.'

'And Manton doesn't know that?'

'He does now.' Lazer turned to Nick. 'I was making conversation with him in the kitchen, trying to be natural. I mentioned about Brady being in hospital and so on in passing. Come to think of it, he and Donner both looked pretty sick about it.'

'They'll have to run,' Garvald said calmly. 'No other choice.'

He sat back, well content, and lit a cigarette. The peelers looked after their own. From this moment on, anything else would have to take second place to the Brady affair and they wouldn't rest till they had Manton and his friends with the cuffs on, which caused him no pain at all. Manton was a rat. He'd had something like this coming to him for years.

Nick's problem was a more immediate one. With no radio telephone he was unable to communicate with Headquarters, and without help it would be quite impossible for him to nail Manton and his two tearaways.

The problem solved itself as Manton's Jaguar skidded out of the lane no more than twenty yards away and drove off fast towards town. Nick didn't hesitate. He pressed the starter and the Mini-Cooper shot away, tyres spinning slightly on the wet asphalt.

'You've got a hope.' Garvald laughed.

'You've been out of circulation a long time,' Nick said. 'This is the original wolf in sheep's clothing.'

The Mini-Cooper touched seventy miles an hour in exactly thirty-one seconds and the needle continued to swing, until on the dual carriageway leading to the outer ring road they almost touched ninety.

'God in heaven, what is this thing?' Ben Garvald shouted.

Nick grinned, concentrating all his attention on the lights of the Jaguar in front, gleaming through the heavy rain. 'The greatest invention since the horse.'

As they emerged from the dual carriageway, he braked, then accelerated into a shallow corner and the Mini-Cooper shot round, all four wheels glued to the ground.

The Jaguar was no more than fifty yards ahead now and going well. Garvald leaned over the seat and touched Nick on the shoulder. 'You'll be on your own, have you thought of that, copper? Three to one and Donner's the kind who'd sell his sister if he was short of beer money.'

Nick ignored him, concentrating wholly on the Jaguar, gauging the distance between them, timing his move in advance to the last fraction of a second. He was right on the big car's tail now. Quite suddenly, he dropped into third, pulled out and jammed his foot hard on the accelerator. The Mini-Cooper moved alongside the Jaguar and he took the little car in close and started to brake.

As he swung the wheel, he glanced across. Only one man sat in the other car, the driver, and as he too braked hard, the Jaguar skidded, its nearside wheels cutting into the grass banking at the side of the road. As it came to a halt, Nick pulled in ahead, switched off his own engine and jumped out.

Jango was just a little slower. He scrambled out of the Jaguar and started to run. A hand grabbed him by the shoulder, spun him round and sent him crashing back against the car.

He reacted with the habitual criminal's usual blend of outraged innocence and aggression. 'Hey, what in the hell is this?'

A hand was clamped around his throat so viciously that he cried out in agony and swung wildly at the pale blur of the face in front of him.

For the second time that night a fist lifted into his stomach. As he lay with his face in the wet grass, his arms were jerked behind him, steel bracelets snapped into place with a cold finality and fear moved in his very bowels.

Lazer had got out of the passenger seat and stood beside the open door of the Mini-Cooper staring through the darkness towards the Jaguar. He was aware of a sudden movement inside and turned quickly. Ben Garvald was sliding behind the wheel.

He grinned as he reached for the starter. 'I've got things to do, Chuck. Maybe I'll be seeing you, but it isn't likely. Give Miller my respects. In other circumstances, I'd have enjoyed hating him.'

As the engine roared into life he pushed hard, catching Lazer full in the face, sending him staggering backwards. As the American recovered his balance, the door slammed and the Mini-Cooper faded into the night.

19

It was just after three and for at least twenty or thirty of the guests who refused to go home, the party was still going strong. Harry Faulkner had taken over the barman's duties in the Long Room and half a dozen couples danced to a record player.

Bella had long since reached the stage when the gin was beginning to stick in her throat and all at once a strange thing happened. Every face she looked into seemed weak and evil and selfish and when she turned quickly to a mirror, what she saw there repelled her most of all.

Too much to drink, that's what it was. What she needed was a good soak in a hot tub and about twelve solid hours of sleep. She crossed the hall, went into the library and locked the door.

The bathroom was in black-veined marble and gold, the bath itself half-set into the tiled floor. She turned on the water, then returned to the bedroom and undressed quickly, throwing her dress and underclothes carelessly on the bed.

She stood in front of the dressing-table mirror for a full minute, examining her magnificent body in detail. The breasts were still high and firm, her flesh unmarked, but there was a perceptible thickening around the waist and the way the skin was starting to bulge beneath her chin boded ill.

She went into the bathroom and stepped down into the hot water, revelling in the sense of physical release it always gave her. She lay there looking up at the ceiling, going over the evening's events in her mind, thinking about Ben. The strange thing was that she could form no clear mental picture of how he looked. Still, it had been a long time. She sat up and reached for the soap and was immediately conscious of a slight draught as if the door was open. When she turned, Ben was standing there smiling down at her.

He stuck a cigarette in his mouth and grinned. 'A long time, angel, but you still look good to me.'

And she wasn't afraid, which was strange because she had thought that she would be. She looked up at him and something stirred in her. A memory of her youth, perhaps, when nothing had ever seemed to matter very much except having a good time. And then Ben had come into her life, this handsome, smiling Irish devil who could put the fear of God in any man who ever crossed him, but who was everything a woman could desire.

She pushed herself up and stood there, the water draining from her breasts, steam curling from her rounded limbs. 'You'd better pass me a towel.'

He was still smiling, the sight of her having no apparent effect. He dropped his cigarette to the floor, pulled a bath towel from the rack and crossed to her. 'What do you want me to do, angel, dry your back?'

'It wouldn't be the first time,' she said calmly.

He draped the towel around her shoulders, then in one quick movement scooped her up into his arms. She could feel the heart move in her, the hollowness in her stomach as she looked up at him and a sudden indolent warmth seeped through her limbs.

She slid her damp arms around his neck, the towel slipping to her waist, her breasts crushed against him, and as he turned and walked into the bedroom, her mouth found his, her tongue working passionately.

She pulled away and rubbed her cheek against his. 'Ben, oh Ben,' she whispered.

'I know, angel, isn't love grand?' He dropped her on the bed and stood back, a grin on his face. 'By God, you must warm the cockles of poor old Harry Faulkner's heart.'

She lay there, raised on one elbow, the towel covering less than half of her beautiful body and glared up at him, fire in her eyes.

'All right then, what *do* you want?'

'My money, angel, that's all. Seven thousand eight hundred and fifty quid. No fortune, but what my old grannie back in County Antrim would have called a respectable portion. Not much to show for nine years in the nick, but it'll give me a start.'

She lay there staring up at him, a slight fixed frown on her face, and he stopped smiling. 'You've still got it, haven't you?'

She nodded and sat up, pulling the towel around her shoulders. 'Not here though.'

He frowned. 'That's not so good. I was hoping to be out of town by breakfast. I would have thought that would have suited you, too.'

'I've got a motor cruiser moored at Hagen's Wharf on the river,' she said. 'Harry bought it for my birthday last year. The money's there. I'll be glad to see the back of it.'

'That's fine,' Garvald said. 'I've got a car. I'd say it shouldn't take us more than ten minutes to get there from here.'

She got to her feet and stood there, still holding the towel about her. 'If you'd kindly get to hell out of here, I could get dressed. You'll find a drink in the other room.'

'Time was,' he said and started to laugh. He was still laughing when he went into the library.

The moment the door closed, Bella sat on the edge of the bed and reached for the telephone. She dialled a number quickly and the receiver at the other end was lifted almost at once.

'He's here,' she said. 'We'll be leaving in ten minutes.'

The receiver at the other end was replaced immediately and Bella dropped her own into its cradle and dressed quickly in slacks, knee-length Cossack boots and a heavy sheepskin coat. She stood in front of the dressing-table mirror to fasten a silk scarf peasant-fashion around her head.

Last of all, she moved across to a bureau, unlocked a drawer with a small key and took out a Smith & Wesson .38 calibre automatic. For a long moment she looked down at it, gripping the handle so tightly that her knuckles gleamed white to the bone, and then she slipped the gun into her pocket and went into the library.

Bluey Squires sat at the kitchen table and stared vacantly into space, a glass in one hand, a bottle in the other. He was thinking about his dog and he looked across at the bundle in the corner by the fire covered with an old sack.

The strange thing was that he didn't blame Garvald. It was all Manton's fault. Manton and that wall-eyed bastard, Donner. If they hadn't brought Garvald to The Grange in the first place, the whole damn thing would never have happened.

There was the sound of a car drawing up outside in the yard and he got to his feet, went to the window and peered into the rain. The Jaguar was parked a couple of feet from the front door and he unlocked it quickly.

What happened then was like something out of a strange, distorted dream. The nearside door of the Jaguar opened and a large man moved out with surprising speed, a man with creased, weatherbeaten features which Squires instantly recognized.

He stood there with his mouth open and a hand like a dinner plate wrapped itself around his throat and Grant said softly: 'Where are they, Bluey? I want 'em and I want 'em quick.'

He released his grip and Squires took a great sobbing breath. 'Upstairs, Mr Grant. Manton's got an office on the first floor. It's the only other room in the house that's furnished.'

He moved back as the room seemed to fill with policemen and Grant said, 'Right then, Bluey. If you want to come out of this with a whole skin, this is what you're going to do.'

Manton swallowed his whisky and looked at his watch for the fifth time in as many minutes. 'He's taking his own sweet time.'

Donner laughed harshly. 'Maybe the scuffers have got him.'

He sat on the edge of the desk, the shotgun across his

knees, a cigarette smouldering in one corner of his mouth, his good eye half closed, the other fixed, staring unpleasantly. He was more than a little drunk and he reached for the bottle to pour himself another.

'Lay off that stuff,' Manton said angrily. 'You're going to need all your wits about you if we're to see this night through.'

'Your days of telling me what to do are over, Mr Manton,' Donner said, pouring himself another whisky.

Manton took a step towards him and pulled up short as someone knocked on the door. He moved across quickly.

'Who is it?'

'It's me, Mr Manton,' Bluey Squires called. 'Jango's back.'

Manton felt the relief surge through him in a great wave and he turned the key. In the same moment, the door swung in on him. He was aware of Grant with a face like some avenging God and Miller at his side, eyes like dark holes in a bone-white face. And beyond them, the others, big men in blue uniforms surging forward like a tidal wave, pouring over him.

Donner started to swing the shotgun too late. As it came up, Nick tossed an office stool that deflected the barrel and the weapon discharged harmlessly into the floor. Grant jumped the last ten feet, one great fist connecting solidly high on Donner's right cheekbone.

A moment later, Donner was struggling on the floor beneath the weight of four good men. It took another two to get him down to the van.

20

As they neared the centre of the town, the fog became thicker and Garvald turned the Mini-Cooper off the main road and continued towards the river, keeping to the back streets.

'Where did you get the car?' Bella asked.

'A friend loaned it to me.'

They continued in silence for a little while longer and then she spoke again. 'It's been a long time, hasn't it, Ben? Since we were together like this, I mean.'

'Too long, angel,' he replied and there was a sharp finality in his voice.

She seemed to realize it, took out a gold case and put a cigarette in her mouth. 'What are you going to do next?'

'Once I have the money?' He grinned. 'I'm going home, Bella. Back to the old country. An uncle of mine has a farm in Antrim and no one to follow him. I've had enough of cities.'

She stared at him in genuine astonishment and then started to laugh. 'You, a farmer? I'll believe that when I see it.'

'Stranger things have happened.'

'Name me one.'

'You selling yourself as an old man's bed warmer,' he said with a brutality that stunned her into silence.

As they approached the river, they saw no other traffic and moved into an area of dark canyons flanked by great warehouses shuttered and barred for the night. Garvald braked to a halt at her direction underneath a lamp in a narrow alley beside a gate. Through the iron bars he could see the riding lights of barges moored on the far side of the river glowing through the fog, but the only sound was the lapping of water against the wharf pilings.

'We'll have to walk from here,' she told him.

He got out and moved round to join her. The main gates were locked, but a small judas at one side opened to her touch and they passed through.

One or two ancient gas lamps bracketed to the warehouse walls gave some kind of light, but the fog rolling in from the river reduced visibility considerably.

They passed a door with a sign above it which read *Hagen's Wharf – General Office* and continued across the black shining cobbles to the final lamp at the end of the old warehouse. Beyond that, the railings and wooden planks of the wharf disappeared into the fog and darkness of the river.

'Damn!' Bella said. 'The light's out at the end of the pier. You can't trust these blasted watchmen for more than ten minutes at any one time.'

'Is the boat tied up out there?'

She nodded. 'You wait here. I'll go back to the office for a hand lamp. I've got a key.'

She walked away quickly, the sound of her leather boots on the cobbles dying away almost at once. Garvald took out a cigarette, lit it and stood there staring gloomily into the fog.

By rights, he should have been feeling great because for the first time in his life he was really trying to break out of something. Instead, he felt strangely sad. The lamp above his head, the wharf in front of him stretching into darkness, seemed unreal and transitory as if they might dissolve into the fog at any moment.

The years that the locusts have eaten. As the quotation jumped into his mind, it carried with it a memory of his old grandmother, her Bible on her knee, reading on a Friday night to a boy who still had life ahead of him with all its hopes and dreams and breathless wonderment.

He heard her steps on the cobbles again and started to turn. 'That didn't take long.'

He was aware of only one thing in that final frozen second of life when time seemed to stand still – the muzzle of the gun that was thrust out towards him. Flame exploded in the night and he staggered backwards against the wooden railing of the wharf. He half-turned, clutching at it for support, and as the railing splintered and broke the second bullet caught him in the back and sent him over the edge into an eternal darkness.

21

When Harry Faulkner went into the main C.I.D. office at Police Headquarters it was exactly four-fifteen. The first person he saw was Chuck Lazer, who sat at a vacant desk playing Patience, a mug of tea beside him.

'What in the hell are you doing here?' Faulkner demanded in bewilderment.

'I'm what they call an aide to the C.I.D.,' Lazer said. 'Fascinating work, but the pay stinks.'

The door to Grant's office opened and a young constable came out. 'In here, Mr Faulkner. Superintendent Grant would like a few words with you.'

Grant was sitting at his desk in his overcoat. Sweat glistened on his forehead and he wiped it away with his sleeve, took a strip of Aspro from his pocket and popped two into his mouth. He swallowed some tea from the pint pot at his elbow and made a face.

'Fill it up with something drinkable, there's a good lad.'

The constable took the pot and retired and Faulkner sat down in the chair on the other side of the desk, a frown on his face.

'And what's all this about then?'

'We've arrested Fred Manton,' Grant said, applying a match to his pipe. 'I thought you'd like to know, you being his employer and so on.'

Faulkner was too old a bird to be drawn. He took a

cigarette from his case and lit it with a brass lighter. 'What's the charge?'

'At the moment I'd say attempted murder of a police officer.'

Faulkner's face went grey. 'You know what you're doing?'

'Too bloody right I do,' Grant said. 'If you're interested, he was going to do a bunk with all the ready cash he could lay his hands on. Your money, of course.'

'The bastard,' Faulkner said. 'After all I've done for him.'

'I'm sending a couple of officers to the Flamingo now,' Grant said. 'They'll have a warrant empowering them to make a thorough search of Manton's office and apartment. I think you should be there as owner, just to confirm that everything's in order. I'd particularly like to see an inventory of the contents of the safe.'

'Anything to help,' Faulkner said calmly. 'You know me.'

'Somehow that's what I thought you'd say. You'll find Detective Constable Carter and a uniformed officer waiting for you downstairs.'

Faulkner moved to the door, opened it and stood back as the young constable entered with Grant's tea. 'Just one more thing, Mr Faulkner,' Grant said. 'If you could return here with the two officers when the search has been completed. I'd like a general statement from you concerning Manton.'

'Is that really necessary?'

'I'd appreciate any help you can give me. Any help at all.'

Faulkner looked at him, a slight frown on his face as if he couldn't quite understand which way things were going and then he shrugged.

'See you later, then.'

The door closed behind him and Grant reached for the pot of tea and carried it to his lips. He made a face and hurriedly put the pot down again.

'It's freshly made, sir,' the young constable said defensively.

'It's not your fault, lad,' Grant said. 'It's me. I'm getting too damned old for this game. I last saw a bed twenty hours ago, I've a temperature of 102 and my mouth tastes like a Russian wrestler's armpit.'

'Is there anything I can do, sir?'

'Yes, find yourself a decent job while you're still young enough to get out.' Grant got to his feet, moved to the door, opened it and turned. 'If you quote me on that, I'll have you skinned.'

As he moved through the outer office, Lazer looked up and shook his head. 'You look like something the tomb just threw up.'

'Nothing to how I feel.'

Grant walked along the corridor, opened the door of the Interrogation Room and went in. Manton sat at the table in the centre, his head in his hands. The uniformed constable in the chair by the door got to his feet. Grant nodded, moved across to the table, sat in the chair opposite Manton and lit a cigarette.

Rain drummed against the window and the grey-green walls seemed to swim out of the shadows. There was a smell of stale cigarette smoke and fog, sharp and acrid. Manton's head was aching and when he touched the side of his face, there was a three-inch split in the skin, swollen and tender where someone's fist had landed during the fight at The Grange.

'All right, we'll try again.' Grant's voice seemed to come from deep under the sea. 'From the beginning.'

'I want a lawyer,' Manton said in a washed-out voice. 'I know my rights.'

'You're going to need one before I'm through with you,' Grant said. 'Now let's have it.'

'All right, damn you. For the third time, it was Ben Garvald. He was upstairs at the club visiting me when Brady arrived. Garvald wanted to get away and Brady tried to stop him. It was as simple as that.'

'So Garvald tossed him downstairs?'

'They were fighting. I don't think Ben meant to play it that way. It just happened.'

'And what a sweet touch that remark is. They broke the mould the day they made you.'

'That's my story and I'm sticking to it,' Manton said stubbornly.

'Until Jack Brady regains consciousness. What happens if he tells us something different?'

'Maybe he won't come round. He fell a long way.'

'Tell me again what happened after the fall. I like that bit.'

'Garvald had a car parked round the back. He thought Brady was dead so he carted him away over his shoulder. Said he was going to dump him somewhere and make the whole thing look like an accident.'

'And you and Donner and Stavrou just stood around and watched?'

'Garvald told us to stay out of it. He said he might just as easily swing for two as one.'

'Which frightened you all to death, I'm sure.'

The door opened and Nick entered. 'How's he doing? Still the same yarn?'

'Word for word. He and Donner must have been doing their homework together.'

Nick handed him a foolscap form without a word. Grant read it quickly and started to laugh. 'This is fine by me. Let our friend here see it, then take him downstairs and book him.'

He slapped the form down on the table and walked out without a word to Manton who picked it up with shaking hands, a frown on his face.

City Police
PRISONER'S VOLUNTARY STATEMENT

In all cases where a prisoner is arrested on a charge of felony, or other serious charge, the Officer arresting should at once, when charging him, warn him that he is not obliged to say anything, but that anything he may say may be taken down in writing and used in evidence. Having administered this caution, the Officer will write on this form as nearly as possible, word for word, any statement bearing on the charge which the prisoner may make. This statement must then be forwarded through the Superintendent of the Division to the Chief Constable to be retained by him until the trial of the prisoner . . .

My name is Alexias Stavrou, known to my friends as Jango Stavrou, and I am employed as assistant manager at the Flamingo Club in Gascoigne Square. I was near the staff entrance just after midnight when Mr Brady comes in and says he wants Ben Garvald. I told him I didn't even know who Garvald was, not knowing then that he was upstairs with Mr Manton. Frank Donner arrived and there was more argument. Mr Brady forced his way upstairs, but Garvald had gone so he started to search the rooms. Donner told Mr Manton to give him a couple of fivers to get rid of him. Mr Brady got very angry. There was an argument. Donner kicked him in the crutch and Mr Brady fell down the stairs to the private entrance. Garvald then came out of the linen cupboard where he'd been hiding. He left by the side door and Mr Manton told me to go after him. I followed Garvald to the Regent Hotel in Gloyne Street. When I went back, I found Mr Manton hiding in Stank's Yard near the club. He told me that Brady was dead and that Donner had gone to lift a van. They were going to dump Mr Brady in a street somewhere and make it look like a hit-and-run accident. I told Mr Manton I didn't want to be mixed up in it, but he threatened me. He knows I was a member of EOKA for five years during the troubles in Cyprus and that I am in this country on a false passport. We left Mr Brady in a street near the river after making it look like an accident. Donner wanted to run over him with the van just to make it look good, but another car came and we had to leave. Donner dumped the van off Grainger's Wharf. Afterwards, on Mr Manton's orders, we picked up Garvald at the Regent Hotel and took him to The Grange at Ryescroft, because he was a witness to what had happened, but he got away. Mr Manton told me to take his Jaguar and go to the Flamingo and bring him what was in the safe. He said his boss, Mr Faulkner, had been on the phone and needed ready cash because of a run on the house at one of his gambling clubs. On my way to the club I was arrested by Mr Miller who told me the true facts and how Mr Brady wasn't dead after all. That's all I got to say and it's the truth, I swear this on my mother's grave.

SIGNED: Alexias Stavrou

Manton sat staring at the statement for a long moment after he had finished it. Nick reached over and took it from his hands.

'Anything to say?'

'If you can make it stick, if you can't . . .'

Manton helped himself to a cigarette from the packet on the table and Nick gave him a light. 'Fair enough, Manton. There's just one more thing. What about Garvald? Why did he come back? Is the cash from that Steel Amalgamated job still lying around somewhere?'

'Why should I make it easy for you bastards, they're paying you enough, aren't they?' Manton pushed back his chair. 'Take me downstairs and let's get it over with. I could do with some sleep.'

'You'll have plenty of time for that where you're going. There isn't much else to do.'

As they turned to the door, it opened and Grant entered. His face was hard and set, the lines scoured deep. He nodded to the constable. 'Take him down, will you? I'd like a word with Sergeant Miller.'

The door closed behind them and Nick shook his head. 'He'll hang on to that lie until he sees whether Jack Brady pulls through or not. Understandable, I suppose. He's got nothing to lose now.'

'They've found your car,' Grant said.

'Where?'

'Hagen's Wharf on the river. Parked just up the street from the entrance. The gate was open so the beat man thought he'd have a look round in case Garvald was there.'

'And was he?'

Grant nodded. 'He's lying on a mudbank at the far end of the wharf. From the sound of it, he's been shot to death.'

22

The big black van that was known throughout the Department as the Studio was already parked by the pier at the end of Hagen's Wharf when Nick and Grant arrived.

A couple of constables were rigging an arc lamp powered by the van's emergency lighting system under the supervision of Henry Wade, the Detective Sergeant in charge of the Studio.

Wade was a large, fat man with several chins and horn-rimmed spectacles that made him look deceptively benign. He wore a heavy overcoat and Homburg hat and looked like a prosperous back-street bookie. When he moved, he moved slowly, but in his line of country, only brains counted and those he had to a remarkable degree.

'Quick work, Henry,' Grant said as they approached.

'Makes a change to get something interesting,' Wade replied. 'We were at a break-in at Parson's Foundry when I got the call.' He looked at Nick curiously. 'Who's this, the college boy?'

Nick ignored him and moved past the van to the end of the pier as someone switched on the arc lamp and light flooded down across the splintered rail.

Ben Garvald lay on his back in the mud, one leg twisted underneath him, right arm outstretched, fingers curling slightly. The eyes were wide open, fixed on a point in eternity a million light years away, and there was a slight, bewildered smile on his mouth as if he couldn't quite believe in what was happening to him. It was almost as if he might scramble to his feet at any moment, but that wasn't possible because of the ragged hole in the neck just beneath his chin and the bloodsoaked rent in his raincoat below the left breast where the second bullet had emerged.

Nick stared down at the body, hands in pockets, dark eyes brooding in the white face. Six or seven hours since he'd heard Ben Garvald's name for the first time. Since then, a composite picture of the man had emerged from records, at first shadowy and insubstantial, flesh growing on the bones as people who had known him had their say and finally, ten minutes' conversation face to face.

And in the end, he'd known Ben Garvald better than any of them. Did this explain the strange sense of personal loss he now felt as he looked down at the body below?

'He doesn't look too good, does he?' Grant commented.

Nick shook his head. 'I don't know what happened, but he deserved better than this.'

Grant stared at him curiously, then turned to Wade who was pulling on a pair of gumboots. 'Going down now, Henry?'

'In a minute. You want the lot, do you?'

'Every damn thing in the book. Casts of any footprints, just in case the killer went down to make sure he was dead, and photograph everything in sight. And don't forget Miller's car.' He turned to Nick. 'Sorry about that, but you'll have to leave it.'

As Wade went over the edge of the pier to the mudbank, Grant beckoned to the young constable who had been standing patiently by the van, his cap streaming with the heavy rain.

'Johnson, sir, 802. Central Division.'

'You're the lad who found him, eh?'

'That's right, sir.'

'Let's have it then.'

'I got the nod about Detective Sergeant Miller's car when I made a point with my sergeant at three-thirty, sir. It was exactly four-fifteen when I came across it.'

'Did you examine it at all?'

'Only to try the doors, sir. They were locked.'

'So you decided to have a look inside?'

'It seemed the logical place and the judas gate was unlocked. I thought whoever it was might still be around so I took a walk along the wharf and checked the doors. I was just going to turn back when my torch picked out the smashed railing.'

Grant glanced at the mud encrusted leggings. 'I see you went down to him.'

'With his eyes open like that I wasn't sure whether he was alive or dead at first. I pulled his wallet out and found his discharge papers and so on. That told me who he was. I made straight for the nearest telephone and reported. Then I came back and waited.'

Which must have taken nerve, Grant reflected, thinking of the fog and the darkness and what lay in the mud below the pier. 'Ever done any aides to C.I.D. work, lad?'

'No, sir.'

'We'll have to see what we can do then, won't we? Hang on here until I tell you to go. I might need you later on and there should be a cup of tea going in a minute or two if I know the Studio bunch.'

Johnson tried hard to conceal his pleasure and failed. At that moment, Henry Wade, who had been crouching beside Garvald's body, looked up, the light from the arc lamp glinting on his spectacles.

'I'll tell you one thing, sir. He hasn't been here long.'

Grant turned to Nick. 'He couldn't have been, could he? When was it he took off in your car?'

'About three o'clock.'

'Let's assume he'd been dead for at least half an hour when Johnson found him. That leaves about forty-five minutes to fill. I wonder what he was doing?'

'He only had one purpose in coming back,' Nick said. 'I'm sure of that now.'

'The cash from the Steel Amalgamated job? You still believe in that?'

'More than ever.'

Grant leaned against the van and took the cigarette Nick offered. 'Let's assume you're right. If that cash existed, who would Garvald have left it with? His driver, the man we couldn't catch? If Manton was the wheelman on that job, it would give us another motive for some of the things that have happened tonight.'

Nick shook his head. 'Ben wrote to Bella from prison just before he got out. He said, "See you soon – Ben." Why?

He didn't love her any more. He told me himself he wouldn't have touched her with a ten-foot pole and I believed him.'

'Which means he wanted to see her for only one reason?'

'To recover the money she'd been looking after for him all these years. The only weakness I can see in the argument is Bella herself. Knowing her, I would have thought she would have spent it long ago.'

'Not a chance,' Grant said. 'I kept tabs on her for at least a year after Ben went down the steps, just in case she started spending heavily and proved us wrong about that cash going up in flames. She never did. Worked as a waitress for most of the time, then got a job at one of Harry's clubs. From then on she was in clover. He chased her for long enough, believe me, and she made him pay for the privilege.'

A car drew up behind them and a tall, ascetic-looking man in a dark overcoat, a University scarf wrapped around his neck, got out. He carried an old black bag in one hand and nodded to Grant in a familiar manner.

'Can't they pick a more convenient time, for God's sake?'

'Sorry, Professor,' Grant said. 'You'll need gumboots for this one. They'll let you have a pair inside.'

The Professor leaned over the rail and shuddered. 'I see what you mean.'

He put down his bag and turned to the van and Grant took Nick by the arm and led him a few paces away. 'I've been thinking. By a stroke of luck, Harry Faulkner can only be in one of two places. At the Flamingo or back at Headquarters waiting to see me about the Brady affair. That leaves Bella on her own. It might be an idea if you paid her a visit.'

'What line shall I take?'

'You can start by saying we need her to identify Garvald's body. As his ex-wife she's the nearest thing to next of kin he's got.'

'The news could hit her pretty hard. I got the impression she still had a soft spot for him.'

'That's what I'm counting on. See what her reaction is. If she breaks down, get to work on her straight away while the going's good. No telling what you might come up with. You can take my car. If anything unusual happens, let me know by radio.'

He turned as the Professor emerged from the van in a pair of gumboots a size too large and Nick moved away quickly, glad to be going. At least this gave him something concrete to do that might conceivably lead somewhere.

Grant's car was parked outside the gate in the alley and the driver sat behind the wheel smoking a cigarette. 'The Superintendent's staying here,' Nick told him. 'You can run me up to Harry Faulkner's place in St Martin's Wood.'

He reached for the door handle and the driver said: 'What about the Yank, Sergeant? He's been walking up and down the alley like a cat on hot bricks since you went in.'

Chuck Lazer moved out of the shadows into the light of the solitary lamp above the gate. He looked like a dead man walking, the skin stretched tightly over the emaciated face, the dark fringe beard accentuating the sallowness of his skin.

His eyes asked the question and Nick gave him the answer. 'It's Ben I'm afraid. Shot twice at close quarters from the look of it. Do you want to go in?'

The shock was obviously very great and something seemed to go out of Lazer in a long sigh. He shook his head. 'What would be the point?'

'Can I give you a lift?'

'Where to?' Lazer shook his head. 'He was a nice guy. Too nice to go out this way.'

He turned to walk away and Nick said urgently: 'Chuck, you wouldn't do anything silly, would you?'

Lazer shrugged. 'Does it matter, General? Does anything really matter in this lousy world?'

'We'll find who did it. We'll run them down.'

'So what? It won't bring Ben back. Christ Jesus, General, don't you ever stop to ask yourself what it's all supposed to be about?'

He started to walk away and Nick went after him quickly, catching his arm. 'I'm going up to see Bella, Chuck. We'll need her for the official identification. Come with me. You can stay in the car if you like.'

'What's the angle?'

'Let's just say one good man gone is enough for one night. I probably couldn't take another.'

Lazer stared at him sombrely for several moments without speaking and then nodded twice as if understanding. Together, they walked back to the car.

23

The house in St Martin's Wood was still ablaze with lights as they drove up, but only four cars were parked in the drive. Music from the record player still sounded faintly through the curtained windows of the Long Room and Nick turned to Lazer.

'Want to come in with me? Sounds as if the party's still going strong.'

'Why not? Maybe they could do with a good piano man.'

They went up the steps together. The door was locked and Nick pressed the bell button hard, keeping his thumb in place for a good half minute.

When the door finally opened, Craig stared out. The side of his face was swollen and angry looking, a purpling bruise already in evidence. From the look of his eyes he had been drinking and he glared.

'What in the hell do you want? The party's over.'

'Doesn't sound that way to me.'

Nick pushed him back with a good stiff arm and walked inside. The hall was empty, but in the Long Room two couples still circled the floor aimlessly and a man in a dinner jacket slept on a Regency divan near the fireplace.

Lazer walked down the room to the record player, turned it off, sat at the piano and started to play. Craig slammed the front door, grabbed Nick by the arm and jerked him round.

Nick pulled himself free with no difficulty. 'Do that again and I'll put you through the wall. Where's Mrs Faulkner?'

'Got a warrant?'

'As it happens I don't need one. Now where is she?'

'I saw her going to her room about half an hour ago. I think she'd had enough.'

'Go and dig her out. Tell her I want a word with her.'

Craig opened his mouth to give an angry reply, but obviously thought better of it. He moved away along the hall and Nick walked down to the piano.

Lazer grinned tiredly. 'We've been here before, General.'

'A long night, Chuck. A hell of a long night,' Nick said. 'How about a drink?'

'I could certainly use one.'

Nick went behind the bar, found a couple of clean glasses and a bottle of Scotch and went back to the piano. He gave Lazer a generous measure, filled his own glass to the brim and took it down in one easy swallow.

'Careful, General, that way it can get to be a habit,' Lazer said.

As the warm glow spread throughout his entire body, Nick poured himself another, then leaned against the piano, the music reaching out to enfold him. It was five o'clock in the morning at the fag end of a long night and he was tired. Too tired to think straight and that wouldn't do, because somewhere, just below the level of consciousness, something was nagging away at him, one piece of the jigsaw that was the key to this whole business and he was damned if he could think what it was.

Craig appeared at his elbow and bowed ironically. 'She isn't feeling too well. You'll have to wait till tomorrow, copper.'

'Tomorrow's already here.' Nick shook his head. 'You want to get with it, Craig. You're slipping.'

He walked down the room, disregarding Craig's sudden cry and moved along the hall to the library. As he opened the door to go in, Craig caught up with him and grabbed at his shoulder. Nick sent him staggering back across the hall, slammed the door and locked it.

The fire in the grate had burned low, but the lamp was still lit on the desk. He moved across to the bedroom door and knocked. There was no reply and when he tried to open the door, he found it was locked.

He knocked again. 'Bella, this is Nick Miller. I've got to speak to you.'

There was silence for a moment, then a soft foot-fall, the click of a key. When he opened the door, she was moving across to the fireplace.

She wore a négligé of black silk, the sleeves trimmed with mink and her face was very pale, the eyes like dark shadows. She picked up a glass from the side table, poured a double gin and turned to face him, curiously defiant.

'What's Harry been up to then? Don't tell me you've managed to pin something on him after all these years?'

'Harry?' Nick frowned and then he remembered. 'You've got it all wrong, Bella. Fred Manton's the one who's gone in too deep. He was going to make a run for it with the contents of the safe at the Flamingo. Harry was invited down to check on things, that's all.'

A stranger stared out from the mirror behind her. A man in a blue raincoat whose dark eyes beneath the peak of the semi-military cap stared through and beyond.

She shivered and swallowed some of her gin hurriedly. 'Is that all you wanted to say?'

'No, I came to tell you that Ben won't bother you any more.'

There was something in her eyes, but only for a moment and her head went back. 'Is that a fact? Well you can tell him to go to hell as far as I'm concerned.'

'He wouldn't hear me,' Nick said calmly. 'He's lying on his back in the mud at the end of Hagen's Wharf, Bella. Somebody put a couple of bullets in him.'

Until then it had been only a nightmare compounded of the rain and the fog and the night, something to be shrugged off in the light of morning, to be forgotten as quickly as any bad dream.

But now, in one terrible visionary moment of clarity she saw him lying there in the mud, the smile hooked into place, and it was only then that the full force of what had happened hit her.

She dropped the glass and put out a hand as if to ward him off and her head turned from side to side, her face contorting until the vomit rose in her throat and she staggered across to the bathroom, a hand to her mouth.

She leaned over the sink, her shoulders heaving, and Nick stood in the door and watched her, strangely calm. It was as if he stood outside himself, outside of both of them, but that was the whisky talking. He stood in the shadows of the other room looking in at himself and this woman and knew with the most tremendous certainty that he was standing right on the brink of something.

He caught her by the shoulder and jerked her round. 'Why did Ben come back in the first place, Bella? It was to pick up the money, wasn't it? The money you've been keeping for him all these years. His share of the Steel Amalgamated hoist?'

She pushed him hard against the wall and staggered

into the other room. 'Get out!' she screamed. 'Go on, get out!'

'He was here tonight, wasn't he?'

'No, it isn't true. I haven't seen Ben Garvald in nine years.'

She tried to rush past him, he grabbed her by the arm and swung her back across the bed. She lay there staring up at him, terror in her eyes, and he leaned over her.

'He told me he wouldn't touch you with a ten-foot pole and I believed him, so why else would he want to see you? It had to be the money.'

He reached into his inside breast pocket and pulled out his wallet and various papers, scattering them on the bed, searching through them with one hand while he held her wrist with the other.

He found the letter, opened it quickly, and held it in front of her. 'He wrote from prison warning you he was coming, didn't he? There's his letter.'

Her face shattered like a mirror breaking. He released his grip on her wrist and looked at the letter, a frown on his face, and what he saw there hit him low down in the stomach like a kick from a mule.

As she started to sob hysterically, he grabbed her by the throat and forced back her head. 'Right, you bitch, and now we'll have the truth.'

24

It was almost 6 a.m. when Jean Fleming opened the side gate and went into the school yard. In the grey light of early morning, the fog had receded, but rain still hammered down as relentlessly as ever, drifting in a curtain before the wind.

She ran into the porch, searching for her key with one hand, a carton of milk in the other and a newspaper tucked under one arm. She finally got the door open and paused, a slight frown on her face. Someone was playing the piano in the music room.

Nick was tired, more tired than he had ever known. It had been a long night and now the Graveyard Shift was ending. He glanced up as Jean opened the door. She placed the carton of milk and the newspaper on top of a desk, untied the damp scarf which had covered her head and ran her fingers through her dark hair as she came forward.

She was wearing her heavy sheepskin coat, Cossack boots and a hand-tailored tweed skirt, and stood so close that he only had to reach out to touch her. He wondered whether this ever happened more than once in a lifetime? This strange blend of love and desire and the flesh that was almost physical in its pain.

'You look beautiful,' he said, continuing to play. 'More beautiful than I ever believed a woman could look at this hour in the morning. Did you manage to get some sleep?'

'Not really. I was waiting for you.'

'But I told you I wouldn't be able to make it before the end of my shift.'

'Are you finished now?'

He looked up at the clock on the wall. 'Not quite. Ten minutes to go.'

She smiled. 'You've come to have breakfast with me?'

He shook his head. 'No, Jean, I've come to take you downtown.'

'Downtown?' The smile was still there, but the eyes had frozen hard. 'To Police Headquarters you mean?'

'That's right. I'm arresting you for the murder of Ben Garvald.'

And she didn't try to deny it, that was the strange thing. She stood there looking at him, somehow completely detached, outside of all this, the sallow peasant face quite composed.

Nick stopped playing. He took a packet of cigarettes from his pocket, pushed one in his mouth and searched for matches. He found them, lit his cigarette and coughed as smoke caught at the back of his throat.

'May I have one?'

He pushed the packet along the top of the piano and gave her a light. She inhaled deeply and looked down at him, quite calm.

'Hadn't you better get on with it?'

'All right.' He started to play again, his hands moving slowly over the keys, a progression of quiet, sad chords that were autumn and winter rolled into one. 'One or two things about this business had been nagging away at me all night. The letter, for example. The one Ben was supposed to have sent to Bella.'

'Supposed?'

'He had to go and see Chuck Lazer to find out who she'd married, never mind where she lived. How in the hell could he have written to her? I suppose you helped yourself to a little prison notepaper when you last saw him? Easy enough. There's always a supply on hand in the Visiting Room.'

'You'd have difficulty in proving that.'

'I don't think so.'

He took a folded sheet of blue notepaper from his wallet and laid it down on top of the piano. Printed at the top was the legend:

In replying to this letter, please write on the envelope:
Number ....
Name ....
.... Prison

This side of the sheet was blank. When he turned it over, Jean Fleming's name and telephone number were written on the other side in her own hand. He produced Ben's letter written on the same notepaper and placed it beside the other.

Jean sighed. 'That *was* rather careless of me.'

It was the ease with which she accepted it, her ice-cold calm that horrified him. 'This is all pretty circumstantial, Nick. I'd need a reason.'

'You had one. Ben had to be stopped from ever returning here because once he found there was no money waiting for him, you couldn't be sure how he would react. You checked on his release date, then forged the letter.'

'To frighten Bella?'

'Only partly. You wanted something to show Harry Faulkner. You knew he'd arrange things. A show of force, perhaps, that would frighten Ben away. You made a mistake there. Ben Garvald wasn't the sort of man to be frightened by anything. You came to us just to make it look good.'

'You've been to Bella.'

He nodded. 'Once I told her how much I'd worked out for myself, she soon came across with the rest. She even told me about the divorce. How Ben suggested she go through with it as a blind to allay any possible suspicion by the police that she just might have that money.'

'Did she tell you she was Ben's driver when he pulled the Steel Amalgamated job?'

'You were her alibi. You swore to the police that she hadn't been out of the house all night and, afterwards, blackmailed her. You put the screws on your own sister. She knew that all you had to do was open your mouth and she'd get five years.'

'I needed that money,' she said calmly.

'I realize that now,' he said. 'Four years at University. Did you really work as a barmaid at nights, by the way?

And then there was this place. You said you were paying
Miss Van Heflin a percentage of your profits each year. You
didn't tell me you gave her a down payment of three thousand pounds. She did. I hauled her out of bed and spoke
to her on the phone half an hour ago. A nice old girl. She
hopes you haven't done anything wrong, by the way.'

Her iron composure cracked and she slammed a fist down
hard on top of the piano. 'I had to get out of Khyber Street,
Nick. You can understand that? I had to.'

'And what about Ben?'

'He was going to spoil everything. If he'd had some sense,
if he'd stayed away, none of this would have happened.'

'Bella told me how you arranged things. That if Ben
turned up she was to give him a phoney story about the
money being hidden on board a boat she was supposed to
have moored at Hagen's Wharf. You asked her to bring the
gun for protection only. You were going to bribe Ben to go
away. That's what you told her.'

Jean shrugged. 'Poor Bella, she could never really handle
anything when the going got rough. I had to do it all for
her, even when I was a kid. You'll never find the gun, you
know.'

'That doesn't matter. We'll run a nitrate test on your
hands. That'll show whether you've fired a gun recently.
And the mud on that wharf – a lab analysis of the dirt on
your boots should tie in pretty closely. Then there's your
car. If it was parked for long in the alley outside the wharf,
we can prove that, too.' He shook his head. 'You never
stood a chance.'

'Didn't I?'

'You know what your biggest mistake was? You told
me you hated Ben, that from the age of fourteen on, he
wouldn't leave you alone.' Nick shook his head. 'If there
was one thing I learned during the past eight hours, it was
this. Where women were concerned, Ben Garvald was the

original gentleman. He'd have cut off his right hand before he'd have harmed a fourteen-year-old kid.'

'I wanted him,' Jean said simply. 'Do you know that? I used to lie in bed nights and burn for him and he never laid a finger on me.'

He got to his feet, dropping his cigarette to the floor, and she moved in close, hands sliding around his neck, breasts pushing hard against him.

'Nobody needs to know, Nick. You could handle it somehow, I know you could.'

'If I wanted to,' he said slowly. 'And there's the rub. To use the words of a man who was worth a dozen of you any day, I wouldn't touch you with a ten-foot barge pole, angel.'

She cracked completely, fingers hooked, clawing at his eyes. As he grabbed her wrists, the language came bursting out like a dam overflowing. All the filth of Khyber Street, the gutter years, pushed down, hidden away in some dark corner of the mind, now rising to the surface.

Grant came through the door, moving with incredible speed for a man of his weight, a constable at his shoulder. He caught her wrists, pulling her away. 'All right, lad, I'll take her.'

The constable took her other arm and she went through the door between them, looking over her shoulder, face twisted with hate, the stream of filth never ending, fading across the yard into the rain.

He stood staring into space, feeling for a cigarette mechanically. He placed it in his mouth and a match flared. He turned, looked into the dark, tortured face of Chuck Lazer for a moment, then leaned to the light.

'A long night, General.'

Nick didn't reply. He walked out of the room, passed along the corridor and stood in the porch, staring out at the driving rain.

'A long night,' he repeated slowly.

'Look, I know how you feel,' Chuck Lazer said awkwardly. 'But she's a woman after all. They'll go easy on her.'

'Go easy on her?' Nick turned, eyes burning in the white face and all the anger, the self-loathing, the frustrated passion seemed to erupt from his mouth in a single sentence.

'God damn her, I hope they hang the bitch.'

BOOK TWO

BROUGHT IN DEAD

For Dorothy Limón – a real fan

1

The girl was young and might have been pretty once, but not now. Her right eye was almost closed, the cheek mottled by livid bruises and her lips had been split by the same violent blow that had knocked out three teeth.

She hobbled painfully into the Line-Up room supported by a woman P.C., a pathetic, broken figure with a blanket over her shoulders to conceal the torn dress. Miller and Brady were sitting on a bench at the far end of the room and Brady saw her first. He tapped his companion on the shoulder and Miller stubbed out his cigarette and went to meet her.

He paused, noting her condition with a sort of clinical detachment, and the girl shrank back slightly from the strange young man with the white face and the eyes that seemed to stare right through her like dark glass.

Detective Sergeant Nicholas Miller was tired – more tired than he had been in a long, long time. In the ten hours he had already spent on duty, he had served as investigating officer at two burglaries, a factory break-in and a closing-hours brawl outside a pub near the market in which a youth had been slashed so badly across the face that it was more than likely that he would lose his right eye. This had been followed almost immediately by a particularly vile case of child cruelty which had involved forcible entry, in company with an N.S.P.C.C. inspector, of a house near the docks where they had found three children huddled together like animals, almost naked, showing all the signs of advanced malnutrition, squatting in their own dirt in a windowless boxroom that stank like a pigsty.

And now this. Compassion did not come easily at five o'clock on a dark February morning, but there was fear on this girl's face and she had suffered enough. He smiled and his whole personality seemed to change and the warmth reached out to envelop her so that sudden, involuntary tears sprang to her eyes.

'It's all right,' he said. 'Everything's going to be fine. Another couple of minutes and it'll be all over.' He turned to Detective Constable Brady. 'Let's have them, Jack.'

Brady nodded and pressed a red button on a small control panel on the wall. A hard white light illuminated a stage at the far end of the room and a moment later, a door opened and half a dozen men filed in followed by two constables who marshalled them in line.

Miller took the girl gently by the arm, but before he could speak, she started to tremble violently. She managed to raise her right hand, pointing at the prisoner who stood number one in line, a great ox of a man, his right cheek disfigured by a jagged scar. She tried to speak, something rattled in her throat and she collapsed against Miller in a dead faint.

He held her close against his chest and looked up at the stage. 'Okay, Macek, let's be having you.'

A thick-set, fourteen-stone Irishman with fists like rocks, Detective Constable Jack Brady had been a policeman for twenty-five years. A quarter of a century of dealing with human wickedness in all its forms, of walking daily in squalor and filth and a gradual erosion of the spirit had left him harsh and embittered, a hard, cruel man who believed in nothing. And then a curious thing had happened. Certain villains now serving collectively some twenty-five years in one of Her Majesty's Prisons had thrown him down a flight of stairs, breaking his leg in two places and fracturing his skull, later leaving him for dead in a back street.

Most men would have died, but not Jack Brady. The priest was called, the last rites administered and then the surgeons took over and the nurses and physiotherapists, and in three months he was back on duty with a barely perceptible limp in his left leg.

The same, but not the same. For one thing he was noticed to smile more readily. He was still a good tough cop, but now he seemed gifted with a new understanding. It was as if through suffering himself, he had learned compassion for others.

The girl painfully signed her name at the bottom of the typed statement sheet and he helped her to her feet and nodded to the woman P.C.

'You'll be all right now, love. It's all over.'

The girl left, sobbing quietly, and Miller came in holding a teletype flimsy. 'Don't waste too much sympathy on her, Jack. I've just heard from C.R.O. She's got a record. Four previous convictions including larceny, conspiracy to steal, breaking and entering and illegal possession of drugs. To cap that little lot, she's been on the trot from Peterhill Remand Home since November last year.' He dropped the flimsy on the table in disgust. 'We can certainly pick them.'

'That still doesn't excuse what Macek did to her,' Brady said. 'Underneath that surface toughness she's just a frightened little girl.'

'Sweetness and light.' Miller said. 'That's all I need.' He yawned, reaching for a cigarette. The packet was empty and he crumpled it with a sigh. 'It's been a long night.'

Brady nodded, applying a match to the bowl of his pipe. 'Soon be over.'

The door opened and Macek entered, escorted by a young probationer constable. The Pole slumped down on one of the hard wooden chairs at the table and Miller turned to the probationer.

'I could do with some tea and a packet of cigarettes. See what the canteen can offer, will you?'

The young constable went on his way briskly, for Miller was a particular hero of his – Nick Miller, the man with the law degree who had made Detective Sergeant with only five years' service. All this and an interest, so it was rumoured, in his brother's business that enabled him to live in a style to which few police officers were accustomed.

As the door closed, Miller turned to Macek. 'Now then, you bastard, let's get down to it.'

'I've got nothing to say,' Macek said woodenly.

Brady laughed harshly and there was a heavy silence. Macek looked furtively at Miller, who was examining his fingernails, and said desperately, 'All right, so I knocked her around a little. Bloody little tart. She had it coming.'

'Why?' Brady demanded.

'I took her in,' Macek said. 'Gave her a place to stay. The best of everything. Then I find her sneaking out at two in the morning with my wallet, my watch and everything else of value she could lay her hands on. What would you have done?'

He sounded genuinely aggrieved and Miller picked up the girl's statement. 'She says here that you've been living together for five weeks.'

Macek nodded eagerly. 'I gave her the best – the best there was.'

'What about the men?'

'What men?'

'The men you brought round to the house every night. The men who called because they needed a woman.'

'Do me a favour,' Macek said. 'Do I look like a pimp?'

'Don't press me to answer that,' Miller told him.

'You've kept the girl under lock and key for the past two weeks. When she couldn't take any more, you beat her up and threw her out.'

'You try proving that.'

'I don't need to. You said you've been living together as man and wife.'

'So what? It's a free country.'

'She's just fifteen.'

Macek's face turned grey. 'She can't be.'

'Oh, yes she can. We've got her record card.'

Macek turned desperately to Brady. 'She didn't tell me.'

'It's a hard cruel world, isn't it, Macek?' Brady said.

The Pole seemed to pull himself together. 'I want a lawyer.'

'Are you going to make a statement?' Miller asked.

Macek glared across the table. 'You get stuffed,' he said viciously.

Miller nodded. 'All right, Jack, take him down and book him. Make it abduction of a minor and rape. With any luck and his record, we might get him seven years.'

Macek sat there staring at him, horror in his eyes, and Jack Brady's iron fist descended, jerking from the chair. 'On your way, soldier.'

Macek stumbled from the room and Miller turned to the window and pulled the curtain. Rain drifted across the glass in a fine spray and beyond, the first light of morning streaked the grey sky. The door opened behind him and the young probationer entered, the tea and cigarettes on a tray. 'That'll be six bob, sarge.'

Miller paid him and slipped the cigarettes into his pocket. 'I've changed my mind about tea. You have it. I'm going home. Tell Detective Constable Brady I'll 'phone him this afternoon.'

He walked along the quiet corridor, descended three

flights of marble stairs and went out through the swing doors of the portico at the front of the Town Hall. His car was parked at the bottom of the steps with several others, a green Mini-Cooper, and he paused beside it to light a cigarette.

It was exactly five-thirty and the streets were strangely empty in the grey morning. The sensible thing to do was to go home to bed and yet he felt strangely restless. It was as if the city lay waiting for him and obeying a strange, irrational impulse he turned up the collar of his dark blue Swedish trenchcoat against the rain and started across the square.

For some people the early morning is the best part of the day and George Hammond was one of these. Lock-keeper in charge of the great gates that prevented the canal from emptying itself into the river basin below, he had reported for duty at five-forty-five, rain or snow, for more than forty years. Walking through the quiet streets, he savoured the calm morning with a conscious pleasure that never varied.

He paused at the top of the steps at the end of the bridge over the river and looked down into the basin. They catered mainly for barge traffic this far upstream and they floated together beside the old Victorian docks like basking sharks.

He went down the steps and started along the bank. One section of the basin was crammed with coal barges offering a convenient short-cut to the other side and he started to work his way across.

He paused on the edge of the final barge, judging the gap between the thwart and the wharf. He started his jump, gave a shocked gasp and only just managed to regain his balance.

A woman stared up at him through the grey-green water. In a lifetime of working on the river George Hammond had found bodies in the basin before, but never one like this.

The eyes stared past him, fixed on eternity, and for some inexplicable reason he knew fear.

He turned, worked his way back across the river, scrambled up on the wharf and ran along the bank.

Nick Miller had just started to cross the bridge as Hammond emerged from the top of the steps and leaned against the parapet sobbing for breath.

Miller moved forward quickly. 'Anything wrong?'

'Police!' Hammond gasped. 'I need the police.'

'You've found them,' Miller said crisply. 'What's up?'

'Girl down there in the water,' Hammond said. 'Other side of the coal barges beneath the wharf.'

'Dead?' Miller demanded.

Hammond nodded. 'Gave me a hell of a turn, I can tell you.'

'There's an all-night café on the other side of the bridge. 'Phone for a patrol car and an ambulance from there. I'll go down and see what I can do.'

Hammond nodded, turned away and Miller went down the steps quickly and moved along the bank. It had stopped raining and a cool breeze lifted off the water so that he shivered slightly as he jumped for the deck of the first coal barge and started to work his way across.

He couldn't find her at first and then a sudden eddy of the current swirled, clearing the flotsam from the surface and she stared up at him.

And she was beautiful – more beautiful than he had ever known a woman to be, that was the strangest thing of all. The body had drifted into the arched entrance of a vault under the wharf and hung suspended just beneath the surface. The dress floated around her in a cloud as did the long golden hair and there was a look of faint surprise in the eyes, the lips parted slightly as if in wonder at how easy it had been.

Up on the bridge, there was the jangle of a patrol car's

bell and in the distance, the siren of the approaching ambulance sounded faintly. But he couldn't wait. In some strange
way this had become personal. He took off his trenchcoat
and jacket, slipped off his shoes and lowered himself over
the side.

The water was bitterly cold and yet he was hardly
conscious of the fact as he swam into the archway. At that
moment, the first rays of the morning sun broke through
the clouds, striking into the water so that she seemed to
smile as he reached under the surface and took her.

A line of broad steps dropped into the basin twenty yards
to the right and he swam towards them, standing up when
his knees bumped a shelving bank of gravel, lifting her in
his arms.

But now she looked different. Now she looked dead. He
stood there knee-deep, staring down at her, a lump in his
throat, aware of a feeling of personal loss.

'Why?' he said to himself softly. 'Why?'

But there was no answer, could never be and as the
ambulance turned on the wharf above him he went up the
steps slowly, the girl cradled in his arms so that she might
have been a child sleeping.

2

Detective Superintendent Bruce Grant, head of the city's
Central Division C.I.D., stood at the window of his office
drinking a cup of tea and stared out morosely at the driving
rain. He had a slight headache and his liver was acting up
again. He was getting old, he decided – old and fat through
lack of exercise and the stack of paperwork waiting on his
desk didn't help. He lit a cigarette, his first of the day, sat
down and started on the In-tray.

The first report was headed *Found Dead – Unidentified*. Grant read it through, a slight frown on his face, and pressed the button on his intercom.

'Is Sergeant Miller in?'

'I believe he's in the canteen, sir,' a neutral voice replied.

'Get him for me, will you?'

Miller arrived five minutes later, immaculate in a dark blue worsted suit and freshly laundered white shirt. Only the skin that was stretched a little too tightly over the high cheekbones gave any hint of fatigue.

'I thought you were supposed to be having a rest day?' Grant said.

'So did I, but I'm due in court at ten when Macek is formally charged. I'm asking for a ten-day remand. That girl's going to be in hospital for at least a week.'

Grant tapped the form on his desk. 'I don't like the look of this one.'

'The girl I pulled out of the river?'

'That's right. Are you certain there was no identification?'

Miller took an envelope from his pocket and produced a small gold medallion on the end of a slender chain. 'This was around her neck.'

Grant picked it up. 'St Christopher.'

'Have a look on the back.'

The engraving had been executed by an expert: *To Joanna from Daddy – 1955*. Grant looked up, frowning. 'And this was all?'

Miller nodded. 'She was wearing stockings, the usual in underclothes, and a reasonably expensive dress. One rather sinister point. Just beneath the maker's label there was obviously some sort of name tab. It's been torn out.'

Grant sighed heavily. 'Do you think she might have been put in?'

Miller shook his head. 'Not a chance. There isn't a mark on her.'

'Then it doesn't make sense,' Grant said. 'Suicide's an irrational act at the best of times. Are you asking me to accept that this girl was so cold-blooded about it that she took time off to try to conceal her identity?'

'It's the only thing that makes sense.'

'Then what about the chain? Why didn't she get rid of that, too?'

'When you habitually wear a thing like that you tend to forget about it,' Miller said. 'Or maybe it meant a lot to her – especially as she was a Catholic.'

'That's another thing – a Catholic committing suicide.'

'It's been known.'

'But not very often. There are times when such things as statistical returns and probability tables have their uses in this work – or didn't they teach you that at the staff college? What have Missing Persons got to offer?'

'Nothing yet,' Miller said. 'There's time of course. She looks old enough to have been out all night. Someone could conceivably wait for a day or two before reporting her missing.'

'But you don't think so?'

'Do you?'

Grant looked at the form again and shook his head. 'No, I'd say anything we're going to find out about this one, we'll have to dig up for ourselves.'

'Can I have it?'

Grant nodded. 'Autopsy isn't mandatory in these cases but I think I'll ask the County Coroner to authorize one. You never know what might turn up.'

He reached for the 'phone and Miller went back into the main C.I.D. room and sat down at his desk. There was an hour to fill before his brief court appearance – a good opportunity to get rid of some of the paperwork in his In-tray.

For some reason he found it impossible to concentrate.

He leaned back in his chair, closing his eyes, and her face rose out of the darkness to meet him, still that faint look of surprise in the eyes, the lips slightly parted. It was as if she was about to speak, to tell him something but that was impossible.

God, but he was tired. He settled back in his chair and cat-napped, awaking at exactly five minutes to ten feeling curiously refreshed, but when he went downstairs and crossed the square to the county court building, it wasn't the Macek case he was thinking about.

The City Mortuary was at the back of the Medical School, a large, ugly building in Victorian Gothic with stained glass windows by the entrance. Inside, it was dark and cool with green tiled walls and a strange aseptic smell that was vaguely unpleasant.

Jack Palmer, the Senior Technician, was sitting at his desk in the small glass office at the end of the corridor. He turned and grinned as Miller paused in the doorway.

'Don't tell me – let me guess.'

'Anything for me?' Miller asked.

'Old Murray's handled it himself. Hasn't had time to make out his report yet, but he'll be able to tell you what you need to know. He's cleaning up now.'

Miller peered through the glass wall into the white tiled hall outside the theatre and saw the tall, spare form of the University Professor of Pathology emerge from the theatre, the front of his white gown stained with blood.

'Can I go in?'

Palmer nodded. 'Help yourself.'

Professor Murray had removed his gown and was standing at the sluice, washing his hands and arms, when Miller entered. He smiled, speaking with the faint Scots accent of his youth that he had never been able to lose.

'Hardly the time of year to go swimming, especially in

that open sewer we call a river. I trust you've been given
suitable injections?'

'If I start feeling ill I'll call no one but you,' Miller said,
'that's a promise.'

Murray reached for a towel and started to dry his arms.
'They tell me you don't know who the girl is?'

'That's right. Of course she may be reported missing by
someone within the next day or two.'

'But you don't think so? May I ask why?'

'It's not the usual kind of suicide. The pattern's all wrong.
For one thing, the indications are that she did everything
possible to conceal her identity before killing herself.' He
hesitated. 'There's no chance that she was dumped, is there?
Drugged beforehand or something like that?'

Murray shook his head. 'Impossible – the eyes were still
open. It's funny you should mention drugs though.'

'Why?'

'I'll show you.'

It was cold in the theatre and the heavy antiseptic smell
could not wholly smother the sickly-sweet stench of death.
Her body lay on the slab in the centre of the room covered
with a rubber sheet. Murray raised the edge and lifted the
left arm.

'Take a look.'

The marks of the needle were plainly visible and Miller
frowned. 'She was a junkie?'

Murray nodded. 'My tests indicate that she had an injection consisting of two grains of heroin and one of cocaine
approximately half an hour before she died.'

'And when would you say that was?'

'Let's see now. You pulled her out just before six, didn't
you? I'd say she'd been in the water about five hours.'

'Which means she went in at one a.m.'

'Or thereabouts. One can't be exact. It was a cold night.'

'Anything else?'

'What can I tell you? She was about nineteen, well nurtured. I'd say she'd been raised in more than comfortable surroundings.'

'Was she a virgin?'

'Anything but – two months pregnant.' He shook his head and added dryly, 'A young woman very well acquainted with the sexual act.'

'What about her clothes?'

'A chap was here from your Forensic Department. He took them away along with the usual things. Scrapings from under the fingernails, hair samples and so on.'

Miller moved to the other side of the slab, hesitated and then pulled back the rubber sheet revealing the face. Murray had closed the eyes and she looked calm and peaceful, the skin smooth and colourless.

Murray covered her again gently, his face sombre. 'I think she was someone who had suffered a great deal. Too much for one so young.'

Miller nodded, unable to speak. That strange aching dryness clutched at his throat again and he turned away quickly. As he reached the door, Murray called softly, 'Nick!' Miller turned. 'Keep me posted.'

'I'll do that,' Miller said and the rubber doors swung together behind him.

As he went out into the pale morning sunshine, Jack Brady crossed the car park to meet him.

'Grant thought you might need some help on this one. Have they finished the autopsy?'

Miller nodded. 'Murray says she went into the river somewhere around one a.m. She was pregnant, by the way.'

Brady nodded calmly. 'Anything else?'

'She was a junkie. Heroin and cocaine.'

'That should give us a lead.' Brady took a buff envelope from his overcoat pocket. 'I've checked with Forensic. They'll have a report ready by noon. These are from Photography.'

Miller opened the envelope and examined the prints it contained. Those photography boys certainly knew their job. She might almost have been alive, an illusion helped by the fact that the photos had been taken before Murray had closed her eyes.

Brady took one and frowned. 'A damned shame. She looks like a nice kid.'

'Don't they always?' Miller slipped the other prints into his pocket. 'I think I'll go and see Dr Das. He knows just about every junkie in town.'

'What about me?'

Miller took the gold St Christopher from his breast pocket and handed it over. 'You're a good Catholic, aren't you, Jack?'

'I go to Mass now and then.'

'Maybe the girl did. There's an inscription on the other side. Work your way round the parish priests. Someone may recognize her photo or even the medal.'

'More shoe leather,' Brady groaned.

'Good for your soul this one. I'll drop you off at the Cathedral if you like.'

They got into the car and Brady glanced at his copy of the girl's photograph again before putting it away in his wallet. He shook his head. 'It doesn't make sense, does it? Have you any idea what it's like down there on the docks at that time in the morning?'

'Just about the darkest and loneliest place in the world,' Miller said.

Brady nodded. 'One thing's certain. She must have been pretty desperate. I'd like to know what got her into that state.'

'So would I, Jack,' Miller said. 'So would I,' and he released the handbrake and drove rapidly away.

Drug addicts are possibly the most difficult of all patients to handle and yet Dr Lal Das specialized in them. He was a tall cadaverous Indian, with an international reputation in the field, who persisted in running a general practice in one of the less salubrious parts of the city, a twilight area of tall, decaying Victorian houses.

He had just finished his morning calls and was having coffee in front of the surgery fire when Miller was shown in. Das smiled and waved him to a seat. 'A pleasant surprise. You will join me?'

'Thanks very much.'

Das went to the sideboard and returned with another cup. 'A social call?'

'I'm afraid not.' Miller produced one of the photos. 'Have you ever seen her before?'

Das shook his head. 'Who is she?'

'We don't know. I pulled her out of the river this morning.'

'Suicide?'

Miller nodded. 'Professor Murray did an autopsy. She'd had a fix about half an hour before she died.'

'What was the dosage?'

'Two grains of heroin – one of cocaine.'

'Then she can't have been an addict for long. Most of my regulars are on five, six or seven grains of heroin alone. There were the usual tracks in her arm?'

'Only a few.'

'Which would seem to confirm my theory.' Das sighed. 'What a tragedy. She looks such a pleasant child.' He handed the photo back. 'I'm sorry, I can't help. You have no idea as to her identity at all?'

'I was hoping she might be a registered addict.'

Das shook his head emphatically. 'Definitely not. We have a new scheme operating under which all registered addicts must attend my clinic at St Gregory's Hospital on Saturday mornings.'

'Is this as well as their visits to their own doctor?'

Das nodded. 'Believe me, Sergeant, if she was registered I would know her.'

Miller swallowed the rest of his coffee. 'I'd better get moving. Got a lot of ground to cover.'

'Why not have a chat with Chuck Lazer?' Das said. 'If anyone could help, he could.'

'That's an idea,' Miller said. 'How is he these days? Still dry?'

'For ten months now. A remarkable achievement, especially when one considers that his intake was of the order of seven grains of heroin and six of cocaine daily.'

'I hear he's running a small casino club now.'

'Yes, the Berkley in Cork Square. Very exclusive. Haven't you been?'

'I got an invitation to the opening, but I couldn't make it. Does he still play a good jazz piano?'

'Oscar Peterson at his best couldn't improve on him. I was there last Saturday. We were talking about you.'

'I'll drop in and see him,' Miller said. 'Where's he living now?'

'He has an apartment over the club. Very pleasant. He'll probably be in bed now, mind you.'

'I'll take that chance.'

They went out into the hall. Das opened the front door and shook hands formally. 'If I can help in any way . . .'

'I'll let you know,' Miller said and he ran down the steps to the Mini-Cooper and drove away.

Cork Square was a green lung in the heart of the city, a few sycamore trees scattered here and there, the whole surrounded by quiet, grey-stone Georgian houses, most of them occupied by consultant physicians and barristers.

The entrance to the Berkley Club was a cream-painted door, its brass handle and plate shining in the sunlight. Even the neon sign was in perfect taste with the surroundings and had obviously been specially designed. Miller pulled in to the kerb, got out and looked up at the front of the building.

'Hey, Nick, you old so-and-so! What gives?'

The cry echoed across the square and as he turned, Chuck Lazer moved out of the trees, a couple of Dalmatians straining ahead of him on twin leads. Miller went to meet him, leaving the path and crossing the damp grass.

'Hello there, Chuck. What's all this?' He bent down to pat the eager dogs.

The American grinned. 'Part of my new image. The customers love it. Gives the place tone. But never mind that. How are you? It's been too long.'

He was bubbling over with genuine pleasure, the blue eyes sparkling. When Miller had first met him almost a year previously during a murder investigation, Lazer had been hopelessly hooked on heroin with the gaunt fleshless face of an emaciated saint. Now, there was meat on his bones and the neatly trimmed dark fringe beard combined with the expensive sports coat to give him a positively elegant appearance.

He slipped the dogs' leads and the Dalmatians moved into the flower beds as he and Miller sat down on a bench.

'I've just seen Das. He told me he'd been to the club. Gave me a glowing report.' Miller offered him a cigarette. 'On you too.'

Lazer grinned. 'No need to worry about me, Nick. I'd cut my throat before I'd take another shot.' He lit his cigarette and exhaled smoke in a blue cloud. 'What did you want with Das – business?'

Miller produced one of the photos and passed it across. 'Know her?'

Lazer shook his head. 'Can't say I do.' He frowned suddenly. 'Heh, isn't that a morgue photograph?'

Miller nodded. 'I pulled her out of the river this morning. Trouble is we can't identify her.'

'Suicide?'

'That's right. The autopsy showed she was an addict. I was hoping she might be registered, that Das might know her.'

'And she isn't? That makes it difficult.'

'What's the drug market like now, Chuck?' Miller said. 'Where would she get the stuff?'

'Difficult to say. I've been out of circulation for quite a while, remember. As far as I know, there isn't any really organized peddling if that's what you mean. Remember where you first met me?'

Miller grinned. 'Outside the all-night chemist's in City Square.'

'That's where it changes hands. Most registered addicts see their doctor at his evening surgery and usually get a prescription dated for the following day. Legally, they can have it filled from midnight onwards which is why you always find a bunch waiting in the all-night chemist's in any big city round about that time. The non-registered users hang around outside hoping to buy a few pills. They're usually in luck. Quite a few doctors tend to over-prescribe.'

'So all I have to do is go down to City Square at midnight and pass her photo around?'

'If she was an addict, someone will recognize her, that's for sure. The most exclusive club in the world.'

'Thanks very much,' Miller said. 'I didn't get any sleep last night either.'

'You shouldn't have joined.' Lazer chuckled and then his smile faded.

Miller glanced across to the club as a dark blue Rolls eased in to the kerb. The first man to emerge was built like a pro wrestler, shoulders bulging massively under a dark blue overcoat. The driver came round to join him, a small, wiry man with jet black hair, and held open the rear door.

The man who got out was large and rather fleshy with

hair so pale that it was almost white. He wore a single-breasted suit of dark grey flannel that was straight out of Savile Row, a white gardenia in the buttonhole, and carried himself with the habitual arrogance of a man who believes that he exists by a kind of divine right. The small man said something to him and they all turned and glanced at Lazer and Miller.

'Friends of yours?' Miller said as they moved across the grass.

Lazer shook his head. 'I wouldn't say that exactly. The fancy boy is Max Vernon. Came up from London about four months ago and bought out Harry Faulkner. Took over his betting shops, the Flamingo Club – everything.'

'What about his minders?'

'The big boy's called Carver – Simon Carver. The little guy's the one to watch. Stratton – I don't know his first name.'

'Have they been leaning on you?'

Lazer bared his teeth in a mirthless grin. 'Nothing quite so obvious. Let's say I've got a very nice little business and Mr Vernon would like a piece of the action. For a consideration, of course. All nice and legal. Unfortunately, I'm not interested in selling.'

Vernon paused a couple of yards away, Carver and Stratton on either side of him. 'Hello there, old man,' he said cheerfully. 'I was hoping to find you in. Time we had another little chat.'

'Not in my book it isn't,' Lazer replied.

Carver took a step forward, but before anything could develop, Miller said quickly, 'That's an Old Etonian tie you're wearing, did you know that?'

Vernon turned, his smile still hooked firmly into place. 'How very gratifying. You're the first person to recognize it since I've been here. Of course, we are a little far north.'

'Dangerous country,' Miller said. 'We've been known to

roll boulders down the hillside on unwary travellers – stone strangers.'

'How fascinating.' Vernon turned to Lazer. 'Introduce me to your friend, Chuck.'

'A pleasure,' Lazer said. 'Nick Miller. Detective Sergeant, Central C.I.D.'

Vernon hesitated momentarily and then extended his hand. 'Always a pleasure to meet the law.'

Miller stayed where he was on the bench, hands tucked casually into his pockets. 'I can't say it's mutual.'

'You watch your mouth, copper,' Carver said harshly.

He started to move, Lazer whistled twice and the Dalmatians arrived on the run. They stood beside him, pointing at Carver, something rumbling deep down in their throats.

Carver hesitated, obviously uncertain, and Miller laughed. 'Know why they call them carriage dogs, Carver? They were specially bred during the eighteenth century as travelling companions to take care of highwaymen.'

Something glowed deep in Carver's eyes and Vernon chuckled. 'That's damned good. Damned good.' He grinned at Carver. 'See, you learn something new every day of the week.'

He turned away without another word and walked back to the Rolls, Carver and Stratton hurrying after him. Lazer leaned down to fondle the ears of the two dogs and Miller said softly, 'I think you could have trouble there, Chuck.'

'If it comes, I'll handle it.'

Miller shook his head. 'You mean I'll handle it and that's an order.' He got to his feet and grinned. 'I've got to get moving.'

Lazer stood up and produced a small gold-edged card from his breast pocket. 'I know it's illegal to do it this way, but there's a membership card. Why not drop in? It's been a long time since I heard you play piano.'

'I might just do that,' Miller said and he turned and walked away across the grass.

As the Rolls-Royce moved out into the main traffic stream, Max Vernon leaned forward and slid back the glass panel of the partition.

'This chap Miller,' he said to Carver, 'know anything about him?'

'Not a thing.'

'Then start digging. I want to know everything – everything there is to know.'

'Any special reason?' Carver said.

'Well, let me put it this way. The only other copper I've ever met who made a practice of wearing sixty-guinea suits is doing a five stretch in the Ville for corruption.'

Carver's eyes widened and Vernon closed the glass panel, leaned back in his seat and lit a cigarette, a slight smile on his face.

3

Henry Wade was fat and balding and his several chins and horn-rimmed spectacles gave him the deceptively benign air of a prosperous publican or back street bookie. He was neither. He was head of the department's Forensic section with the rank of Detective Inspector and the ready smile concealed a brain that in action had the cutting edge of a razor.

When Miller went into the small office at one end of the police lab, he found Wade at his desk filling in a report, covering the paper with the neat italic script that was his special pride.

He turned and smiled. 'Hello, Nick, I was wondering when you'd turn up.'

'Anything for me?'

'Not much, I'm afraid. Come on. I'll show you.'

Miller followed him into the lab., nodding to the bench technicians as he passed. The girl's clothing was laid out neatly on a table by the window.

Wade went through the items one by one. 'The stockings are a well-known brand sold everywhere and the underwear she bought at Marks & Spencer's along with just about every other girl in the country these days.'

'What about the dress?'

'Reasonably expensive, but once again, a well-known brand name available at dozens of shops and stores. One interesting point. Just below the maker's label, a name tab's been torn out.'

He picked up the dress pointing with a pair of tweezers and Miller nodded. 'I noticed.'

'I had a hunch about that. We matched up a piece of the tab that was still attached to the dress and my hunch paid off. It's a Cash label. You must have seen them. Little white tabs with the individual's name woven in red. People buy them for schoolchildren or students going away to college.'

Miller nodded. 'Thousands of people, including my sister-in-law. Her two kids have them sewn into just about every damned thing they own. Is that all?'

'No – one other thing. When we checked the nail scrapings we discovered a minute quantity of oil paint. There were one or two spots on the dress, too.'

'An artist?' Miller said. 'That's something.'

'Don't be too certain. Lots of people do a little painting these days.' Henry Wade grinned and slapped him on the shoulder. 'You shouldn't have joined, Nick lad. You shouldn't have joined.'

Grant was still working away at his desk when Miller peered round the door. 'Got a minute?'

'Just about.' Grant sat back and lit a cigarette. 'How's it going?'

'So far, not so good, but it was something else I wanted to mention. What do you know about a man called Vernon?'

'Max Vernon, the bloke from London who took over Faulkner's casino and betting shops?' Grant shrugged. 'Not much. The Chief introduced him to me at the Conservative Ball. Obviously a gentleman. Public school and all that sort of thing.'

'Right down to his Old Etonian tie.' Miller suppressed a strong desire to burst into laughter. 'He's leaning on Chuck Lazer.'

'He's what?' Grant said incredulously.

'It's true enough,' Miller said. 'I was chatting to Lazer in the Square outside his place when Vernon turned up with a couple of heavies named Carver and Stratton. No comic Vaudeville act those two, believe me. Vernon wants a piece of the Berkley Club. He'll pay for it of course, all nice and legal, but Chuck Lazer better play ball or else . . .'

Grant was a different man as he flicked one of the switches on his intercom. 'Records? Get on to C.R.O. in London at once. I want everything they've got on Max Vernon and two men now working for him called Carver and Stratton. Top priority.'

He turned back to Miller. 'What happened?'

'Nothing much. Vernon didn't say anything in the slightest way incriminating. On the face of it, he's making a perfectly legitimate business offer.'

'Did he know who you were?'

'Not until Lazer introduced us.'

Grant got up and walked to the window. 'I don't like the sound of this at all.'

'It certainly raises interesting possibilities,' Miller said. 'Those houses Faulkner was running in Gascoigne Square. His call-girl racket. Has Vernon taken those over too?'

'An intriguing thought.' Grant sighed heavily. 'It never rains but it pours. Try and look in this afternoon at about three. I should have heard from C.R.O. by then.'

When Miller went back into the main C.I.D. room a young P.C. was hovering beside his desk. 'I took a message for you while you were in with the Super, Sergeant.'

'Who from?'

'Jack Brady. He said he was ringing from St Gemma's Roman Catholic Church in Walthamgate. He'd like you to join him there as soon as you can.'

'Anything else?'

'Yes – he said to tell you that he thinks he's traced the girl.'

The lights in the little church were very dim and down by the altar the candles flickered and the figure of the Virgin in the chapel to one side seemed to float there in the darkness.

For Miller, this was unfamiliar territory and he paused, waiting as Jack Brady dipped a knee, crossing himself reverently. The man they had come to see knelt in prayer at the altar and when he got to his feet and came towards them, Miller saw that he was very old, the hair silvery in the subdued light.

Brady made the introductions. 'Father Ryan, this is Detective Sergeant Nick Miller.'

The old man smiled and took Miller's hand in a grip that was surprisingly firm. 'Jack and I are old friends, Sergeant. For fifteen years or more he ran the boxing team for me at the Dockside Mission boys' club. Shall we sit in the porch? A pity to miss the sunshine. It's been a hard winter.'

Brady opened the door and Father Ryan preceded them. He sat on the polished wooden bench that overlooked the quiet graveyard with the row of cypress trees lining the road beyond the high wall.

'I understand you might be able to help us with our enquiry, Father,' Miller said.

The old man nodded. 'Could I see the photo again?'

Miller passed it across and for a moment there was silence as Father Ryan examined it. He sighed heavily. 'Poor girl. Poor wee girl.'

'You know her?'

'She called herself Joanna Martin.'

'Called herself . . . ?'

'That's right. I don't think it was her real name.'

'Might I ask why?'

Father Ryan smiled faintly. 'Like you, I deal with people, Sergeant. Human beings in the raw. Let's say one develops an instinct.'

Miller nodded. 'I know what you mean.'

'She first came to my church about three months ago. I noticed something different about her at once. This is a twilight area, most of the houses in multiple occupation, the tenants constantly coming and going. Joanna was obviously the product of a safer more ordered world. She was out of her element.'

'Can you tell us where she lived?'

'She had a room with a Mrs Kilroy, a parishioner of mine. It's not far from here. I've given Detective Constable Brady the address.'

Somehow, the fact that he had used Brady's official title seemed to underline a new formality in the interchange. It was as if he were preparing himself for the question that he knew must come.

'I know this must be a difficult situation for you, Father,' Miller said gently. 'But this girl had problems and they must have been pretty desperate to make her take the way out that she did. Can you throw any light on them?'

Brady cleared his throat awkwardly and shuffled his feet. The old man shook his head. 'For me, the secrecy of the confessional must be absolute. Surely you must be aware of that, Sergeant.'

Miller nodded. 'Of course, Father. I won't press you any further. You've already helped us a great deal.'

Father Ryan stood up and held out his hand. 'If I can help in any other way, don't hesitate to get in touch.'

Brady was already moving away. Miller started to follow and hesitated. 'One more thing, Father. I understand there could be some difficulty regarding burial because of the manner of death.'

'Not in this case,' Father Ryan said firmly. 'There are several mitigating circumstances. I intend raising the matter with the Bishop personally. I may say with some certainty that I foresee little difficulty.'

Miller smiled. 'I'm glad.'

'Forgive me for saying so, but you appear to have some personal interest here? May I ask why?'

'I pulled her out of the river myself,' Miller told him. 'Something I'm not likely to forget in a hurry. I know one thing – I'd like to get my hands on whoever was responsible.'

Father Ryan sighed. 'It's a strange thing, but in spite of the fact that most people believe priests to be somehow cut off from the real world, I come face to face with more human wickedness in a week than the average man does in a lifetime.' He smiled gently. 'And I still believe that at heart, most human beings are good.'

'I wish I could agree, Father,' Miller said sombrely. 'I wish I could agree.' He turned and walked away quickly to where Jack Brady waited at the gate.

Mrs Kilroy was a large, unlovely widow with flaming red hair that had come straight out of a bottle and a thin mouth enlarged by orange lipstick into an obscene gash.

'I keep a respectable place here, I've never had any trouble before,' she said as she led the way upstairs.

'No trouble, Mrs Kilroy,' Brady said persuasively. 'We just want to see the room, that's all, and ask a few questions.'

The landing was long and dark, its polished lino covered by a thin strip of worn carpeting. The door at the far end was locked. She produced a bunch of keys, opened it and led the way in.

The room was surprisingly large and furnished in Victorian mahogany. The curtains at the only window were partially closed, the traffic sounds outside muted and unreal as if from another world and a thin bar of sunlight fell across the floor adding a new richness to the faded colours of the old Indian carpet.

It was the neatness that was so surprising and the cleanliness. The bed had been stripped, the blankets folded into squares and stacked at one end of the mattress and the top of the dressing table had quite obviously been dusted. Miller opened one or two of the empty drawers, closed them again and turned.

'And this is exactly how you found the room this morning?'

Mrs Kilroy nodded. 'She came and knocked on my door last night at about ten o'clock.'

'Had she been out?'

'I wouldn't know. She told me she'd be moving today.'

'Did she say why?'

Mrs Kilroy shook her head. 'I didn't ask. I was more interested in getting a week's rent in lieu of notice, which was the agreement.'

'And she paid?'

'Without a murmur. Mind you there was never any trouble over her rent, I'll say that. Not like some.'

Brady had busied himself during the conversation in moving around the room, checking all drawers and cupboards. Now he turned and shook his head. 'Clean as a whistle.'

'Which means that when she left, she must have taken everything with her.' Miller turned to Mrs Kilroy. 'Did you see her go?'

'Last time I saw her was about half ten. She knocked on the door and told me she'd some rubbish to burn. Asked if she could put it in the central heating furnace in the cellar.'

'Have you been down there since?'

'No need. It has an automatic stoking system. Only needs checking every two days.'

'I see.' Miller walked across to the window and pulled back the curtains. 'Let's go back to when you last saw her. Did she seem worried or agitated?'

Mrs Kilroy shook her head quickly. 'She was just the same as she always was.'

'And yet she killed herself less than three hours later.'

'God have mercy on her.' There was genuine horror in Mrs Kilroy's voice and she crossed herself quickly.

'What else can you tell me about her? I understand she'd been a tenant of yours for about three months.'

'That's right. She arrived on the doorstep one afternoon with a couple of suitcases. As it happened, I had a vacancy and she offered a month's rent in advance in lieu of references.'

'What did you think of her?'

Mrs Kilroy shrugged. 'She didn't really fit in. Too much of the lady for a district like this. I never asked questions, I always mind my own business, but if anyone had a story to tell it was her.'

'Father Ryan doesn't seem to think Joanna Martin was her real name.'

'I shouldn't be surprised.'

'What did she do for a living?'

'She paid her rent on time and never caused any trouble. Whatever she did was her own business. One thing – she

had an easel set up in here. Used to paint in oils. I once
asked her if she was a student, but she said it was only a
hobby.'

'Did she go out much – at night, for instance?'

'She could have been out all night and every night as
far as I was concerned. All my lodgers have their own keys.'
She shrugged. 'More often than not I'm out myself.'

'Did anyone ever call for her?'

'Not that I noticed. She kept herself to herself. The only
outstanding thing I do remember is that sometimes she
looked really ill. I had to help her up the stairs one day. I
wanted to call the doctor, but she said it was just her
monthly. I saw her later that afternoon and she looked
fine.'

Which was how one would expect her to look after a
shot of heroin and Miller sighed. 'Anything else?'

'I don't think so,' Mrs Kilroy hesitated. 'If she had a
friend at all, it was the girl in number four – Monica Grey.'

'Why do you say that?'

'I've seen them going out together, mainly in the afternoons.'

'Is she in now?'

'Should be. As far as I know, she works nights in one of
these gaming clubs.'

Miller turned to Brady. 'I'll have a word with her. You
get Mrs Kilroy to show you where the furnace is. See what
you can find.'

The door closed behind them and Miller stood there in
the quiet, listening. But there was nothing here – this room
had no personality. It was as if she had never been here at
all and after all, what did he really know about her? At the
moment she existed only as a series of apparently contra-
dictory facts. A well-bred girl, she had come down to living
in a place like this. A sincere Catholic, she had committed
suicide. Educated and intelligent, but also a drug addict.

None of it made any sense at all and he went along the corridor and knocked at number four. There was an immediate reply and he opened the door and entered.

She was standing in front of the dressing table, her back to the door and dressed, as far as he could judge in that first moment, in stockings and a pair of dark briefs. In the mirror, he was aware of her breasts, high and firm, and then her eyes widened.

'I thought it was Mrs Kilroy.'

Miller stepped back into the corridor smartly, closing the door. A moment later it opened again and she stood there laughing at him, an old nylon housecoat belted around her waist.

'Shall we try again?'

Her voice was hoarse but not unattractive with a slight Liverpool accent and she had a turned-up nose that gave her a rather gamin charm.

'Miss Grey?' Miller produced his warrant card. 'Detective Sergeant Miller – Central C.I.D. I wonder if I might have a word with you?'

Her smile slipped fractionally and a shadow seemed to cross her eyes as she stepped back and motioned him in. 'What have I done now? Over-parked or something?'

There were times when the direct approach produced the best results and Miller tried it now. 'I'm making enquiries into the death of Joanna Martin. I understand you might be able to help me.'

It had the effect of a physical blow. She seemed to stagger slightly, then turned, groped for the end of the bed and sank down.

'I believe you were pretty good friends,' Miller continued.

She stared up at him blindly then suddenly got to her feet, pushed him out of the way and ran for the bathroom. He stood there, a slight frown on his face and there was a knock on the outside door. He opened it to find Jack Brady waiting.

'Any luck?' Miller asked.

Brady held up an old canvas bag. 'I found all sorts in the ash-pan. What about this for instance?'

He produced a triangular piece of metal, blackened and twisted by the fire, and Miller frowned. 'This is a corner piece off a suitcase.'

'That's right,' Brady shook the bag in his right hand. 'If the bits and pieces in here are anything to go by, I'd say she must have put every damned thing she owned into that furnace.'

'Including her suitcase? She certainly wasn't leaving anything to chance.' Miller sighed. 'All right, Jack. Take that little lot down to the car and put in a call to H.Q. See if they've anything for us. I shan't be long.'

He lit a cigarette, moved to the window and looked out into the back garden. Behind him the bathroom door opened and Monica Grey emerged.

She looked a lot brighter as she came forward and sat on the edge of the bed. 'Sorry about that. It was rather a shock. Joanna was a nice kid.' She hesitated and then continued. 'How – how did it happen?'

'She jumped in the river.' Miller gave her a cigarette and lit it for her. 'Mrs Kilroy tells me you were good friends.'

Monica Grey took the smoke deep into her lungs and exhaled with a sigh of pleasure. 'I wouldn't say that exactly. I went to the cinema with her sometimes in the afternoons or she came in for a coffee, mainly because she happened to live next door.'

'You never went out with her at any other time?'

'I couldn't – I work nights. I'm a croupier at a gaming club in Gascoigne Square – the Flamingo.'

'Max Vernon's place?'

She nodded. 'Have you been there?'

'A long time ago. Tell me about Joanna? Where did she come from?'

Monica Grey shook her head. 'She never discussed her past. She always seemed to live entirely in the present.'

'What did she do for a living?'

'Nothing as far as I could tell. She spent a lot of time painting, but only as a hobby. I know one thing – she was never short of money.'

'What about boyfriends?'

'As far as I know, she didn't have any.'

'Didn't that seem strange to you? She was an attractive girl.'

'That's true, but she had her problems.' She appeared to hesitate and then went on. 'If you've seen her body you must know what I'm getting at. She was a junkie.'

'How did you know that?'

'I went into her room to borrow a pair of stockings one day and found her giving herself a shot. She asked me to keep quiet about it.'

'Which you did?'

Monica Grey shrugged. 'None of my affair how she got her kicks. It was one hell of a shame, but there was nothing I could do about it.'

'She was a Catholic,' Miller said, 'did you know that?'

She nodded. 'She went to church nearly every day.'

'And yet she killed herself after burning everything she owned in the central heating furnace downstairs and ripping the name tab out of the dress she was wearing when she died. It's only by chance that we've managed to trace her this far and when we do, nobody seems to know anything about her. Wouldn't you say that was peculiar?'

'She was a strange kid. You could never tell what was going on beneath the surface.'

'Father Ryan doesn't seem to think that Joanna Martin was her real name.'

'If that's true, she certainly never gave me any clue.'

Miller nodded, turned and paced across the room. He

paused suddenly. The table against the wall was littered with sketches, mainly fashion drawings, some in pen and ink, others colour-washed. All showed indications of real talent.

'Yours?' he said.

Monica Grey stood up and walked across. 'That's right. Like them?'

'Very much. Did you go to the College of Art?'

'For two years. That's what brought me here in the first place.'

'What made you give it up?'

She grinned. 'Forty quid a week at the Flamingo plus a dress allowance.'

'Attractive alternative.' Miller dropped the sketch he was holding. 'Well, I don't think I need bother you any more.' He walked to the door, paused and turned. 'Just one thing. You do understand that if I can't trace her family, I may have to ask you to make the formal identification?'

She stood there staring at him, her face very white, and he closed the door and went downstairs. There was a pay 'phone fixed to the wall by the door and Brady leaned beside it filling his pipe.

He glanced up quickly. 'Any joy?'

'Not really, but I've a feeling we'll be seeing her again.'

'I got through to H.Q. There was a message for you from Chuck Lazer. Apparently he's been passing round the copy of the photo you gave him. He's come up with a registered addict who sold her a couple of pills outside the all-night chemist's in City Square just after midnight. If you guarantee no charge, he's agreed to make a statement.'

'That's all right by me,' Miller said. 'You handle it, will you? I'll drop you off at Cork Square and you can go and see Chuck right away. I've a 'phone call to make first.'

'Anything special?'

'Just a hunch. The girl liked to paint, we've established

that. Another thing – that name tab she ripped out of her dress was a type commonly bought by students. I'm wondering if there might be a connection.'

He found the number he wanted and dialled quickly. The receiver was picked up almost at once at the other end and a woman's voice said, 'College of Art.'

'Put me through to the registrar's office please.'

There was a momentary delay and then a pleasant Scottish voice cut in, 'Henderson here.'

'Central C.I.D. Detective Sergeant Miller. I'm making enquiries concerning a girl named Joanna Martin and I've good reason to believe she might have been a student at your college during the last couple of years. Would it take you long to check?'

'No more than thirty seconds, Sergeant,' Henderson said crisply. 'We've a very comprehensive filing system.' A moment later he was back. 'Sorry, no student of that name. I could go back further if you like.'

'No point,' Miller said. 'She wasn't old enough.'

He replaced the receiver and turned to Brady. 'Another possibility we can cross off.'

'What now?' Brady demanded.

'I still think there's a lot in this idea of Father Ryan's that Martin wasn't her real name. If that's true, it's just possible she's been listed as a missing person by someone or other. You go and see Chuck Lazer and I'll drop round to the Salvation Army and see if a chat with Martha Broadribb produces anything.'

Brady grinned. 'Don't end up beating a drum for her on Sundays.'

But Miller had to force a smile in reply and as he went down the steps to the car, his face was grim and serious. At the best of times a good copper was guided as much by instinct as solid fact and there was something very wrong here, something much more serious than appeared on the surface of things and all his training, all his experience told him as much.

4

The small office of the Stone Street Citadel was badly over-crowded, half a dozen young men and women working busily surrounded by green filing cabinets, double-banked to save space.

'I'll see if the Major's in her office,' said Miller's escort, a thin, earnest young man in blazer and flannels, and he disappeared in search of Martha Broadribb.

Miller leaned against a filing cabinet and waited, impressed as always at the industry and efficiency so obviously the order of the day. A sheet of writing paper had fallen to the floor and he picked it up and read the printed heading quickly. *Missing Relatives Sought in any part of the World: Investigations and Enquiries carried out in Strictest Confidence: Reconciliation Bureau: Advice willingly Given.*

The biggest drawback to tracing a missing person from the official point of view was that there was nothing illegal about disappearing. Unless there was a suspicion of foul play, the police could do nothing, which produced the ironical situation that the greatest experts in the field were the Salvation Army, who handled something like ten thousand British and foreign enquiries a year from their Headquarters in Bishopsgate, London, and who were constantly in touch with centres throughout the country such as the Stone Street Citadel.

The young man emerged from the inner office, his arm around the shoulders of a middle-aged woman in a shabby coat who had obviously been weeping. He nodded briefly without speaking and Miller brushed past them and went in.

Major Martha Broadribb was exactly five feet tall, her
trim uniformed figure bristling with a vitality that belied
her sixty years. Her blue eyes were enormous behind steel-
rimmed spectacles and she had the smooth, unused face
of an innocent child. And yet this was a woman who
had laboured for most of her life in a China Mission,
who had spent three terrible years in solitary confinement
in a Communist prison camp.

She came forward quickly, a smile of genuine affection
on her face. 'Nicholas, this *is* nice. Will you have a cup of
tea?'

'I wouldn't say no,' Miller said. 'Who was that who just
left?'

'Poor soul. Her husband died a year ago.' She took a
clean cup and saucer from a cupboard and moved to the
tea-tray that stood on her desk. 'She married one of her
lodgers last month. He persuaded her to sell the house and
give him the money she received to buy a business.'

'Don't tell me, let me guess,' Miller said. 'He's cleared
off?'

'That's about the size of it.'

'She's been to the police?'

'Who told her that as he hadn't committed a criminal
offence they were powerless to act.' She stirred his tea
briskly. 'Four lumps and much good may it do you.'

'Do you think you'll find him?'

'Certain to,' she said, 'and he'll face up to his responsi-
bilities and do right by the poor woman after I've had a
chance of talking to him. I'm certain of that.'

Another one who thought most people were good at heart. Miller
smiled wryly, remembering their first meeting. On his way
home one night he had answered an emergency call simply
because he happened to be in the vicinity and had arrived
at a slum house near the river in time to find a graceless,
mindless lout doing his level best to beat his wife to death

after knocking Martha Broadribb senseless for trying to stop him, breaking her right arm in the process. And the very next day she had visited him in the Bridewell, plaster-cast and all.

She lit a cigarette, her one vice, and leaned back in her chair. 'You look tired, Nicholas.'

'I feel tired,' he said. 'A perpetual state these days, but don't let's go into that.' He passed one of the photos across. 'Ever seen her?'

Martha examined it with a slight frown. 'This is a mortuary photo, isn't it?'

'That's right. I pulled her out of the river this morning.'

'Suicide?' There was an expression of real grief on her face. 'Poor child. Poor, poor child.'

'No ordinary suicide,' Miller said. 'This girl did everything she could to destroy her identity before she died.'

He sketched in the main facts and she nodded sombrely. 'So Father Ryan thinks that Joanna Martin wasn't her real name?'

'He got that impression, which the other two people I've spoken to who knew her confirm. Coming to see you was just a hunch really. I was hoping that somebody might have put out a search for her – that you might recognize her photo.'

Martha nodded and held up the medal. 'She still hung on to Joanna. Interesting that – they nearly always do hang on to their Christian name. It's as if they're afraid of losing themselves entirely.'

She gave him back the medal and made a few notes on her pad. 'Let's see what we've got. About nineteen, fair hair, blue eyes. Well spoken, educated, obviously from a superior background and an artist. We'll look under the name of Martin first, just in case, and we'll check the Christian name.'

'I didn't know you could do that?'

'As I said, so many of them hang on to their Christian names that it's worth cross-indexing and Joanna isn't very common these days. We'll see what we've got here and I'll also put through a call to London. Should take about fifteen minutes.'

Before he could reply, the 'phone on her desk rang. She took the call and then held out the receiver. 'For you – Detective Constable Brady.'

Martha went into the outer office and Miller sat on the edge of the desk. 'What have you got?'

'Plenty,' Brady said. 'I've just had a session with a character named Jack Fenner. He's been a registered addict for just over a year now. He makes a living as a dance band drummer.'

'I think I've seen him around,' Miller said. 'Small, fair-haired.'

'That's him. He says he had a prescription for heroin and cocaine filled at the all-night chemist's in City Square at midnight on the dot. Joanna Martin stopped him on his way out and offered him a couple of quid for enough pills for a shot. His story is that he felt sorry for her. Said she had the shakes.'

'No chance of a mistake?'

'Definitely not.' Brady laughed harshly. 'In fact this is where it gets interesting. Fenner says he's seen her before.'

'Where?'

'At Max Vernon's place, the Flamingo, about six weeks ago. The regular drummer was ill that night and Fenner stood in for him. Apparently it was Vernon's birthday and he threw a big private binge. Fenner remembers the girl because Vernon kept her with him for most of the evening, which Fenner says is highly unusual. Apparently our Max prefers variety.'

'Now that *is* interesting,' Miller said. 'Fenner's certain he's never seen her at any other time?'

'Dead certain – is it important that he should have?'

'Could be. Look at it this way. The girl wasn't a registered addict, we know that, so where did she get the stuff from? If she'd been working the prescription racket outside the all-night chemist's regularly, Fenner would have seen her many times. An addict needs at least one fix a day remember. Usually more.'

'Which means that someone must be peddling the stuff?'

'Could be.' Behind Miller, the door opened as Martha Broadribb returned and he added hastily, 'I've got to go now, Jack. I'll see you back at the office in half an hour.'

He turned, eyebrows raised enquiringly, and Martha shook her head. 'I'm sorry, Nicholas. Not a thing. There was one Joanna on file, that's all – a West Indian nurse.'

Miller sighed and stood up. 'Never mind, Martha, it was just a hunch. Thanks for the tea anyway. I'll leave you a copy of the photo just in case.'

He dropped it on the desk and as he turned, she placed a hand on his arm, concern on her face. 'You're worried about this one, aren't you? There's no need to be. Something will turn up. It always does.'

He grinned and kissed her briefly on the forehead. 'Don't work too hard, Martha. I'll be seeing you.'

The door closed behind him. She stood there staring blankly at it for a moment, then took a deep breath, squaring her shoulders, sat down at her typewriter and started to work.

Brady was sitting on the other side of Grant's desk when Miller looked round the door of the Superintendent's office. Grant waved him in at once.

'Jack's been filling me in on your progress so far. You don't seem to be doing too badly. At least you've got a name for her now.'

'Which doesn't seem to mean a great deal,' Miller said. 'I'm afraid Martha Broadribb couldn't help at all.'

'Never mind,' Grant said. 'Something will turn up.'

Miller smiled. 'The second time I've been told that today. Anything through from C.R.O. on Max Vernon and company yet?'

Grant nodded, his face grim. 'And it doesn't make pleasant reading.' Brady started to get up and the Superintendent waved him down. 'You might as well hear this, Jack. I'll be circularizing the information anyway.'

He put on his reading glasses and picked up the white flimsy that had been delivered from Records ten minutes earlier. 'Let's start with his two bully boys and a nice pair they are. Benjamin Carver, 35. Last known profession, salesman. Four previous convictions including five years for robbery with violence; conspiracy to steal; larceny; grievous bodily harm. He's been pulled in for questioning on twenty-three other occasions.'

'And Stratton?'

'Even worse. Mad as a March Hare and twisted with it. William, "Billy" Stratton, 34. Three previous convictions including a five stretch for robbery with violence. Remember the Knavesmire Airport bullion robbery?'

'He was in on that?'

Grant nodded. 'The psychiatrists did what they could for him during his last stretch, but it wasn't much. Psychopathic tendencies and too damned handy with a chiv. The next time he stands in the dock it'll be for murder, mark my words.'

'And Vernon?'

'Nothing.'

'You mean he's clean?' Miller said in astonishment.

'As a whistle.' Grant dropped the flimsy on the table. 'Six years ago he was invited to help Scotland Yard with their enquiries concerning the Knavesmire Airport bullion robbery. The interview lasted exactly ten minutes, thanks to the best lawyer in London.'

'And that's all?'

'All that's official.' Grant picked up another flimsy. 'Now let's look at what they have to say about him unofficially. Believe me, it'll make your hair stand on end.'

'Maxwell Alexander Constable Vernon, 36. Younger son of Sir Henry Vernon, managing director of the Red Funnel shipping line. From Eton he went to Sandhurst and was commissioned in the Guards.'

'Only the best, eh?'

Grant nodded. 'The rot set in when he was seconded for duty with a Malayan infantry regiment during the emergency. Vernon proved so successful at rooting out the Communists in his area that he was awarded the D.S.O. Then they discovered he'd been indulging in an orgy of sadism and torture. No one could afford a public scandal at the time so he was simply persuaded to resign his commission. His family disowned him.'

'He took to crime?'

'That's what it looks like. Organized prostitution – he started with a call-girl racket – illegal clubs, protection, dope peddling – anything that pays, that's our Maxwell. And he's a bright boy – don't make any mistake about that. The Knavesmire Airport heist was only one of half a dozen big jobs he's probably been behind during the past five or six years.'

'Why move up here though?' Brady put in. 'It doesn't make sense.'

'I'm not so sure,' Grant said. 'Since the middle of last year there's been open warfare in London between the four most powerful gangs, mainly over the protection racket. These things always run to a pattern. The villains carve each other up – in this case they're even using shooters – and the police stand by to pick up the pieces when it's all over. Nobody wins that kind of fight and Vernon was clever enough to realize that. As soon as he heard the first rumblings, he sold out to one of his rivals and dropped out of sight.'

'To reappear here?' Brady said.

Grant got to his feet and paced to the window. 'I've always thought this might happen one day. That the London mobs would start looking for fresh fields. I'll have to have a word with the old man about it.' He shook his head. 'I'd love to know what Vernon's been up to since he's been here.'

'Maybe Chuck Lazer could give me a few pointers,' Miller said.

Grant swung round, his face brightening. 'That's a thought. See what you can get out of him.'

'I'll do my best,' Miller said, 'but don't expect too much. To a certain extent Lazer's on the other side of the fence, remember. I'll keep you posted.'

He returned to the main C.I.D. room and Brady followed him. 'What now?'

'About the girl?' Miller shrugged. 'I'm still considering. There are one or two interesting possibilities.'

He pulled a packet of cigarettes out of his pocket and the gold medal and chain fell to the floor. Brady picked it up and examined the inscription again. 'At least we know one thing for certain – her Christian name.'

Miller paused in the act of lighting his cigarette. 'My God, I must be losing my touch.'

'What do you mean?' Brady asked.

'I'm remembering something Martha Broadribb told me. How most people who go missing hang on to their Christian name – there's a pretty obvious psychological explanation for that. It's such a common behaviour pattern that they cross-index missing persons under their Christian names as well.'

'And where does that get us?' Brady demanded looking puzzled. 'She still couldn't help, could she?'

'No, but I'm wondering whether we might have just a little bit more luck at the College of Art,' Miller said simply.

'This must be her,' Henderson said suddenly, turning from the file and handing Miller a white index card.

He was a small, greying Scot with a pleasant, lined face, obviously fascinated by the present situation, which had turned what would otherwise have been a day of dull routine into a memorable one.

Miller read the details on the card aloud and Brady made notes. 'Joanna Maria Craig, address, Rosedene, Grange Avenue, St Martin's Wood.'

Brady pursed his lips in a soundless whistle. 'Pretty exclusive. We were certainly on the ball there.'

'Apparently she dropped out of the course just over three months ago,' Miller said. 'It says here see personal file.'

'That's what I'm looking for.' Henderson had opened another filing cabinet and was flicking rapidly through the green folders it contained. He nodded suddenly, took one out and opened it as he turned.

After a while he looked up and nodded. 'I remember this case now, mainly because of her father.'

'Her father?'

'That's right. A hell of a nice chap. I felt sorry for him at the time. He's managing director of that new firm out on the York Road. Gulf Electronics.'

'Why do you say you felt sorry for him?'

'As I recall, she was giving him a hard time. When she first started here everything was fine and then about four months ago she seemed to go to pieces. Cutting lectures, not turning in her work on time, that sort of thing. We called him in to discuss the position.' He frowned suddenly. 'Now I remember. He brought his other daughter with him. Charming girl. A schoolteacher I believe. It emerged during the interview that he was a widower.'

'What happened?'

'He promised to try and straighten the girl out, but I'm afraid he had no luck in that direction. There was a nasty incident about a week later with one of the women lecturers. Harsh words and then the girl slapped her in the face. Naturally she had to go after that.'

Miller sat there in silence for a moment, thinking about it, and then got to his feet. He held out his hand. 'You've helped us a great deal, Mr Henderson.'

'Anything else I can do don't hesitate to get in touch,' Henderson said.

Outside, the pale afternoon sun picked out the vivid colours of the mosaic in the concrete face of the new shopping precinct on the other side of the road and Miller paused at the top of the steps to light a cigarette.

Jack Brady looked up at him, eyebrows raised, and Miller sighed. 'And now comes the unpleasant bit.'

St Martin's Wood was on the edge of the city, an exclusive residential area not far from Miller's own home. The houses ran very much to a pattern, turn of the century mansions in grey stone, each one standing in an acre or two of garden. The house they were seeking stood at one end of a quiet cul-de-sac behind a high stone wall. Miller turned the Cooper in through the gates and drove along a wide gravel drive, braking to a halt at the bottom of a flight of shallow steps which led to the front door.

The bell push was obviously electronic, the sound echoing melodiously inside, and after a while the door was opened by a pleasant-faced young maid in a nylon working overall.

'Yes, sir?' she said to Miller.

'Is Mr Craig at home by any chance?'

'Colonel Craig,' she said in a tone of mild reproof, 'is in London at the moment, but we're expecting him home tonight.'

'Who is it, Jenny?' a voice called and then a young woman appeared from a door to the right.

'The gentlemen wanted to see the Colonel, but I've told them he isn't at home,' the maid said.

'All right, Jenny, I'll handle it.' She came forward, an open book in one hand. 'I'm Harriet Craig. Is there anything I can do?'

She was perhaps twenty-two or -three and nothing like her sister. The black shoulder-length hair framed a face that was too angular for beauty, the mouth so wide that it was almost ugly. And then, for no accountable reason, she smiled and the transformation was so complete that she might have been a different person.

Miller produced his warrant card. 'I wonder if we could have a word with you, Miss Craig?'

She looked at the card and frowned. 'Is anything wrong?'

'If we could go inside, miss,' Brady said gently.

The drawing room into which she led them was beautifully furnished in excellent taste and purple and white hyacinths made a brave splash of colour in a pewter bowl that stood on the grand piano. She turned, a hand on the mantelshelf.

'Won't you sit down?'

Miller shook his head. 'I think it might be a good idea if you did.'

She stiffened slightly. 'You've got bad news for me, is that it?' And then as if by intuition, 'Is it my sister? Is it Joanna?'

Miller produced one of the photos from his inside pocket. 'Is this her?'

She took the photo from him almost mechanically and her eyes widened in horror. When she spoke, it was in a whisper. 'She's dead, isn't she?'

'I'm afraid so,' Miller said gently. 'She was taken out of the river at dawn today. To the best of our knowledge, she committed suicide.'

'Suicide? Oh, my God.'

And then she seemed to crack, to break into a thousand fragments and as Miller's arms opened to her, she lurched into them, burying her face against his chest like some small child seeking comfort and strength in a world she could no longer understand.

Jack Palmer lifted the sheet and for a brief moment Harriet Craig looked down on the dead face of her sister. She swayed slightly and Miller's grip tightened on her elbow.

'All right to use your office for ten minutes, Jack?'

'Help yourself.'

It was warm in the tiny glass office after the cold outside. Miller sat her in the only chair and perched on the edge of the desk. Jack Brady leaned against the door, notebook and pencil ready.

'I'm afraid I'm going to have to ask you some questions,' Miller said.

She nodded, gripping her handbag so tightly that her knuckles gleamed white. 'That's all right.'

'Were you aware that for the past three months your sister was living at a house in Grosvenor Road under the name of Joanna Martin?'

She shook her head. 'No – in fact it doesn't make sense. We understood she was in London. We've had three letters from her and they were all postmarked Chelsea.'

'I understand there was some trouble at the College of Art?' Miller said. 'That she had to leave? Could you tell me about that?'

'It's rather difficult to explain. Joanna was always a sweet kid. Very talented, but a little naïve, that's why my father thought it would be better to let her attend the local college and live at home instead of going away.'

She took a deep shuddering breath and when she continued, her voice was much stronger. 'And then, about

four months or so ago she seemed to change overnight. It
was as if she'd become a different person.'

'In what way exactly?'

'Her whole temperament altered. She became violently
angry on the slightest excuse. It became almost impossible
to handle her. She came home drunk a couple of times and
then she started staying out all night. Naturally my father
didn't like that, but he's often away on business and in any
case, she was hardly a child.'

'How old was she?'

'Twenty last month. After a while, there was trouble at
the college. She behaved so badly that she was asked to
leave.'

'What happened then?'

'She had a furious row with my father and ended by
packing her bags and leaving. She said she intended to
continue her studies at one of the London colleges.'

'What about money? Did your father agree to support
her?'

'There was no need. She had some of her own. Just over
a thousand pounds. A legacy from an old aunt a year or
two ago.'

'What about boyfriends? At the college, for instance?'

'In the two years she was there, she never brought a
single one home. As I've said, until that sudden dreadful
change in her she was a shy, rather introverted girl, very
much bound up in her work.'

'Did she ever mention a man named Max Vernon at all?'

Harriet Craig frowned slightly. 'Not that I recall. Who is
he?'

'Just someone who apparently knew her, but it's of no
consequence.' Miller hesitated and went on, 'Your sister was
a drug addict, Miss Craig. Were you aware of that fact?'

His answer was plain in the incredulous horror in her eyes
as she looked up at him sharply. Her head moved slightly

from side to side, her mouth opened as if to speak, but no sound was uttered.

Miller stood up as she buried her face in her hands and broke into a storm of weeping. He patted her gently on the shoulder and turned to Brady.

'Take her home, Jack. You can use my car.'

'What about you?'

'I think I'll have another little chat with Monica Grey and this time I'll have some straight answers. You can catch up with me there.'

He went out quickly, fastening the belt of his trenchcoat as he moved along the corridor, and the expression on his face was like the wrath of God.

5

The door of her room was unlocked and when he opened it gently and went in, she was sitting on the edge of the bed buffing her nails. She glanced up sharply and Miller closed the door.

'Sergeant Miller,' she said and then her voice faltered.

Miller produced one of the photos and held it up. 'Joanna Maria Craig.' He slipped the photo back into his pocket. 'Why did you lie to me?'

'I don't know what you mean.'

'Joanna Craig was a student at the College of Art for the best part of two years. So were you. And don't try to tell me you never came across her. You were in the same year group. I've just checked.'

She stared up at him, her face white, and he took his time over lighting a cigarette. 'Another thing. Mrs Kilroy told me that Joanna had just arrived on the doorstep one day complete with baggage; that there just happened to be a vacancy. Now that isn't true, is it? She knew there was a vacancy because you told her.'

She shook her head vigorously. 'It isn't true.'

'Isn't it? Then try this for size. You work for Max Vernon, don't you?'

And this time he had her. Her eyes widened in horror, and he went on relentlessly, 'Joanna was his girlfriend – I've got proof. Are you going to try to tell me you didn't know that as well?'

She tried to get to her feet and he flung her back across the bed fiercely. 'Come on, damn you! What about the truth for a change?'

She turned her face into the pillow and burst into a flood of tears, her whole body shaking. Miller stood looking down at her, something close to pity in his eyes, and then he moved across the room quickly and went into the small kitchen. He found half a bottle of gin in one of the cupboards, poured a generous measure into a tumbler and went back.

He sat on the edge of the bed and she turned her tear-stained face towards him. 'He'll kill me. I know he will.'

'No one's going to kill you.' Miller held out the glass. 'Drink this. You'll feel better.'

She struggled up against the pillows. 'You don't know what he can be like.'

'Max Vernon?'

She nodded and sipped some of her gin. 'He's a devil – a walking devil. Cruel, arrogant – anything he wants, he takes.'

'And that included Joanna Craig?'

Her eyes widened in amazement. 'How did you know that?'

'Just a hunch. But tell me about it – everything that happened.'

'All right.' She swung her legs to the floor, stood up and paced restlessly about the room as she talked. 'You were

right about the College of Art. I knew Joanna for nearly
two years. Not that we were close friends or anything like
that. I liked to live it up. Joanna was more interested in
her work.'

'What about boyfriends?'

'She hardly ever bothered. This may sound crazy to you,
but she had something about her. She was sort of untouched
by life if you know what I mean.'

'I think I do,' Miller said.

'Not that there was anything weird about her. Everybody
liked her. She was the sweetest person I've ever known,
but they treated her with respect, particularly the men.
That's something for art students, believe me.'

'And yet she changed,' Miller said. 'So utterly and
completely that she might have been a different person.
Why?'

'She met Max Vernon.'

'I wouldn't have thought he was her type.'

'He wasn't – that was the whole trouble.' She swallowed
the rest of her gin and sat on the edge of the bed. 'I answered
an advertisement for female croupiers at the Flamingo. As
I told you earlier, the money was so good that I dropped
out of the college course and started working there. Max
was always throwing big parties and he was pretty free and
easy about us bringing our friends along.'

'You took Joanna to one?'

'That's right. About four months ago. I bumped into her
one afternoon quite by chance. There was a party that
evening and I asked her to come on impulse. I never
expected her to say yes, but she did.'

'What happened?'

'Max took a fancy to her. I don't know what it was –
maybe it was just her innocence. She was certainly different
from every other girl there.'

'Did she respond?'

'Anything but and he tried everything, believe me. Then she passed out. I thought that maybe she'd had one gin too many or something. Max took charge. He said she could sleep it off there.'

'And you left her?'

'There was nothing I could do.' She got to her feet and crossed to the window. 'She 'phoned me here next day and asked me to meet her in town. Poor kid, she was in a hell of a state.'

'I'm not surprised.'

She swung round to face him. 'Oh, no, it was worse than that. Much worse. You see someone had given her a fix while she was unconscious.'

The bile rose in Miller's throat, threatening to choke him. He got to his feet and walked towards the door, fists clenched and when he turned, she recoiled from the terrible anger on his face.

'Max Vernon?'

'I don't know – I haven't any proof.'

Miller crossed the room in three quick strides and grabbed her savagely by the shoulders. 'Was it Max Vernon?'

'Well who the hell else could it have been?' she cried.

For a long moment he held her and when he turned away, she dropped down on to the bed. 'She didn't know what had happened to her. All she knew was that her body needed something.'

'And only one person was able to supply it,' Miller said bitterly. 'She wasn't only hooked on heroin and cocaine. She was hooked on Max Vernon.'

When Monica Grey continued, her voice was dry and lifeless. 'She had a lot of trouble at home and then they asked her to leave at the college. Her whole personality changed. That's how it affects them. I've seen it before.'

'So she came to live here with you?'

'Max thought it was a good idea. It's a funny thing, but

for a while there I thought he was really gone on her. He had her at the club all the time and if any other man even went near her . . .' She shuddered. 'He keeps a couple of heavies around called Carver and Stratton. One night at a party some bloke made a pass at Joanna and they took him out into the alley and half killed him. I heard he lost his right eye. That's the kind they are.'

'When did the rot set in?'

She looked up at him quickly. 'You don't miss much do you?'

'In my job I can't afford to.'

'I don't know what happened, but Max changed towards her just like that about two or three weeks ago.'

'She was pregnant, did you know that?'

She shook her head quickly. 'No – no I didn't. Maybe that would explain it.'

'Did he drop her completely?'

She nodded. 'Told her to stay away from the club. She did, too, until last night.'

'What happened then?'

'Max was throwing a private party – just a small affair. Mainly personal friends.'

'You were there?'

'I'm always there,' she said. 'All part of the job. Something else he didn't tell me at the interview. Anyway, it must have been about nine o'clock. Things had just started to swing when the door opened and Joanna walked in.'

'Just like that?'

'Apparently she still had a key to the private door in the alley. Max was furious. He dragged her into a corner and started telling her where to get off. I couldn't hear what she was saying, but you'd only to see her face to know that she was pleading with him.'

'What happened?'

'As I say, I couldn't hear what she said, but he laughed

right in her face and said, "There's always the river, isn't there?" I wasn't the only one who heard that.'

There was a long silence and then Miller said calmly, 'It would seem she took him at his word.' Monica Grey didn't reply and he got to his feet. 'Does he know she's dead?'

'Not as far as I'm aware.'

'You haven't been in touch with him since I was last here?'

She shook her head and he nodded, moved to the door and opened it. 'You do and I'll crucify you.'

As he went downstairs, Brady opened the front door. He paused, waiting for Miller to join him. 'Any luck?'

'You could say that. How about Harriet Craig?'

'She'll be fine once she gets over the initial shock. She's got a lot about her that one. Where to now?'

'The Flamingo Club,' Miller said, 'to have a few words with Mr Maxwell Vernon. I'll explain on the way.'

He went down the steps quickly and when he slipped behind the wheel of the Cooper, his hands were shaking.

Max Vernon's office was a showpiece in cream and gold and furnished in perfect taste, the walls lined with expensive military prints, a fire flickering brightly in the Adam grate. He made a handsome figure sitting there at his desk, the last rays of the afternoon sun lighting up the fair hair, picking out the colours of the green velvet smoking jacket, the Guards Brigade scarf at his throat.

There was a knock on the door, it opened and Stratton came in. 'I've got those figures you wanted.'

Vernon put down his pen and sat back. 'Good show, Billy. Just leave 'em on the desk. Anything else?'

'Yes, this copper you were asking about.'

'Miller?'

'That's right. You're on a bum steer there. He's anything but bent. It seems his brother owns a chain of television shops. Miller's a sleeping partner, that's where all his gelt comes from.'

'But that's illegal,' Vernon said. 'Coppers aren't encouraged to have business interests on the side.'

Stratton nodded. 'Apparently they all know about it on the force, but they simply look the other way. It seems Miller's a blue-eyed boy. He's been to University, got a law degree and that sort of thing.'

'Has he now?' Vernon said. 'Now that *is* interesting.'

There was a sudden disturbance in the corridor outside and then the door was thrown open and Miller walked in. Behind him, Jack Brady and Carver glowered at each other, chest to chest. Stratton took one quick, fluid step forward like a ballet dancer, his right hand sliding into his pocket, and Miller raised a finger warningly.

'You do and I'll break your arm.'

Vernon sat there, apparently unmoved, a slight smile hooked firmly into place. 'Do come in,' he said ironically.

'I intend to,' Miller told him. 'Get rid of these two. We've got business.'

'Now look here, you bastard,' Carver began and Vernon's voice rang across the room like cold steel.

'I'll call if I need you.'

Carver and Stratton obeyed without another murmur and as the door closed behind them, Vernon grinned. 'Good discipline – that's what I like to see.'

'Once a Guardsman, always a Guardsman, is that it?' Miller said.

'The most exclusive private club in the world.' Vernon fitted a cigarette into a green jade holder and gave a mock sigh. 'You've been checking up on me, Sergeant.'

'And how,' Miller said. 'The Yard was more than interested to hear you'd turned up again.'

'Let's get one thing clear,' Vernon said. 'I run a perfectly legitimate business here and that applies to everything else

I own. If you've anything else to say, I suggest you discuss it with my lawyers.'

He reached for the telephone and Miller said calmly, 'We pulled Joanna Craig out of the river this morning, Vernon.'

For a brief moment only Vernon's hand tightened on the 'phone and then an expression of shock appeared on his face.

'Joanna – in the river? But this doesn't make sense. You're quite sure it is her?'

'Why shouldn't we be?'

'The fact is, I understood she'd been living under an assumed name. Nothing sinister – just to stop her family from running her down. She'd had trouble at home.' He shook his head. 'This is terrible – terrible.'

It was all there, beautifully detailed by a steeltrap mind which had assessed the situation in a matter of seconds and had come up with the only possible counter with the speed of a computer.

'When did you first meet her?'

The answer came without the slightest hesitation.

'About four months ago. Someone brought her along to one of my parties. I discovered she was a very talented artist. I wanted some murals for the club and she agreed to accept the commission. It was as simple as that.'

'And that was all – just a business arrangement?'

'The murals are on the wall of the main casino, you can see them for yourself,' Vernon said. 'Anything else that was between us is no damned business of yours. She wasn't a child. She had a good body and she liked the pleasures of the flesh as much as the rest of us.'

'So you did have an affair with her?'

'If you mean by that did she ever sleep with me, the answer is yes. If you're really interested, so do lots of other women, though I can't see what in the hell it has to do with you.'

'Did you know she was a junkie – that she was main-lining on heroin?'

'Good heavens, no.'

'Not good enough. You didn't even bother to look surprised.' Miller shook his head. 'You're a liar.'

Something glowed deep in Vernon's eyes. 'Am I?'

Miller gripped the edge of the desk to keep his hands from shaking. 'I know this girl, Vernon. The first time I clapped eyes on her, she was floating off the central quay two feet under the surface and yet I know more about her now than I do about my own sister. She was a sweet, shy girl, a little bit introverted, interested only in her work. To use an old-fashioned word for these times, she was a lady – a term that wouldn't mean a damned thing to you in spite of Eton, Sandhurst and the Guards.'

'Is that a fact now,' Vernon said softly.

'You're from under a stone, Vernon, did you know that?' Miller said. 'Now let me tell you what really happened between you and Joanna Craig. She was brought to one of your parties by an old student friend and she must have looked as fresh as the flowers in spring compared to the usual rubbish you keep around. You wanted her, but she didn't want you and that wasn't good enough for the great Maxwell Vernon because what he wants he takes. You got her boozed up and gave her a fix and from then on she was hooked because she had to have one every day of the week and that meant coming to you – accepting your terms. That's the terrible thing about addiction to heroin. There's no degradation to which the victim won't stoop to get the stuff and you must have been just about as low as she could get.'

Vernon's face was white, the eyes burning. 'Have you quite finished?'

'I'll let you know when I have. When you'd had enough, you threw her out and then last night she forced her way

into your party to beg you to help her because she was
going to have a baby. You laughed in her face, Vernon. You
told her there was always the river and she took you at
your word.' Miller straightened up and took a deep breath.
'I'm going to get you for that.'

'Are you now?' Vernon said calmly. 'Well let me tell you
something, Mr Bloody Miller. I knew a girl called Joanna
Craig just like I know a hell of a lot of other girls. She
painted some murals in the main casino downstairs. You
or anyone else can see them whenever you like. Anything
else is pure fantasy. You try bringing it out in an open court
and I'll knock you down so hard you'll never get up again.
Now I'm giving you one minute to get out of here or I'm
calling my lawyer and you know what that means.'

'Perfectly,' Miller said. 'It means you're frightened to
death.' He smiled coldly. 'See you in court, Vernon.'

He turned and nodded to Brady who opened the door
and they went out. For a while Vernon sat there staring
into space and then he lifted the 'phone and pushed a
button.

'Is that you, Ben?' he said. 'Send Stratton up right away.
I've got a little job for him.'

Monica Grey came out of the bathroom listlessly. She'd
hoped a good hot tub would make her feel better. Instead,
she felt depressed, drained of all energy. How she was going
to get through the long night at the Flamingo, she didn't
know.

The knock, when it came, was so faint that at first she
thought she'd imagined it. She hesitated, fastening the belt
of her robe quickly, and it sounded again.

When she opened the door, she had a vague impression
of someone standing there, of an arm sweeping up and
then liquid splashed across her face. She staggered back, a
scream rising in her throat, her hands covering her eyes as

they began to burn. She was aware of the door closing and then a hand slammed against her shoulder, spinning her round so that she fell across the bed.

Someone laughed coldly and fingers fastened in her hair, jerking her head back painfully. 'Come on now, dearie, open up for Uncle Billy.'

She opened her eyes, aware that the smarting had somehow eased, and looked into Billy Stratton's white, bloodless face. Only his lips had any colour and he smiled showing a row of sharp, even teeth.

'Water, dearie, mixed with a little disinfectant to make your eyes sting. Just imagine what it could have been – vitriol, for instance.' He chuckled mirthlessly. 'You'd have been blind now.'

She was absolutely terrified and lay there staring up at him in horror as he patted her on the cheek. 'You've been a naughty girl, haven't you? You've been talking to the wrong people. Mr Vernon doesn't like that – he doesn't like that at all. Now get your clothes on. You're coming with me.'

It was almost dusk when Miller turned the Cooper in through the gates of the house in Grange Avenue and braked to a halt at the bottom of the steps leading up to the front door. It had been a long day and he was so tired that he sat at the wheel for a moment before getting out.

When he rang the bell, the door was opened by Jenny, the young maid, and her eyes were red and swollen from weeping. 'Sergeant Miller,' she said. 'You'd better come in.'

'There was a message for me at Headquarters,' Miller said. 'Apparently Colonel Craig called at the mortuary to view his daughter's body. I understand he'd like to see me.'

'The Colonel and Miss Harriet are out walking in the garden,' Jenny said. 'I'll get him for you.'

'That's all right,' Miller told her. 'I'll find him for myself.'

It was cold in the garden and rooks cawed uneasily in the bare branches of the beech trees as he crossed the lawn already damp with the evening dew. Somewhere there was a low murmur of voices above the rattle of a small stream over stones and then a familiar voice called to him on the quiet air. 'Over here, Sergeant Miller.'

Harriet Craig leaned against the rail of a tiny rustic bridge. The man who stood with her was perhaps a shade under six feet in height with iron grey hair cut close to his skull.

The eyes were very calm above high cheekbones. For a moment they considered Miller and then he held out his hand. 'It was good of you to come so quickly.'

There was an extraordinary impression of vitality about him, of controlled force that Miller found strangely disturbing. He must have been at least forty-eight or -nine and yet he carried himself with the easy confidence of a man half his age.

'Your message said that you'd like to talk things over with me,' Miller said. 'I'll be happy to help in any way I can.'

'I've seen your Superintendent Grant,' Colonel Craig said. 'He gave me as comprehensive a report as he could, but felt that the full details would be better coming from you.' He hesitated and then went on, 'I believe Harriet gave you some indication of the trouble we were having with Joanna.'

'That's right.'

'I've been given to understand that she'd become addicted to the drug heroin.'

'Which explains what otherwise would have been her completely inexplicable change in character,' Miller told him. 'You must understand that heroin produces a feeling of well-being and buoyancy, but in between fixes an addict is sick, unwell and has only one thought in mind – to get another fix. They become paranoid, irritable, subject to extremes of emotion.'

'And that's what happened to Joanna?'

'The girl who gave you all that trouble wasn't your daughter, Colonel,' Miller said gently. 'She only looked like her.'

For a long, long moment there was silence and then Colonel Craig said, 'Thank you for that, Sergeant. And now, if you don't mind, I'd like you to tell me everything – everything there is to know about this whole sorry affair.'

It didn't take long, that was the strange thing, and when he had finished, Harriet Craig leaned against the rail crying quietly, her father's arm about her shoulders.

'This man Vernon,' Craig said. 'He'll be called as a witness at the inquest?'

'That's right.'

'Is there any possibility of a criminal charge being preferred against him?'

Miller sighed heavily and shook his head. 'I might as well be honest with you. I don't hold out much hope.'

'But he murdered Joanna,' Harriet Craig cried passionately. 'Murdered her as surely as if he'd used a gun or a knife.'

'I know that,' Miller said. 'Morally he's as guilty as any man could be, but the facts are all that matters and this is how it will look in court. Your sister committed suicide. She was pregnant and she was also a drug addict. One witness, Monica Grey, has indicated that someone gave your daughter an injection of heroin at a party at Max Vernon's after she'd passed out, but even she can't swear definitely that it was Vernon. She wouldn't last five minutes on the stand with the kind of counsel he'd bring in. Another thing, this isn't a criminal matter at the moment. All she's done is give me a general verbal statement that she might change completely once she's on the stand.'

'But Vernon was responsible,' Harriet said. 'He was responsible for everything. You believe that yourself.'

'Proving it is something else again.'

There was another long silence and then Craig said, 'There's just one thing I don't understand. Joanna did everything she could to conceal her identity before she killed herself. Why would she do that?'

'Do you really want me to answer that, colenel?'

'More than anything else in the world.'

'All right. I'd say she did it for you.'

The expression on Craig's face didn't alter. 'Please go on.'

'In those final moments, I think she must have been thinking more clearly than she had for a long time. She'd let you down enough. She didn't want to shame you any more. I think she wanted the river to swallow her up as if she'd never been.'

When Craig replied, only the slightest of tremor disturbed the even tenor of his voice. 'Thank you, Sergeant. Somehow I thought it might be something like that.'

6

When Brady opened the door of the Coroner's Court and peered inside, proceedings had already started. In spite of the fact that there were no more than half a dozen members of the public present, the court seemed overcrowded with the jury taking up almost one side of the room and the coroner high above them on the bench, the court officers below.

Miller was just leaving the stand. He noticed Brady at once and they went outside quietly and closed the door.

'Sorry I'm late,' Brady said. 'I had a remand. How's it going?'

'I've just done my little act. Craig's down front with Harriet. Vernon's got Henry Baxter with him.'

'That old shark?' Brady whistled. 'He'll charge him plenty.'

'Any word from Grant?'

Brady nodded. 'Not good I'm afraid. He's just heard from the office of the Director of Public Prosecutions. They've considered the matter and as far as they're concerned, there isn't even the beginnings of a case against Vernon.'

'Never mind. It was worth a try and there's still the hearing. You can never be sure what's going to happen at a coroner's inquest.'

They went back inside and sat down in time to hear Monica Grey take the oath.

'You are Monica Alice Grey and you reside at 15, Argyle Road?'

'That's right.'

'When did you first meet the deceased?'

'About two years ago. We were both students at the College of Art.'

'We have heard from Detective Sergeant Miller that she came to reside at the same address as yourself under the name of Joanna Martin. Why was that?'

'She was having trouble at home. She decided to leave, but she didn't want her father to know where she was living.'

Miller leaned forward slightly, intent on the proceedings. In his own case he had been compelled to stick strictly to the facts and what Monica Grey said from now on was going to be of crucial importance.

'You were on close terms with the deceased?'

'We were good friends – yes.'

'She confided in you – discussed her troubles. For example, were you aware that she was a drug addict?'

'I was, but only found out by accident. I happened to go into her room one day and found her giving herself a fix.'

The coroner glanced over the top of his spectacles sharply. 'I beg your pardon?'

'An injection of heroin.'

'And did she tell you what had started her on the habit?'

'Yes, she said she'd passed out after having too much to drink at some party or other. Someone had given her an injection while she was unconscious.'

'Why would anyone do that?'

'I don't know. For a giggle, maybe.'

'Indeed.' The coroner examined the papers in front of him, his face impassive. 'Did she ever suggest to you that the party in question was at a gaming club called the Flamingo owned by Mr Maxwell Vernon?'

'Definitely not.'

The coroner looked at her steadily for a moment and then nodded. 'You were aware that she was pregnant?'

'Yes, she told me a couple of weeks ago.'

'In what circumstances?'

'She was very upset. She asked me if I knew anyone who could help her.'

'To get rid of the child?'

'That's right.'

The coroner made another note. 'One final question. As regards the state of mind of the deceased. Would you say she was a balanced individual?'

Monica Grey shook her head. 'Not during the time she lived with me. She sometimes had terrible bouts of depression, but I think that was the drugs.'

'Thank you, that will be all.'

The fat, well-dressed man who was sitting at the front beside Vernon half rose and the coroner stayed Monica Grey with his hand. 'Yes, Mr Baxter.'

'I appear on behalf of Mr Maxwell Vernon, called as a witness in this matter. Certain rumours seem to be circulating which connect my client and the deceased. I think we might be able to clarify the situation if I could put a question or two to Miss Grey.'

'By all means.'

'I shan't keep you long, Miss Grey,' Baxter said. 'I'd like to return to this question of the deceased's pregnancy. Did she ever tell you who the father was?'

'I asked her, but she wouldn't disclose his name.'

'It has been alleged in certain quarters that my client was responsible.'

'He couldn't have been.'

'You seem very positive. Might I ask why?'

Monica Grey hesitated, glanced across at Vernon and said with obvious reluctance, 'To tell you the truth, I knew Joanna had been out with Mr Vernon a few times and I thought it might be him. When I put it to her she said definitely not. That it was someone else entirely.'

'A last question, Miss Grey. I understand you were present at a private party given by Mr Vernon at his flat at the Flamingo Club on the night the deceased died.'

'That's right.'

'Please tell us what happened.'

'It was about nine o'clock. The party had just got started when Joanna walked in. She was in a bit of a state so Mr Vernon took her into the corner to calm her down.'

'Could you hear their conversation?'

'Not really. She was obviously very upset and Mr Vernon seemed to be trying to take her out of herself. After a while she just turned and walked out.'

'What did Mr Vernon do?'

'He took me on one side and said he hadn't liked the way she was talking. He asked me to keep an eye on her, to let him know if there was anything he could do.'

'Thank you, Miss Grey.'

Monica Grey returned to her seat as Baxter sat down and Vernon was called. He made an impressive figure in the dock, erect and manly in a well-cut suit, the Guards tie standing out against a snow white shirt. His occupation was given as company director, which made the impression on the jury that Miller had expected.

'Mr Vernon, how long had you known the deceased?'

'About four months,' Vernon said. 'Miss Monica Grey, an employee of mine, brought her to a party at my place one night. I understood they'd been students together.'

'And you became close friends?'

'I think it would be fair to say that.' Vernon shrugged. 'As an artist, she had real talent and I admired her work. I commissioned her to paint a series of murals at my club.'

'I see.' The coroner's voice was dry, remote. 'Was the relationship ever anything more than a business one?'

'I took her to dinner now and then or to the theatre. We got on very well together. I liked her immensely.'

'And on occasion you were intimate with her?'

Vernon managed to inject just the right amount of outrage into his voice when he replied. 'The girl's dead, damn you! Can't she be left in peace!'

There was a flurry of movement amongst the jury, an outburst of whispering. One man even nodded approvingly and the coroner had to call for silence.

He removed his spectacles and leaned back in his chair.

'Mr Vernon, I can respect your feelings in this matter, but I must insist on a reply – and you are still under oath, sir.'

Vernon's shoulders sagged. 'Yes, we were intimate.' He drew himself up suddenly and glared fiercely at the coroner. 'And why not? She wasn't a child. It was our own affair.'

The coroner replaced his spectacles and examined the papers before him again. 'Were you aware that she had become a drug addict?'

'Certainly not. Do you think I could have stood by and done nothing if I'd known?'

'We've already heard that on the night she died, she appeared at a private party you were giving at your club.'

'That's right.'

'What happened on that occasion?'

'There really isn't much to tell. She was depressed and unhappy. She told me that she'd lost the urge to paint, that life didn't seem worth living any longer. I realize, in retrospect, that it was the drugs which had reduced her to that state. I advised her to go home. She'd told me previously that she and her father hadn't been seeing eye to eye, but it seemed to me that didn't matter any longer. That home was the best place for her.'

'How did she react to that advice?'

'She didn't, I'm afraid. I went to get her a drink. When I returned, she'd gone.'

'Thank you, Mr Vernon. You may stand down.'

As Vernon went back to his seat, Baxter rose again. 'If I might insert a word at this time on my client's behalf?'

The coroner nodded and Baxter continued, 'Certain allegations do seem to have been made in connection with this unfortunate young woman's death, allegations which would suggest that my client was in some way responsible. I would suggest his complete honesty in answering the question put to him, and his bearing on the stand, added to the statement of Miss Monica Grey, an independent witness, make nonsense of these allegations, which are completely without foundation. My client is Managing Director of a company which controls several important enterprises. I might also add, although he has attempted to dissuade me from so doing, that he was at one time a regular officer in the Brigade of Guards and in 1951 was awarded the Distinguished Service Order for gallantry and outstanding leadership during the Malayan Emergency.'

Vernon looked suitably embarrassed as Baxter sat down. 'Thank you, Mr Baxter,' the coroner said. 'Call Colonel Craig, please.'

All eyes turned on Craig as he got to his feet and moved to the stand. He stood there, hands resting lightly on the rail, the eternal soldier in spite of his dark suit and tie.

'You are Colonel Duncan Stuart Craig and you reside at Rosedene, Grange Avenue, St Martin's Wood?'

'That is correct.'

'Did you see the body of a woman at the City Mortuary on Tuesday of this week?'

'I did.'

'Who was she?'

'My daughter – Joanna Maria Craig.'

'I will issue you with a burial order.' There was a pause as the coroner made a note and he continued, 'I know this must be most distressing for you, Colonel Craig, so I shan't keep you long. Until four months ago or thereabouts, your daughter was a perfectly normal young woman for her age in every way?'

'That is so. The change, when it came, was inexplicable to us. Temper tantrums, extremely emotional behaviour, that sort of thing. She became a completely different person. I realize now that her general deterioration was a direct consequence of her addiction to heroin.'

'From the time your daughter left home until her death did she ever communicate with you?'

'There were three letters, all postmarked Chelsea. They are before the court.'

The coroner nodded. 'I have read them. They would seem to imply that she was residing in London and studying at a College of Art there. Presumably some acquaintance posted them for her.' He hesitated and then went on, 'Colonel Craig, you have heard the evidence before the court. Have you anything to add?'

Miller felt Brady stir beside him and held his breath, waiting for Craig's answer. 'I have nothing to add, sir. The evidence in this matter seems clear enough.'

'And you can make of that what you like,' Brady whispered to Miller.

And then, with a rush, it was all over. The jury didn't even bother to retire and the foreman, a small, greying bank clerk, rose self-consciously. 'We find that the deceased took her own life while the balance of her mind was disturbed.'

'And that is the verdict of you all.' The foreman nodded and sat down. 'Let it so be entered.'

There was a sudden hush as people sat up expectantly, waiting for the coroner's closing words. 'It is not within my province to make moral judgements. It is sufficient for me to say that on the evidence presented I must agree completely with the verdict of the jury. There is one disturbing feature of this case and it is this. Joanna Craig was not a registered drug addict and yet somehow or other she managed to obtain a daily supply. I trust that the representatives of the police present in court will see that this aspect of the affair is most thoroughly investigated.'

'The court will rise for Her Majesty's Coroner.'

There was a general move towards the exit and Brady turned towards Miller, his face grim. 'And that's that. The swine's got away with it.'

'What else did you expect?' Miller said.

Colonel Craig and Harriet were still sitting down at the front and Vernon and Baxter had to pass them. For a moment, Vernon hesitated as if about to speak and then obviously thought better of it. He nodded to Miller and Brady as he passed them, face grave, and went out.

'I wonder what Craig would have done if the bastard had tried to speak to him?' Brady said.

Craig came towards them, Harriet hanging on to his arm. He smiled tightly. 'Have you gentlemen time for a drink?'

Brady shook his head reluctantly. 'Not me, I'm afraid. I'm in court again in ten minutes.' He nodded to Miller. 'I'll catch up with you later.'

For the moment, they had the court to themselves and Harriet Craig said bitterly, 'Justice – is that what they call it?'

'I'm sorry,' Miller said. 'More sorry than I can say. We tried the Director of Public Prosecutions but he told us we hadn't got even the shadow of a case. I was hoping something might come out at the hearing. As you probably noticed, things are pretty informal in a coroner's court. No one gets worked up over procedure and so on which usually means that things have a chance to break through to the surface.'

'But not in this case, it would appear.'

Craig put an arm around her shoulders and gave her a quick squeeze. 'Let's have that drink, shall we? Do us all good.'

They sat in the saloon bar of the George across the square and Craig ordered brandy all round and offered Miller a cigarette while they waited. Behind them, the bar was lined with solicitors and their clerks and counsels in wig and gown, most of them snatching a beer and a sandwhich between cases and talking shop.

Harriet leaned across and covered one of Miller's hands with her own. 'I'm sorry I sounded off back there in court. I wasn't getting at you. You believe that, don't you?'

'That's all right.'

'You know Vernon's a very clever man,' Craig said. 'He handled himself superbly. Made an excellent impression on the jury.'

'And the girl helped, don't forget that,' Miller said.

'Yes, she lied, didn't she?'

'Too true she did, probably under extreme coercion.' Miller hesitated and then went on. 'It wasn't her fault, you know. She's just as much a victim of circumstances as Joanna was. Actually, she's quite a nice girl.'

Craig swirled the brandy around in his glass and drank some. 'You know I've been finding out a few things about our Mr Vernon. He's quite a character.'

'Is that so?' Miller said carefully.

'Come off it, Sergeant, you know what I mean.' Craig swallowed the rest of his brandy and waved to the waiter for another. 'You've heard of Pedlar Palmer, I suppose?'

'Detective Superintendent Palmer of the Special Branch at Scotland Yard?'

'That's right. We did some soldiering together in the Middle East back in '43. I gave him a ring yesterday, just to ask him what he could tell me about Vernon. He owes me a favour or two. That's in confidence, mind you.'

'Naturally.'

'Quite a boy, Max Vernon. Do you think he's getting up to the same sort of capers in these parts as he did in London?'

'Leopards don't change their spots.'

'That's what I thought.' Craig nodded, a slight, abstracted smile on his face. 'What is it they say about justice, Sergeant? It must not only be done, it must be seen to be done? But what happens when society falls down on the job? What happens when the law isn't adequate? Wouldn't you say the individual was entitled to take matters into his own hands?'

'I know one thing,' Miller said. 'It wouldn't be the law he was taking.'

'You've got a good point there.' Craig glanced at his watch. 'Good heavens, is that the time? I must go. Can you get a taxi, Harriet?'

Miller cut in quickly before she could reply. 'I'll see she gets home all right. I have my own car.'

'Thanks a lot. I'll see you later then, my dear.' He squeezed Harriet's shoulder briefly and was gone.

'Another drink, Miss Craig?'

'No, I don't think so. I'd like to go if you don't mind. I'm feeling rather tired. These past few days have been something of a strain.'

The Mini-Cooper was in for servicing and he was using his brother's E-type Jaguar that day. She was suitably impressed. 'I didn't know police pay had improved quite this much.'

'It hasn't,' he said as he handed her in and closed the door. 'This belongs to my brother. He has more money than he knows what to do with and he worries about me.'

He took the car out into the main traffic stream expertly. 'You're a teacher, aren't you?'

She nodded. 'That's right. Dock Street Secondary Modern. I took the day off.'

'A pretty rough neighbourhood.'

'Good experience. They're pulling the school down soon. There'll be a new Comprehensive opening about half a mile away.'

They drove in silence for a while and then he said, 'You don't think your father will try to do anything silly, do you?'

She frowned. 'What on earth do you mean?'

'I wasn't too happy about that conversation we had back at the pub. All that stuff about taking the law into one's own hands when society falls down on the job.'

'It's worth a thought, isn't it?'

Miller shook his head. 'Not if he wants to stay alive. Max Vernon's a powerful, ruthless criminal without the slightest scruples about who he hurts or how he does it. He'd crush your father like an ant under his foot.'

She turned on him, her mouth slack with amazement. 'Crush Duncan Craig – that worm?' She laughed wildly. 'Don't you know who my father is? If he's made the decision I think he has, then Maxwell Vernon is a dead man walking.'

7

When Monica Grey opened her door and found Duncan Craig standing there, she tried to close it quickly, but he was inside before she could stop him.

She backed away, her throat going dry, and he shook his head slowly. 'I'm not going to hurt you, I'm not going to harm you in any way. Just sit down like a good girl and listen to me.'

Suddenly she was no longer afraid. In fact for some strange reason she felt like crying and she did as she was told and slumped down on the bed.

'You lied at the inquest, didn't you?'

'I had to. God knows what would have happened to me if I hadn't done as I was told.'

'Then your original statement to Sergeant Miller was true? It was Max Vernon who first gave my daughter heroin?'

'It had to be him,' she said. 'It couldn't have been anyone else.'

'And Vernon who continued to supply her.'

She nodded. 'One of his little sidelines.'

'You know a great deal about him, don't you?'

'Plenty,' she said, 'but you needn't think I'm going to sing out in open court for you or anyone else.'

'You won't have to. Have you got a passport?'

She nodded. 'Somewhere around the place. Why?'

He took a large buff envelope from his inside breast pocket. 'You'll find traveller's cheques in here for one thousand pounds plus a ticket on the four-thirty flight to London Airport.'

'And just how long do you think it would take Max Vernon to catch up with me?'

'At least a couple of days. Long enough for you to complete any formalities, have any necessary inoculations and so on. You'll find another plane ticket in the envelope – a first-class single to Sydney. You could be on your way by Wednesday.'

'You mean Sydney, Australia?'

'That's right. You'll also find a letter to a business friend of mine out there. He'll fix you up with a job and help you get started. You'll be all right. He owes me a favour.'

Her eyes were shining and the lines had been wiped clean from her forehead. Colonel Craig laid the envelope down on the bed beside her.

'In return I want you to tell me everything there is to know about Max Vernon.'

She didn't hesitate. 'It's a deal. You talk and I'll pack.'

'They tell me he was the brains behind one or two big jobs in the London area. The Knavesmire Airport bullion robbery for instance. Has he pulled anything like that up here?'

'Not as far as I know, but I think there's something in the wind. There's been some funny customers in and out of the place lately.'

'What about the Flamingo? Is the game honest?'

'It has to be.' She pulled a suitcase down from the top of the wardrobe. 'It caters for the most exclusive clientele in town.'

'You wouldn't have a key to the place by any chance?'

'Sure – to the back door.' She opened her hand-bag, produced a Yale key and threw it across. 'My pleasure.'

'What other little enterprises does Vernon operate?'

'There's the betting shops.'

'I'm looking for something rather more illegal.'

'That's easy. He runs a cut liquor still up the York Road. Gibson's Furniture Factory it says outside, but it's a front. Supplies clubs all over the north.'

'Where does the liquor come from in the first place?'

'Your guess is as good as mine. Some from long distance lorries that took the wrong turning. Some they make on the premises. He's got money tied up in that place.'

'But more still in the Flamingo?'

She fastened the lid on one suitcase and took down another. 'Better than a hundred thousand. Without the

Flamingo he's nothing. He had to take what he could get when he sold up in London. They say he dropped a bundle.'

'And what about the betting shops?'

'He operates them on a day-to-day basis using the cash from the previous night's take at the Flamingo. He still hasn't got on his feet up here yet.'

'So everything revolves around the Flamingo.'

'I suppose you could say that.' She frowned suddenly. 'What are you getting at?'

'Never you mind, you've got other things to think about now.' He glanced at his watch. 'We'll have to get moving. We've got exactly half an hour to get you to the airport.'

The Bull & Bell Yard was not far from the market, a dirty and sunless cobbled alley named after the public house which had stood there for more than two hundred years. Beside the entrance to the snug stood several overflowing dustbins and cardboard boxes and packing cases were thrown together in an untidy heap.

It was raining slightly and an old man squatted against the wall, a bottle of beer in one hand, a sandwich in the other. He wore an ancient army greatcoat and his hair and beard were long and matted.

The door opened and a barman appeared in the entrance, a bucket in one hand. He was a large, hefty young man in a white apron with long dark sideburns and a cold, rather dangerous face. He emptied the bucket of slops across the cobbles and looked down at the old man in disgust.

'You still here, Sailor? Christ Jesus, I don't know how you can stand it.'

'Go on, Harry,' the old man said hoarsely. 'Ain't doing any 'arm, am I?'

The barman went back inside and Sailor raised the bottle of beer to his lips. He lowered it slowly, his mouth gaping in amazement. The man who stood facing him had the

most extraordinary eyes the Sailor had ever seen, quite dark
and completely expressionless. He wore a three-quarter
length British warm, a bowler hat and carried a tightly
rolled umbrella.

His hand disappeared into a pocket and came out holding
a pound note. 'Do you know Mr Vernon?' he said. 'Mr Max
Vernon?' Sailor nodded. 'Is he inside?'

'In the snug, governor.'

The man in the bowler hat dropped the pound note into
his lap. 'I'm very much obliged to you,' he said and went
inside.

Sailor waited for no more than a moment and then he
scrambled to his feet, pushed open the door an inch or two
and peered in.

The Bull & Bell did ninety-five per cent of its trade in the
evenings, which was why Max Vernon preferred to patronize
it in the afternoon. For one thing it meant that he could
have the snug to himself, which was handy for business of
a certain kind.

He sat on a stool at the bar finishing a roast beef sandwich, a pint of bitter at his elbow, and Carver and Stratton
lounged on the window seat chatting idly.

It was Carver who first noticed Craig standing in the
doorway. 'Christ Almighty,' he said and then there was a
long silence.

Craig moved into the snug and paused against the bar
three or four feet away from Vernon. 'There you are, Vernon.
You know you're a damned difficult fellow to run down.
I've been looking everywhere for you.'

'I'm in the telephone book, Colonel,' Vernon said calmly.

'Ah, but that wouldn't have suited my purpose at all,
I'm afraid,' Craig said. 'What I was hoping for was a private
chat – just the two of us.'

He glanced at Carver and Stratton and Vernon shrugged.

'There's nothing you can say to me that these two can't hear.'

'Suit yourself.' Craig took a cigarette from a pigskin case and lit it carefully. 'I expect you'll be wondering why Monica Grey didn't turn up for work last night. She gave me a message for you.'

'Did she now?'

'I'm afraid you'll have to manage without her in future.' Craig blew smoke up towards the ceiling in a long streamer. 'Actually I had a very informative chat with her after which I put her on a plane with a first-class ticket to somewhere so far away that she can forget she ever knew a man called Max Vernon.'

'What is this?' Vernon said. 'A declaration of war?'

'To the knife,' Craig said pleasantly. 'First of all I'm going to destroy the things that are important to you, Vernon. After that, and only when I'm ready, I'm going to destroy you.'

Stratton took a sudden step forward and Vernon raised his hand quickly. 'Stay where you are!' He looked Craig up and down and shook his head slowly. 'It's been tried, Colonel. It's been tried by the best in the business and they all ended up flat on their faces.'

'But you did have to get out of London in rather a hurry.'

'So what – I'll be up there on top again. I'm on my way now. I'll run this town before I'm finished.'

'The great Max Vernon,' Craig said. 'He always gets what he wants.'

'That's it.'

'Including my daughter.'

'Including your daughter. She saw things my way by the time I was through with her.'

For the first time, Craig's iron composure cracked and his hand tightened around the handle of his umbrella. He half raised it as if to strike, but quickly regained control.

'Thank you for saying that, Vernon. You've made it a lot easier for me.'

Vernon's easy smile vanished in an instant. 'You know something, you remind me of my old colonel. I couldn't stand him either. Harry!' he called. 'Get in here!'

Harry came in from the other bar drying a pewter tankard. 'Yes, Mr Vernon?'

Vernon nodded towards Craig and picked up his newspaper. 'Get rid of him.'

'Certainly, Mr Vernon.' Harry lifted the bar flap and moved out. 'Right, on your way, mate.'

'I'll go when I'm ready,' Craig said pleasantly.

Harry's right hand fastened on Craig's collar and they went through the door with a rush to a chorus of laughter from Stratton and Carver. As the door to the alley burst open, Sailor ducked behind a packing case and waited.

Harry was grinning widely, an arm around Craig's throat. 'We don't like fancy sods like you coming around here annoying the customers.' He didn't get the chance to say anything else. Craig's right elbow swung back sharply connecting just beneath the ribs and, as Harry swung back gasping, he pivoted on one foot.

'You should never let anyone get that close. They haven't been teaching you properly.'

Harry gave a cry of rage and sprang forward, his right fist swinging in a tremendous punch. Craig grabbed for the wrist with both hands and twisted it round and up so that he held him in a Japanese shoulder lock. Harry cried out in agony and still keeping that terrible hold in position, Craig ran him head-first into the stack of packing cases. As he bent down to retrieve his umbrella, Vernon appeared in the doorway, Carver and Stratton crowding behind him. Craig nodded briefly. 'I'll be in touch, Vernon,' he said and walked briskly away.

*

It was perhaps ten minutes later that the 'phone rang on Nick Miller's desk in the main C.I.D. room. He picked up the receiver at once and a familiar voice roughened by years of drink and disease sounded in his ear.

'That you, Sergeant Miller? This is Sailor – Sailor Hagen. I'm ringing from a call box in City Square. I've got something good for you. What's it worth?'

'Depends what it's about,' Miller said.

'The bloke who took over Harry Faulkner's place, the Flamingo. Max Vernon.'

Miller was already on his feet. 'I'll meet you by the fountain in five minutes,' he said and hung up.

When Miller was shown in, Vernon was in the main casino looking over arrangements for the evening opening. 'You're getting to be a permanent fixture around here,' he said.

'You can cut out the funny stuff,' Miller told him. 'What happened at the Bull & Bell?'

'I haven't the slightest idea what you're talking about.'

'Duncan Craig visited you there no more than an hour ago. As I understand it, he threatened to kill you.'

Vernon leaned against the edge of the roulette table and laughed gently. 'Someone's been pulling your leg, old man.'

'This is serious, Vernon,' Miller said. 'I don't give a damn what happens to you, but I do care what happens to Duncan Craig.'

Vernon shrugged. 'As far as I'm concerned the whole thing's over and done with.' He glanced at his watch. 'They're burying his daughter at St Gemma's Church at four o'clock. I sent a wreath. Could I do more than that?'

'You did what?' Miller said incredulously.

Vernon smiled blandly. 'One does have to do the right thing on these occasions.'

When Miller's hands came out of their pockets, they were both tightly clenched. For a long, long moment he stood

there fighting the impulse to knock Vernon's teeth down
his throat and then he swung on his heel and walked rapidly
towards the exit. Behind him, Vernon started to laugh gently.

It was raining quite hard when Miller drove up to St
Gemma's. He parked the Cooper in the main road and went
in through the side gate and along a narrow path lined
with poplars leading to the cemetery.

He could hear Father Ryan's voice as he went forward
and then he saw them. There were no more than half a
dozen people grouped around the open grave and the old
priest's voice sounded brave and strong as the rain fell on
his bare head.

Miller moved off the path and stood behind a large marble
tomb and after a while, Father Ryan finished and the group
broke up. Harriet Craig was crying steadily and moved away
in company with Jenny, the young maid, and Father Ryan
followed them. Craig was left standing on his own beside
the grave and Miller went forward slowly.

'It wouldn't work,' he said softly. 'It wouldn't bring
Joanna back.'

Craig turned to face him. 'What are you, a mind reader
or something?'

'I know what happened at the Bull & Bell this afternoon.'

'I haven't the slightest idea what you're talking about.'

'That's what Vernon said when I called on him. But
someone dislocated Harry Parson's shoulder and broke his
nose. Who the hell was that? Mr Nobody?'

Craig looked down into the open grave. 'She was a nice
kid, Sergeant. A lot of dreams gone up in smoke there.'

'I'm sorry about the wreath,' Miller said.

Craig turned, frowning. 'What wreath?'

'The wreath Vernon sent. God knows where he gets his
gall from.'

'I'm happy to say you've been misinformed,' Duncan
Craig said. 'We've certainly received no wreath from Max

Vernon.' As the rain increased into a solid downpour he turned up his collar. 'You must excuse me now, but Harriet's taken this afternoon rather hard. I'd like to get her home as soon as possible.'

'Of course. If there's anything I can do . . .'

'I don't think so.' Craig smiled briefly, shook hands and walked briskly away.

Miller watched him until he had disappeared round the side of the church and then he turned and went back to his car.

It was just after ten on the following morning and Max Vernon was having a late breakfast at a small table in front of the fire when there was a knock on the door and Carver came in.

'Now what?' Vernon demanded irritably.

Carver held up a large and very beautiful wreath of white lilies without a word.

'What is it, for God's sake?'

'It's the wreath you told me to get for the Craig girl's funeral. The one I had delivered yesterday. The porter's just found it pinned to the private door in the alley.'

'Has he now?' Vernon said softly.

'But that's not all, Max,' Carver said. 'This came with it.'

Vernon took the small pasteboard card that Carver offered and held it up to the light. It was edged in black and the inscription was simple and to the point. *In memory of Maxwell Vernon. 1929–1967. R.I.P.*

8

Miller came awake slowly and stared up at the ceiling through the early morning gloom. He checked his watch.

It was just coming up to six and then he remembered that he was on a rest day. He gave a sigh of pleasure and turned over.

The outside door opened suddenly and as he struggled up on one elbow, there was laughter and the pounding of feet across the floor of the lounge. A moment later, the bedroom door was flung open and his nephews erupted into the room, a large and very eager Airedale leading the way.

The dog scrambled onto the bed and Miller shoved it away with a curse. 'Get down, you brute.'

Tommy was eight and Roger ten and they moved in on him from both sides gurgling with laughter. 'Come on, Uncle Nick, we're taking Fritz to the park for a run.'

'Not with me you aren't,' Miller said, hitching the blankets over his shoulders.

'Uncle Nick, you promised.'

'When?'

'Oh, ages ago.'

Fritz leapt clear across the bed and circled the room briskly and Miller sighed. 'All right, I know when I'm beaten. But get that brute out of here. You can wait for me in the yard.'

After they had gone, he went into the bathroom, splashed cold water on his face and dressed quickly in cord slacks, polo necked sweater and suede boots. He lit a cigarette and went outside.

His brother's house stood in two acres of garden, a large Victorian villa in grey Yorkshire stone, and Miller's flat was above the garage block at the rear. As he went down the fire escape, an engine roared into life inside the garage and the Mini-Cooper reversed into the yard.

Tommy and Fritz were in the rear, Roger at the wheel and Miller opened the door quickly and pushed him into the passenger seat. 'Don't you ever let your mother catch you doing that,' he said. 'You'll get me shot.'

When they reached the park, they left the car near the main gates, but instead of going inside, walked down the road to the public playing fields where Miller released Fritz. The Airedale bounded away and the boys ran after him, shouting and laughing.

Miller followed at his own pace, hands in pockets. The morning was cold and grey and yet the wind was bracing and he felt alive again for the first time in weeks.

The boys had reached the line of iron railings that marked the boundary of the park. Suddenly Roger gave a cry that was echoed by Tommy and they disappeared over the skyline.

Miller hurried after them and when he squeezed through a gap in the fence and looked down into the sports arena, a man in a black track suit was running round the grass track, Fritz in hot pursuit. Roger and Tommy were hopping about in the centre calling ineffectually.

By the time Miller reached the bottom of the hill the runner had secured a grip on Fritz's collar and was leading him to the boys. They stood together in a little group and Miller heard a burst of laughter.

'Sorry about that,' he said as he approached.

The man in the track suit turned and grinned. 'Surprise, surprise.' It was Duncan Craig.

'You're right, it is,' Miller said. 'You're up early.'

'The best part of the day. Besides I like to keep fit.' He ruffled Roger's hair. 'These two imps yours?'

'My nephews,' Miller said. 'For my sins. Roger and Tommy. Boys, this is Colonel Craig.'

They were enormously impressed. 'Were you in the war?' Roger demanded.

Craig grinned. 'I'm afraid so.'

'Commandos?'

'Nothing so romantic.'

They looked disappointed and Miller snapped the lead

to Fritz's collar. 'Don't you believe him. Colonel Craig was something a whole lot more romantic than any commando.'

Craig glanced sharply at him. 'Been doing a little research, Sergeant?'

'You could say that.' Miller brought Fritz to heel and nodded to the boys. 'We'd better be getting back.'

They turned and ran across the arena and Miller nodded to Craig. 'I'll be seeing you.'

'I'm sure you will.'

When he reached the top of the hill, the boys were waiting for him and Miller paused to catch his breath. Below, Craig was already half-way round the track.

'I say, Uncle Nick,' Roger said, 'he certainly likes running, doesn't he?'

'I suppose he does,' Miller said, a slight frown on his face, and then he smiled. 'I don't know about you two, but I'm starving. Come on, I'll race you to the car.'

Their excited laughter mingled with the dog's barking died into the distance and below in the silent arena, Duncan Craig started on his second circuit, running strongly.

There was a time when Nick Miller had aspired to a black belt in karate or judo, but the pressure of work had interfered with that pursuit as it had with so many things. When he entered the premises of the Kardon Judo Centre on the following morning, it was his first visit in a month.

Bert King, the senior instructor, was dressed for the mat, but sat at his desk reading the morning paper, a cup of coffee in his hand. He was a small, shrunken man whose head seemed too big for his body and yet in the dojo, he was poetry in motion, a third dan in both judo and aikido.

'Hello, Mr Miller, long time no see,' he said cheerfully.

'I don't seem to have time to turn round these days,' Miller said, 'but I've got an hour to spare this morning. Any chance of a private lesson?'

Bert shook his head. 'Sorry, I've got a client in the dojo now warming up. I was just going to go in.'

'Anyone I know?'

'I don't think so, he isn't one of the regulars. A chap called Craig.'

Miller paused in the act of lighting a cigarette. 'Colonel Duncan Craig?'

'That's right. Do you know him?'

'We've met. Is he any good?'

'You're telling me he is,' Bert King said emphatically. 'His aikido is murder – brown belt standard at least. Maybe even first dan and the strange thing is, he isn't even graded. He's been coming in two hours each day for a fortnight now and it's taking me all my time to hold him, I can tell you.'

'Mind if I watch?'

'Help yourself.' He moved out of the office, opened the door to the dojo and went inside. Miller hesitated for a moment and then followed him.

Craig and King faced each other in the centre of the mat. The Colonel was wearing an old judogi and looked fit and active, vibrant with energy like an unexploded time bomb.

'Free practice?' Bert King said.

Craig nodded. 'All right by me.'

The contest which followed lasted just under fifteen minutes and was one of the finest Miller had seen. When it finished, both men were damp with sweat and Bert King looked shaken for the first time since Miller had known him.

'I must be getting old,' he said. 'Ten minutes' rest and then we'll brush up on some of the finer points.'

'That's fine by me.' Craig picked up his towel from the bench to wipe the sweat from his face and noticed Miller in the doorway. 'Hello, Sergeant, we seem to be running into each other all over the place.'

'We'll have to get Sergeant Miller on the mat with you one of these days,' Bert said.

Miller shook his head. 'No thanks. He's too rich for my blood.'

'Don't you believe it,' Bert told Craig. 'He'll give you a run for your money.'

'I'm sure he will.' Craig dropped his towel on the bench. 'I'll go through a few routines till you're ready, Bert.'

There was a full-length mirror on the wall and he stood in front of it and started to practise karate kicks, knee raised, flicking each foot forward in turn with lightning speed.

'He's good, isn't he?' Bert King observed.

'Too damned good for comfort,' Miller said and he turned and went out quickly, his face grim.

'So he likes to take early morning runs in the park and he's keen on judo,' Grant said. 'So what? Plenty of men of his age like to keep fit. Wish I had the time myself.'

'But Duncan Craig is no ordinary man,' Miller said. 'I've been doing a little research on him. He took a B.Sc. in Electrical Engineering at Leeds University in 1939, joined a tank regiment at the outbreak of war and was captured at Arras when the Panzers broke through in 1940. His grandmother was French and he speaks the language fluently, which helped when he escaped from prison camp and walked to Spain. Special Operations Executive recruited him when he got home and dropped him into France on four separate occasions to organise the *maquis*. On his last job, he was betrayed, but managed to slip through the net again. They posted him to the Middle East after that and he spent the rest of the war working for the Special Air Service organizing guerrillas in the Cretan Mountains.'

'He must have been a pretty hard apple,' Grant observed.

'You're telling me. When the war ended he was twenty-seven and a Lieutenant-Colonel. D.S.O. and bar, M.C., Legion of Honour – you name it, he's got it.'

The early March wind drove hail like bullets against the window of Grant's office and he sighed. 'Look here, Nick, don't you think you're getting this thing completely out of proportion?'

'Do I hell,' Miller said. 'Can you imagine a man like that sitting back while his daughter's murderer walks the streets a free man?'

'Now you're being melodramatic.' Grant shook his head. 'I don't buy this one, Nick. I don't buy it at all. Not that I don't want you to stop keeping a fatherly eye on Max Vernon. He'll make his move sooner or later and when he does, I want us to be ready for him. As for Craig – just forget about him.'

Miller crumpled the sheet of paper he was holding into a ball of paper and Grant lost his temper. 'Just let me put you straight on one or two things before you go. In this town alone crime has quadrupled over the past seven years. We've a clear-up rate for housebreaking of sixteen per cent, the average week in the C.I.D. is seventy hours and you want to waste your time on a thing like this? Go on, get out of here and get on with some work.'

Miller went back into the outer office and sat down at his desk. Jack Brady came across, a sympathetic grin on his face, and leaned against the wall as he filled his pipe.

'You did ask for it, you know.'

Miller sighed and ran his hands over his face. 'I'm right, Jack – I know I am.'

'Perhaps you are, but I fail to see what you can do about it until something happens. Did you see that note I left for you?'

'This one?' Miller picked a sheet of paper from his In-tray.

'That's right. It came in half an hour ago. You did say you wanted to know of anything concerning Chuck Lazer's place, didn't you?'

Miller read the report quickly and then picked up the

telephone. 'Get me the District Inspector for the R.S.P.C.A.'
He looked up at Brady. 'This could mean trouble.'

'That's what I thought.'

A voice clicked in on the other end of the wire. 'Forbes
here.'

'Good morning, Inspector. Detective Sergeant Miller,
Central C.I.D. You've sent us a routine report on two
poisoned dogs – Dalmatians. I wonder if you'd mind telling
me what happened?'

'We got a call from a Mr Lazer of the Berkley Club in
Cork Square at nine o'clock this morning. He found his
dogs dead in the alley at the side of the club. Arsenical
poisoning, which was why I reported it.'

'Did he have any idea who was responsible?'

'He said very little. He was obviously quite distressed –
and I don't blame him. They were beautiful animals.'

Miller thanked him and replaced the receiver.

'What do you think,' Brady said, 'a declaration of war?'

'I should imagine so.' Miller stood up and took down his
trenchcoat from the stand. 'We'd better go round and see
if we can damp down this little affair before it bursts into
flame.'

Chuck Lazer was sitting at the piano in the empty casino,
a glass at his elbow. He gave a tired grin when Miller and
Brady entered and kept right on playing.

'Bad news travels fast.'

'It certainly does,' Miller said. 'Why didn't you let me
know?'

'My affair.'

'Not in my book.' Miller pulled a chair forward and sat
astride it, arms resting on the back. 'He's going to squeeze
you out, Chuck. This is only the first step.'

Lazer shrugged and moved into a pushing, intricate
arrangement of *Blue Moon*. 'I can look after myself.'

'What with – a gun?'

Lazer cracked suddenly and completely. 'What in the hell do you expect me to do? Bow out gracefully and let him take over? I've put a lot of sweat into this place, Nick. I run an honest game for a nice class of people, which suits me and suits them. I'm damned if I'm going to let Max Vernon walk all over me.'

Miller got to his feet, walked across to one of the green baize tables and picked up a pair of dice. He rattled them in his hand and turned, a frown on his face.

'When do you think they'll start, Jack?'

'Probably tonight if what happened to the dogs is anything to go by,' Brady said. 'Half a dozen heavies mingling with the regular members, complaining about the service, starting a punch-up or two. The usual pattern. Before you know where you are this place will be as dead as the Empire music hall.'

Lazer's face had gone grey and his shoulders sagged as he stopped playing. 'Okay – you win. What do I do?'

'You do nothing,' Miller said. 'Just leave everything to us. What time do you open?'

'Eight o'clock, but things don't really get moving till nine-thirty or ten.'

Miller turned to Brady enquiringly. 'Feel like a night on the town, Jack?'

'Suits me,' Brady grinned. 'Naturally I'll expect my chips to be on the house.'

Lazer managed a faint smile. 'I might as well get ruined that way as the other.'

Miller clapped him on the shoulder. 'Don't worry, Chuck, we'll have the heavy brigade standing by. Anyone who starts anything tonight is in for the shock of their lives.'

On returning to Headquarters, Miller went in to see Grant to report on this latest development and then sat down at his desk and started to work his way through some of the paper that had accumulated in his In-tray. It was just before one and he was thinking about going down to the canteen for a sandwich when the 'phone rang.

It was a woman's voice, cool, assured and faintly familiar. 'Detective Sergeant Miller?'

'Speaking.'

'Harriet Craig here.'

'What can I do for you, Miss Craig?'

'I was wondering if we could have a chat.'

'I don't see why not. Are you free this afternoon?'

'No, I'm afraid not, and this evening I'm going to the symphony concert at the George Hall with friends.' She hesitated as if slightly uncertain. 'It finishes at ten. I could meet you then or would that be too late?'

'Not at all,' Miller said. 'Shall I pick you up outside?'

'No, I'd rather not if you don't mind. There's a bar in Gascoigne Square – the Romney. Do you know it?'

'I certainly do.'

'I'll meet you in the lounge at ten fifteen.'

Miller replaced the receiver and stared into space, thinking about Gascoigne Square by night and the lounge bar of the Romney, the neon lights of the Flamingo Club flashing across from the other side.

'And now what's she up to?' he asked himself softly.

9

The evening started slowly at the Berkley as it did at most gaming clubs, but from eight o'clock on, Miller and Brady waited, sitting in comfort in Chuck Lazer's office, watching the activities in the main casino through a two-way mirror.

Lazer was at the piano as always, working his way

through one standard after another, stopping occasionally to chat with a favoured customer. He looked cool and immaculate in a mohair evening suit and showed no sign of strain.

Gradually the numbers built up until most of the tables were surrounded by those who came only to watch and all seats were taken. It was just after nine-thirty when Brady gave a sudden exclamation and touched Miller's sleeve.

'Coming through the door now. The three at the back.'

Miller nodded. 'I've got them.'

'The man at the front is Manchester Charlie Ford, followed by Frank Butcher. I sent him down for G.B.H. once. Three years. The little bloke with hair like patent leather is Sid Tordoff – a right villain.'

'They aren't local lads?'

'Are they hell – Manchester. They've been imported specially – probably via a middle man. You know how it goes. A pound to a penny they don't even know who they're working for.'

They waited and a few moments later he nodded again. 'I thought so. Arthur Hart and Martin Dereham – he's the good-looking one with the buttonhole and the moustache. Tries to come the public school touch, but the highest he ever got up the educational ladder was class four at Dock Street Elementary.'

'Okay,' Miller said, getting to his feet. 'I'm going in. Better put a call through to H.Q. We'll have the heavy brigade standing by just in case.'

It was a quiet, well-behaved crowd, mostly moneyed people, the kind who'd run for cover and never come back at the slightest hint of violence or trouble of any sort. Miller scanned the faces quickly, noting that the gang had dispersed themselves, which probably indicated outbursts of trouble in several different places at once.

And then he saw Manchester Charlie Ford on the other

side of the roulette wheel. Ford was of medium height with powerful sloping shoulders, the scar tissue beneath his eyes indicating that he had once been a prize fighter. He was wearing a surprisingly well-cut suit and pushed his way through the crowd with an arrogance that was obviously beginning to alarm several people.

He paused behind a rather attractive woman. It was impossible to see what actually happened, but she turned sharply and her escort, a dark-haired young man, rounded on Ford. 'What's the game?'

So this was how it was to start? Miller slipped through the crowd, arriving from the rear, and secured a grip on Ford's left wrist before he knew what had hit him.

'Get moving!' he said softly into Ford's ear. 'Try anything funny and I'll break your arm.'

Before the young couple could say a word, Miller and Ford had been swallowed up by the crowd. They came to rest behind a pillar, Miller still retaining his grip. Ford's right hand dived into his pocket. As it came out again, Jack Brady arrived on the scene and relieved him of a wicked-looking spiked knuckle-duster.

'Well, well, if it isn't my old friend Manchester Charlie Ford.'

Ford looked ready to commit murder and when Miller turned and glanced over the crowd, he saw the others making rapidly for the exit.

'Are they leaving you then, Charlie?' Brady said. 'Isn't that a shame?'

They hustled him into Lazer's office between them and Miller shoved him down into a chair. 'Who's paying the piper on this little caper?'

'Why don't you get knotted?' Ford said.

Brady dangled the knuckle-duster in front of him between thumb and forefinger. 'Carrying an offensive weapon, Charlie, and with your record? Good for six months that.'

'I can do that standing on my head.' Ford turned as Lazer entered the room, a worried look on his face. 'Are you Lazer?' He laughed harshly. 'Had to bring in the bloody scuffers, eh? That's your lot, boyo. I hope you realize that. You're dead meat.'

'Why don't you shut up?' Miller said and glanced at his watch. 'I'll have to go, Jack. I've got a date. Will you book him for me?'

'My pleasure.'

Brady yanked Ford to his feet and took him out through the side door and Miller turned to Lazer. 'Don't take any notice of that goon, Chuck. We've made a good start. They'll think twice the next time.'

'Oh, sure – sure they will,' Lazer said, but his eyes were unhappy and Miller knew that he didn't believe him for a moment.

The lounge bar of the Romney was only half full when Miller entered shortly after ten, but there was no sign of Harriet Craig. He sat on a stool at the end of the bar, ordered a brandy and ginger ale and lit a cigarette. When he glanced up, he could see her in the mirror standing in the doorway behind him.

She was wearing an evening coat in green grosgraine which hung open at the front to reveal a simple black cocktail dress and when she smiled on catching sight of him, she looked quite enchanting.

'Am I late?' she asked as she sat on the stool beside him.

'No, I was early. How about a drink?'

'Please. A dry martini.'

'How was the concert?'

'Fine – Mendelssohn's *Ruy Blas* and a Mozart piano concerto. Do you like classical music?'

'Some – I'm a jazz man myself. How's your father?'

'Fine – just fine.' She stared down into her glass and

sighed. 'Look, I'm afraid I've rather got you here under false pretences.'

'You mean you don't want to chat after all?'

She nodded. 'As a matter of fact I was hoping you might take me out.'

'Now there's an attractive idea,' he said. 'Where would you like to go?'

'I'd like to go to the Flamingo.'

'May I ask why?'

'Those murals Joanna painted for Vernon – I'd like to see them. The only other way would be to ask his permission and I'd hate that.' She opened her bag and took out a gold-edged card. 'I've got a membership card – one of Daddy's business friends arranged it for me and members are allowed to take guests in with them.'

Miller sat there looking down at the card for a long moment, a slight frown on his face and she put a hand on his arm. 'Please, Nick? I'd feel safe with you.'

'You make a very appealing liar,' Miller said, 'but I'll still take you. In fact I wouldn't miss it for the world. I'm sure it will prove more than interesting.'

The Flamingo had altered a lot since Miller's last visit, but that had been in the old days when Harry Faulkner had owned it and it had been more a night club than anything else, with gambling relegated to a strictly illegal small back room. The Gaming Act had changed all that and now there was money to burn.

The small, thickly carpeted foyer had been decorated in excellent taste and the man who moved forward to check Harriet's membership card was greying and distinguished and wore hunting pink. They went through a door at the end of a short passage and found themselves at the top of a flight of steps which dropped into the main casino.

'Oh, look, Nick! Look!' Harriet clutched at his arm.

The murals were astonishingly good. There were four of

them in enormous panels, two on either side of the long
room. They were all battle scenes, the Foot Guards figuring
largely in each one, and had been executed in a rather
stylistic seventeenth-century manner and yet had a life and
originality that was all their own.

Miller shook his head slowly. 'I just didn't realize she
was that good.'

'She could have been a great painter, Nick,' Harriet said.
'Something special.' She took a deep breath and smiled as
though determined to be cheerful. 'Well, as long as we're
here we might as well have a look round.'

There were the usual games – Chemmy, Roulette,
Blackjack and, in a small side room, Poker was on offer.
But it was the clientele which Miller found most interesting.
There was little doubt that Vernon was catering for the top
people with a vengeance. The kind of money being wagered
would have been sufficient to indicate that, but in any case,
Miller recognized faces here and there. Wool barons, indus-
trialists, the managing director of one of the world's largest
ready-made clothing factories. There were at least four
millionaires present to his personal knowledge.

The whole place had the atmosphere of a West-End club,
only a low buzz of conversation disturbed the silence and
grave-faced waiters in hunting pink moved from table to
table dispensing free drinks.

Manchester Charlie Ford and his boys would never
have got past the door, but if they had, they would have
closed the place down by just one visit. With the kind of
clientele it catered for, a club like the Flamingo depended
on its reputation. Take that away from it and it was
finished.

They stood by the roulette wheel watching the play and
she turned suddenly. 'I'd like to have a go. What do I do?'

'Decide how much you can afford to lose, that's lesson
number one.'

She opened her handbag and produced two five-pound notes. 'Will this be all right?'

He grinned. 'It won't go far in a place like this, but never mind. Who knows? You may even break the bank. Wait here, I'll get you some chips.'

Max Vernon sat at his desk, magnificent in a midnight blue dinner jacket, a white gardenia in his buttonhole. For supper, the chef had presented him with a mixed grill done to perfection and a glass of champagne was at his elbow.

The man who stood on the other side of the desk, an open ledger in his hand, was Claudio Carelli, the casino manager, and he looked worried.

'But it isn't good, Mr Vernon. We put a lot of money into this place. The new décor and refurnishing came to twenty-two thousand and then there are the running expenses. At the moment, we're virtually living from day to day.'

'You worry too much, Claudio,' Vernon said. 'It takes time to build up a prestige club like this. But they're coming now – all the right people. Another three months and we'll be in the clear.'

'I certainly hope so.'

As Carelli opened the door to leave, Stratton came in, his face pale with excitement. 'Miller's downstairs in the casino.'

'How did he get in?'

'He's with the Craig girl. Ben saw them come in. He checked with Bruno on the door. She's a member all right, everything square and above board. She brought Miller in as her guest.'

'Who put her up?'

'Bruno says it was Sir Frank Wooley. Shall we get rid of them?'

'You bloody fool.' Vernon reached across the desk and

grabbed him by the tie. 'How many times have I got to tell you? No trouble in the club. What do you want to do – bankrupt me?' He shoved Stratton away from him and poured another glass of champagne. 'Keep an eye on them. I'll be down myself in ten minutes.'

Harriet had a small, but exciting run of luck at Roulette that took her up to seventy pounds.

'I think I'd better try something else while I'm ahead,' she said. 'What are they playing over there?'

'One of the oldest games of chance in the world,' Miller told her. 'You simply throw the dice and pray that the right number comes up.'

'Any skill required?'

'Not to my knowledge.'

'Then that's the game for me.'

The table was a popular one and not only were all the seats taken, but a fair-sized crowd stood around watching. Harriet had to wait for five minutes before her chance came. The first time she threw, she didn't cast the dice far enough and the croupier handed them back to her with a whispered instruction. There were one or two good-humoured remarks and then she made two straight passes and doubled her money.

There were encouraging smiles from the crowd and she laughed excitedly. 'These dice can't possibly have any more luck in them. Can I have a new pair?'

'Certainly, madame.'

The croupier passed them across and removed the others. Harriet rattled the dice in one hand and threw a pair of ones. 'Snakes' eyes,' said a military-looking gentleman with a curving moustache who was standing next to her. 'Bad luck.'

She tried again with no better luck and the third throw cleaned her out. 'How strange,' she said with a little laugh. 'I just keep getting a pair of ones, don't I?'

'The luck of the game, my dear,' the military-looking man said.

She picked up the dice and rolled them gently no more than a foot or so. 'Look, there they are again. It just isn't my night.'

The croupier's rake reached out, but the military man beat him to it, a frown on his face. 'Not so fast there.'

'I hope monsieur is not suggesting that there could be anything wrong with the dice?'

'We'll see, shall we?'

He rattled the dice together and threw them the length of the table. *Snakes' eyes.* The croupier's rake moved out, but the military man beat him to it again. 'Oh, no you don't, my friend. These dice are loaded.' There was a sudden hubbub amongst the crowd and he turned to an elderly, white-haired man at his side. 'See for yourself.'

The elderly man tossed the dice across the table and the result was plain for all to see. Voices were raised suddenly, people got up from other tables and came across as the news spread like wildfire.

Harriet Craig moved through the crowd to Miller's side. 'They *are* getting excited, aren't they?'

Before he could reply, Vernon appeared on the scene, pushing his way through the crowd, his face angry. 'What's going on here?'

'I was just going to ask you the same question, Vernon,' the white-haired man said. 'To start with you'll oblige me by throwing these dice.'

Vernon stood there, holding them in his hand, a bewildered frown on his face and then he threw. There was a roar from the crowd and the white-haired man gathered them up quickly.

'That settles it. Somebody better get the police.' He turned and addressed the crowd. 'I don't know about the rest of you, but I've dropped four hundred pounds here during the past couple of weeks and I'm not leaving till I get it back.'

'Ladies and gentlemen – please.' Vernon raised his arms in an attempt to placate them, but it was no use.

The voices rose angrily on either side and Miller pushed his way forward and tapped the white-haired man on the shoulder. 'I think I'd better have those, sir.'

'And who the devil might you be?'

'Detective Sergeant Miller, Central C.I.D.' Miller produced his warrant and the dice were passed over without a murmur.

Miller looked across at Vernon. 'Are these your dice, sir?'

'Of course not.'

'I notice that in accordance with a specific regulation of the Gaming Act, they carry this club's registered mark as placed there by the makers. What you are saying is that you have a full set without this pair? That these are forgeries?'

'But that's rubbish,' the white-haired man put in. 'What on earth would be the point of a player substituting for the real dice a pair that would make him lose every time he threw.'

Vernon's shoulders sagged and his knuckles gleamed whitely as he gripped the edge of the table. He glared across at Miller, who returned his stare calmly.

'Right – I think that's it for tonight, Mr Vernon.'

'What in hell do you mean?' Vernon demanded furiously.

'I mean that I'm closing you up.'

'Yes, closing you up for good, you damned crook,' the white-haired man said, leaning across the table.

For a moment, Vernon gazed wildly about him and then he turned, pushed his way through the crowd and disappeared upstairs.

It was just after eleven when Miller went down the Town Hall steps to the Cooper. The radio was playing faintly and when he opened the door, Harriet Craig sat in the passenger seat, humming softly to herself.

'All finished?' she said brightly.

Her handbag was at her feet and he picked it up without answering and searched it quickly.

'What on earth are you looking for?'

'The other pair of dice – the ones you palmed. Where are they?'

'I haven't the slightest idea what you're talking about.'

Miller tossed the handbag into her lap, switched on the engine and drove away. 'I don't like being used.'

'Not even in a good cause?'

'For God's sake, Harriet, don't you realize what you've done? You've finished the Flamingo. An exclusive gaming house lives on its reputation. All it takes is one tiny scandal – just one and the clientele disappear like the snow in the springtime.'

'Poor Mr Vernon. What rotten luck.'

'If you imagine for one moment he's going to take it lying down, you've got another thought coming.'

'We'll see, shall we?' She settled back in her seat, arms folded and sighed. 'Those murals were wonderful – really wonderful. Who knows? Maybe he'll be willing to sell them now.'

'You'll come in for a drink?' she said when they reached the house.

'Are you sure it isn't too late?'

'Of course not. We'll have something to eat if you like. I'm starving.'

She unlocked the front door and led the way into the hall and Miller was at once aware of the low persistent hum of a dynamo. 'Daddy must still be working,' she said. 'Come on. I'll take you through to the workshop. You two can chat while I make some supper.'

When she opened the door at the end of the corridor Miller paused in astonishment. The room had been expertly equipped and fitted, of that there could be no doubt. The walls were lined with shelves which seemed to carry just about every kind of spare imaginable in the electrical field. There was an automatic lathe, a cutter and several other machines whose purpose was a complete mystery to him.

Duncan Craig leaned over a bench, spot-welding a length of steel rod to what looked like the insides of a computer. He glanced up as the door opened, killed the flame on the blow torch and pushed up his goggles.

'Hello there,' he said. 'And what have you two been up to?'

'Nick took me to the Flamingo,' Harriet said. 'Quite an experience, but I'll tell you all about it later. Keep him occupied while I get the supper.'

The door closed behind her and Craig offered Miller a cigarette. 'She seems to have enjoyed herself.'

'How could she fail to? Seeing Max Vernon fall flat on his face must have quite made her day.'

Craig's expression didn't alter. 'Oh, yes, what happened then?'

'Apparently the casino was using crooked dice. There was quite a fuss when it was discovered.'

'My God, I bet there was.' Craig contrived to look shocked. 'This won't do Vernon much good, will it?'

'He might as well close up shop. There'll be a prosecution of course, but even if it doesn't get anywhere, the damage is done.'

'How did he react?'

'Oh, he said he'd been framed. That the loaded dice must have been passed by one of the players.'

'But that's ridiculous,' Craig said. 'I could imagine a player trying to substitute dice that would win for him, but not a pair that would lose. Anyway, a club's dice have to be specially manufactured and accounted for. It's a regulation of the Gaming Act expressly aimed at stamping out this sort of thing.'

Miller moved along the bench and picked up a small stick of lead. 'Easy enough for a man with some technical know-how to inject a little lead into a pair of plastic dice.'

'But what would be the point of the exercise?'

'I think that's been achieved, don't you?'

'Well, I'm hardly likely to shed tears over Max Vernon, am I?'

'I suppose not.'

Miller wandered round the bench and paused beside a curious contrivance – a long, chromium tube mounted on a tripod. It had a pistol grip at one end and what appeared to be a pair of small headphones clipped to a hook.

'What's this – a secret weapon?'

Craig chuckled. 'Hardly – it's a directional microphone.'

Miller was immediately interested. 'I've heard of those. How do they work?'

'It's a simple electronic principle. The tube is lined with carbon to exclude side noises, traffic for instance. You aim it by ear through the headphones. It can pick up a conversation three hundred yards away.'

'Is that so?'

'Of course these are even handier.' He picked up a small metal disk that was perhaps half an inch thick and little larger than a wrist watch. 'Not only a microphone but also a radio transmitter. Works well up to a range of a hundred yards or so if you use a fountain pen receiver. Wire that up to a pocket tape recorder and you're in business.'

'What as?' Miller asked.

'That depends on the individual, doesn't it?'

'I suppose you're aware that all these gadgets are illegal?'

'Not for the Managing Director of Gulf Electronics.'

Miller shook his head. 'You're a fool, Colonel. Carry on like this and you'll be in trouble up to your neck.'

'I don't know what you're talking about.' Craig smiled blandly. 'By the way, harking back to what you said earlier about doctoring the dice. One would have to get hold of them first.'

'Easy enough to get into a place like the Flamingo, especially in the small hours just after they've closed.'

'I should have thought that might have presented some difficulty.'

'Not for the kind of man who broke into a Vichy prison in 1942 and spirited away four resistance workers who were due to be executed next morning.'

Craig laughed. 'Now you're flattering me.'

'Warning you,' Miller said grimly. 'It's got to stop. Carry on like this and you'll go too far and no one will be able to help you – just remember that.'

'Oh, I will,' Craig said, his smile still hooked firmly into place.

'Good.' Miller opened the door. 'Tell Harriet I'm sorry, but I've suddenly lost my appetite.'

The door closed behind him. Craig's smile disappeared instantly. He stood there staring into space for a while, then pulled down his goggles, re-lit the blow torch and started to work again.

Max Vernon walked to the fireplace and back to his desk again, restless as a caged tiger, and Carver and Stratton watched him anxiously.

'This is serious,' he said. 'Don't you stupid bastards realize that? One single scandal – that's all you need in a prestige club like this and you're finished. My God, did you see their faces? They'll never come back.'

'Maybe things aren't as bad as you think, Mr Vernon,' Carver ventured and Vernon turned on him.

'You bloody fool, we've been living from day to day, waiting for things to build up. I've been using the take from the Flamingo to keep the betting shops running. Now what happens?'

He sat down behind his desk and poured himself a brandy. 'Who's done this to me – who?'

'Maybe it was Chuck Lazer,' Stratton suggested.

'Do me a favour?' Vernon drained his glass. 'I know one thing. Whoever it is will wish he'd never been born before I'm through with him.'

He slammed his fist down hard on the desk and something dropped to the floor and rolled across the carpet. Vernon leaned over and frowned. 'What was that?'

Stratton picked up the small steel disk and passed it over. 'Search me, Mr Vernon. It fell off the desk when you hit it. Must have been underneath.'

Vernon stared down incredulously and then grabbed a paper knife and forced off the top. 'I've seen one of these before,' he said. 'It's an electronic gadget – a microphone and transmitter.' His face was suddenly distorted with fury and he dropped the disk on the floor and ground his heel into it. 'We've been wired for sound. Some bastard's been listening in.'

He reached for the brandy bottle and paused, eyes narrowing. 'Just a minute – Craig's Managing Director of an electronics firm, isn't he?'

Stratton nodded eagerly. 'That's right and his daughter was here tonight remember.'

'So she was,' Vernon said softly. 'Plus that nosy copper, Miller. Come to think of it, that's twice he's stuck his nose into my business in one night. That won't do – that won't do at all.'

'Do you want Ben and me to handle it?' Stratton said.

Vernon shook his head and poured himself another glass of brandy. 'Not on your life. Contract it out, Billy. A couple of real pros should be enough. One of the south London mobs might be interested. Just make sure they don't know who they're working for, that's all.'

'How much can I offer?' Stratton asked.

'Five hundred.'

'For Craig?' Stratton's eyes widened. 'That's a good price, Mr Vernon.'

'For both of them, you fool. Miller and Craig.' Vernon raised his glass of brandy in an ironic salute. 'Down the hatch,' he said and smiled grimly.

10

It was dark in the office except for the pool of light falling across the drawing board from the anglepoise lamp. Duncan Craig put down his slide-rule and stretched with a sigh. It was almost eight o'clock and for the past two hours he had worked on alone after the rest of his staff had left.

There were footsteps in the corridor and as he turned, the door opened and the night guard entered, a black and tan Alsatian on a lead at his side. He put a thermos flask on the desk and grinned.

'Just checking, Colonel. I've brought you a cup of tea.'

'Thanks very much, George.' Craig ruffled the dog's ears. 'What time's your next round – nine o'clock isn't it?'

'That's right, sir. Will you still be here?'

'The way this thing is going I'll probably be here all night.'

The door closed behind George and Craig stood there listening to his footsteps move along the corridor outside. When they had finally faded away, he went into the wash-room quickly and closed the door.

When he reappeared five minutes later he presented a

strange and sinister picture in dark pants and sweater, and wearing an old balaclava helmet, his face darkened by a brown make-up stick. In his left hand he carried a canvas hold-all. He dropped it on the floor beside his desk, picked up the telephone and dialled a number.

The receiver was lifted instantly at the other end. 'Yes?'

'I'm leaving. I'll ring you again in thirty-five minutes.'

'I'll be waiting.'

He replaced the receiver, picked up the hold-all and opened the door, listening for a moment before moving into the corridor.

He took the service lift down to the basement, walked through the work's garage, helping himself to a jerry can full of petrol on the way, and left through a small judas gate. It was raining slightly and he crossed the yard, keeping to the shadows, scrambled over the low wall and dropped down onto the grass bank that sloped into the canal.

He crouched at the water's edge, opened the hold-all and pulled out the collapsible dinghy it contained. When he activated the compression cylinder, the boat inflated with a soft hiss and he dropped it into the water and pushed off into the darkness.

He'd kept Gibson's Furniture Factory under careful observation for three days now from the top floor of his own factory, even going to the lengths of obtaining a ground-floor plan of the place from the City Engineer's Department, for most of the area was scheduled for demolition and municipal development.

It was no more than four hundred yards up the York Road from Gulf Electronics and an approach from the rear via the canal had seemed obvious. He grinned as he paddled out into mid-stream to pass the barge and moved back into the shadows again. Just like the old days – other times, other places when to live a life like this had seemed as natural as breathing.

He passed the coaling wharf of the steel plant, dark and lonely in the light of a solitary yellow lamp. The furniture factory was the second building along from there and he paddled in quickly, scrambled out onto a narrow strip of mud and pulled the dinghy clear.

The brick wall above his head was about nine feet high, but old and crumbling and in spite of being encumbered with the jerry can he found no difficulty in scaling it. For a moment he sat there peering into the darkness and then dropped into the yard below.

A light glowed dimly through the dirty windows and he moved round to the front of the building keeping to the shadows. The whole area was enclosed by a crumbling brick wall. The main gates were of wood, ten feet high and secured by a massive iron bar which dropped into sockets on either side.

In one corner of the yard was a jumbled mass of packing cases and rubbish which had obviously accumulated over the years and it was for this that he had brought the petrol. He emptied the jerry can quickly, scattering its contents as widely as possible, and then returned to the gates and removed the holding bar.

He checked his watch. It was exactly fifteen minutes since he had left his office. From now on, speed was essential.

He hit his first snag when he reached the main door of the factory. It was locked. He hesitated only for a moment and then tried his alternative route up an old fire escape to the second floor. The door at the top was also locked, but several panes of glass in the window beside it were broken and it opened with little difficulty.

He stood in the darkness listening, aware of voices somewhere in the distance, and moved along a short corridor. There was a door at the end with a broken panel through which light streamed. He opened it cautiously and was at once aware of a strong smell of whisky.

He was on a steel landing. The hall below was crowded with crates, and a large six-wheeler truck, which certainly didn't look as if it belonged, was parked a yard or two away from the main doors.

The voices came from his left and he went along the landing, passing a small glass-walled office which stood in darkness. There was a light in a room at the very end of the landing and he peered round the edge of the glass partition and found three men playing poker.

He withdrew quietly, went back along the landing and descended the iron stairs to the hall below. The truck was loaded with crates of whisky consigned to London Docks and when he looked inside the cab, the ignition key was in the dashboard.

The main doors were the real snag. They were chained together and secured by a large padlock. He examined it carefully, turned and went back upstairs.

He crouched in the darkness of the little office, the 'phone on the floor beside him, and dialled the number he wanted carefully.

The reply was instant. 'Police Headquarters. Can I help you?'

'Central C.I.D. – Detective Sergeant Miller,' Craig said in a hoarse voice. 'I think you'll find he's on duty tonight.'

Miller was sitting behind his desk listening to a well-known housebreaker indignantly deny the offence with which he was charged when the 'phone rang.

'All right, Arnold, you can take a breather,' he said and nodded to Brady, who leaned against the wall cleaning his fingernails with a penknife. 'Give him a cigarette, Jack, while I see what we've got here.'

He picked up the telephone. 'Detective Sergeant Miller.'

The voice at the other end was strangely hoarse and completely unfamiliar to him. 'Gibson's Furniture Factory on the York Road – interesting place – they even make their own booze. You'd better get round here quick and bring the Fire Brigade with you.' He chuckled harshly. 'I do hope Vernon's insured.'

Craig replaced the receiver and looked at the luminous dial of his watch. He was running late, but there was nothing he could do about that now. He waited exactly four minutes, went back downstairs and climbed into the cab of the truck.

He pulled out the choke, pressed the starter and the engine burst into life with a shattering roar. There was a cry of alarm from the landing above his head and he rammed the stick into first gear, let in the clutch sharply and accelerated. The doors burst open and the truck rolled out into the yard. Craig swerved sharply, braking to a halt near the outside gates, switched off and jumped to the ground taking the ignition key with him.

He struck a match quickly and tossed it onto the stacked crates, picked up his jerry can, turned and ran into the shadows. Somewhere in the night, the jangle of a police car's bell sounded ominously.

When he drifted into the side of the canal below the wall of his own factory yard five minutes later, there was already a considerable disturbance in the vicinity of the furniture factory and a red glow stained the darkness, flames leaping into the night from the stack of burning crates.

He took a knife from his pocket and slashed the dinghy in several places, forcing out all air so that he was able to stuff it into the hold-all again, then he tossed it over the wall with the jerry can and followed them.

He left the can with a stack of similar ones on his way through the garage and returned to the tenth floor in the service lift. The moment he was safely inside his office, he reached for the 'phone and dialled his home. As before, the receiver was lifted instantly at the other end.

'You're late,' Harriet said.

'Sorry about that. I must be getting old.'

She chuckled. 'That'll be the day. Everything go off okay?'

'Couldn't be better. I won't be home just yet, by the way. I want to finish the details on the vibrator modification in time for the staff conference tomorrow.'

'How long will you be?'

'Another couple of hours should do it.'

'I'll have some supper waiting.'

He replaced the receiver, went into the washroom, scrubbed the filth from his body and changed quickly. He had hardly returned to the other room when there was a knock on the door and George came in.

'Hell of a fuss going on up the road, sir. Don't know what it's all about, but everybody seems to be there. Fire, police – the lot.'

'Go and have a look if you like,' Craig said.

'Sure you don't mind, sir?'

'Not at all. I'd be interested to know what's happening myself.'

He sat down at the drawing board and picked up his slide-rule and George went out quickly.

Miller and Grant stood by the ashes of the fire and surveyed the scene. The Fire Brigade had left, but the big black van that was known throughout the Department as the Studio was parked just inside the gates and the boys from Forensic were already getting to work on the truck.

'So no one was around when the first car got here?' Grant asked, for he had only just arrived on the scene and was seeking information.

'That's right, sir. Whoever was here must have cleared off pretty sharpish. Of course the fire was bound to attract attention.'

'What about the truck?'

'Hi-jacked two days ago on the A1 near Wetherby. Carrying

a consignment of export Scotch to the London Docks. Valued at £30,000.'

Grant whistled softly. 'That's going to bring the county's crime figures down a bit. And you say you didn't recognize the informer's voice?' he added incredulously.

'I'm afraid not.'

'Well, all I can say is you've got a good snout there, by God.'

Jack Brady emerged from the factory and came towards them, an open document in one hand. 'We've found the lease on this place in a filing cabinet in the office, sir,' he said. 'It's made out in the name of Frank O'Connor. The property's been made the subject of a demolition order so it's owned by the city. O'Connor's a citizen of Eire by the way.'

'And probably on his way back there as fast as he can run at this very moment,' Grant observed and turned to Miller. 'You're sure the snout mentioned Vernon's name?'

'Absolutely.'

'Doesn't make sense then, does it?'

'It does if O'Connor was just a front man.'

'I suppose so. Just try proving that and see where it gets you. I know one thing – if it is Vernon's place then someone certainly has it in for him.' He glanced at his watch. 'My God, it's almost eleven. Too late for me. See you two in the morning.'

He moved away and Brady turned to Miller. 'Ready to go, Nick? Not much more we can do here.'

'You know, Grant's right,' Miller said. 'Whoever set this little lot up for us must really have it in for Vernon. Hang on a minute. I want to make a 'phone call.'

'Checking on someone?'

'That's right – Duncan Craig.'

'Not that again, Nick,' Brady groaned. 'Why don't you leave it alone?'

Miller ignored him and went to the 'phone box on the corner. Harriet Craig sounded cool and impersonal. 'Harriet Craig speaking.'

'Nick Miller.'

'Hello, Nick.' There was a new warmth in her voice. 'When are you coming round to finish your supper?'

'Almost any day now. I'm just waiting for the crime figures to fall. Is your father in? I'd like a word with him.'

'I'm sorry, he isn't. He's working late tonight. Was it important?'

'Not really. I've got a rest day Saturday and I thought he might be interested in a game of golf.'

'I'm sure he would. Shall I tell him to give you a call?'

'Yes, you do that. I'll have to go now, Harriet, we're having a hard night.'

'Poor Nick.' She laughed. 'Don't forget to keep in touch.'

'How could I?'

He replaced the receiver and went back to Brady. 'Now there's a thing – guess where Craig is at this very moment? Working late at the factory.'

'Gulf Electronics is only just down the road,' Brady said. 'The big new block. You can see it from here. There's a light in one of the top-floor offices.'

As Miller turned, the light went out. 'Let's take a look.'

'Suit yourself,' Brady said as they moved to the car. 'But I think you're making a big mistake.'

As they drove away there was a low rumble of thunder in the distance and quite suddenly, the light rain which had been falling steadily for the past hour turned into a solid driving downpour. The main gates of Gulf Electronics stood open and Miller pulled into the side of the road and switched off.

At the same moment, the glass entrance doors opened and Duncan Craig appeared, the night guard at his side with the Alsatian.

'That's old George Brown,' Brady said. 'Sergeant in "B" Division for years. Got himself a nice touch there.'

Brown went back inside, locking the doors, and Craig stood at the top of the steps, belting his raincoat and pulling on his gloves. He turned up his collar, went down the steps and hurried into the darkness of the car park. A second later, two men moved out of the shadows at the side of the door and went after him.

'I don't like the look of that one little bit,' Miller said, wrenching open the door. 'Come on!'

He turned in through the gates, running hard, and from somewhere in the darkness of the car park there came a scream.

Duncan Craig had almost reached his car when he heard the rush of feet through the darkness behind and swung round. A fist lifted into his face as he ducked and he staggered back against the car, flinging himself to one side. One of his assailants raised an iron bar two-handed above his head and brought it down with such force that he dented the roof of the Jaguar.

A razor gleamed in the diffused light from the street lamps on the other side of the railings and he warded off the descending blow with a left block, and kicked the man sharply in the stomach so that he screamed in agony.

There was another rush of feet through the darkness and Miller and Brady arrived. The man with the iron bar started to turn and Brady delivered a beautiful right to the jaw that had all his fourteen stone behind it.

There was a sudden silence and Craig laughed. 'Right on time. I don't know what I'd have done without you.'

Miller snapped the cuffs on the man who was lying on the ground and hauled him to his feet. 'Anyone you know, Jack?'

Brady held the other one against Craig's car. 'They're not

off our patch, that's certain. Specially imported I shouldn't wonder.'

Miller turned on Craig savagely. 'Maybe you'll listen to reason from now on.' He sent his prisoner staggering into the darkness in front of him. 'Come on, Jack, let's take them in.'

Craig stood there in the darkness without moving until the Cooper had driven away and then he unlocked the door of the Jaguar and climbed behind the driving wheel. He knew something was wrong the moment she refused to start. He tried several times ineffectually, then took a flashlight from the glove compartment, got out and raised the bonnet. The rotor arm had been removed, an obvious precaution in case he'd beaten them into the car. He sighed heavily, dropped the bonnet and moved across to the main gates.

It was only twenty past eleven and there were plenty of late buses about, but in any case, he would be able to get a taxi in City Square. He crossed the road quickly, head down against the driving rain.

Someone moved out of a doorway behind him, he was aware of that, and then the pain as a sharp point sliced through his raincoat and jacket to touch bare flesh.

'Keep walking,' Billy Stratton said calmly. 'Just keep walking or I'll shove this right through your kidneys.'

They turned into a narrow alley a few yards further along, Craig walking at the same even pace, hands thrust deep into his pockets. A lamp was bracketed to the wall at the far end and beyond, the river roared over a weir, drowning every other sound.

'A good thing I came along, wasn't it?' Stratton said. 'But then I have an instinct for these things. I knew something would go wrong just as I knew you were trouble from the first moment I clapped eyes on you. But not any more, you bastard. Not any more.'

Craig took to his heels and ran and Stratton cried out in fury and went after him. The cobbles at the end of the alley were black and shiny in the light of the old gas lamp and beyond the low wall that blocked the end, the river rushed through the darkness.

As Craig turned, Stratton paused, the knife held ready, a terrible grin splitting the white face, and then he moved with incredible speed, the blade streaking up. To Duncan Craig, it might have been a branch swaying in the breeze. He pivoted cleanly to one side, secured the wrist in a terrible aikido grip and twisted the hand back in the one way nature had never intended it should go, snapping the wrist instantly.

Stratton screamed soundlessly, his agony drowned by the roaring of the river. He staggered back clutching his broken wrist, mouthing obscenities, and as Craig picked up the knife and moved towards him, turned and stumbled away.

Craig went after him, but Stratton thundered along the alley as if all the devils in hell were at his heels, emerged into the main road and ran headlong into the path of a late-night bus.

There was a squeal of brakes as the bus skidded, a sudden cry and then silence. A moment later voices were raised and when Craig reached the end of the alley, passengers were already beginning to dismount, men crouching down to peer under the wheels.

'Oh, my God, look at him!' A woman sobbed suddenly and Craig turned up his collar and walked away quickly through the heavy rain.

11

The disk shot high into the air, poised for one split second at the high point of its trajectory and disintegrated, the sound of the gunshot reverberating through the quiet morning.

The rooks lifted into the air from their nests in the beech trees at the end of the garden, crying in alarm, and Duncan Craig laughed and lowered the automatic shotgun.

'I'm not too popular, it would seem. Let's have another.'

As Harriet leaned over the firer to insert another disk, Jenny came out through the French windows. 'There's a gentleman to see you, Colonel Craig. A Mr Vernon.'

Craig paused in the act of reloading the Gower and turned to Harriet, who straightened slowly. 'Does he now?' he said softly. 'All right, Jenny, show him out here.'

Harriet came to him quickly, anxiety on her face, and he slipped an arm about her shoulders. 'Don't get alarmed. There's nothing to worry about. Not a damned thing. Let's have another one.'

The disk soared into the air and this time he caught it on the way down, a difficult feat at the best of times, snap-shooting from the shoulder, scattering the fragments across the lawn.

'Am I supposed to be impressed?' Vernon said and Craig turned to find him standing in the French windows, Ben Carver at his shoulder.

'Well, well, if it isn't Mr Vernon,' Craig said. 'And to what do we owe the honour?'

Vernon nodded towards Harriet. 'What about her?'

Craig smiled faintly. 'Anything you say to me, you say to Harriet. She's my right arm.'

Vernon took a cigarette from a platinum case and Carver gave him a light. 'All right, Colonel, I'll put my cards on the table. I made a mistake about you, that I freely admit, but I know when I'm beaten.'

'I wish I knew what you were talking about,' Craig said.

Vernon obviously had difficulty in restraining himself. 'Let's stop beating about the bush. I've lost the Flamingo

and my place up the York Road and then Billy Stratton
meets with a nasty accident. You aren't going to tell me
I'm just experiencing a run of bad luck?'

'It can happen to the best of us.'

'All right – I'll lay it on the line. You've had your fun
– you've broken me, so I'm getting out just as soon as I
can find a buyer for what's left. I'm asking you to leave it
alone from now on – all right?'

'Oh, no, Mr Vernon,' Craig said softly. 'Not in a thousand
years. I'll see you in hell first and that's a very definite promise.'

'That's all I wanted to know.' Far from being angry Vernon
now smiled amiably. 'You're being very silly, old man. I
mean it isn't as if you've only got yourself to consider, is
it? There's Harriet here . . .'

He got no further. There was an ominous click and the
barrel of the shotgun swung round to touch his chest. Craig's
eyes seemed to look right through him and the voice was
cold and hard.

'If you even try, Vernon, I'll shoot you down like a dog.
In your own home, in the street – you'll never know when
it's coming – never feel safe again.'

For a long moment Vernon held his gaze and then quite
suddenly he nodded to Carver. 'Let's go.'

They walked across the lawn and disappeared round the
side of the house. Harriet moved to her father's side. 'Why
did he come?'

'For another look at the opposition I think. Nothing like
knowing the enemy – a cardinal rule of war and Vernon
was a good officer, make no mistake about that.'

'But what was the point of all that business about selling
out and asking you to lay off?'

'Who knows? It might have worked – perhaps that's what
he was hoping. He may even be up to something.' Duncan
Craig smiled. 'We'll have to find out, won't we?'

*

'What now, Mr Vernon?' Ben Carver said as he turned the Rolls into the main road.

'We'll go back to the club,' Vernon told him. 'After lunch I want you to drive down to Doncaster to pick up Joe Morgan. I told him to leave the London train there just in case.'

'Do I bring him back to the Flamingo?'

Vernon shook his head. 'No more indoor meetings – too risky. I'll be waiting on one of those benches next to the fountain in Park Place.'

'Thinking of Craig?'

Vernon nodded. 'There's always the odd chance that he has more of those gadgets of his planted around the place.'

'When are we going to do something about him?'

'Thursday morning,' Vernon said. 'Right after the job and just before we leave.' He leaned forward and his voice was cold. 'And you can forget about the *we* part right now. I settle with Craig personally – understand?'

It was cold in the mortuary and when Jack Brady lifted the sheet to reveal Billy Stratton's face it was pale and bloodless.

'But there isn't a mark on him,' Grant said.

'I wouldn't look any lower if I were you,' Miller told him.

'What a way to go. You're satisfied with the circumstances?'

'Oh, yes, the driver of that bus didn't stand a chance. It was raining heavily at the time and Stratton simply plunged across the road, head-down. He'd been drinking, by the way.'

'Much?'

'Five or six whiskies according to the blood sample.'

Grant nodded to Brady, who replaced the sheet. 'Who did the formal identification?'

'Ben Carver – reluctantly, I might add.'

Brady chuckled. 'I had to twist his arm a little. He wasn't too pleased.'

'Oh, well, I'm not going to weep crocodile tears over the likes of Billy Stratton,' Grant said. 'We're well rid of him.' He shivered. 'I don't know why, but this place always makes me thirsty. They must be open by now. Let's go and have one.'

The saloon bar of the George had just opened and they had the place to themselves. They stood at the bar and Grant ordered brandies all round.

'What about these two villains who had a go at Craig last night?' he asked Miller. 'Have you got anywhere with them?'

'Hurst and Blakely?' Miller shook his head. 'A couple of real hard knocks. We've had a sheet on each of them from C.R.O. a yard long.'

'Which means they were specially imported,' Brady said.

Grant nodded. 'I don't like the sound of that at all.' He swallowed some of his brandy and gazed down into the glass reflectively. 'You know I'm beginning to think I may have been wrong about this whole thing, Nick. It's just that it seemed such an incredible idea.'

'Duncan Craig's a pretty incredible person,' Miller said. 'I tried to make that clear at the very beginning.'

'Have you seen him since last night?'

Miller shook his head. 'I tried this morning, but he wasn't available. Gone to Manchester on business I was told. Of course he'll have to come in to swear a formal complaint.'

'When he does, let me know. I think I'd better have a word with him myself.'

'You'll be wasting your time, sir,' Miller said. 'He'll insist that the whole thing was quite simply a common assault and we can't prove otherwise.'

'But Hurst and Blakely won't get more than six months apiece for that.'

'Exactly.'

Grant frowned. 'There's no chance at all that they might crack and admit who hired them?'

'If I know Max Vernon, they won't even know his name,' Miller said.

Grant sighed and emptied his glass. 'All in a day's work I suppose. Let's have another one.'

'On me,' Miller said.

'Oh no you don't,' a cheerful voice interrupted. 'My round. The same again, Maggie, and make them big ones.'

Chuck Lazer grinned hugely as he climbed onto a stool next to Brady.

'What's all this?' Miller demanded. 'Last time I saw you, you were on your knees.'

'With the world falling in on me, but not now, boy. Not with the pressure off.'

'What are you talking about?'

'Max Vernon.' Lazer shrugged. 'I mean he's on the run, isn't he? Everyone knows his betting shops have taken a hammering since the Flamingo closed and now last night's little affair.'

'And what little affair would that be?' Brady put in.

'Come off it,' Chuck said. 'You know what I'm talking about. That place he was running up the York Road. The cut liquor racket.' He chuckled. 'He was making a packet there, too.'

'You mean Max Vernon was behind that place?'

'Sure – everyone knows that.' Lazer looked surprised. 'Didn't you?'

Miller looked at Grant. 'See what I mean, sir?'

Grant sighed. 'All right. So I was wrong, but just try proving it, that's all. Just try proving it.'

Park Place was a green oasis on the fringe of the city centre surrounded by old Victorian terrace houses already scheduled for demolition to make way for an inner Ring Road.

It was much favoured by office workers during their lunch-break, but at three-thirty when Max Vernon arrived it was quite deserted except for the cars parked round the edges and the small, greying man in the camel-hair coat who sat on a bench near the fountain.

He was reading a newspaper and didn't even bother to look up when Vernon sat beside him. 'I hope you aren't wasting my time?'

'Did I ever, Joe?'

'What about that Cable Diamonds job? I got nicked – five hard years while you sat laughing your head off in some fancy club or other.'

'Luck of the draw.'

'You never get involved personally, do you, Vernon? You never dirty your hands.'

'Two hundred to two hundred and ten thousand quid, Joe. Are you in or out?'

Morgan's jaw dropped. 'Two hundred grand? You must be joking.'

'I never joke. You should know that by now.'

'What's in it for me?'

'Half – you provide your own team and pay them out of your cut.'

'And what in the hell do you do?'

'I've done my share.' Vernon patted his briefcase. 'It's all here, Joe. Everything you could possibly need and it'll go like clockwork – you know me. I never miss a trick.'

'Not where you're concerned you don't.' Morgan shook his head. 'I don't know. Fifty per cent. That's a big slice to one man.'

'You'll only need three men in the team. Give them ten thousand each – contract it beforehand. That still leaves you with seventy – maybe more.' Morgan sat there, a frown on his face, and Vernon shrugged. 'Please yourself. I'll get somebody else.'

He started to his feet and Morgan pulled him back. 'All right – no need to get shirty. I'm in.'

'On my terms?'

'Whatever you say. When do we make the touch?'

'Wednesday night.'

'You must be joking. That only gives us two days.'

'No, it's got to be then – you'll see why in a moment. There's an express to London in an hour. You'll catch it easily. That'll give you plenty of time to recruit your team, gather your gear together and be back here by tomorrow night.'

'What will I need?'

'That depends. You'll do the vault yourself?'

'Naturally. What is it?'

'Bodine-Martin 53 – the latest model. Burglar proof naturally.'

'They always are.' Morgan chuckled. 'A snip.'

'What will you use – nitro?'

'Not on your life.' Morgan shook his head. 'There's some new stuff the Army's been experimenting with going the rounds. Handles like nitro, but three times as powerful. It'll open that vault up like a sardine can.'

'How long will you need?'

'On the vault itself?' He shrugged. 'I'll have to cut a hole into the lock. Let's say forty-five minutes.'

'And twenty to get you inside.' Vernon nodded. 'Just over an hour. Let's say an hour and a half from going in to coming out.'

'Sounds too good to be true.'

'You'll need a good wheelman to stand by with the car.'

'Frankie Harris is available. He's just out of the Ville. Could do with some gelt.'

'What about a labourer?'

'That's settled to start with – Johnny Martin. He knows how I like things done.'

'And a good heavy and I don't mean some punch-drunk old has-been. You'll need someone who can really handle himself, just in case of trouble, though I don't think he'll even have to flex his muscles.'

'I know just the man,' Morgan said. 'Jack Fallon. He used to run with Bart Keegan and the Poplar boys, but they had a row.'

Vernon nodded approvingly. 'That's a good choice. I remember Fallon. He's got brains, too.'

'Okay – now that's settled let's get down to brass tacks. What's the pitch?'

'Chatsworth Iron & Steel down by the river. Only five minutes from where we are now as a matter of fact. Nine thousand workers and the management are still daft enough to pay them in cash. It takes the staff two days to make the wages up, which means there's never less than two hundred thousand, sometimes as much as two hundred and twenty in the vault Wednesday and Thursday, depending on earnings of course.'

'Isn't there a night shift?'

'Only for the workers. The admin. side closes down at five-thirty on the dot. It's housed in a brand-new ten-storey office block between the factory and the river and they've installed just about every kind of alarm known to man.'

'Bound to with loot like that lying around. How do we get in?'

'About a hundred yards from the factory there's a side street called Brag Alley. I've marked it on the map I'm giving you. Lift the manhole at the far end and you'll find yourself in a tunnel about three feet in diameter that carries the Electricity Board main cables. You'll know when you've reached Chatsworth Steel because they've been obliging enough to paint it on the wall. There's a single-course brick wall between you and the cellars of the office block. If it takes you longer than ten minutes to get through that I'll eat my hat.'

'What about the alarm system?'

'I'm coming to that. When you get into the cellar you'll find a battery of fuse boxes on the far wall and they're all numbered. I've numbered the ones you'll have to switch off in your instructions, but the most important thing to remember is to cut the green cable you'll find running along the skirting board. It looks innocent enough, but it controls an alarm feeder system in case the others fail.'

'Are the vaults on the same level?'

'That's right – at the far end of the corridor.'

'What about night guards?'

'They only have one.' Morgan raised his eyebrows incredulously and Vernon grinned. 'I told you they'd installed every gadget known to man. The whole place is rigged for closed-circuit television, which is operated by one man from a control room off the main entrance hall. The moment you leave that cellar and walk down the passage you'll be giving a command performance. All he does is lift the 'phone and the coppers are all over you before you know it.'

'Okay,' Morgan said. 'The suspense is killing me. How do we sort that one out?'

'They run a three-shift system and our man takes over at eight. He always stops in at a little café near the main gates for sandwiches and a flask of coffee. On Wednesday night he'll get more than he bargained for.'

'Something in his coffee?'

Vernon grinned. 'Simple when you know how.'

Morgan looked dubious. 'What if he hasn't had a drink by the time we arrive? We'd be in dead lumber.'

'I've thought of that. You won't break in till midnight. That gives him four hours. If he hasn't had a drink by then, he never will.'

There was a long silence as Morgan sat staring into the distance, a slight frown on his face. After a while he sighed and shook his head.

'I've got to give it to you, Max. It's good – it's bloody good.'

'See you tomorrow night then,' Vernon said calmly and passed him the briefcase. 'Everything you need is in there. Your train leaves at five o'clock. You've got twenty minutes.'

He watched Morgan disappear into the side street in the far corner of the square and nodded. So far, so good. The sun burst through the clouds, touching the fine spray of the fountain with colour and he smiled. There were times when life could really be very satisfying. He lit a cigarette, got to his feet and strolled away.

Duncan Craig watched him leave from the rear window of the old Commer van which was parked on the far side of the square. He, too, was smiling, but for a completely different reason. He turned and patted the chromium barrel of the directional microphone mounted on its tripod and started to dismantle it.

12

It was raining hard when the van turned into Brag Alley and braked to a halt, the light from the headlamps picking out the faded lettering of the sign on the wooden doors that blocked the far end. *Gower & Co – Monumental Masons.*

'This is it,' Morgan said. 'Right – let's have you, Jack.'

Fallon, a large, heavily built Irishman, jumped out, a pair of two-foot cutters in his hands that sliced through the padlock that secured the gates like a knife through butter. The gates swung open and Harris, the wheelman, took the van into the yard and cut the engine.

Fallon was already levering up the manhole in the alley and Morgan and Martin unloaded the van quickly and joined him. He dropped into the tunnel and they passed down the heavy cylinders for the oxy-acetylene cutter and the other equipment and followed him.

Harris dropped to one knee and Morgan whispered 'Replace the manhole, shut yourself into the yard and sit tight. An hour and a quarter at the most.'

The manhole clanged into place above his head as he dropped down to join the others. He switched on the powerful battery lantern he carried and its beam cut into the darkness. In spite of the thick cables, there was room to crawl and he moved off without a word, Fallon and Martin following, each dragging a canvas hold-all containing the equipment.

It was bitterly cold, the insulating jackets of the heavy cables damp with condensation, and at one point there was a sudden whispering like dead leaves rustling through a forest in the evening and a pair of eyes gleamed through the darkness.

'Jesus Christ, rats,' Jack Fallon said. 'I can't stand them.'

'At these prices you can afford to,' Morgan said and paused as his torch picked out the name Chatsworth Steel painted in white letters on the wall. 'Here we are.'

'Not much room to swing,' Martin commented.

'Never mind that. Get the bloody gear out and let's have a go.'

Martin was a small, undersized man with prematurely white hair, but his arms and shoulders were over-developed from a spell of working in the rock quarry at Dartmoor and he lay on his side and swung vigorously with a seven-pound hammer at the cold chisel which Fallon held in position.

When the wall gave, it was not one, but a dozen bricks which collapsed suddenly into the cellar on the other side. Martin grinned, his teeth gleaming in the light of the lamp.

'There's present-day British workmanship for you. I don't know what the country's coming to.'

Morgan shone his lantern into the darkness on the other side and picked out the control panel at once. 'Come on, let's get in there,' he said. 'We're right on time. Let's keep it that way.'

It was the work of a couple of minutes to enlarge the hole sufficiently to allow him to pass through and he left the others to manage the equipment and made straight for the control panel.

There were thirty-seven boxes on the board, each one numbered, and he had to pull the switch on nine of them. He had memorized the numbers, but checked them from the list Vernon had given him just to make sure.

'Everything okay?' Martin said at his shoulder.

'Couldn't be sweeter.' Morgan dropped to one knee, located the green cable running along the edge of the skirting board and severed it neatly with a pair of pocket cutters. 'That's it unless Vernon's made a mistake somewhere, which I doubt.'

When he opened the door, the outside corridor was brilliantly lit by neon light. 'What in the hell is the idea of that?' Martin demanded.

'For the television cameras, you fool. They wouldn't see much in the dark, would they?' Morgan led the way out into the corridor and grinned tightly. 'Keep your fingers crossed. If that bloke upstairs is still awake, he's seen us already.'

'I can't see any cameras,' Martin said in bewilderment.

'No, but they can see you.' Morgan paused at the foot of the service stairs. 'You stay here. Jack and I will go and take a look.'

He went up the stairs quickly. The door at the top had a Yale lock and therefore opened from the inside with no difficulty.

The hall was tiled in black and white and brilliantly illuminated, its great glass doors protected by a bronze security grill. Morgan knew exactly where he was making for. He crossed the hall quickly, found the third door on the right with *Control Room* painted on it in black letters and turned the handle gently.

The guard had obviously tumbled from the black leather swivel chair in front of the control panel and sprawled on his face. The thermos flask stood open on a small table at one side and Morgan poured a little into the empty cup and tested it.

'Cold – he's been out for ages.'

'Would you look at this now?' Fallon said in wonder.

There were at least thirty separate screens on the control panel. Not only was every entrance to the building covered, but cameras had obviously been positioned at strategic sites in all the main corridors.

'There's Johnny,' Fallon said, pointing.

They could see Martin clearly as he stood in the basement corridor, the two canvas hold-alls at his feet.

'Looks nervous, doesn't he?' Morgan said and leaned forward. 'There's the entrance to the strongroom and that's a picture of the vault door. Look, they've even got a shot of the interior. Would you credit it.'

'It's fantastic,' Fallon said. 'You can see everything from up here.'

Morgan nodded. 'Come to think of it, it might be a good idea if you stayed up here, Jack. You've got every entrance to the building covered. If anyone did turn up, you'd know in a flash. Johnny and I can manage below.'

'And how will I know when to join you?' Fallon said.

'You'll see on the screen, won't you?'

Fallon grinned delightedly. 'And so I will. Off you go then, Joe, and God bless the good work.'

*

Morgan went down the service stairs quickly and rejoined Martin. 'Let's get moving,' he said and picked up one of the canvas hold-alls.

The entrance to the strongroom was at the end of the passage, a steel door with a double padlock that took him exactly three minutes to pick.

He crossed the room quickly and examined the face of the vault door, testing the handles. Behind him, Martin had already got the first cylinder out of his hold-all. He screwed home one end of the flexible hose that connected it to the blow torch and ignited the flame.

Morgan pulled on a pair of protective goggles and held out his hand. 'Okay, let's get to work,' he said.

A few moments later he was cutting into the steel face of the vault, six inches to the right of the locking mechanism, with the precision of an expert.

For something like forty-five minutes, Jack Fallon had a seat at the show that couldn't have been bettered if he'd been sitting in the front circle at his local cinema. He leaned back in the swivel chair, smoking one cigarette after the other, intent on the drama that was being enacted below.

He was at Morgan's side when he finished cutting the hole and waited, biting his fingernails, while the explosive was gently poured inside the lock, sealed with a plastic compound and fused.

He heard no noise, but the visual effect of the explosion was dramatic enough. The door seemed to tremble, then a portion of it around the lock seemed to disintegrate before his eyes and smoke rose in a cloud.

He saw Morgan and Martin rush forward, heaving on the door together, swinging it open, and switched his gaze to the next screen in time to see them enter the interior of the vault itself.

He jumped to his feet, excitement racing through him,

started to turn away and paused, a cold chill spreading through his body.

He was looking at another screen – the one that gave a view of the passageway linking the cellar by which they had entered the building with the strongroom. A man was moving along the passage cautiously, tall and dark in sweater and pants, gloves on his hands and a nylon stocking pulled over his face.

Fallon cursed savagely, turned and ran to the door, knocking over the chair in his haste.

Beyond the van a monumental cross reared into the night and here and there, marble tombstones gleamed palely. The mason's yard was dark and lonely, a place of shadows that was too much like a cemetery for comfort and Frankie Harris huddled into the driver's seat miserably, hands thrust deep into the pockets of his overcoat.

He was getting old, that was the trouble – too old for this sort of action by night. He seemed to have been waiting there for hours and yet it was no more than forty-five minutes since his three companions had entered the manhole.

His feet were so cold that he could no longer feel them and after a while he opened the door and stepped into the rain. He walked up and down for a minute or two, stamping his feet to restore the circulation, and then paused to light a cigarette, his hands cupped around the flaring match.

He gave a sudden, terrible start as the light picked a face out of the night – a dark, formless face lacking eyes and mouth that could belong to nothing human.

He staggered back in horror, the match dropping from his nerveless fingers, and his throat was seized in a grip of iron.

'Frank Harris?' The thing had a voice. 'You're just out of the Ville, aren't you?'

The pressure was released and Harris nodded violently. 'That's right.'

'How long?'

'Ten days.'

'You bloody fool.' Suddenly he found himself being jerked round and propelled towards the gate. 'Now start running,' the voice said harshly, 'and don't stop. Anything that happens to you after this, you deserve.'

Harris ran along the alley as he hadn't run since he was a boy and when he reached the end, paused, leaning against the wall.

'Christ Jesus,' he sobbed. 'Oh, Christ Jesus.'

After a while he pulled himself together, turned into the main road and started walking briskly in the direction of the Central Station.

Duncan Craig moved rapidly along the tunnel towards the patch of light that streamed in through the broken wall from the cellar. When he reached the opening he paused to examine his watch, wondering if he had timed things right and a sudden, muffled explosion reverberating throughout the basement told him that he had.

He dropped into the cellar and moved out into the passage, a strange and sinister figure in his dark clothing, a nylon stocking pulled down over his face.

A cloud of dust and smoke filtered out through the half open door of the strongroom at the far end of the passage and he moved towards it cautiously and peered inside.

The room was full of dust and smoke and beyond through the half open vault door, he was aware of a vague movement. He stepped back into the passageway and slammed the strongroom door shut, jerking down the handle, the locking bolts clanging into their sockets with a grim finality. Without the key he was unable to actually lock the door, but the important thing was that it would be impossible for it to be opened from the inside. He turned and moved back along the passage.

As he passed the entrance to the service stairs, Fallon

jumped on him from five steps up, fourteen stone of bone and muscle driving Craig into the floor.

For the moment, he was winded and as he struggled for air, the Irishman's massive forearm wrapped itself around his throat. As the pressure increased, Craig rammed the point of his right elbow back hard, catching Fallon in the stomach just under the rib cage. Fallon gasped and again Craig drove his elbow home with all his force. As the Irishman's grip slackened, Craig twisted round and slammed him backwards with the heel of his hand.

Fallon rolled against the wall, the instinct derived from a hundred street fights bringing him to his feet in a reflex action, but Craig was already up and waiting for him. As Fallon moved in, Craig's right foot flicked out in a perfectly executed karate front kick that caught the Irishman in the stomach. He started to keel over, and Craig's knee lifted into his face like a battering ram, sending him into darkness.

Ruth Miller waved the last of her guests goodbye and closed the door. She looked at her watch and smothered a yawn. One o'clock. A good party and the clearing up could wait till morning. She started across the hall and the 'phone rang.

Nick Miller and his brother were having a final drink in front of the fire when she looked in. 'It's for you, Nick. He wouldn't say who he was. I do hope you don't have to go out.'

'On a night like this? Not on your life.' He went out into the hall and picked up the 'phone.

'That you, Miller?'

'Yes, who is it?'

'Never mind that. Chatsworth Iron & Steel – they usually keep a couple of hundred thousand in their vault on a Wednesday night, don't they? You'd better get down there

quick. They almost lost it.' There was a hoarse chuckle.
'Poor old Maxie. Talk about the best-laid schemes . . .'

But Miller had already cut him off and was dialling the
best-known telephone number in England furiously.

The main C.I.D. office was a hive of industry when Grant
entered at two a.m. and Miller got up from his desk and
went to meet him.

'Well, this is a turn up for the book and no mistake,'
Grant said.

'You've had a look at Chatsworth's, sir?'

'Never seen anything like it. Any chance of a cup of tea?'

Miller nodded to a young D.C. who disappeared at once
and they went into Grant's office.

'What about the guard?'

'I've just had a 'phone call from the man I sent with him
to the Infirmary. Apparently his coffee was laced with
enough chloral hydrate to put him asleep for twelve hours
so he still hasn't come round.'

'Who have we got in the bag?'

'Joe Morgan for one.'

'Have we, by George?' Grant's eyebrows went up. 'We
certainly don't need a scratch sheet on him. One of the best
petermen in the game. Was Johnny Martin with him?'

Miller nodded. 'That's right.'

'I thought so – they usually work together. Who else?'

'We found a nasty-looking piece of work lying in the
basement passageway. He'd taken quite a beating.'

'Is he okay now?'

'Alive and kicking, but making things awkward for us.
Jack Brady's running his fingerprints through C.R.O. now.
We found their transport, by the way, parked in a monumental mason's yard in Brag Alley at the other end of the
tunnel which they used to gain access. No sign of a
wheelman.'

'Maybe they didn't use one.'

'Could be – I've put out a general call anyway, just in case.'

The tea arrived and Grant drank some gratefully, warming his hands around the cup. 'Fantastic, Nick – that's the only word for it. This thing was planned to the last inch, you realize that don't you? They'd have been in London by morning. God knows where after that.'

'Except for an elusive someone who shut the strongroom door on Morgan and Martin and left this other bloke lying unconscious in the passageway.'

'Your informer, presumably. And he mentioned Vernon?'

'As far as I'm concerned he did. Vernon's the only Maxie I know and planning a job like this would be right up his street.'

Grant emptied his cup and sighed. 'I suppose you think it's Craig?'

'I can't see who else it could be.'

'No, I suppose not.'

'Do I pull him in for questioning?'

'On what charge?' Grant spread his hands. 'We'd have to think up a brand-new one just for him.'

'What about accessory before the fact? He knew the caper was coming off – he should have passed on the information to us.'

'I can't imagine a judge giving him more than a stern wigging for that. Anyway, how could Craig have obtained such detailed information?'

'Simple,' Miller said. 'He's an electronics expert. Directional microphones, transistor transmitters the size of matchboxes, fountain pen receivers. You name it, he's got it.'

'Nothing illegal in that considering the nature of his business.' Grant shook his head. 'Proof, Nick – real proof. That's what you need. You haven't got it and you never will have unless I miss my guess.'

'All right,' Miller said. 'You win. What about Vernon? Do we bring him in?'

Grant hesitated. 'No, let him stew for a while. He's always covered his tracks perfectly in the past so there's no reason to think things will be any easier for us this time. If we're going to get him, it must be through Morgan and his boys. Put two men on watch at his club and leave it at that for the moment.'

Brady knocked on the door and entered, a sheaf of tele-type flimsies in his hand. 'I thought I'd get the facts on all of them while I was at it. Our awkward friend is a bloke called Jack Fallon – a real tearaway. He's even done time for manslaughter.'

'He certainly met his match this time,' Grant said.

Miller was reading the reports quickly and he suddenly frowned. 'Cable Diamonds – that has a familiar sound.'

'It should have,' Brady said. 'It was mentioned in that confidential file on Vernon that we got from C.R.O. in London. Another of the jobs he was supposed to be behind.'

Miller grinned. 'You're going to love this, sir,' he said to Grant and passed one of the flimsies across. 'Joe Morgan was nicked for that job after getting clean away. He did five years, but the diamonds were never recovered.'

'He doesn't seem to be having much luck with Max Vernon, does he?' Brady said.

Grant nodded and got to his feet. 'Let's go and remind him of that fact, shall we?'

13

From one-thirty onwards Max Vernon knew in his heart that something had gone badly wrong. By two-fifteen he was sure of it. He poured himself a large brandy, went to his desk and flicked one of the switches on the intercom.

'Get in here, Ben.'

The door opened a few moments later and Carver entered. 'Yes, Mr Vernon?'

'Something's up – they're way over time. Take the car and go for a drive past Chatsworth's. See if you can see any action.'

Carver nodded obediently and left and Vernon lit a cigarette and moved across to the fire. He stared down into the flames, a frown on his face. What could have possibly gone wrong? It didn't make any kind of sense. The thing was foolproof.

The door swung open behind him and Carver came in looking pale and excited. 'A couple of coppers out front, Mr Vernon.'

'Are you sure?'

'Certain – I can smell 'em a mile away. I'll show you.'

Vernon followed him out into the corridor and Carver turned into the cloakroom and paused by the window. 'I came in for my overcoat. Lucky I didn't turn on the light.' He pointed across to the sycamore on the other side of the fence beyond the first street lamp. 'There, in the shadows.'

'Yes, I've got them.'

'What do you think?'

'I think it stinks to high heaven,' Vernon said, and the telephone started to ring in the other room.

He moved back quickly, Carver at his heels, and stood by the desk looking down at the 'phone.

'It's Morgan,' Carver said. 'It has to be. Who else would be ringing in at this time in the morning?'

'We'll see shall we? You take it on the extension.' Vernon lifted the receiver. 'Max Vernon here.'

'That you, old man?' Craig's voice rang mockingly in his

ear. 'I'm afraid Joe Morgan and his boys won't be able to join you after all. They ran into a little trouble.'

Vernon sank down in his chair. 'I'll kill you for this, Craig.'

'You've had it,' Craig said cheerfully. 'Joe Morgan and his boys are being squeezed dry at this very moment. How long do you think it will be before one of them spills his guts? You're on borrowed time, Vernon.'

'As long as I've enough left for you that's all I ask,' Vernon said.

'Sorry, old man. I've decided to take myself off into the country for a couple of days' shooting. Nothing like a change of pace. If you want me, you'll have to come looking.'

He was still chuckling as Vernon slammed down the receiver. Carver replaced the extension 'phone, a bewildered look on his face. 'But how could he have known?'

'How the hell do I know? Another of his damned gadgets probably.'

'What do we do now?'

'Get out while the going's good – on foot the back way. I've got an old Ford brake parked in a lock-up garage on the other side of the river. I always did believe in covering every eventuality.'

'Where are we going, Mr Vernon – Ireland?'

'You can if you like. I can manage a couple of hundred. That should see you through.'

'What about you?'

Vernon unlocked a drawer in his desk and took out a Luger pistol. 'I've got an account to settle.'

'With Craig? You don't even know where he's going.'

'I shouldn't imagine I'll have any difficulty in finding out.'

Carver frowned in bewilderment. 'I don't get it.'

'A challenge, Benny. A challenge – something you wouldn't understand.'

'You mean Craig wants you to follow him?'

Vernon opened the wall safe and took out a black cash box. 'That's the general idea.' He returned to his desk with the cash box and unlocked it. 'This is what he's been aiming at from the beginning – him and me in a final showdown, but he's made a big mistake.' When Vernon smiled he looked like the Devil incarnate. 'I was a good man in the jungle, Ben – the best there was. Craig's still got to find that out.'

He opened the cash box, tossed two packets of fivers across and started to fill his pockets with the rest. 'There's two hundred there and good luck to you.'

Carver shook his head slowly and threw the money back. 'We've been together a long time, Mr Vernon. I'm not dropping out now.'

Vernon stared at him incredulously. 'Loyalty at this stage, Ben?' And then he laughed harshly and clapped him on the shoulder. 'All right then. Let's see if we can't show the bastard a thing or two.'

'But who turned you in, Morgan, that's what I can't understand?' Miller said.

It was just after four a.m. and the pale green walls of the Interrogation Room seemed to float out of the shadows, unreal and transitory as if they might disappear at any moment.

Joe Morgan sat at the plain wooden table under a strong central light that made him look old and sunken. Brady leaned against the wall near the window and a young constable stood stolidly in the corner.

'Nobody turned us in. The whole thing went sour, that's all.'

'Then who closed the strongroom door on you and Martin?'

'I don't know – maybe it just slammed shut.'

'All right, miracles sometimes happen. That still doesn't

explain how we found Jack Fallon lying beaten and unconscious in the passageway.'

Morgan didn't reply and Brady said helpfully, 'Maybe
Fallon just doesn't like you any more. Maybe he decided
to lock you and Martin in the strongroom just for kicks and
took off. Unfortunately he tripped and fell in the passage,
knocking himself unconscious.'

Morgan turned away contemptuously. 'You ought to see
a psychiatrist.'

'We'll provide you with one for free,' Miller said. 'You're
going to need him badly, Morgan. You're going to sit for
the next ten years staring at the wall, asking yourself the
same question over and over again until it drives you out
of your mind.'

Morgan snapped, suddenly and completely. 'But I don't
know what went wrong. I don't know.' He hammered on
the table with a clenched fist. 'Can't you get that through
your thick skull?'

In the silence which followed Grant peered round the
door, eyebrows raised. Miller shook his head, nodded to
Brady and they joined the Superintendent in the corridor.

'Anything?' Grant said.

Miller shook his head. 'No more success than we've had
with the others.'

'He seems genuinely bewildered to me,' Brady put in. 'I
get the impression he'd like to know what happened as
much as anybody.'

'Right,' Grant said briskly. 'This is where keeping them
separate might have paid off. Put them together in cell 15
and let's see what happens.'

When the constable pushed Joe Morgan into the cell, Martin
was sitting despondently on a bench against the wall. Morgan
frowned in bewilderment as the door closed behind him.

'What is this?'

Martin shrugged. 'Search me.'

'Maybe the place is wired for sound?'

Morgan looked the walls over carefully and behind him, the door opened again and Jack Fallon was pushed into the cell. He looked a mess. His lips were swollen and gashed, several teeth missing and the front of his shirt was soaked in blood.

He staggered forward, a wild look in his eyes and grabbed Morgan by the lapels. 'What happened for Christ's sake? Who was he?'

Morgan tore himself free with some difficulty. 'Who was who?'

'The bloke who came in through the tunnel and locked you and Johnny in the strongroom.'

'What are you talking about?' Morgan demanded.

'I'm trying to tell you. I saw him on the bloody television screen. Big bloke all in black with a stocking over his face. He locked you and Johnny in the strongroom and I jumped him from the stairs.'

'You had a barney?'

'Not for long. Henry Cooper couldn't have hit me any harder than he did.'

'Maybe it was Harris?' Martin said.

'Do me a favour.' Fallon laughed harshly. 'I could break him in two with one hand tied behind my back. It wouldn't make sense anyway. What would he stand to gain?'

'Then why haven't they put him in with the rest of us?'

'Search me.'

Morgan turned away, his hands gripped tightly together. 'Only one man knew we were pulling this caper,' he said. 'The man who organized it.'

'Vernon?' Martin's eyes widened. 'It don't make sense, Joe.'

'I've just got one prayer,' Morgan said. 'That one day they put him in the same nick as me. That's all I ask.'

In the next cell, Grant reached up to switch off the tannoy and nodded to Miller and Brady. 'That'll do me. In we go.'

They went out into the passage and the constable who was standing at the door of cell 15 unlocked it quickly and stood back.

'Did I hear somebody mention Max Vernon's name?' Grant said as he led the way in.

'Why don't you take a running jump at yourself,' Morgan told him bitterly.

'Oh, to hell with it.' Jack Fallon cursed savagely. 'If you think I'm going to rot while that bastard goes free you can think again. If you don't tell him, I will.'

'You don't have much luck with Vernon, do you?' Grant said to Morgan. 'Remember that Cable Diamond affair? I suppose he saw you all right when you came out.'

'Five hundred,' Morgan said. 'Five hundred quid for five bloody years in the nick.' The anger came pouring out of him in an uncontrollable flood. 'All right – Vernon's your man and much good it'll do you. We were supposed to be back at his place no later than one-thirty. If he's still there when you call then I'm Santa Claus.'

It was almost five-thirty when Miller went into Grant's office. The Superintendent was reading through the statements made by Morgan and his cronies and looked up sharply.

'Any luck?'

'Not a sign. Must have cleared out the back way on foot. I've put out a general call. We've alerted the County and the Regional Crime Squad as well.'

'He'll probably try for the Irish boat at Liverpool.' Grant said. 'He won't get far.'

'I'm not so sure, sir. What if he's still in town?'

'Why should he be?'

'There's always Craig. He has a score to settle there.'

'I shouldn't think he'd be foolish enough to hang around while he still had time to get out.'

'All the same, sir, I'd like your permission to give Craig a ring. I'd feel happier.'

Grant leaned back in his chair and looked at him reflectively. 'You like him, don't you?'

'I suppose the simple answer to that is yes – a hell of a lot.'

Grant indicated the 'phone on his desk with a sweep of his hand. 'Be my guest.'

The 'phone rang for a long time at the other end before it was lifted and Harriet Craig said sleepily, 'Yes, who is it?'

'Harriet – is that you? Nick Miller here.'

'Nick?' There was a pause and he had a mental picture of her struggling up onto one elbow, a be-wildered frown on her face. 'Nick, what time is it?'

'Twenty to six. I was hoping to speak to your father.'

'I'm afraid he's gone away for a few days.' Suddenly, her voice changed and she came wide awake.

'What is it, Nick? Is something wrong?'

There was genuine alarm in her voice and he hastened to reassure her. 'Everything's all right, I promise you. Are you on your own?'

'No, Jenny's here.'

'Tell you what. How would you like to give me breakfast? I'll tell you all about it then.'

'That's fine by me. What time?'

'Seven-thirty too early?'

'Not at all. If you think I could go to sleep again after this you're mistaken.'

Miller replaced the receiver and turned to Grant. 'She's on her own – her father's out of town. Mind if I put a car on watch up there? Just in case.'

'Just in case?' Grant said and smiled. 'Young love – it's marvellous. Go on – get out of here.'

*

It was raining heavily when Miller drove up to the house and the patrol car was parked by the entrance to the drive. He got out of the Cooper and walked across and the driver wound down his window.

'Anything?' Miller asked.

'Not a thing, sarge. Some bird came out of the door about five minutes ago and took a walk in the garden, that's all. She must be nuts in this weather.'

'Okay,' Miller said. 'I'll take over. You can shove off now.'

The patrol car moved away and he got back into the Cooper and drove up to the house. As he got out, a voice hailed him and he turned to find Harriet crossing the lawn. She was wearing an old trenchcoat of her father's and a scarf was bound around her head peasant-fashion.

'I saw the police car at the gate when I came downstairs,' she said, her face grave. 'What is it, Nick?'

'Maybe we'd better go inside.'

'No, I'd rather not. Jenny's in the kitchen . . .'

'And she doesn't know what you and your father have been up to, is that it?'

She turned away, an angry flush staining her cheeks, and he pulled her round to face him. 'You said your father had gone away for a few days. Is that the truth?'

'Of course it is.'

'And you didn't know what he was up to last night?'

She shook her head, her eyes anxious. 'Please, Nick – I don't know what you're talking about.'

He looked at her searchingly for a moment and then nodded. 'All right – I believe you.'

He sketched in the events of the night briefly and when he finished, she looked pale and drawn. 'I can't believe it.'

'But you knew about the other things.'

She gazed up at him searchingly. 'Are you here as a friend, Nick, or as a policeman?'

'As a friend, damn you.' He took her hands and held them fast. 'You must believe that.'

She nodded. 'Yes, I knew about the other things. It seemed wrong somehow that Max Vernon should get away with what he did.' She looked up at him fiercely. 'I'm not sorry.'

'You will be if he gets his hands on your father.'

'You think that's possible?'

'Not really, he's too many other problems facing him at the moment, but you never can tell what a man like Vernon might pull. We'd better give your father a ring just in case.'

'But there isn't a 'phone,' she said. 'He's staying in our houseboat on the river at Grimsdyke.'

'In the marshes?'

'That's right, he goes for the shooting.'

'That's about twenty miles, isn't it?'

'Eighteen on the clock.'

'Good – we'll drive down and see him. It's early yet and the roads will be quiet. Shouldn't take more than half an hour.'

She nodded briefly. 'I'd better tell Jenny. I'll only be a moment.'

She turned and ran across the lawn to the terrace and Miller walked back to the car.

It was no more than ten minutes after they had left when the 'phone rang and Jenny answered it on the kitchen extension.

'Colonel Craig's residence.'

The voice was smooth and charming. 'Good morning – my name's Fullerton. Gregory Fullerton. I'm a colleague of Colonel Craig's. He told me he was going away for a few days and gave me his address so that I could get in touch with him if anything came up. Damned stupid of me, but I've mislaid it.'

'It's the houseboat you'll be wanting, sir,' Jenny said. 'That's on the river at Grimsdyke in the marshes about a mile south of Culler's Bend.'

'So kind of you.'

'Not at all.' She replaced the receiver and went back to her work.

When Max Vernon emerged from the telephone box at the end of the small country lane he was grinning wolfishly. He opened the door of the brake and climbed into the passenger seat next to Carver.

'Right, Benny boy, we're in business,' he said. 'Let's have a look at that map.'

14

The marsh at Grimsdyke on the river estuary was a wild lonely place of sea-creeks and mud flats and great pale barriers of reeds higher than a man's head. Since the beginning of time men had come here for one purpose or another – Roman, Saxon, Dane, Norman, but in the twentieth century it was a place of ghosts, an alien world inhabited mainly by the birds, curlew and redshank and the brent geese coming south from Siberia to winter on the flats.

Miller turned the Cooper off the main road at Culler's Bend and followed a track no wider than a farm cart that was little more than a raised causeway of grass. On either side, miles of rough marsh grass and reeds marched into the heavy rain and a thin sea mist was drifting in before the wind.

Harriet lowered the window and took a deep breath of the salt-laden air. 'Marvellous – I love coming here. It's like nowhere else on earth – a different world.'

'I must say I'm impressed,' he said. 'I've never been here before.'

'Lost in a marsh punt in a sea mist it can be terrifying,' she said. 'In some places there are quicksands and mud-holes deep enough to swallow a cart.'

The closer they got to the estuary, the more the mist closed in on them until visibility was reduced to no more than twenty yards. Finally the track emerged into a wide clearing of rough grass surrounded by thorn trees. Craig's Jaguar was parked under one of them and Miller braked to a halt.

'We have to walk from here,' Harriet said. 'It isn't very far.'

They followed a narrow path through the reeds. Wildfowl lifted out of the mist in alarm and somewhere a curlew called eerily. The marsh was stirring now, water swirling through it with an angry sucking noise, gurgling in crab holes, baring shining expanses of black mud.

'If we don't hurry we might miss him,' Harriet said. 'The tide's on the ebb. The best time for duck.'

She half-ran along the track and Miller followed her and suddenly, the wind was cold on his face and she called through the rain, waving her hand.

The mist had cleared a little so that one could see the river, the houseboat moored to the bank forty or fifty yards away. Duncan Craig was about to step into a flat-bottomed marsh punt and straightened, looking towards them.

He was wearing an old paratrooper's beret and combat jacket and carried a shotgun under one arm. He stood there staring at them, one hand shielding his eyes from the rain and then ran forward suddenly.

His face was white and set when he grabbed Harriet by the arm, the first time Miller had known him to show real emotion. 'What the hell are you doing here?'

Harriet was bewildered by the anger in his voice. 'What is it, Daddy? What's wrong?'

'We tried to arrest Max Vernon early this morning, but he gave us the slip,' Miller told him. 'I thought you ought to know he was on the loose.'

Craig gave Harriet a quick push forward. 'Get her out of here, Miller! Get her out now before it's too late!'

Harriet swung round, her face white, and Miller said softly, 'My God, you're actually expecting him, aren't you? You've arranged the whole damned thing?'

'Every step of the way.' Craig patted the shotgun. 'Vernon shall have his chance – all part of the game.'

'It isn't a game any longer, you bloody fool,' Miller said. 'Can't you get that through your head? If Max Vernon comes looking for you he'll have only one thought on his mind.'

'Which suits me just fine.' Suddenly there was iron in his voice. 'No more arguments. Just get Harriet out of here.'

Miller shrugged and said evenly, 'All right, if that's the way you want it. I might point out that the first thing I shall do is contact the County Police.'

'Good luck to you. There's a village bobby at Culler's Bend two miles up the road – Jack Berkley. He's fifty years of age and it takes him all his time to get on his bicycle.'

'They do have such things as patrol cars.'

'Fair enough – it'll be interesting to see just how efficient they are.'

'He isn't worth it, Craig,' Miller said desperately. 'He isn't worth what it would do to you.'

'He murdered my daughter,' Craig said calmly. 'He wasn't even fit to tie her shoes, but I'm still giving him his chance, Nick. God help me, but I can't play the game any other way.'

'Which means only one thing in the final analysis. That you won't be able to kill him,' Miller said. 'Can't you see that? It's the essential difference between you and Vernon.'

Craig didn't reply and Harriet simply stood there, white

and terrified. Miller sighed and took her arm. 'All right.
Let's get going.'

When they reached the clearing, he helped Harriet into the
passenger seat of the Cooper, climbed behind the wheel
quickly and started the engine. He slid back the window
and leaned out.

'For the last time, Duncan – please.'

Craig smiled strangely and leaned down. 'Thanks, Nick
– for everything. Now get her out of it, there's a good chap.'

Miller moved into gear and took the Cooper back along
the track and beside him Harriet started to sob bitterly.

'Oh, Nick, I'm so afraid,' she said. 'He isn't like Vernon
– not when it comes down to it. He's going to die. I know
he is.'

'Not if I can help it.' Miller said and braked violently as
a Ford station wagon appeared from the mist.

The two cars were not more than twenty feet apart. For
one horrified moment they stared at Max Vernon and Carver
and then Miller slammed the stick into reverse and took
the Cooper back along the track.

Vernon jumped out of the Ford, the Luger in his hand,
and fired twice, his second shot punching a hole in the
Cooper's windscreen. It slewed wildly and went half over
the edge of the track.

As Miller got the door open Duncan Craig appeared on
the run. He dropped to one knee and fired once in the
direction of the Ford.

'You two all right?'

Harriet nodded shakily. 'I think so.'

'Get her down into the reeds,' he told Miller briskly. 'I'll
lead them off. As soon as they pass, get her out of here.'

He scrambled to his feet before Miller could argue and
ran through the mist towards the Ford.

*

Vernon waited, the Luger ready, and Carver crouched on the other side of the Ford, a Smith & Wesson revolver in his hand.

'Do you think it was Craig who fired that shot, Mr Vernon?'

Craig answered for himself, his voice drifting mockingly out of the mist. 'So you got here, Vernon? All right, then. Let's see how good you really are.'

For a brief moment he appeared from the mist and turned and ran and Vernon went after him, cold with excitement.

They reached the Cooper half-blocking the track and Craig called, 'This way, Vernon! This way!'

As they disappeared into the mist, Miller emerged from the reeds pulling Harriet behind him. They ran back along the track and paused beside the Ford. The key was missing from the dashboard, but he reached underneath, wrenched out the ignition wires and looped them together quickly. A moment later the engine roared into life.

He turned to Harriet. 'Can you get this thing out of here?'

'I think so.'

'Good – I noticed a telephone box about a mile up the road on the way in. Ring through to Grant – he'll know what to do. The County boys would probably wonder what in the hell you were talking about.'

'What about you?'

'You don't think I'm going to let him cut his own throat at this stage do you?' He shoved her into the car. 'Go on – get out of it!'

As the Ford reversed away, a pistol shot echoed across the marshes that was answered by the blast of a shotgun. Miller turned and ran along the track in the direction of the sound.

Duncan Craig turned off the path to the left, ran across an expanse of coarse marsh grass into the shelter of the mist and doubled back on his tracks. He paused and listened intently. The only sound was the lapping of water and further along, geese lifted into the sky, voicing their annoyance at being disturbed.

By all the rules he should now be behind Vernon and Carver and he moved out of the shelter of the mist and approached the path cautiously. Somewhere to the right, there was the sound of running footsteps and as he crouched, shotgun ready, Nick Miller ran out of the mist.

'Over here!' Craig called softly and Miller paused on the edge of the raised path and looked down at him, chest heaving.

'Thank God – I didn't think it would be this easy.'

There was a sudden cold laugh and Max Vernon scrambled onto the path from the other side about twenty yards to the left. 'It never is,' he called harshly and his hand swung up.

The bullet caught Miller in the upper arm, knocking him back off the path into the soft earth as Craig fired his shotgun in reply. Max Vernon had already slipped back into cover and Craig reached down and dragged Miller to his feet.

'Can you still run?'

Miller nodded, his face white with shock. 'I think so.'

'Then let's get out of here.'

They stumbled across the rough ground into the mist, two more bullets chasing them on their way, and suddenly the water was knee-deep and the reeds lifted to meet them.

Another bullet echoed wildly through the mist and Miller crouched instinctively, stumbling to one knee. Craig pulled him to his feet and they moved on through a thick glutinous slime covered by water, which in places was thigh deep.

Miller was conscious of the pain in his arm as the first shock wore off, of the coldness of the water as it ate into his flesh like acid, and struggled for breath.

Suddenly Craig disappeared with a startled cry, the water

closing over his head. Miller lurched forward, reaching out, and followed him in. It was a terrible sensation as the filthy, stinking water forced its way into his mouth and nostrils. His feet could find no bottom as he struggled frantically and then an iron hand had him by the collar. A moment later, he was on his hands and knees amongst the reeds and breathing again.

Craig crouched beside him. He had lost his red beret and his face was streaked with black mud and slime. 'All right?'

Miller coughed and brought up a little marsh water.

'What about you?'

'Lost the shotgun, I'm afraid. If you think you can keep on the move, we've a chance of circling round to the houseboat. There are a couple of sporting rifles and an extra shotgun there.'

Miller nodded, getting to his feet, and they moved forward again. A couple of minutes later the reeds started to thin and a dyke lifted out of the mist. They scrambled up out of the water and Craig started to run at a jogtrot, Miller stumbling after him.

The pain in his arm was much worse now and there was a stitch in his side. He stumbled into a thorn tree at the top of a grassy knoll above a small, scum-covered pool and managed to cry out.

'No use, Duncan. I can't go on.'

Craig didn't even attempt to argue. 'Get out of sight and wait,' he said crisply. 'I'll be back in ten minutes.'

There was a clump of bushes just below the path and Miller rolled underneath. He pillowed his cheek against the wet earth, struggling for breath, and was suddenly aware of footsteps approaching from the direction in which they had come. A moment later, Ben Carver came into view.

He paused, his feet no more than a yard away from Miller's head, the Smith & Wesson held in his left hand, and Miller didn't hesitate. He grabbed for the ankles with all his force. Carver fell on top of him, the Smith & Wesson flying out of his hand into the pool below.

Miller cried out in agony as the pain in his arm seemed to spread throughout his entire body and he reached for Carver's throat with his right hand. Together, they burst out of the bushes and rolled down the slope.

For the briefest of moments Miller was on top as they reached the bottom and he used it well. His right hand rose and fell, the edge catching Carver full across the throat. He screamed and turned over, tearing at his collar.

Miller tried to get to his feet and Max Vernon said, 'Hold it right there – where's Craig?'

He was standing half-way down the slope, the Luger ready, his face pale. 'Right here, Vernon!' Craig called.

He came down the slope like a rugby forward, head down, catching Vernon round the waist. The Luger exploded once and then they were locked together and falling backwards.

The waters of the pool closed over them and they rose separately. Vernon seemed bewildered, his face black with mud and Craig surged forward and hit him again and again, solid, heavy punches that drove him into the centre of the pool.

Vernon lost his balance and went under the surface. As he got to his feet, he screamed suddenly. 'My legs – I can't move my legs! I'm sinking!'

Craig floundered back towards the edge of the pool, the mud releasing him reluctantly with great sucking noises. When he reached firm ground he turned, a slightly dazed expression on his face and wiped the back of a hand wearily across his eyes.

Vernon was going fast, the quagmire under the surface of the water drawing him down. 'For God's sake, help me, Craig! Help me!'

Miller pushed himself to his feet and staggered forward clutching his arm, blood oozing between his fingers. Vernon was already chest-deep and he went to pieces completely, babbling hysterically, arms thrashing the water.

Miller started forward and Craig pulled him back. 'And I thought it was going to be so easy,' he said bitterly.

He unzipped his combat jacket, taking it off as he waded into the pool. He held it by the end of one sleeve and reached out to Vernon.

'Hold on tight if you want to live.'

Vernon grabbed for the other sleeve with both hands like a drowning man and Craig started backwards. He was already beginning to sink himself and for a moment, nothing seemed to be happening. Miller moved to help him, extending his one good arm, and Craig grabbed at his hand. A moment later, Vernon came out of the slime with a rush.

He crawled from the water and lay face down at the side of the pool, his whole body racked by sobbing. Miller and Craig moved back to the bottom of the slope and slumped down.

'So you were right and I was wrong?' Craig sighed wearily. 'I should have known I couldn't go through with it.'

'All part of the service,' Miller said.

Craig turned with a wry grin. 'It's been fun, hasn't it? We must do it again sometime.'

As they started to laugh, a police whistle sounded somewhere in the distance and scores of brent geese rose in a protesting cloud and flew out to sea.

BOOK THREE

HELL IS ALWAYS TODAY

PROLOGUE

The police car turned the end of the street and pulled into the kerb beside the lamp. The driver kept the motor running, and grinned at his passenger.

'Rather you than me on a night like this, but I was forgetting. You love your work, don't you?'

Police Constable Henry Joseph Dwyer's reply was unprintable and he stood at the edge of the pavement, a strangely melancholy figure in the helmet and cape, listening to the sound of the car fade into the night. Rain fell steadily, drifting down through the yellow glow of the street lamp in a silver spray and he turned morosely and walked towards the end of the street. It was just after ten and the night stretched before him, cold and damp. The city was lonely and for special reasons at that time, rather frightening even for an old hand like Joe Dwyer. Still, no point in worrying about that. Another ten months and he'd be out of it, but his hand still moved inside his cape to touch the small two-way radio in his breast pocket, the lifeline that could bring help when needed within a matter of minutes.

He paused on the corner and looked across the square towards the oasis of light that was the coffee stall on the other side. No harm in starting off with something warm inside him and he needed some cigarettes.

There was only one customer, a large, heavily built man

in an old trenchcoat and rain hat who was talking to Sam
Harkness, the owner.

As Dwyer approached, the man turned, calling goodnight
over his shoulder and plunged into the rain head down so
that he and the policeman collided.

'Steady on there,' Dwyer began and then recognized him.
'Oh, it's you, Mr Faulkner. Nasty night, sir.'

Faulkner grinned. 'You can say that again. I only came
out for some cigarettes. Hope they're paying you double
time tonight.'

'That'll be the day, sir.'

Faulkner walked away and Dwyer approached the stall,
'He's in a hurry, isn't he?'

Harkness filled a mug with tea from the urn, spooned
sugar into it and pushed it across. 'Wouldn't you be if you
was on your way home to a warm bed on a night like this?
Probably got some young bird lying there in her underwear
waiting for him. They're all the same these artists.'

Dwyer grinned. 'You're only jealous. Let's have twenty
of the usual. Must have something to get me through the
night. How's business?'

Harkness passed the cigarettes across and changed the
ten-shilling note that Dwyer gave him. 'Lucky if I make
petrol money.'

'I'm not surprised. You won't get many people out on a
night like this.'

Harkness nodded. 'It wouldn't be so bad if I still had the
Toms, but they're all working from their flats at the moment
with some muscle minding the door if they've got any sense.
All frightened off by this Rainlover geezer.'

Dwyer lit a cigarette and cupped it inside his left hand.
'He doesn't worry you?'

Harkness shrugged. 'He isn't after the likes of me, that's
for certain, though how any woman in her right mind can
go out at the moment on a night when it's raining beats

me.' He picked up the evening paper. 'Look at this poor
bitch he got in the park last night. Peggy Nolan. She's been
on the game round here for years. Nice little Irish woman.
Fifty if she was a day. Never harmed anyone in her life.'
He put the paper down angrily. 'What about you blokes,
anyway? When are you going to do something?'

The voice of the public, worried, frightened and looking
for a. scapegoat. Dwyer nipped his cigarette and slipped it
back into the packet. 'We'll get him, Sam. He'll over-reach
himself. These nut-cases always do.'

Which didn't sound very convincing even to himself and
Harkness laughed harshly. 'And how many more women
are going to die before that happens, tell me that?'

His words echoed back to him flatly on the night air as
Dwyer moved away into the night. Harkness watched him
go, listening to the footsteps fade and there was only the
silence and beyond the pool of light, the darkness seemed to
move in towards him. He swallowed hard, fighting back the
fear that rose inside, switched on the radio and lit a cigarette.

Joe Dwyer moved through the night at a measured pace,
the only sound the echo of his own step between the tall
Victorian terraces that pressed in on either side. Occasionally
he paused to flash his lamp into a doorway and once he
checked the side door of a house which was by day the
offices of a grocery wholesaler.

These things he did efficiently because he was a good
policeman, but more as a reflex action than anything else.
He was cold and the rain trickled down his neck, soaking
into his shirt, and he still had seven hours to go, but he was
also feeling rather depressed, mainly because of Harkness.
The man was frightened, of course, but who wasn't? The
trouble was that people saw too much television. They were
conditioned to expect their murders to be neatly solved in
fifty-two minutes plus advertising time.

He flashed his lamp into the entry called Dob Court a few yards from the end of the street hardly bothering to pause, then froze. The beam rested on a black leather boot, travelled across stockinged legs, skirt rucked up wantonly, and came to rest on the face of a young woman. The head was turned sideways at an awkward angle in a puddle of water, eyes staring into eternity.

And he wasn't afraid, that was the strange thing. He took a quick step forward, dropping to one knee and touched her face gently with the back of his hand. It was still warm, which could only mean one thing on a night like this . . .

He was unable to take his reasoning any further. There was the scrape of a foot on stone. As he started to rise, his helmet was knocked off and he was struck a violent blow on the back of the head. He cried out, falling across the body of the girl, and someone ran along the entry behind him and turned into the street.

He could feel blood, warm and sticky, mingling with the rain as it ran across his face and the darkness moved in on him. He fought it off, breathing deeply, his hand going inside his cape to the two-way radio in his breast pocket.

Even after he had made contact and knew that help was on its way, he held on to consciousness with all his strength, only letting go at the precise moment that the first police car turned the corner at the end of the street.

1

It had started to rain in the late evening, lightly at first, but increasing to a heavy, drenching downpour as darkness fell. A wind that, from the feel of it, came all the way from the North Sea, drove the rain before it across the roofs of the city to rattle against the enormous glass window that stood at one end of Bruno Faulkner's studio.

The studio was a great barn of a room which took up the entire top floor of a five storey Victorian wool merchant's town house, now converted into flats. Inside a fire burned in a strangely mediaeval fireplace giving the only light, and on a dais against the window four great shapes, Faulkner's latest commission, loomed menacingly.

There was a ring at the door bell and then another.

After a while, an inner door beyond the fireplace opened and Faulkner appeared in shirt and pants, a little dishevelled for he had been sleeping. He switched on the light and paused by the fire for a moment, mouth widening in a yawn. He was a large, rather fleshy man of thirty whose face carried the habitually arrogant expression of the sort of creative artist who believes that he exists by a kind of divine right. As the bell sounded again he frowned petulantly, moved to the door and opened it. 'All right, all right, I can hear you.' He smiled suddenly, 'Oh, it's you, Jack.'

The elegant young man who leaned against the wall

outside, a finger held firmly against the bell push, grinned, 'What kept you?'

Faulkner turned and Jack Morgan followed him inside and closed the door. He was about Faulkner's age, but looked younger and wore evening dress, a light overcoat with a velvet collar draped across his shoulders.

He examined Faulkner dispassionately as the other man helped himself to a cigarette from a silver box and lit it. 'You look bloody awful, Bruno.'

'I love you too,' Faulkner said and crossed to the fire.

Morgan looked down at the telephone which stood on a small coffee table. The receiver was off the hook and he replaced it casually. 'I thought so. I've been trying to get through for the past couple of hours.'

Faulkner shrugged. 'I've been working for two days nonstop. When I finished I took the phone off the hook and went to bed. What did you want? Something important?'

'It's Joanna's birthday, or had you forgotten? She sent me to get you.'

'Oh, my God, I had – completely. No chance that I've missed the party, I suppose?'

'I'm afraid not. It's only eight o'clock.'

'Pity. I suppose she's collected the usual bunch of squares.' He frowned suddenly. 'I haven't even got her a present.'

Morgan produced a slim leather case from one pocket and threw it across. 'Pearl necklace . . . seventy-five quid. I got it at Humbert's and told them to put it on your account.'

'Bless you, Jack,' Faulkner said. 'The best fag I ever had.'

He walked towards the bedroom door and Morgan turned to examine the figures on the dais. They were lifesize, obviously feminine, but in the manner of Henry Moore's early work had no individual identity. They possessed a curious group menace that made him feel decidedly uneasy.

'I see you've added another figure,' he said. 'I thought you'd decided that three was enough?'

Faulkner shrugged. 'When I started five weeks ago I thought one would do and then it started to grow. The damned thing just won't stop.'

Morgan moved closer. 'It's magnificent, Bruno. The best thing you've ever done.'

Faulkner shook his head. 'I'm not sure. There's still something missing. A group's got to have balance . . . perfect balance. Maybe it needs another figure.'

'Surely not?'

'When it's right, I'll know. I'll feel it and it's not right yet. Still, that can wait. I'd better get dressed.'

He went into the bedroom and Morgan lit a cigarette and called to him, 'What do you think of the latest Rainlover affair?'

'Don't tell me he's chopped another one? How many is that – four?'

Morgan picked up a newspaper that was lying on a chair by the fire. 'Should be in the paper.' He leafed through it quickly and shook his head. 'No, this is no good. It's yesterday evening's and she wasn't found till nine o'clock.'

'Where did it happen?' Faulkner said as he emerged from the bedroom, pulling on a corduroy jacket over a polo neck sweater.

'Not far from Jubilee Park.' Morgan looked up and frowned. 'Aren't you dressing?'

'What do you call this?'

'You know what I mean.'

'Who for, that bunch of stuffed shirts? Not on your life. When Joanna and I got engaged she agreed to take me exactly as I am and this is me, son.' He picked up a trench-coat and draped it over his shoulders. 'I know one thing, I need a drink before I can face that lot.'

'There isn't time,' Morgan said flatly.

'Rubbish. We have to pass The King's Arms, don't we? There's always time.'

'All right, all right,' Morgan said. 'I surrender, but just one. Remember that.'

Faulkner grinned, looking suddenly young and amiable and quite different. 'Scouts' honour. Now let's get moving.'

He switched off the light and they went out.

When Faulkner and Morgan entered the saloon bar of The King's Arms it was deserted except for the landlord, Hal, Meadows, a genial bearded man in his mid-fifties, who leaned on the bar reading a newspaper. He glanced up, then folded the newspaper and put it down.

''Evening, Mr Faulkner . . . Mr Morgan.'

''Evening, Harry,' Faulkner said. 'Two double brandies'

Morgan cut in quickly. 'Better make mine a single, Harry. I'm driving.'

Faulkner took out a cigarette and lit it as Meadows gave two glasses a wipe and filled them. 'Quiet tonight.'

'It's early yet,' Morgan said.

Meadows pushed the drinks across. 'I won't see many tonight, you mark my words.' He turned the newspaper towards them so that they could read the headline *Rainlover strikes again*. 'Not with this bastard still on the loose. Every time it rains he's at it. I'd like to know what the bloody police are supposed to be doing.'

Faulkner swallowed some of his brandy and looked down at the newspaper. 'The Rainlover – I wonder which bright boy dreamed that one up.'

'I bet his editor gave him a fifty pound bonus on the spot.'

'He's probably creeping out at night every time it rains and adding to the score personally, just to keep the story going.' Faulkner chuckled and emptied his glass.

Meadows shook his head. 'It gives me the shakes, I can

tell you. I know one thing . . . you won't find many women on the streets tonight.'

Behind them the door swung open unexpectedly and a young woman came in. She was perhaps nineteen or twenty and well made with the sort of arrogant boldness about the features that many men like, but which soon turns to coarseness. She wore a black plastic mac, a red mini-skirt and knee-length leather boots. She looked them over coolly, unbuttoning her coat with one hand, then sauntered to the other end of the bar and hoisted herself on to a stool. When she crossed her legs, her skirt slid all the way up to her stocking tops. She took a cheap compact from her bag and started to repair the rain damage on her face.

'There's someone who doesn't give a damn for a start,' Faulkner observed.

Morgan grinned. 'Perhaps she doesn't read the papers. I wonder what the Rainlover would do to her?'

'I know what I'd like to do to her.'

Meadows shook his head. 'Her kind of custom I can do without.'

Faulkner was immediately interested. 'Is she on the game then?'

Meadows shrugged. 'What do you think?'

'What the hell, Harry, she needs bread like the rest of us. Live and let live.' Faulkner pushed his glass across. 'Give her a drink on me and I'll have a refill while you're at it.'

'As you say, Mr Faulkner.'

He walked to the other end of the bar and spoke to the young woman, who turned, glanced briefly at Faulkner, then nodded. Meadows poured her a large gin and tonic.

Faulkner watched her closely and Morgan tapped him on the shoulder. 'Come on now, Bruno. Don't start getting involved. We're late enough as it is.'

'You worry too much.'

The girl raised her glass and he toasted her back. She

made an appealing, rather sexy picture sitting there on the
high stool in her mod outfit and he laughed suddenly.

'What's so funny?' Morgan demanded.

'I was just thinking what a sensation there would be if
we took her with us.'

'To Joanna's party? Sensation isn't the word.'

Faulkner grinned. 'I can see the look on Aunt Mary's
weatherbeaten old face now – the mouth tightening like a
dried prune. A delightful thought.'

'Forget it, Bruno,' Morgan said sharply. 'Even you
couldn't get away with that.'

Faulkner glanced at him, the lazy smile disappearing at
once. 'Oh, couldn't I?'

Morgan grabbed at his sleeve, but Faulkner pulled away
sharply and moved along the bar to the girl. He didn't waste
any time in preliminaries.

'All on your own then?'

The girl shrugged. 'I'm supposed to be waiting for somebody.' She had an accent that was a combination of Liverpool
and Irish and not unpleasant.

'Anyone special?'

'My fiancé.'

Faulkner chuckled. 'Fiancé's are only of secondary importance. I should know. I'm one myself.'

'Is that a fact?' the girl said.

Her handbag was lying on the bar, a large and ostentatious letter G in one corner bright against the shiny
black plastic. Faulkner picked it up and looked at her
enquiringly.

'G for . . .?'

'Grace.'

'How delightfully apt. Well, G for Grace, my friend and
I are going on to a party. It occurred to me that you might
like to come with us.'

'What kind of a party?'

Faulkner nodded towards Morgan. 'Let's put it this way. He's dressed for it, I'm not.'

The girl didn't even smile. 'Sounds like fun. All right, Harold can do without it tonight. He should have been here at seven-thirty anyway.'

'But you weren't here yourself at seven-thirty, were you?'

She frowned in some surprise. 'What's that got to do with it?'

'A girl after my own heart.' Faulkner took her by the elbow and moved towards Morgan, who grinned wryly.

'I'm Jack and he's Bruno. He won't have told you that.

She raised an eyebrow. 'How did you know?'

'Experience . . . mostly painful.'

'We can talk in the car,' Faulkner said. 'Now let's get moving.'

As they turned to the door, it opened and a young man entered, his hands pushed into the pockets of a hip-length tweed coat with a cheap fur collar. He had a narrow white face, long dark hair and a mouth that seemed to be twisted into an expression of perpetual sullenness.

He hesitated, frowning, then looked enquiringly at the girl. 'What gives?'

Grace shrugged. 'Sorry, Harold, you're too late. I've made other arrangements.'

She took a single step forward and he grabbed her arm. 'What's the bloody game?'

Faulkner pulled him away with ease. 'Hands off, sonny.'

Harold turned in blind rage and swung one wild punch that might have done some damage had it ever landed. Faulkner blocked the arm, then grabbed the young man's hand in an aikido grip and forced him to the ground, his face remaining perfectly calm.

'Down you go, there's a good dog.'

Grace started to laugh and Harry Meadows came round the bar fast.

'That's enough, Mr Faulkner. That's enough.'

Faulkner released him and Harold scrambled to his feet, face twisted with pain, something close to tears in his eyes.

'Go on then, you cow,' he shouted. 'Get out of it. I never want to see you again.'

Grace shrugged. 'Suit yourself.'

Faulkner took her by the arm and they went out laughing. Morgan turned to Meadows, his face grave. 'I'm sorry about that.'

Meadows shook his head. 'He doesn't change, does he, Mr Morgan? I don't want to see him in here again – okay?'

Morgan sighed helplessly, turned and went after the others and Meadows gave some attention to Harold who stood nursing his hand, face twisted with pain and hate.

'You know you did ask for it, lad, but he's a nasty piece of work that one when he gets started. You're well out of it. Come on, I'll buy you a drink on the house.'

'Oh, stuff your drink, you stupid old bastard,' Harold said viciously and the door swung behind him as he plunged wildly into the night.

2

Detective Sergeant Nicholas Miller was tired and it showed in his face as he went down the steps to the tiled entrance hall of the Marsden Wing of the General Infirmary. He paused to light a cigarette and the night sister watched him for a moment before emerging from her glass office. Like many middle-aged women she had a weakness for handsome young men. Miller intrigued her particularly for the dark blue Swedish trenchcoat and continental raincap gave him a strange foreign air which was hardly in keeping with his profession. Certainly anything less like the conventional idea of a policeman would have been hard to imagine.

'How did you find Mr Grant tonight?' she asked as she came out of her office.

'Decidedly restless.' Miller's face was momentarily illuminated by a smile of great natural charm. 'And full of questions.'

Detective Superintendent Bruce Grant, head of the city's Central C.I.D., had been involved in a car accident earlier in the week and now languished in a hospital bed with a dislocated hip. Misfortune enough considering that Grant had been up to his ears in the most important case of his career. Doubly unfortunate in that it now left in sole charge of the case Detective Chief Superintendent George Mallory of Scotland Yard's Murder Squad, the expert his superiors had insisted on calling in, in response to the growing public alarm as the Rainlover still continued at large.

'I'll tell you something about policemen, Sister,' Miller said. 'They don't like other people being brought in to handle things that have happened on their patch. To an old hand like Bruce Grant, the introduction of Scotland Yard men to a case he's been handling himself is a personal insult. Has Mallory been in today, by the way?'

'Oh yes, but just to see Inspector Craig. I don't think he called in on Superintendent Grant.'

'He wouldn't,' Miller said. 'There's no love lost there at all. Grant's one satisfaction is that Craig was in the car with him when the accident happened which leaves Mallory on his own in the midst of the heathen. How is Craig?'

'Poorly,' she said. 'A badly fractured skull.'

'Serves him right for coming North.'

'Now then, Sergeant, I was a Londoner myself twenty years ago.'

'And I bet you thought that north of High Barnet we rolled boulders on to travellers as they passed by.'

He grinned wickedly and the night sister said, 'It's a change to see you smile. They work you too hard. When did you last have a day off?'

'A day? You must be joking, but I'm free now till six a.m. As it happens, I've had an invitation to a party, but I'd break it for you.'

She was unable to keep her pleasure at the compliment from showing on her pleasant face and gave him a little push. 'Go on, get out of it. I'm a respectable married woman.'

'In that case I will. Don't do anything I would.' He smiled again and went out through the swing doors.

She stood there in the half-light, listening to the sound of the car engine dwindle into the distance, then turned with a sigh, went back into her office and picked up a book.

Nick Miller had met Joanna Hartmann only once at a dinner party at his brother's place. The circumstances had been slightly unusual in that he had been in bed in his flat over the garage block at the rear of the house when his brother had arrived to shake him back to reality with the demand that he get dressed at once and come to dinner. Miller, who had not slept for approximately thirty hours, had declined with extreme impoliteness until his brother indicated that he wished him to partner a national television idol who had the nation by the throat twice-weekly as the smartest lady barrister in the game. It seemed that her fiancé had failed to put in an appearance, which put a completely different complexion on the whole thing. Miller had got dressed in three minutes flat.

That evening had been interesting and instructive. Like most actresses, she had proved to be not only intelligent, but a good conversationalist and for her part she had been intrigued to discover that her host's handsome and elegant younger brother was a policeman.

A pleasant evening, but nothing more, for a considerable

amount of her conversation had concerned her fiancé, Bruno Faulkner the sculptor, who had followed her north when she had signed to do her series for Northern Television and Nick Miller was not a man to waste his time up blind alleys.

Under the circumstances her invitation was something of a surprise, but it had certainly come at the right moment. A little life and laughter was just what he needed. Something to eat, a couple of stiff drinks and then home to bed or perhaps to someone else's? You never knew your luck where show people were concerned.

She had the top flat in Dereham Court, a new luxury block not far from his own home and he could hear cool music drifting from a half-open window as he parked the green Mini-Cooper and went up the steps into the hall.

She opened the door to him herself, a tall, elegant blonde in a superb black velvet trouser suit who looked startlingly like her public image. When she greeted him, he might have been the only person in the world.

'Why Nick, darling, I was beginning to think you weren't going to make it.'

He took off his coat and cap and handed them to the maid. 'I nearly didn't. First evening off for a fortnight.'

She nodded knowingly. 'I suppose you must be pretty busy at the moment.' She turned to the handsome greying man who hovered at her elbow, a glass in one hand. 'Nick's a detective, Frank. You'll know his brother, by the way, Jack Miller. He's a director of Northern Television. This is Frank Marlowe, my agent, Nick.'

Marlowe thawed perceptibly. 'Why, this is real nice,' he said with a faint American accent. 'Had lunch with your brother and a few people at the Midland only yesterday. Let me get you a drink.'

As he moved away, Joanna took Miller's arm and led him towards a white-haired old lady in a silver lamé gown

who sat on a divan against the wall watching the world go
by. She had the face of the sort of character actress you've
seen a thousand times on film and television and yet can
never put a name to. She turned out to be Mary Beresford,
Joanna's aunt, and Miller was introduced in full. He resisted
an insane impulse to click his heels and kiss the hand that
she held out to him, for the party was already turning out
to be very different from what he had imagined.

That it was a very superior sort of soirée couldn't be
denied, but on the whole, the guests were older rather than
younger, the men in evening wear, the women exquisitely
gowned. Certainly there were no swinging young birds from
the television studios in evidence – a great disappointment.
Cool music played softly, one or two couples were dancing
and there was a low murmur of conversation.

'What about the Rainlover then, Sergeant Miller?' Mary
Beresford demanded.

The way she said *sergeant* made him sound like a lavatory attendant and she'd used the voice she kept for grand
dowager parts.

'What about him?' he said belligerently.

'When are you going to catch him?' She said it with all
the patience of an infant teacher explaining the school rules
to a rather backward child on his first day. 'After all, there
are enough of you.'

'I know, Mrs Beresford,' Miller said. 'We're pretty hot on
parking tickets, but not so good on maniacs who walk the
streets on wet nights murdering women.'

'There's no need to be rude, Sergeant,' she said frostily.

'Oh, but I'm not.' Behind him Joanna Hartmann moved
in anxiously, Frank Marlowe at her shoulder. Miller leaned
down and said, 'You see the difficulty about this kind of case
is that the murderer could be anyone, Mrs Beresford. Your
own husband – your brother even.' He nodded around the
room. 'Any one of the men here.' There was an expression

of real alarm on her face, but he didn't let go. 'What about Mr Marlowe, for instance?'

He slipped an edge of authority into his voice and said to Marlowe, 'Would you care to account for your movements between the hours of eight and nine last night, sir? I must warn you, of course, that anything you say may be taken down and used in evidence.'

Mary Beresford gave a shocked gasp, Marlowe looked decidedly worried and at that precise moment the record on the stereogram came to an end.

Joanna Hartmann grabbed Miller's arm. 'Come and play the piano for us.' She pulled him away and called brightly over her shoulder to Marlowe who stood there, a drink in each hand, mouth gaping. 'He's marvellous. You'll swear it was Oscar Peterson.'

Miller was angry, damned angry, but not only at Mary Beresford. She couldn't help being the woman she was, but he was tired of the sort of vicious attack on the police that met him every time he picked up a newspaper, tired of cheap remarks and jibes about police inefficiency from members of the public who didn't seem to appreciate that every detective who could be spared had been working ninety to a hundred hours a week since the Rainlover had first killed, in an attempt to root him out. But how did you find one terrifyingly insane human being in a city of three-quarters of a million? A man with no record, who did not kill for gain, who did not even kill for sexual reasons. Someone who just killed out of some dark compulsion that even the psychiatrists hadn't been able to help them with.

The piano was the best, a Bechstein grand, and he sat down, swallowed the double gin and tonic that Marlowe handed him and moved into a cool and complicated version of 'The Lady is a Tramp'. One or two people came across to stand at the piano watching, because they knew talent when they heard it and playing a good jazz piano was

Miller's greatest love. He moved from one number into another. It was perhaps fifteen minutes later when he heard the door bell chime.

'Probably Jack and Bruno,' Joanna said to Marlowe. 'I'll get it.'

Miller had a clear view of the door as she crossed the room. He looked down at the keyboard again and as he slowed to the end of his number, Mary Beresford gave a shocked gasp.

When Miller turned, a spectacularly fleshy-looking young tart in black plastic mac, mini-skirt and knee-length leather boots stood at the top of the steps beside the maid who had apparently got to the door before Joanna. A couple of men moved into the room behind her. It was pretty obvious which was Bruno Faulkner from what Miller had heard, and it was just as obvious what the man was up to as he helped the girl off with her coat and looked quickly around the room, a look of eager expectancy on his face.

Strangely enough it was the girl Miller felt sorry for. She was pretty enough in her own way and very, very nubile with that touch of raw cynicism common to the sort of young woman who has slept around too often and too early. She tilted her chin in a kind of bravado as she looked about her, but she was going to be hurt, that much was obvious. Quite suddenly Miller knew with complete certainty that he didn't like Bruno Faulkner one little bit. He lit a cigarette and started to play 'Blue Moon'.

Of course Joanna Hartmann carried it all off superbly as he knew she would. She walked straight up to Faulkner, kissed him on the cheek and said, 'Hello, darling, what kept you?'

'I've been working, Joanna,' Faulkner told her. 'But I'll tell you about that later. First, I'd like you to meet Grace. I hope you don't mind us bringing her along.'

'Of course not.' She turned to Grace with her most charming smile. 'Hello, my dear.'

The girl stared at her open-mouthed. 'But you're Joanna Hartmann. I've seen you on the telly.' Her voice had dropped into a whisper. 'I saw your last film.'

'I hope you enjoyed it.' Joanna smiled sweetly at Morgan. 'Jack, be an angel. Get Grace a drink and introduce her to one or two people. See she enjoys herself.'

'Glad to, Joanna.' Morgan guided the girl away expertly, sat her in a chair by the piano. 'I'll get you a drink. Back in a jiffy.'

She sat there looking hopelessly out of place. The attitude of the other guests was what interested Miller most. Some of the women were amused in a rather condescending way, others quite obviously highly indignant at having to breathe the same air. Most of the men on the other hand glanced at her covertly with a sort of lascivious approval. Morgan seemed to be taking his time and she put a hand to her hair nervously and tilted her chin at an ageing white-haired lady who looked her over as if she were a lump of dirt.

Miller liked her for that. She was getting the worst kind of raw deal from people who ought to know better, but seldom did, and she was damned if she was going to let them grind her down. He caught her eye and grinned. 'Anything you'd like to hear?'

She crossed to the piano and one or two people who had been standing there moved away. 'What about "St Louis Blues"?' she said. 'I like that.'

'My pleasure. What's your name?'

'Grace Packard.'

He moved into a solid, pushing arrangement of the great jazz classic that had her snapping her fingers. 'That's the greatest,' she cried, eyes shining. 'Do you do this for a living?'

He shook his head. 'Kicks, that's all. I couldn't stand the

kind of life the pro musicians lead. One-night stands till the early hours, tour after tour and all at the union rate. No icing on that kind of cake.'

'I suppose not. Do you come here often?'

'First time.'

'I thought so,' she grinned with a sort of gamin charm. 'A right bunch of zombies.'

Morgan arrived with a drink for her. She put it down on top of the piano and clutched at his arm. 'This place is like a morgue. Let's live it up a little.'

Morgan didn't seem unwilling and followed her on to the floor. As Miller came to the end of the number someone turned the stereogram on again, probably out of sheer bloody-mindedness. He wasn't particularly worried, got to his feet and moved to the bar. Joanna Hartmann and Faulkner were standing very close together no more than a yard from him and as he waited for the barman to mix him a large gin and tonic, he couldn't help but overhear their conversation.

'Always the lady, Joanna,' Faulkner said. 'Doesn't anything ever disturb your poise?'

'Poor Bruno, have I spoiled your little joke? Where did you pick her up, by the way?'

'The public bar of The King's Arms. I'd hoped she might enliven the proceedings. At least I've succeeded in annoying Frank from the look on his face. Thanks be for small mercies.'

Joanna shook her head and smiled. 'What am I going to do with you?'

'I could make several very pleasant suggestions. Variations on a theme, but all eminently worthwhile.'

Before she could reply, Mary Beresford approached and Faulkner louted low. 'Madam, all homage.'

There was real disgust on her face. 'You are really the most disgusting man I know. How dare you bring that dreadful creature here.'

'Now there's a deathless line if you like. Presumably from one of those Victorian melodramas you used to star in.' She flinched visibly and he turned and looked towards the girl who was dancing with Morgan. 'In any case what's so dreadful about a rather luscious young bird enjoying herself. But forgive me. I was forgetting how long it was since you were in that happy state, Aunt Mary.' The old woman turned and walked away and Faulkner held up a hand defensively. 'I know, I've done it again.'

'Couldn't you just ignore her?' Joanna asked.

'Sorry, but she very definitely brings out the worst in me. Have a Martini.'

As the barman mixed them, Joanna noticed Miller and smiled. 'Now here's someone I want you to meet, Bruno. Nick Miller. He's a policeman.'

Faulkner turned, examined Miller coolly and sighed. 'Dammit all, Joanna, there's a limit you know. I do draw the line at coppers. Where on earth did you find him?'

'Oh I crawled out of the woodwork,' Miller said pleasantly, restraining a sudden impulse to put his right foot squarely between Faulkner's thighs.

Joanna looked worried and something moved in the big man's eyes, but at that moment the door chimes sounded. Miller glanced across, mainly out of curiosity. When the maid opened the door he saw Jack Brady standing in the hall, his battered, Irish face infinitely preferable to any that he had so far met with that evening.

He put down his glass and said to Joanna, 'Looks as if I'm wanted.'

'Surely not,' she said in considerable relief.

Miller grinned and turned to Faulkner. 'I'd like to say it's been nice, but then you get used to meeting all sorts in my line of work.'

He moved through the crowd rapidly before the big man

could reply, took his coat and cap from the maid and gave
Brady a push into the hall. 'Let's get out of here.'

The door closed behind them as he pulled on his trenchcoat. Detective Constable Jack Brady shook his head sadly.
'Free booze, too. I should be ashamed to take you away.'

'Not from that lot you shouldn't. What's up?'

'Gunner Doyle's on the loose.'

Miller paused, a frown of astonishment on his face. 'What
did you say?'

'They moved him into the Infirmary from Manningham
Gaol yesterday with suspected food poisoning. Missed him
half an hour ago.'

'What's he served – two and a half years?'

'Out of a five stretch.'

'The daft bastard. He could have been out in another ten
months with remission.' Miller sighed and shook his head.
'Come on then, Jack, let's see if we can find him.'

3

Faulkner ordered his third Martini and Joanna said, 'Where
have you been for the past two days?'

'Working,' he told her. 'Damned hard. When were you
last at the studio?'

'Wednesday.'

'There were three figures in the group then. Now there
are four.'

There was a real concern in her voice and she put a hand
on his arm. 'That's really too much, Bruno, even for you.
You'll kill yourself.'

'Nonsense. When it's there, it's got to come out, Joanna.
Nothing else matters. You're a creative artist yourself. You
know what I mean.'

'Even so, when this commission is finished you're taking a long holiday.'

Frank Marlowe joined them and she said, 'I've just been telling Bruno it's time he took a holiday.'

'What an excellent idea. Why not the Bahamas? Six months . . . at least.'

'I love you too.' Faulkner grinned and turned to Joanna. 'Coming with me?'

'I'd love to, but Frank's lined me up for the lead in Mannheim's new play. If there's agreement on terms we go into rehearsal next month.'

'But you've only just finished a film.' Bruno turned to Marlowe and demanded angrily, 'What's wrong with you? Can't you ever see beyond ten per cent of the gross?'

As Marlowe put down his glass, his hand was shaking slightly. 'Now look, I've taken just about as much as I intend to take from you.'

Joanna got in between them quickly. 'You're not being fair, Bruno. Frank is the best agent there is, everyone knows that. If a thing wasn't right for me he'd say so. This is too good a chance to miss and it's time I went back to the stage for a while. I've almost forgotten how to act properly.'

The door bell chimed again and the maid admitted another couple.

'It's Sam Hagerty and his wife,' Joanna said. 'I'll have to say hello. Try to get on, you two. I'll be back soon.'

She moved away through the crowd and Marlowe watched her go, his love showing plainly on his face.

Faulkner smiled gently. 'A lovely girl, wouldn't you say?'

Marlowe glared at him in a kind of helpless rage and Faulkner turned to the barman. 'Two brandies, please. Better make it a large one for my friend. He isn't feeling too well.'

*

Jack Morgan and Grace Packard were dancing to a slow cool blues. She glanced towards Faulkner who was still at the bar. 'He's a funny one, isn't he?'

'Who, Bruno?'

She nodded. 'Coming to a do like this in those old clothes. Bringing me. Have you known him long?'

'We were at school together.'

'What's he do for a living?'

'He's a sculptor.'

'I might have known it was something like that. Is he any good?'

'Some people would tell you he's the best there is.'

She nodded soberly. 'Maybe that explains him. I mean when you're the best, you don't need to bother about what other people think, do you?'

'I wouldn't know.'

'Mind you, he looks a bit of a wild man to me. Look at the way he handled Harold at the pub.'

Morgan shrugged. 'He's just full of pleasant little tricks like that. Judo, aikido, karate – you name it, Bruno's got it.'

'Can he snap a brick in half with the edge of his hand? I saw a bloke do that once on the telly.'

'His favourite party trick.'

She pulled away from him abruptly and pushed through the crowd to Faulkner.

'Enjoying yourself?' he demanded.

'It's fabulous. I never thought it would be anything like this.'

Faulkner turned to Marlowe who stood at his side drinking morosely. 'There you are, Frank. Fairy tales do come true after all.'

'Jack says you can smash a brick with the edge of your hand,' Grace said.

'Only when I'm on my second bottle.'

'I saw it on television once, but I thought they'd faked it.'

Faulkner shook his head. 'It can be done right enough. Unfortunately I don't happen to have a brick on me right now.'

Marlowe seized his chance. 'Come now, Bruno,' he said, an edge of malice in his voice. 'You mustn't disappoint the little lady. We've heard a lot about your prowess at karate . . . a lot of talk, that is. As I remember a karate expert can snap a plank of wood as easily as a brick. Would this do?'

He indicated a hardwood chopping block on the bar and Faulkner grinned. 'You've just made a bad mistake, Frank.'

He swept the board clean of fruit, balanced it across a couple of ashtrays and raised his voice theatrically. 'Give me room, good people. Give me room.'

Those near at hand crowded round and Mary Beresford pushed her way to the front followed by Joanna who looked decidedly uncertain about the whole thing.

'What on earth are you doing, Bruno?'

Faulkner ignored her. 'A little bit of hush, please.'

He gave a terrible cry and his right hand swung down, splintering the block, scattering several glasses. There was a sudden gasp followed by a general buzz of conversation. Grace cried out in delight and Mary Beresford pushed forward.

'When are you going to start acting your age?' she demanded, her accent slipping at least forty-five years. 'Smashing the place up like a stupid teenage lout.'

'And why don't you try minding your own business, you silly old cow?'

The rage in his voice, the violence in his eyes reduced the room to silence. Mary Beresford stared at him, her face very white, the visible expression one of unutterable shock.

'How dare you,' she whispered.

'Another of those deathless lines of yours.'

Marlowe grabbed at his arm. 'You can't talk to her like that.'

Faulkner lashed out sideways without even looking, catching him in the face. Marlowe staggered back, clutching at the bar, glasses flying in every direction.

In the general uproar which followed, Joanna moved forward angrily. 'I think you'd better leave, Bruno.'

Strangely, Faulkner seemed to have complete control of himself. 'Must I?' He turned to Grace. 'Looks as though I'm not wanted. Are you coming or staying?' She hesitated and he shrugged. 'Suit yourself.'

He pushed his way through the crowd to the door. As he reached it, Grace arrived breathless. 'Changed your mind?' he enquired.

'Maybe I have.'

He helped her on with her plastic mac. 'How would you like to earn a fiver?'

She looked at him blankly. 'What did you say?'

'A fiver . . . just to pose for me for a couple of minutes.'

'Well, that's a new name for it.'

'Are you on?' he said calmly.

She smiled. 'Okay.'

'Let's go then.'

He opened the door and as Grace Packard went out into the hall, Joanna emerged from the crowd and paused at the bottom of the steps. Faulkner remembered her birthday present and took the leather case from his pocket. 'Here, I was forgetting.' He threw the case and as she caught it, called, 'Happy birthday.'

He went out, closing the door and Joanna opened the case and took out the pearls. She stood there looking at them, real pain on her face. For a moment she was obviously on the verge of tears, but then her aunt approached and she forced a brave smile.

'Time to eat, everybody. Shall we go into the other room?' She led the way, the pearls clutched tightly in her hand.

*

In Faulkner's studio the fire had died down, but it still gave some sort of illumination and the statues waited there in the half-light, dark and menacing. The key rattled in the lock, the door was flung open and Faulkner bustled in, pushing Grace in front of him.

'Better have a little light on the situation.'

He flicked the switch and took off his coat. Grace Packard looked round her approvingly. 'This is nice . . . and your own bar, too.'

She crossed to the bar, took off her mac and gloves, then moved towards the statues. 'Is this what you're working on at the moment?'

'Do you like it?'

'I'm not sure.' She seemed a trifle bewildered. 'They make me feel funny. I mean to say, they don't even look human.'

Faulkner chuckled. 'That's the general idea.' He nodded towards an old Victorian print screen which stood to one side of the statues. 'You can undress behind that.'

She stared at him blankly. 'Undress?'

'But of course,' he said. 'You're not much use to me with your clothes on. Now hurry up, there's a good girl. When you're ready, get up on the dais beside the others.'

'The others?'

'Beside the statues. I'm thinking of adding another. You can help me decide.'

She stood looking at him, hands on hips, her face quite different, cynical and knowing. 'What some people will do for kicks.'

She disappeared behind the screen and Faulkner poured himself a drink at the bar and switched on the hi-fi to a pleasant, big-band version of 'A Nightingale Sang in Berkeley Square'. He walked to the fire, humming the tune, got down on one knee and started to add lumps of coal to the flames from a brass scuttle.

'Will this do?' Grace Packard said.

He turned, still on one knee. She had a fine body, firm and sensual, breasts pointed with desire, hands flat against her thighs.

'Well?' she said softly.

Faulkner stood up, still holding his drink, switched off the hi-fi, then moved to the bedroom door and turned off the light. The shapes stood out clearly in silhouette against the great window and Grace Packard merged with the whole, became like the rest of them, a dark shadow that had existence and form, but nothing more.

Faulkner's face in the firelight was quite expressionless. He switched on the light again. 'Okay . . . fine. You can get dressed.'

'Is that all?' she demanded in astonishment.

'I've seen what I wanted to see if that's what you mean.'

'How kinky can you get.'

She shook her head in disgust, vanished behind the screen and started to dress again. Faulkner put more coal on the fire. When he had finished, he returned to the bar to freshen his drink.

She joined him a moment later carrying her boots.

'That was quick,' he told her.

She sat on one of the bar stools and started to pull on her boots. 'Not much to take off with this year's fashions. I can't get over it. You really did want me to pose.'

'If I'd wanted the other thing I'd have included it in our arrangement.' He took a ten-pound note from his wallet and stuffed it down the neck of her dress. 'I promised you a fiver. There's ten for luck.'

'You *must* be crazy.' She examined the note quickly, then lifted her skirt and slipped it into the top of her right stocking.

He was amused and showed it. 'Your personal bank?'

'As good as. You know, I can't make you out.'

'The secret of my irresistible attraction.'

'Is that a fact?'

He helped her on with her mac. 'Now I've got some work to do.'

She grabbed for her handbag as he propelled her towards the door. 'Heh, what is this? Don't say it's the end of a beautiful friendship.'

'Something like that. Now be a good girl and run along home. There's a taxi rank just round the corner.'

'That's all right. I haven't far to go.' She turned as he opened the door and smiled impishly. 'Sure you want me to leave?'

'Goodnight, Grace,' Faulkner said firmly.

He closed the door, turned and moved slowly to the centre of the room. There was a dull ache just to one side of the crown of his skull and as he touched the spot briefly, feeling the indentation of the scar, a slight nervous tic developed in the right cheek. He stood there examining the statues for a moment, then went to the cigarette box on the coffee table. It was empty. He cursed softly and quickly searched his pockets without success.

A search behind the bar proved equally fruitless and he pulled on his raincoat and hat quickly. As he passed the bar, he noticed a pair of gloves on the floor beside one of the stools and picked them up. The girl had obviously dropped them in the final hurried departure. Still, with any luck he would catch up with her before she reached the square. He stuffed them into his pocket and went out quickly.

Beyond, through the great window, the wind moaned in the night, driving the rain across the city in a dark curtain.

4

When they carried Sean Doyle into the General Infirmary escape couldn't have been further from his mind. He was sweating buckets, had a temperature of 104 and his stomach seemed to bulge with pieces of broken glass that ground themselves into his flesh and organs ferociously.

He surfaced twenty-four hours later, weak and curiously light-headed, but free from pain. The room was in half-darkness, the only light a small lamp which stood on the bedside locker. One of the screws from the prison, an ex-Welsh Guardsman called Jones, nodded on a chair against the wall as per regulations.

Doyle moistened cracked lips and tried to whistle, but at that moment the door opened and a staff nurse entered, a towel over her arm. She was West Indian, dark and supple. To Doyle after two and a half years on the wrong side of the wall, the Queen of Sheba herself couldn't have looked more desirable.

As she moved across to the bed, he closed his eyes quickly. He was aware of her closeness, warm and perfumed with lilac, the rustle of her skirt as she turned and tiptoed across to Jones. Doyle watched her from beneath lowered eyelids as the Welshman came awake with a start.

'Here, what's going on?' he said in some alarm. 'Is the Gunner all right?'

She put out a hand to restrain him. 'He's still asleep. Would you like to go down to the canteen?'

'Well, I shouldn't really, you know,' Jones told her in his high Welsh voice.

'You'll be all right, I'll stay,' she said. 'Nothing can possibly happen – he's still asleep. After what he's been through he must be as weak as a kitten.'

'All right then,' Jones whispered. 'A cup of tea and a smoke. I'll be back in ten minutes.'

As they moved to the door she said, 'Tell me, why do you call him the Gunner?'

Jones chuckled. 'Well, that's what he was, you see. A gunner in the Royal Artillery. Then when he came out and went into the ring, that's what they called him. Gunner Doyle.'

'He was a prizefighter?'

'One of the best middleweights in the game.' Jones was unable to keep the enthusiasm from his voice for like most Welshmen he was a fanatic where boxing was concerned. 'North of England champion. Might have been a contender if he could have left the skirts alone.'

'What was his crime?' she whispered, curiosity in her voice.

'Now there he did really manage to scale the heights, as you might say.' Jones chuckled at his own wit. 'He was a cat burglar – one of the best in the game and it's a dying art, believe me. Climb anything he could.'

The door closed behind him and the staff nurse turned and looked across at the Gunner. He lowered his eyelids softly as she came across to the bed. He was acutely aware of her closeness, the perfume filled his nostrils, lilac, heavy and clinging, fresh after rain, his favourite flower. The stiff uniform dress rustled as she leaned across him to put the towel on the table on the other side.

The Gunner opened his eyes and took in everything. The softly rounded curves, the dress riding up her thighs as she leaned across, the black stockings shining in the lamplight. With a sudden fierce chuckle he cupped his right hand around her left leg and slid it up inside her skirt to the band of warm flesh at the top of her stocking.

'By God, that's grand,' he said.

Her eyes were very round as she turned to look at him. For a frozen moment she stared into his face, then jumped backwards with a little cry. She stared at him in astonishment and the Gunner grinned.

'I once shared a cell at the Ville with a bloke who did that to a big blonde who was standing in front of him in a bus queue one day. Just for a laugh. They gave him a year in the nick. Makes you wonder what the country's coming to.'

She turned without a word and rushed out, the door bouncing back against the wall before closing. It occurred to the Gunner almost at once that she wasn't coming back. Add that to the fact that Jones would be at least fifteen minutes in the canteen and it left a situation that was full of possibilities.

It also occurred to him that with full remission he had only another ten months of his sentence to serve, but at that sudden exciting moment, ten months stretched into an infinity that had no end. He flung the bedclothes to one side and swung his legs to the floor.

An athlete by profession all his life, the Gunner had taken good care to keep himself in first-class physical trim even in prison, and this probably accounted for the fact that, apart from a moment of giddiness as he first stood up, he felt no ill effects at all as he crossed to the locker against the wall and opened it. There was an old dressing-gown inside, but no slippers. He pulled it on quickly, opened the door and peered out into the corridor.

It was anything but deserted. Two doctors stood no more than ten yards away deep in conversation and a couple of porters pushed a floor polisher between them, its noiseless hum vibrating on the air. The Gunner turned and walked the other way without hesitation. When he turned the corner at the far end he found himself in a cul-de-sac. There was a service elevator facing him and a door at the side of it opened on to a dark concrete stairway. The elevator was on its way up so he took the stairs, running down lightly, the concrete cold on his bare feet.

Ten floors down, he arrived at the basement, opened the door at the bottom and found himself in a small entrance hall. One door opened into a side courtyard, heavy rain slanting down through the lamp that was bracketed to the wall above the entrance. But he wouldn't last five minutes out there on a night like this without shoes and some decent clothes. He turned and opened the other door and immediately heard voices approaching. Without hesitation he plunged into the heavy rain, crossed the tiny courtyard and turned into the street keeping close to the wall.

'So you were only out of the room for fifteen minutes?' Brady said.

'As long as it took me to get down to the canteen, have a cup of tea and get back again.' Jones' face was white and drawn. 'The dirty bastard. Why did he have to do this to me? God knows what might happen. I could lose my pension.'

'You've only yourself to blame,' Miller said coldly. 'So don't start trying to put it on to Doyle. He saw his chance and took it. Nobody can blame him for that.'

He dismissed the prison officer with a nod and turned to the young staff nurse. 'You told Jones you'd stay in the room till he got back. Why did you leave?'

She struggled with the truth for a moment, but the thought of recounting in detail what had happened to the two police officers was more than she could bear.

'I'd things to do,' she said. 'I thought it would be all right. He was asleep.'

'Or so it seemed. I understand you told the first officer you saw that there was only an old dressing-gown in the cupboard?'

'That's right.'

'But no shoes or slippers?'

'Definitely not.'

Miller nodded and went out into the corridor, Brady at his heels. 'All right, Jack, you're Doyle in a hurry in bare feet and a dressing-gown. What do you do?'

Brady glanced left along the quiet end of the corridor

and led the way. He paused at the lift, frowned, then opened the door and peered down into the dark well of the concrete stairway. 'On a hunch I'd say he went this way. A lot safer than the lift.'

They went down quickly and at the bottom Miller pushed open the outside door and looked out into the rain. 'Not very likely. He'd need clothes.'

The other door led into a narrow corridor lined on one side with half a dozen green painted lockers. Each one was padlocked and carried an individual's name on a small white card. They were aware of the gentle hum of the oil-fired heating plant somewhere near at hand and in a small office at the end of the corridor, they found the Chief Technician.

Miller showed him his warrant card. 'Looking for the bloke that skipped out are you?' the man said.

'That's right. He'd need clothes. Anything missing down here?'

'Not a chance,' the Chief Technician shook his head. 'I don't know if you noticed, but all the lads keep their lockers padlocked. That was on advice from one of your blokes after we had a lot of pinching last year. Too easy for people to get in through the side door.'

Miller thanked him and they went back along the corridor, and stood on the steps looking out at the driving rain.

'You're thinking he just walked out as he was?' Brady suggested.

Miller shrugged. 'He didn't have much time, remember. One thing's certain – he couldn't afford to hang about.'

Brady shook his head. 'He wouldn't last long in his bare feet on a night like this. Bound to be spotted by someone sooner or later.'

'As I see it he has three possible choices,' Miller said. 'He can try to steal a car, but that's messy because he's got to nose his way round till he finds one that some idiot's forgotten to lock and in that rig-out of his, he's certain to be noticed.'

'He could always hang around some alley and wait his chance to mug the first bloke who went by.'

Miller nodded. 'My second choice, but it's still messy and there aren't many people around the back streets on a night like this. He could get pneumonia waiting. My own hunch is that he's making for somewhere definite. Somewhere not too far away perhaps. Who were his friends?'

'Come off it, he didn't have any.' Brady chuckled. 'Except for the female variety. The original sexual athlete, the Gunner. Never happy unless he had three or four birds on the go at once.'

'What about Mona Freeman?' Miller said. 'He was going to marry her.'

'She was a mug if she believed him.' Brady shook his head. 'She's still in Holloway. Conspiracy to defraud last year.'

'All right then,' Miller said. 'Get out the street directory and let's take a look at the map. Something might click while you're looking at it.'

Brady had grown old on the streets of the city and had developed an extraordinary memory for places and faces, the minutiae of city life. Now he unfolded the map at the back of his pocket directory and examined the area around the Infirmary. He gave a sudden grunt. 'Doreen Monaghan.'

'I remember her,' Miller said. 'Little Irish girl of seventeen just over from the bogs. She thought the sun shone out of the Gunner's backside.'

'Well, she isn't seventeen any longer,' Brady said. 'Has a flat in a house in Jubilee Terrace less than a quarter of a mile from here. Been on the game just over a year now.'

'Let's go then.' Miller grinned. 'And don't forget that right of his whatever happens. He's only got to connect once and you won't wake up till next Friday.'

5

When the Gunner hurried across the courtyard and turned into the side street at the rear of the Infirmary, he hadn't the slightest idea what he was going to do next. Certainly he had no particular destination in mind although the icy coldness of the wet flags beneath his bare feet told him that he'd better find one quickly.

The rain was hammering down now which at least kept the streets clear and he paused on a corner to consider his next move. The sign above his head read Jubilee Street and triggered off a memory process that finally brought him to Doreen Monaghan who at one time had worshipped the ground he walked on. She'd written regularly during the first six months of his sentence when he was at Pentonville, but then the letters had tailed off and gradually faded away. The important thing was that she lived at 15 Jubilee Terrace and might still be there.

He kept to the back streets to avoid company and arrived at his destination ten minutes later, a tall, decaying Victorian town house in a twilight area where a flat was high living and most families managed on one room.

The fence had long since disappeared and the garden was a wilderness of weeds and brambles, the privet hedge so tall that the weight of the heavy rain bowed it over. He paused for a moment and looked up. Doreen had had the top floor flat stretching from the front of the house to the rear and light showed dimly through a gap in the curtains which was encouraging.

When he went into the porch there was an innovation, a row of independent letter boxes for mail, each one neatly labelled. Doreen's name was there all right underneath the one at the end and he grinned as he went in through the hall and mounted the stairs. She was certainly in for one hell of a surprise.

The lady in question was at that moment in bed with an able seaman of Her Majesty's Royal Navy home on leave from the Far East and already regretting the dark-skinned girls of Penang and Singapore who knew what it was for and didn't charge too much.

A member of the oldest profession in the world, she had long since discovered that its rewards far exceeded anything that shop or factory could offer and salved her conscience with a visit to the neighbouring church of Christ the King every Monday for confession followed by Mass.

Her sailor having drifted into the sleep of exhaustion, she gently eased herself from beneath the sheets, pulled on an old kimono and lit a cigarette. Having undressed in something of a hurry, his uniform lay on the floor beside a chair and as she picked it up, a leather wallet fell to the floor. There must have been eighty or ninety pounds in there – probably his leave money. She extracted a couple of fivers, slipped them under the edge of the mat, then replaced the wallet.

He stirred and she moved across to the dressing-table and started to put on her stockings. He pushed himself up on one elbow and said sleepily, 'Going out, then?'

'Three quid doesn't get you squatter's rights, you know,' she said. 'Come on now, let's have you out of there and dressed. The night isn't half over and I've things to do.'

At that moment there was a knock at the door. She straightened, surprise on her face. The knocking continued, low but insistent.

She moved to the door and said softly, 'Yes?'

The voice that replied was muffled beyond all recognition. 'Come on, Doreen, open up,' it called. 'See what Santa's brought you.'

'Who is it?' the sailor called, an edge of alarm in his voice.

Doreen ignored him, opened the door on its chain and peered out. Sean Doyle stood there in a pool of water, soaked to the skin, hair plastered to his skull, the scarlet hospital dressing-gown clinging to his lean body like a second skin.

He grinned, the old wicked grin that used to put her on her back in five seconds flat. 'Come on then, darling, I'm freezing to death out here.'

So complete was the surprise, so great the shock of seeing him that she unhooked the chain in a kind of dazed wonder and backed slowly into the room. As the Gunner moved in after her and closed the door the sailor skipped out of bed and pulled on his underpants.

'Here, what's the bloody game?' he demanded.

The Gunner ignored him, concentrating completely on Doreen, whose ample charms were prominently displayed, for the girdle of her kimono, loosely fastened, had come undone.

'By God, but you're a sight for sore eyes, he said, sincere admiration in his voice.

Having had time to take in the Gunner's bedraggled appearance, the sailor's alarm had subsided and there was an edge of belligerency in his voice when he spoke again, 'I don't know who the hell you are, mate, but you'll bloody well get out of it fast if you know what's good for you.'

The Gunner looked him over and grinned amiably. Why don't you shut up, sonny?'

The sailor was young, active and muscular and fancied himself as a fighting man. He came round the end of the bed with a rush, intending to throw this rash intruder out on his ear and made the biggest mistake of his life. The Gunner's left foot slipped forward, knee turned slightly in. The sailor flung the sort of punch that he had seen used frequently and with great success on the films. The Gunner swayed a couple of inches and the punch slid across his shoulder. His left fist screwed into the sailor's solar plexus, his right connected with the edge of the jaw, slamming him back against the far wall from which he rebounded to fall on his face unconscious.

The Gunner turned, untying the cord of his dressing-gown, 'How've you been keeping them, darlin'?' he demanded cheerfully.

'But Gunner – what happened?' she said.

'They had me in the Infirmary for a check-up. One of the screws got a bit dozy so I took my chance and hopped it. Got any clothes?'

She opened a drawer, took out a clean towel and gave it to him, an expression of wonder still on her face. 'No – nothing that would do for you.'

'Never mind – I'll take this bloke's uniform.' He turned her round and slapped her backside. 'Find me something to drink, there's a girl. It was no joke out there in this rig-out on a night like this.'

She went into the kitchen and he could hear her opening cupboards as he stripped and scrubbed himself dry. He had the sailor's trousers and shirt on and was trying to squeeze his feet into the shoes when she returned.

He tossed them into the corner in disgust. 'No bloody good. Two sizes too small. What have you got there?'

'Sherry,' she said. 'It's all I could find. I was never much of a drinker – remember?'

The bottle was about half-full and he uncorked it and took a long swallow. He wiped a hand across his mouth with a sigh of pleasure as the wine burned its way into his stomach.

'Yes, I remember all right.' He emptied the bottle and dropped it on the floor. 'I remember lots of things.'

He opened her kimono gently, and his sigh seemed to

echo into forever. Still sitting on the edge of the bed, he pulled her close to him, burying his face in her breasts.

She ran her fingers through his hair and said urgently, 'Look, Gunner, you've got to get moving.'

'There's always time for this,' he said, and looked up at her, his eyes full of grey smoke. 'All the time in the world.'

He fell back across the bed, pulling her down on top of him and there was a knock on the door.

Doreen jumped up, pulling her kimono about her and demanded loudly, 'Who is it?'

The voice that replied was high and clear. 'Mrs Goldberg, dear. I'd like a word with you.'

'My landlady,' Doreen whispered and raised her voice. 'Can't it wait?'

'I'm afraid not, dear. It really is most urgent.'

'What am I going to do?' Doreen demanded desperately 'She's a funny old bird. She could make a lot of trouble for me.

'Does she know you're on the game?' the Gunner demanded.

'At fifteen quid a week for this rat-trap? What do you think?'

'Fair enough.' The Gunner rolled the unconscious sailor under the bed, lay on it quickly, head propped up against a pillow and helped himself to a cigarette from a packet on the bedside locker. 'Go on, let her in now. I'm just another client.'

Mrs Goldberg called out again impatiently and started to knock as Doreen crossed to the door and opened it on the chain. The Gunner heard the old woman say, 'I must see you, my dear. It's very, very urgent.'

Doreen shrugged and unfastened the chain. She gave a cry of dismay as the door was pushed back sending her staggering across the room to sprawl across the Gunner on the bed.

Nick Miller moved in, Brady at his side, the local patrolman behind them, resplendent in black crash helmet and foul-weather gear.

'All right then, Gunner,' Miller said cheerfully. 'Let's be having you.'

The Gunner laughed out loud. 'Another five minutes and I'd have come quietly, Mr Miller, but to hell with this for a game of soldiers.'

He gave the unfortunate Doreen a sudden, violent push that sent her staggering into Miller's arms, sprang from the bed and was into the kitchen before anyone could make a move. The door slammed in Brady's face as he reached it and the bolt clicked home. He turned and nodded to the young patrolman, a professional rugby player with the local team, who tucked his head into his shoulder and charged as if he was carving his way through a pack of Welsh forwards.

In the kitchen, the Gunner tugged ineffectually at the window, then grabbed a chair and smashed an exit. A second later, the door caved in behind him as the patrolman blasted through and sprawled on his face.

There was a fallpipe about five feet to one side. Without hesitation, the Gunner reached for the rotting gutter above his head, swung out into the rain and grabbed at the pipe as the gutter sagged and gave way.

He hung there for a moment, turned and grinned at Miller, who leaned out of the window, arm outstretched and three feet too short.

'No hard feelings, Mr Miller. See you in church.'

He went down the pipe like a monkey and disappeared into the darkness and rain below. Miller turned and grinned at Brady. 'Still in his bare feet, did you notice? He always was good for a laugh.'

They returned to the bedroom to find Doreen weeping passionately. She flung herself into Brady's arms the moment he appeared.

'Oh, help me, Mr Brady. As God's my judge I didn't know that divil was coming here this night.'

Her accent had thickened appreciably and Brady patted her bottom and shoved her away. 'You needn't put that professional Irish act on with me, Doreen Monaghan. It won't work. I'm a Cork man meself.'

There was a muffled groan from under the bed. Brady leaned down and grabbed a foot, hauling the sailor into plain view, naked except for his underpants.

'Now I'd say that just about rounds the night off,' Miller said to the big Irishman and they both started to laugh.

Mrs Goldberg, seventy and looking every year of it with her long jet earrings and a patina of make-up that gave her a distinct resemblance to a death mask, peered round the door and viewed the splintered door with horror.

'Oh, my God,' she said. 'The damage. Who's going to pay for the damage?'

The young patrolman appeared behind her, looking white and shaken. Miller moved forward, ignoring Mrs Goldberg for the moment. 'What happened to you?'

'Thought I'd better get a general call out for Doyle as soon as possible, Sergeant, so I went straight down to my bike.'

'Good lad,' Brady said. 'That's using your nut.'

'They've been trying to get in touch with Sergeant Miller for the last ten minutes or so.'

'Oh, yes,' Miller said. 'Anything important?'

'Chief Superintendent Mallory wants you to meet him at Dob Court, Sergeant. That's off Gascoigne Street on the north side of Jubilee Park. The beat man found a woman there about twenty minutes ago.' Suddenly he looked sick. 'Looks like another Rainlover killing.'

There were at least a dozen patrol cars in Gascoigne Street when Miller and Brady arrived in the Mini-Cooper and the

Studio, the Forensic Department's travelling laboratory, was just drawing up as they got out and moved along the wet pavement to Dob Court.

As they approached, two men emerged and stood talking. One was Detective Inspector Henry Wade, Head of Forensic, a fat balding man who wore horn-rimmed spectacles and a heavy overcoat. He usually smiled a lot, but now he looked grim and serious as he wiped rain from his glasses with a handkerchief and listened to what Detective Chief Superintendent George Mallory of Scotland Yard's Murder Squad was saying to him.

He nodded and moved away and Mallory turned to Miller. 'Where were you?'

He was forty-five years of age, crisp, intelligent, the complete professional. The provincials he had to work with usually didn't like him, which suited him down to the ground because he detested inefficiency in any form and had come across too much of it for comfort on his forays outside London.

He thoroughly approved of Miller with his sharp intelligence and his law degree, because it was in such men that the salvation of the country's out-dated police system lay. Under no circumstances would he have dreamt of making his approval apparent.

'Brady and I had a lead on Doyle.'

'The prisoner who escaped from the Infirmary? What happened?'

Miller told him briefly and Mallory nodded. 'Never mind that now. Come and have a look at this.'

The body lay a little way inside the alley covered with a coat against the heavy rain until the Studio boys could get a tarpaulin rigged. The constable who stood beside it held his torch close as Mallory lifted the raincoat.

'From the looks of it her neck is broken just like the others,' Mallory said, 'but the first thing we've got to do is find out who she is. Typical of a lot of these girls these days there isn't any kind of identification whatsoever in her handbag.'

Miller looked down at the waxen face turned sideways awkwardly, the eyes staring into eternity. When he spoke, it was with difficulty.

'I think I can help you there, sir.'

'You know her?'

'Her name is Packard, sir,' Miller said hoarsely. 'Grace Packard.'

6

The Gunner went through the back gate of the yard at the rear of Doreen's house and ran like a hare, turning from one street into another without hesitation, completely forgetting his bare feet in the excitement of the moment.

Then he paused in a doorway for a breather; his heart was pounding like a trip-hammer, but not because he was afraid. On the contrary, he found himself in the grip of a strange exhilaration. A psychologist might have found a reason in the sudden release from confinement after two and a half years in a prison cell. The Gunner only knew that he was free and he lifted his face up to the rain and laughed out loud. The chase was on.

He would lose it in the end, he knew that, but he'd give them a run for their money.

He moved towards the end of the street and paused. A woman's voice said clearly, 'Able-fox-victor come in please. I have a 952 for you.'

He peered round the corner and saw a police car parked, window open as a beat constable in helmet and cape leaned down to speak to the driver. The Gunner retreated hastily and trotted towards the far end of the street. He was no more than half-way along when a police motorcyclist turned the corner and came towards him. The man saw him at once and came on with a sudden burst of speed, engine roaring. The Gunner ran across the street and ducked into a narrow entry between two houses.

He found himself in a small courtyard faced by a stone wall a good fifteen feet high and in one corner was an old washhouse of the type common to late Victorian houses. He pulled himself up on to the sloping roof as the patrolman pounded into the entry blowing his whistle, and reached for the top of the wall, sliding over silently as the policeman arrived.

The sound of the whistle faded as he worked his way through a network of backyards and alleys that stretched towards the south side of Jubilee Park. He stopped once as a police car's siren sounded close by and then another lifted on the night air in the middle distance. He started to run again. The bastards were certainly doing him proud.

Ten minutes later he had almost reached the park when another siren not too far in front of him made him pause. It was standard police procedure on this sort of chase, he knew that, intended to confuse and bewilder the quarry until he did something stupid.

But the Gunner was too old a fox for that one. The park was out. What he needed now was somewhere to lie up for a few hours until the original excitement had died down.

He retraced his steps and turned into the first side street. It was flanked by high walls and on the left, a massive wooden gate carried the sign *Henry Crowther and Sons – Transport*. It seemed just the sort of place he was looking for and for once his luck was in. There was the usual small judas with a yale lock set in the main gate. Someone had left it on the latch for it opened to his touch.

He found four trucks parked close together in a cobbled

yard. There was a house at the other end and light streamed between the curtains of a ground floor window.

When he peered inside he saw a white-haired old woman sitting in front of a bright coal fire watching television. She had a cigarette in one hand and what looked like a glass of whisky in the other. He envied her both and was conscious of his feet for the first time since leaving Doreen's flat. They were cold and raw and hurt like hell. He hobbled across the yard towards a building on the right of the house and went in through doors which stood open. It had been a stable in years gone by, but from the looks of things was now used as a workshop or garage.

Wooden stairs went up through a board floor to what had obviously been the hayloft. It was in almost total darkness and seemed to be full of drums of oil and assorted junk. A half-open wooden door creaked uneasily and rain drifted in on the wind. A small wooden platform jutted out ten feet above the cobbles and a block and tackle hung from a loading hook.

He had a good view of the house and the yard, which was important, and sank down on an old tarpaulin and started to massage his feet vigorously. They hadn't felt like this since Korea and he shuddered as old memories of frostbite and comrades who had lost toes and even feet in that terrible retreat south during the first winter campaign, came back to him.

The gate clicked in the darkness below and he straightened and peered out. Someone hurried across the yard and opened the front door. As light streamed out, he saw that it was a young woman in a raincoat with a scarf bound around her head, peasant-fashion. She looked pretty wet and the Gunner smiled as she went inside and closed the door.

He leaned against the wall and stared into the rain, hunger gnawing at his stomach. Not that there was anything he could do about that. Later, perhaps, when all the lights had gone out in the house he might see if he had lost any of his old skill. Shoes and something to eat and maybe an old raincoat – that's all he needed. If he could make it as far as the Ring Road there were any one of half a dozen transport cafés where long-distance lorry drivers pulled up for rest and a meal. All he had to do was get himself into the back of a truck and he could be two hundred miles away by breakfast.

He flinched, dazzled by light that poured from one of the second floor windows. When he looked across he could see the girl standing in the doorway of what was obviously her bedroom. The wind lifted, driving rain before it and the judas gate creaked. The Gunner peered cautiously into the darkness, imagining for a moment that someone else had arrived, then turned his attention to the bedroom again.

The girl didn't bother to draw the curtains, secure in the knowledge that she was cut off from the street by the high wall and started to undress, obviously soaked to the skin.

The Gunner watched with frank and open admiration. Two and a half years in the nick and the only female company a monthly visit from his Aunty Mary, a seventy-year-old Irish woman with a heart of corn whose visits with their acid asides on authority, the peelers as she still insisted on calling them, and life in general, always kept him laughing for at least a week afterwards. But this? Now this was different.

The young woman dried off with a large white towel, then examined herself critically in the mirror. Strange how few women looked their best in the altogether but she was more than passable. The black hair almost reached the pointed breasts and a narrow waist swelled into hips that were perhaps a trifle too large for some tastes, but suited the Gunner down to the ground.

When she dressed again, she didn't bother with a suspender belt. Simply pulled on a pair of hold-up stockings, black pants and bra, then took a dress from the wardrobe. He'd heard they were wearing them short since he'd gone down, but this was ridiculous. Not only was it half-way up her thighs, but crocheted into the bargain so you could see through it like the tablecloth Aunty Mary had kept in the parlour when he was a kid.

She stood at the dressing table and started to brush her hair, perhaps the most womanly of all actions, and the Gunner felt strangely sad. He'd started off by fancying a bit of the usual and why not? He'd almost forgotten what it tasted like and the business with Doreen had certainly put him in the mood. But now, lying there in the loft with the rain falling, he felt like some snotty-nosed kid with his arse out of his pants, looking in at what he could never have and no one to blame but himself.

She tied her hair back with a velvet ribbon, crossed to the door and went out, switching off the light. The Gunner sighed and eased back slightly and below in the yard there was the scrape of a foot on stone.

Jenny Crowther was twenty-two years of age, a practical, hard-headed Yorkshire girl who had never visited London in her life, but in her crocheted mini-dress and dark stockings she would have passed in the West End without comment.

'Feeling better, love?' her grandmother enquired as she entered the room.

Jenny nodded, rubbing her hands as she approached the fire. 'It's nice to be dry.'

'Eh, Jenny love,' the old woman said. 'I don't know how you can wear yon dress. I can see your knickers.'

'You're supposed to, Gran.' The old woman stared in blank amazement across a gulf that was exactly fifty years wide and the girl picked up the empty coal scuttle. 'I'll get some coal, then we'll have a nice cup of tea.'

The coal was in a concrete bunker to the left of the front door and when she opened it, light flooded across the yard, outlining her thighs clearly through the crocheted dress as she paused, looking at the rain. She took an old raincoat from a peg, hitched it over her shoulders, went down the steps and lifted the iron trap at the base of the coal bunker. There was no sound and yet she turned, aware from some strange sixth sense of the danger that threatened her. She caught a brief glimpse of a dark shape, the vague blur of a face beneath a rain hat, and then great hands had her by the throat.

The Gunner went over the edge of the platform, hung for a moment at the end of the block and tackle, then dropped to the cobbles. He moved in fast, smashing a fist into the general area of the other man's kidneys when he got close enough. It was like hitting a rock wall. The man flung the girl away from him and turned. For a moment, the Gunner saw the face clearly, lips drawn back in a snarl. An arm swept sideways with amazing speed, bunched knuckles catching him on the side of the head, sending him back against one of the trucks, The Gunner went down on one knee and the girl's attacker went past him in a rush. The judas banged and the man's running steps faded along the back street.

As the Gunner got to his feet, Ma Crowther called from the doorway, 'Make another move and I'll blow your head off.'

She was holding a double-barrelled shotgun, the barrels of which had been sawn down to nine inches in length, transforming it into one of the most dangerous and vicious weapons in the book.

Jenny Crowther moved away from the wall, a hand to

her throat and shook her head. 'Not him, Gran. I don't
know where he came from, but it was a good job he was
around.'

The Gunner was impressed. Any other bird he'd ever
known, even the really hard knocks, would have been on
their backs after an experience like that, but not this one.

'Which mob were you in then, the Guards?' he demanded.

The girl turned to look at him, grinning instantly and
something was between them at once, unseen perhaps, but
almost physical in its strength. Like meeting like, with
instantaneous recognition.

She looked him over, taking in the sailor's uniform, the
bare feet and laughed, a hand to her mouth. 'Where on
earth did you spring from?'

'The loft,' the Gunner told her.

'Shall I get the police, love?' Ma Crowther asked.

The Gunner cut in quickly. 'Why bother the peelers about
a little thing like this? You know what it's like on a Saturday
night. A bloke has a few pints, then follows the first bit of
skirt he sees. Sometimes he tries to go a bit too far like the
geezer who just skipped, but it's all come out in the wash.
Once it's reported in the papers, all the old dears will think
he screwed you, darlin', even if he didn't,' he assured the
girl gaily.

'Here, just a minute,' the old woman said. Bare feet and
dressed like a sailor. I know who you are.' She turned to
the girl and said excitedly, 'They've just had a flash on
Northern Newscast. This is Gunner Doyle.'

'Gunner Doyle?' the girl said.

'The boxer. Your dad used to take me to see him. Topped
the bill at the Town Hall a couple of times. Doing five years
at Manningham Gaol. They took him into the Infirmary
because they thought he was ill and he gave them the slip
earlier this evening.'

The girl stood looking at him, legs slightly apart, a hand

on her hip and the Gunner managed a tired, tired grin. 'That's me, the original naughty boy.'

'I don't know about that,' she said. 'But you're bleeding like a stuck pig. Better come inside.' She turned and took the shotgun from the old woman's grasp. 'It's all right, Gran. He won't bite.'

'You forgot something,' the Gunner said.

She turned in the doorway. 'What's that, then?'

'What you came out for in the first place.' He picked up the coal scuttle. 'Lad's work, that's what my Aunty Mary always used to say.'

He got down on his knees to fill it. When he straightened and turned wearily, the girl said, 'I don't know why, but I think I like your Aunty Mary.'

The Gunner grinned. 'She'd go for you, darlin'. I'll tell you that for nothing.'

He swayed suddenly and she reached out and caught his arm in a grip of surprising strength. 'Come on then, soldier, you've had enough for one night,' and she drew him into the warmth.

7

Faulkner frowned, enormous concentration on his face as he leaned over the drawing board and carefully sketched in another line. When the door bell rang he ignored it and continued working. There was another more insistent ring. He cursed softly, covered the sketch with a clean sheet of cartridge paper and went to the door.

He opened it to find Chief Superintendent Mallory standing there, Miller at his shoulder. Mallory smiled politely. 'Mr Faulkner? Chief Superintendent Mallory. I believe you've already met Detective Sergeant Miller.'

Faulkner showed no particular surprise, but his eyes

widened slightly when he looked at Miller. 'What is all this? Tickets for the policeman's ball?'

Mallory's manner was dangerously gentle. 'I wonder if we could have a few words with you, sir?'

Faulkner stood to one side, ushering them into the studio with a mock bow. 'Be my guest, Superintendent.'

He closed the door and as he turned to face them, Mallory said in a calm, matter-of-fact voice, 'We're making enquiries concerning a Miss Packard, Mr Faulkner. I understand you might be able to help us?'

Faulkner lit a cigarette and shrugged. 'To the best of my knowledge I've never even heard of her.'

'But she was with you earlier this evening at Joanna Hartmann's party,' Miller put in.

'Oh, you mean Grace?' Faulkner nodded. 'I'm with you now. So the viper's discovered it can sting, has it? Has he made a formal complaint?'

'I'm afraid I don't understand you, sir,' Mallory said. 'Grace Packard is dead. Her body was found in an alley called Dob Court not far from here less than an hour ago. Her neck was broken.'

There was a short silence during which both policemen watched Faulkner closely, waiting for some reaction. He seemed genuinely bewildered and put a hand to his forehead. 'Either of you feel like a drink?'

Mallory shook his head. 'No thank you, sir.'

'Well, I do.' He moved to the fire and tossed his cigarette into the flames. 'You say she was found about an hour ago?'

'That's right.' Faulkner glanced up at the clock. It was just coming on to eleven thirty-five and Mallory said, 'What time did she leave here?'

Faulkner turned slowly. 'Who said she was here at all?' He looked at Miller with a frown. 'Have you been bothering Joanna?'

Miller shook his head. 'When I telephoned, the party was still going strong from the sound of things. I spoke to the maid. She told me that you and the girl had left together.'

'All right – she was here, but for no more than ten minutes. I left at half-ten.'

'Which would indicate that she was murdered almost immediately,' Mallory said.

'Is this another of those Rainlover things?'

'We can't be sure yet. Let's say it falls into a familiar pattern.'

'Two in two days.' Faulkner was by now quite obviously over the initial shock. 'He's getting out of hand.'

Miller watched his every move, slightly puzzled. The man actually seemed to be enjoying the whole sorry business. He wondered what Faulkner had in his veins instead of blood and the big man said, 'I hope you won't mind me asking, but am I first on the list?'

'This is an informal interview, sir, solely to help us in our enquiries,' Mallory told him. 'Of course you're perfectly entitled to have your solicitor present.'

'Wouldn't dream of dragging him away from the party,' Faulkner said. 'He deserves it. You just fire away. I'll do anything I can to help.'

'You made a rather puzzling remark when we first came in,' Miller said. 'Something about a viper discovering that it could sting. What did you mean by that?'

'I might as well tell you, I suppose. I've been working rather hard lately and completely forgot about Joanna's birthday party. A friend, Mr Jack Morgan, called for me and we stopped in at The King's Arms in Lazer Street for a quick one. While we were there, the girl came in.'

'And you got into conversation?' Mallory said.

'On the contrary, I picked her up quite deliberately. She was waiting for her boyfriend and he was late. I invited her to the party.'

'Why did you do that, sir?'

'Because I knew it would be infested by a miserable bunch of stuffed shirts and I thought she might liven things up a bit. She was that sort of girl. Ask Miller, he was paying enough attention to her from what I could see. An honest tart. Hair out of a bottle and a skirt that barely covered her backside.'

'You were at the party for about twenty minutes before I left,' Miller said. 'You couldn't have stayed for long.'

'About half an hour in all.'

'And the girl left with you?'

'You already know that, for Christ's sake.' He swung on Mallory. 'Are you sure you won't have that drink?'

'No, sir.'

'Then I will.' He went behind the bar and reached for a bottle. 'All of a sudden, things seem to be taking a rather nasty turn.'

Mallory ignored the remark. 'You say she was here for no more than ten minutes.'

'That's right.'

'I would have thought she'd have stayed longer.'

'If I'd brought her back to sleep with me, the poor little bitch would be alive now, but I didn't.'

'Why *did* you bring her back?'

'To pose for me.' He swallowed a large whisky and poured himself another. 'I offered her five quid to come back and pose for me.'

For a brief moment Mallory's composure slipped. He glanced at Miller in bewilderment and Faulkner said, 'As it happens I'm a sculptor. That little lot on the dais behind you is a commission I'm working on at the moment for the new Sampson building. The Spirit of Night. This is just a rough draft, so to speak – plaster on wire. I thought a fifth figure might give more balance. I brought Grace back with me to stand up there with the others so I could see.'

'And for that you paid her five pounds?'

'Ten, as a matter of fact. I wanted to know and I wanted to know right then. She happened to be available.'

'And what did you decide, sir?' Mallory asked.

'I'm still thinking about it. Well, what happens now?'

'Oh, we'll have to make further enquiries, sir,' Mallory said. 'We'll probably have to see you again, of course, you realize that.'

They walked to the door and Faulkner opened it for them. 'What about her boyfriend, Superintendent? Harold, I think she called him.'

'I don't follow you, sir.'

Faulkner laughed boyishly. 'I suppose I'd better come clean. He arrived just as we were leaving The King's Arms. There was something of a scene. Nothing I couldn't handle, but he was pretty angry at the girl more than me.'

'That's very interesting, sir,' Mallory said. 'I'll bear it in mind.'

He went out. As Miller moved to follow him, Faulkner tapped him on the shoulder. 'A private word, Sergeant,' he said softly and the smile had left his face. 'Stay away from my fiancée in future. One likes to know when a friend is a friend. The trouble with all you bloody coppers is that you're on duty twenty-four hours a day.'

There was a sudden viciousness in his voice, but Miller refused to be drawn. 'Good night, Mr Faulkner,' he said formally and went out.

Faulkner slammed the door and turned with a frown. For a while he stood there looking thoughtful, then moved back to the drawing board. He removed the clean sheet of cartridge paper, disclosing a sketch of the four statues. After a while he picked up his pencil and started to add an additional figure with bold, sure strokes.

*

Outside in the street, it was still raining heavily as Miller
and Mallory got into the Chief Superintendent's car where
Jack Brady waited with the driver.

'What did you think?' Mallory demanded.

Miller shrugged. 'It's hard to say. He's not the sort you
meet every day of the week. Did you buy his story about
taking the girl back to the studio to pose for him?'

'It's crazy enough to be true, we just can't tell at this
stage. He's certainly right about one thing – the girl's
boyfriend wants checking out.' He turned to Brady. 'You
can handle that one. The fiancé's name is Harold, that's all
we know. The girl's father should be able to give you the
rest. When you get the address, go straight round and bring
him down to Central for questioning.'

'What about me, sir?' Miller asked.

'You can go back to that damned party. See Joanna
Hartmann and check Faulkner's story. I still don't understand why he left so early. I'll see you at Central as well
when you've finished. Get cracking then – I'll drop Brady
off.'

His car moved away into the rain. Miller watched it go
and sighed heavily as he got into the Mini-Cooper. His
second visit to Joanna Hartmann's that night was something
he didn't fancy one little bit.

8

The party had just about folded and the guests had departed
except for Jack Morgan and Frank Marlowe who sat at the
bar with Joanna and her aunt, having a final drink before
leaving.

The door bell chimed and Joanna looked up in surprise.
'Now, who on earth can that be?'

'Probably Bruno,' her aunt remarked acidly. 'Returning to tell you that all is forgiven.

'Well, it won't work – not this time.' Joanna was annoyed. 'He can stew for a while.'

There was another ring and Frank Marlowe started to rise. 'I'd better go . . .'

'No I'll handle it. I'll see him myself.'

She opened the door, braced for her encounter and found Nick Miller standing there. 'Why, Nick,' she said in bewilderment.

'Could I come in for a moment?'

'Certainly.' She hesitated. 'I'm afraid nearly everyone's gone home. We're just having a final drink. Why don't you join us?'

'I'd better not,' he said. 'To tell you the truth, I'm here on business.'

As she closed the door, she stiffened then turned very slowly. 'Bruno? Something has happened to Bruno?'

Miller shook his head quickly. 'He's perfectly all right – I've just been speaking to him. There was a girl here earlier – a girl called Grace Packard. He brought her with him, didn't he?'

Jack Morgan got up from his stool and came forward. 'That's right, but she left some time ago. Look here, Miller, what is this?'

'As I said, I've already spoken to Faulkner. She went back to his studio with him and left at approximately ten-thirty. She was found by a police officer less than fifteen minutes later in an alley a couple of streets away.'

There was a shocked gasp from Mary Beresford and Marlowe said in a whisper, 'You mean she's dead?'

'That's right. Murdered. Her neck was broken, probably by a sharp blow from the rear.'

'The Rainlover,' Mary Beresford said so quietly that it might have been a sigh.

'It could be,' Miller said. 'On the other hand that kind of killer tends to work to a pattern and it's a little close to his last one.' He turned to Morgan. 'You've been here all the time?'

'Since I arrived at eight-thirty or so.'

'I can confirm that,' Joanna said quickly. 'We all can.'

'Look here,' Marlowe said. 'Can we know where we stand? Is this an official call?'

'Just an enquiry.' Miller turned to Joanna again. 'I understand from your fiancé that he didn't stay very long. Isn't that rather unusual considering that it was your birthday party?'

'Bruno's very much a law unto himself,' she said calmly.

Mary Beresford came in under full sail. 'Oh, for heaven's sake tell the truth about him for once, Joanna. He didn't stay long because he was asked to leave.'

'And why was that?'

'I should have thought it sufficiently obvious. You were here – you saw what happened. He picked that little tart up in a saloon bar and brought her here with the deliberate intention of ruining the party for everyone.'

'Aunt Mary – please,' Joanna said.

'It's true, isn't it?' The old woman's eyes glittered fiercely. 'He arrived dressed like a tramp as usual and within twenty minutes was trying to break the place up.'

Miller turned enquiringly. Jack Morgan picked up the two halves of the wooden chopping block that lay on the bar. 'Bruno's latest parlour trick.'

'Karate?'

'That's right. Imagine what a blow like that would do to somebody's jaw.'

A brown belt who was soon to face re-grading to first Dan, Miller could have told him in detail. Instead he looked at Marlowe speculatively. 'That bruise on your face – did he do that?'

'Look here,' Marlowe said angrily. 'I don't know what

all this is leading up to, but if you think I'm laying a complaint against him you're mistaken. There was a rather undignified squabble – there usually is when Bruno's around. Nothing more.

'And he left with Grace Packard. You must have found that rather upsetting, Joanna.'

'God knows, but she's had enough practice by now,' Mary Beresford said. 'You say he took her home with him?'

'That's right, but apparently she only stayed ten minutes or so.'

'A likely story.'

'Confirmed by the time the body was found. He says that he gave her ten pounds to pose for him. Would you say that was likely?'

Frank Marlowe laughed harshly. 'More than that – typical.'

Joanna had gone very white, but hung on to her dignity with, everything she had left. 'As I've already said, he's very much a law unto himself.'

'He's been working on a special commission,' Jack Morgan said. 'One of the most important he's had. It started as a single figure four or five weeks ago and now comprises a group of four. He was discussing with me earlier the question of adding a fifth to give the thing balance.'

Miller nodded. 'Yes, he did mention that.'

'Then why did you have to ask?' Joanna said sharply.

Miller frowned. 'I'm afraid I don't follow you.'

'Are we to take it that my fiancé is under some kind of suspicion in this business?'

'Routine, Joanna, pure routine at the moment. But it has to be done, you must see that surely.'

'I don't at all,' she said hotly. 'What I do see is that you were a guest in my house earlier this evening because I had imagined you a friend.'

'Rubbish,' Miller said crisply. 'You asked me to your party

for one reason only. Because my brother is probably the most influential man in Northern Television and you're worried because you've heard there's talk of taking off your series at the end of this season.'

'How dare you?' Mary Beresford said. 'I'll complain to your superiors.'

'You can do what you damned well like,' Miller helped himself to a cigarette from a box on the table and smiled calmly. 'With my present service and including certain special payments my annual salary at the moment as a Detective Sergeant is one thousand three hundred and eighty-two pounds, Mrs Beresford. It might interest you to know that every penny of it goes for income tax. Gives me a wonderful feeling of freedom when I'm dealing with people like you.'

He turned back to Joanna Hartmann. 'Whether you like it or not you've got a few unpleasant facts to face. Number one as far as I'm concerned is that Grace Packard was murdered within an hour of leaving this flat in company with your fiancé, so don't start trying to get on your high horse because we have the impudence to suggest that he might be able to help us with our enquiries.'

'I'm Mr Faulkner's solicitor,' Jack Morgan said. 'Why wasn't I present when he was questioned?'

'Why not ask him? He was certainly offered the privilege.' Miller turned very quickly, moved to the door and opened it. 'I'll probably have to see you again, Miss Hartmann,' he said formally. 'We'd appreciate it if you'd make yourself available during the next couple of days.'

'But Miss Hartmann's due in London tomorrow for an important business conference,' Frank Marlowe said.

'I can't prevent her going,' Miller said, 'but it would certainly be a great pity if Faulkner happened to need her and she wasn't here.'

He closed the door and chuckled grimly as he went along the corridor to the lift. He'd certainly stirred things up there.

It would be more than interesting to see what the outcome, if any, would be.

The heavy silence after Miller had gone out was first broken by Frank Marlowe. 'I don't like the smell of this – don't like it at all.'

'Neither do I,' Jack Morgan said.

Joanna went up the steps to the door, opened a cupboard and took out a sheepskin coat. She pulled it on quickly.

'Did you come in your car, Jack?'

'Yes.'

'Good . . . I'd like you to run me round to Bruno's.'

Her aunt put a hand on her arm as if she would restrain her. 'For goodness' sake, Joanna, don't be a fool. Stay out of this.'

Joanna turned on her fiercely. 'You don't like him, do you, Aunt Mary? You never did. Because of that you want to believe that he's somehow mixed up in this business. Well, I never will.'

The old woman turned away, suddenly looking her age and Frank Marlowe said, 'Want me to come?'

Joanna shook her head. 'Better not. Would you mind. hanging on till we get back?'

'I'll be here.'

Jack Morgan opened the door for her and as Joanna turned, her aunt made a final try, 'Joanna,' she said sharply. 'You must listen to me. It's for your own good. Think of your career. You can't afford to get mixed up in the kind of scandal this could cause.'

Joanna ignored her completely. 'Ready, Jack?' she said and led the way out.

They didn't talk during the drive to Bruno's place, but when Morgan pulled in at the kerb and switched off the engine, she put a hand on his arm.

'You've known Bruno a long time, Jack, longer than any of us. You don't believe he could . . .'

'Not a chance,' he told her emphatically. 'He's a wild man, I'll give you that, but I couldn't accept the kind of suspicions Nick Miller obviously holds for a moment.'

'That's all I wanted to hear.' She smiled her relief. 'Now let's go up and have a word with him.'

But they were wasting their time. There was no reply to their insistent knocking at Bruno's door. After five minutes of fruitless effort, Morgan turned to her and said gently, 'Better leave it for now, Joanna. He's probably had enough for one night.'

She nodded wearily. 'All right, Jack, take me home. We'll try again in the morning. I'll cancel my trip to London.'

On the other side of the door, Faulkner listened to the footsteps fade as they descended the stairs. His head was hurting again. My God, but it was hurting. He took a couple of the pills the doctor had given him, poured himself a large whisky and stood at the window and looked out into the night.

Rain spattered against the glass and he rested his aching forehead against it. But it didn't help. Quite suddenly it was as if he was suffocating. Air, that's what he needed – the cold air of night to drive away this terrible pain. He grabbed his trenchcoat and hat and let himself out quickly.

9

'Last time I saw you in the ring was when you fought Terry Jones for the area title,' Ma Crowther said. 'I thought you had it in your pocket till he gave you that cut over the eye and the ref stopped the fight in the third.'

'I always did cut too easily,' the Gunner said. 'If it hadn't been for that I could have gone right to the top. The Boxing Board took my licence away after the Terry Jones fight on medical advice. Just a vale of tears, isn't it?'

He looked anything but depressed sitting there at the table wearing an old sweater the girl had found him and a pair of boots that had belonged to her father. He had already worked his way through three fried eggs, several rashers of bacon and half a loaf of bread and was now on his third cup of tea.

'You're a funny one and no mistake.' Jenny Crowther shook her head. 'Doesn't anything ever worry you?'

'Life's too short, darlin'.' He helped himself to a cigarette from the old woman's packet. 'I shared a cell once with a bloke who was big on this yoga lark. You've got to learn to relaxez-vous. Live for today and use the talents the good Lord's given you.'

Jenny laughed helplessly. 'I think that's marvellous. Considering the way you make a living.'

He wasn't in the least embarrassed. 'So I scrounge a few bob where I can. The kind of people I hit can afford it. Insured up to the hilt they are. I don't go around duffing up old women in back street shops.'

'The original Robin Hood,' she said acidly. 'And what happens when someone gets in your way on a job? Do you go quietly or try to smash your way through?'

She piled the dirty dishes on to a tray and went into the kitchen. The Gunner moved across to the fire and sat in the opposite chair to the old woman. 'Is she always as sharp as that?'

'She has to be, lad, running an outfit like this.'

'You mean she's in charge?'

'Her dad passed on a couple of months back – cerebral haemorrhage. Jenny was a hairdresser, a good one too, but she dropped that and took over here. Been trying to keep things going ever since.'

'Having trouble, then?'

'Only what you'd expect. We've eight drivers and two mechanics and there isn't one who wouldn't take advantage if he could. And then there's the foreman, Joe Ogden. He's the worst of the lot. He's shop steward for the union. Always quoting the book at her, making things as difficult as he can.'

'And why would he do that?'

'You've seen her, haven't you?' She poured herself another whisky. 'What about you? Where do you go from here?'

He shrugged. 'I don't know, Ma. If I can get to the Ring Road I could snatch a lift to any one of a dozen places.'

'And then what?' He made no answer and she leaned across and put a hand on his knee. 'Don't be a fool, lad. Give yourself up before it's too late.'

Which was exactly what the Gunner had been thinking, but he didn't say so. Instead, he got to his feet and grinned. 'I'll think about it. In any case there's nothing for you or Jenny to worry about. I'll clear out of here in an hour or so when it's a bit quieter, if that's all right with you.'

He went into the kitchen and found the girl at the sink, an apron around her waist, washing the dishes. 'Need any help?'

'You can dry if you like.'

'Long time since I did this.' He picked up a tea towel.

'Even longer before you do it again.'

'Heh, what have I done?' he demanded.

'It's just that I can't stand waste,' she said. 'I mean look at you. Where on earth do you think you're going to go from here? You won't last long out there with every copper for miles around on the watch for you.'

'Whose side are you on then?'

'That's another thing. You can't be serious for a moment – not about anything.'

She returned to the dishes and the Gunner chuckled. 'I'm glad you're angry anyhow.'

'What's that supposed to mean?'

'Better than no reaction at all. At least you're interested.'

'You'll be lucky. The day I can't do better I'll jump off Queen's Bridge.'

But she was smiling and some of the tension had gone out of her when she returned to the washing-up. 'I was having an interesting chat with your gran,' the Gunner said. 'Seems you've got your hands full at the moment.'

'Oh, we get by.'

'Sounds to me as if you need a good man round the place.'

'Why, are you available?'

He grinned. 'I wish I was, darlin'.'

The judas gate banged outside and steps echoed across the yard. Jenny Crowther frowned. 'That's funny, I dropped the latch when I went out earlier.'

'Anyone else got a key?'

'Not as far as I know. I'll see who it is. You'd better stay here.' He waited, the kitchen door held open slightly so that he could see what took place. Ma Crowther appeared from the other room and watched as Jenny opened the front door.

The man who pushed his way inside wore a donkey jacket with leather patches on the shoulders and had obviously had a drink. He was hefty enough with arms that were a little too long, but his face was puffed up from too much beer and the weak mouth the biggest giveaway of all.

'And what might you want at this time of night, Joe Ogden?' Ma Crowther demanded.

'Leave this to me, Gran,' Jenny said calmly. 'Go on now. I'll be in in a minute.'

The old woman went back into the sitting-room reluctantly

and Jenny closed the door and turned to face Ogden. She held out her hand. 'You used a key to open the outside gate. I don't know where you got it from, but I want it.'

He smiled slyly. 'Nay, lass, I couldn't do that. I like to be able to come and go.' He took a step forward and put his hand on the wall so that she was caged in the corner by the sitting-room door. 'We could get along just fine, you and me. Why not be sensible? A lass like you's got better things to be doing than trying to run a firm like this. Keeping truckies in their place is man's work.'

He tried to kiss her and she twisted her head to one side. 'I'm going to give you five seconds to get out of here. If you don't, I'll send for the police and lay a complaint for assault.'

He jumped back as if he had been stung. 'You rotten little bitch,' he said, his face red and angry. 'You won't listen to reason, will you? Well, just remember this – I'm shop steward here. All I have to do is say the word and every man in the place walks out through that gate with me – they'll have no option. I could make things very awkward for you.'

She opened the door without a word. He stood there glowering at her, then moved out. 'All right, miss,' he said viciously. 'Don't say I didn't warn you.'

She closed the door and turned, shaking with rage. 'I'll kill him. I'll kill the bastard,' she said and then broke down and sobbed, all the worry and frustration of the weeks since her father's death welling up to the surface.

Strong arms pulled her close and a hand stroked her hair. 'Now then, darlin', never say die.' She looked up and the Gunner grinned down at her. 'Only one way to handle a situation like this. Put the kettle on, there's a good girl. I'll be back in five minutes.'

He kissed her full on the mouth and before she could say anything, opened the door and went out into the night.

*

Joe Ogden paused on the corner, swaying slightly for he was still about three-parts drunk. So she wanted it the hard way did she? Right – then that was the way she could have it. He'd show the bitch – by God he would. By the time he was finished she'd come crawling, begging him to sort things out for her and then he'd call the tune all right.

He crossed the street and turned into a narrow lane, head down against the driving rain, completely absorbed by a series of sexual fantasies in which Jenny Crowther was doing exactly as she was told. The lane was badly lit by a number of old-fashioned gas lamps, long stretches of darkness in between and the pavement was in a bad state of repair, the flags lifting dangerously.

The Gunner descended on him like a thunderbolt in the middle of one of the darker stretches and proceeded to take him apart savagely and brutally in a manner that was as exact as any science.

Ogden cried out in pain as he was propelled into the nearest brick wall with a force that took the breath out of his body. He swung round, aware of the pale blur of a face and swung a fist instinctively, catching the Gunner high on the right cheekbone.

It was the only hit he was to make that night. A boot caught him under the right kneecap, a left and a right screwed into his stomach and a knee lifted into his face as he keeled over, for the Gunner was never one to allow the Queensberry rules to get in his way in this sort of affair.

Ogden rolled over in the rain and the Gunner kicked him hard about the body half a dozen times, each blow judged to a nicety. Ogden lay there, face against the pavement, more frightened than he had ever been in his life, expecting to meet his end at any moment.

Instead, his assailant squatted beside him in the darkness and said in a strangely gentle voice, 'You don't know who I am, but I know you and that's all that matters. Now listen carefully because I'm only going to say this once. You'll get your cards and a week's pay in the post Monday. In the future, you stay away from Crowther's yard. Make any kind of trouble at all, union or otherwise, and I'll get you. He grabbed a handful of Ogden's hair. 'Understand?'

'Yes.' Ogden could hardly get the word out as fear seized him by the throat.

'See that you do. Now where's the key to the outside gate?'

Ogden fumbled in his left hand pocket, the Gunner took the yale key from him, slammed him back hard against the pavement and walked away.

Ogden got to his knees, dizzy with pain and pulled himself up against the wall. He caught a brief glimpse of the Gunner running through the lighted area under one of the lamps and then he was alone again. Quite suddenly, and for the first time since childhood, he started to cry, dry sobs tearing at his throat as he turned and stumbled away through the darkness.

Crouched by the open doorway in the loft above the old barn in the exact position the Gunner had occupied earlier, the Rainlover waited patiently, wondering whether the man would return.

The door opened for the second time in ten minutes and the girl appeared, framed against the light, so close that he could see the worry on her face. He started to get up and beyond through the darkness, there was the creaking of the judas gate as it opened. A moment later, the Gunner appeared.

He paused at the bottom of the steps and tossed the key up to Jenny. 'This is yours.'

She glanced at it briefly. 'What happened?'

'Oh, you might say we came to an understanding. He's agreed not to come back. In return he gets his cards and a week's pay, first post Monday morning.'

She tilted his head to one side and examined the bruise that was spreading fast under his right eye. 'Some understanding. You'd better come in and let me do something about that.'

She turned and the Gunner followed her. After he had closed the door, the yard was dark again, but something moved there in the shadows making no more noise than the whisper of dead leaves brushing across the ground in the autumn. The judas gate creaked slightly and closed with a soft click. In the alley, footfalls faded into the rain.

The Gunner emptied the glass of whisky she had given him with a sigh of satisfaction and turned his head to the light as she gently applied a warm cloth to the bruise under his eye.

'What happened to the old lass, then?'

'I told her to go to bed. It's late.'

He glanced at the clock. 'You're right. I'll have to be off soon.'

'No hurry. You'll stand a better chance later on.'

'Maybe you're right.'

He was suddenly tired and with the whisky warm in his stomach, contented in a way that he hadn't been for years. It was pleasant there by the cheerful fire with just the one lamp in the corner and the solid, comfortable furniture. She gave him a cigarette and lit a paper spill at the fire for a light.

He took one of the easy chairs and she sat on the rug, her legs tucked underneath her. The Gunner smoked his cigarette slowly from long habit, making it last, and watched her. Strange, but he hadn't felt like this about a woman before. She had everything a man could ever want – a body to thank God for, a pleasant face, strength, character. He pulled himself up short. This was beginning to get out of hand. Trouble was it had been so damned long since he'd

been within smelling distance of a bird that probably one
of those forty-five-year old Toms from the back of the market
would have looked remarkably like the Queen of the May.

She turned and smiled. 'And what's going on inside that
ugly skull of yours now?'

'Just thinking how you're about the best-looking lass I've
seen in years.'

'Not much of a compliment,' she scoffed. 'Not when you
consider where you've been lately.'

'Been reading up on me, have you?'

She shrugged. 'I caught the final newscast on television.
You'd plenty of competition, by the way. There's been a
woman murdered earlier tonight on the other side of Jubilee
Park.'

'Another of these Rainlover things?'

'Who else could it be?' She shivered and added slowly.
'when I was alone in the kitchen earlier I got to thinking
that maybe that man out there in the yard . . .'

'Was the Rainlover?' The Gunner shook his head emphatically. 'Not a chance. The fact that he's seen off this poor
bitch earlier is proof enough of that. They always work to
a pattern these blokes. Can't help themselves. The chap
who jumped you had something a damned sight more old-
fashioned on his mind.'

She frowned. 'I don't know, I was thinking that maybe
I should report it to the police.'

She hesitated as well she might. Her father had left mother
and daughter a business which was worth in cash and
property some fifteen thousand pounds yet he had never
considered himself as anything other than working class.
His daughter was of the same stubborn breed and had been
raised to obey the usual working class code which insisted
that contact with the police, no matter what the reason,
was something to be avoided at all costs.

'And what were you going to tell them?' demanded the

Gunner. 'That Sean Doyle, with every copper for miles around on his tail, stopped to save you from a fate worse than death, so you fed him and clothed him and sent him on his way rejoicing because you figured you owed him something?' He chuckled harshly. 'They'll have you in a cell in Holloway before you know what's hit you.'

She sighed. 'I suppose you're right.'

'Of course I am.' With some adroitness he changed the subject. 'So I was on the telly, was I?'

'Oh, they did quite a feature on the great Gunner Doyle.'

'Free publicity is something I can always use. I hope they mentioned I was the best second-storey man in the North of England.'

'Amongst other things, including the fact that you were the most promising middle-weight since the war, a contender for the crown until women and booze and fast cars got in the way. They said you were the biggest high-liver the ring had seen since somebody called Jack Johnson.'

'Now there's a compliment if you like.'

'Depends on your point of view. The commentator said that Johnson had ended up in the gutter without a penny. They seemed to be drawing some kind of comparison.'

There was a cutting edge to her voice that needled the Gunner and he said hotly, 'Well just for the record, darlin', there's a few things they've missed out like the way I cut so badly that refs used to stop fights I was winning because they'd get worried about the blood pouring all over my face. In that last fight with Terry Jones I got cut so much I was two weeks in hospital. I even needed plastic surgery. They took my licence away so I couldn't box any more. Any idea how I felt?'

'Maybe it was rough, Gunner, life often is, but it didn't give you a licence to steal.'

'Nay, lass, I don't need any excuses.' He grinned. 'I had a few sessions with a psychiatrist at the Scrubs first time I

got nicked. He tried to make out that I'd gone bent to get
my own back on society.'

'What's your version?'

'Chance, darlin', time and chance, that's what happened
to me. When the fight game gave me up I'd about two
hundred quid in the bank and I was qualified to be just
one thing. A bloody labourer. Anything seemed better than
that.'

'So you decided to try crime?'

'Not really. It just sort of happened. I was staying in the
Hallmark Hotel in Manchester, trying to keep up appearances while I tried to con my way into a partnership with
a bloke I knew who was running a gambling club. When
the deal folded, I was so broke I couldn't even pay the bill.
One night I noticed a bloke in the bar with a wallet full of
fivers. Big bookie in from the races.'

He stared into the fire, silent for a moment and as he
started to speak again, she realized that in some strange
way he was re-living that night in every detail.

'He was staying on the same floor as me five rooms along.
There was a ledge outside my window, only about a foot
wide mind you, but it was enough. I've always had a head
for heights ever since I was a kid, always loved climbing. I
don't know, maybe if things had been different I might have
been a real climber. North face of the Eiger and all that sort
of stuff. Those are the blokes with the real guts.'

'What happened?' she said.

'I worked my way along the ledge at about two in the
morning, got in through his window and lifted the wallet
and him snoring the whole time.'

'And you got away with it?'

'No trouble at all. Just over six hundred nicker. I ask
you, who'd have gone labouring after a touch like that?
My fortune was made. As I said, I've always had a head
for heights and that kind of thing is a good number. You

don't need to work with anyone else which lowers the chance of getting nicked.'

'They got you though, didn't they?'

'Twice, that's all, darlin'. Once when I fell forty feet at the back of the Queen's Hotel in Leeds and broke a leg. The second time was when I got nicked at that new hotel in the Vandale Centre. Seems they had one of these electronic eyes switched on. The scuffers were in before I knew what hit me. Oh, I gave them quite a chase over the roofs, but it was all for laughs. I'd been recognized for one thing.'

He yawned and shook his head slightly, suddenly very, very tired. 'Better get moving I suppose. You don't want me hanging round here in the morning.'

The cigarette dropped from his hand to the carpet. She picked it up and tossed it into the fire and the Gunner sighed, leaning back in the comfortable old chair. Very softly Jenny Crowther got up and reached for the rug that was draped over the back of the settee.

As she covered the Gunner, his hand slid across her thigh and he said softly, 'Best looking lass I've seen in years.'

She didn't move, aware that he was already asleep, but gently disengaged his hand and tucked it under the rug. She stood there for quite a while looking down at that reckless face, almost childlike in repose. In spite of the scar tissue around the eyes and the permanently swollen cheekbones, it was handsome enough, a man's face whatever else he was and her thigh was still warm where he had touched her.

Perhaps it was as well that sleep had overtaken him so suddenly before things had taken their inevitable course – although she would have had no particular objections to that in principle. By no means promiscuous, she was like most young people of her generation, a product of her day and the sexual morality of earlier times meant nothing to her.

But loving, even in that sense, meant some kind of involve-ment and she couldn't afford that. Better that he should go after an hour or two's sleep. She turned off the light and went and stood at the window, her face against the cold glass, rain hammering hard against it, wondering what would happen to him, wondering where he would run to.

10

Narcia Place lay in an area that provided the local police force with one of its biggest headaches. The streets followed each other upon a pattern that was so exact as to be almost macabre. Sooty plane trees and solid terrace houses, once the homes of the lower middle classes on their way up, but now in multiple occupation due to an influx of immigrants since the war. Most of the whites had left. Those who found it impossible stayed and hated.

It was almost 12.15 when Jack Brady arrived in a Panda car provided by the local station. The whole street was dark and still in the heavy rain and when he rapped the old-fashioned cast-iron knocker on the door of number ten there was no immediate response. The driver of the Panda car vanished into the entry that led to the back yard without a word and Brady tried again.

It was at least five minutes before a window was pushed up above his head and a voice called, 'What the hell you think you're playing at this time in the morning?'

'Police,' Brady replied. 'Open up and be sharp about it. I haven't got all night.'

The window went down and the driver of the Panda car emerged from the entry. 'Any joy?'

'Just stuck his head out of the window,' Brady said. 'Get round to the back yard, just in case he tries to scarper.'

But there was no need for at that moment, the bolt was drawn and the front door opened. Brady pushed it back quickly and went in. 'Harold Phillips?'

'That's me – what is this?'

His feet were bare and he wore an old raincoat. Brady looked him over in silence and Harold swallowed, his black eyes flickering restlessly. He looked hunted and was very obviously scared.

Brady smiled in an avuncular manner and put a hand on his shoulder. 'I'm afraid I've got some bad news for you, son. I understand you're engaged to be married to a Miss Grace Packard?'

'That's right.' Harold went very still. 'What's happened? She been in an accident or something?'

'Worse than that, son. She was found dead earlier tonight in an alley called Dob Court on the other side of Jubilee Park.'

Harold stared at him for a long moment, then started to puke. He got a hand to his mouth, turned and fled into the kitchen. Brady found him leaning over the sink, a hand on the cold water tap.

After a while Harold turned, wiping his mouth with the back of one hand. 'How did it happen?'

'We're not certain. At the moment it looks as if her neck was broken.'

'The Rainlover?' The words were almost a whisper.

'Could be.'

'Oh, my God.' Harold clenched a fist convulsively. 'I had a date with her tonight. We were supposed to be going dancing.'

'What went wrong?'

'I was late. When I turned up she'd got involved with another bloke.'

'And she went off with him.' Harold nodded. 'Do you know who he was?'

Harold shook his head. 'Never seen him before, but the landlord seemed to know him. That's the landlord of The King's Arms near Regent Square.'

'What time was this?'

'About half eight.'

'Did you come straight home afterwards?'

'I was too upset so I walked around in the rain for a while. Then I had a coffee in the buffet at the railway station. Got home about half nine. Me mum was in bed so I took her a cup of tea and went myself.'

'Just you and your mother live here?'

'That's right.'

'She goes to bed early then?'

'Spends most of her time there these days. She isn't too well.'

Brady nodded sympathetically. 'I hope we haven't disturbed her.'

Harold shook his head. 'She's sleeping like a baby. I looked in on my way down.' He seemed much more sure of himself now and a strange half-smile played around his mouth like a nervous tic that couldn't be controlled. 'What happens now?'

'I'd like you to come down to Central if you wouldn't mind, just to have a few words with Chief Superintendent Mallory – he's in charge of the case. The girl's father is already there, but we need all the assistance we can get. You could help a lot. Give us details of her friends and interests, places she would be likely to visit.'

'Glad to,' Harold said. 'I'll go and get dressed. Only be five minutes.'

He went out and the Panda driver offered Brady a cigarette. 'Quite a technique you have. The silly bastard thinks he's got you eating out of his hand.'

'Glad you noticed,' Brady said, accepting the cigarette and a light. 'We'll make a copper out of you yet.'

There was a white pill box on the mantelpiece and he picked it up and examined the label. It carried the name of a chemist whose shop was no more than a couple of streets away. *The Capsules—one or two according to instructions—it is dangerous to exceed the stated dose.*

Brady opened the box and spilled some of the white and green capsules into his palm. 'What you got there?' the Panda man demanded.

'From the look of them I'd say it's what the doctor gave my wife last year when she burnt her hand and couldn't sleep for the pain. Canbutal. Half a dozen of these and you'd be facing your Maker.'

He replaced the box on the mantelpiece, a slight frown on his face.

'Tell you what,' he said to the Panda driver. 'You go and wait for us in the car and bang the door as hard as you like on the way out.'

The young constable, old before his years and hardened to the vagaries of C.I.D. men, left without a word, slamming the door so hard that the house shook. Brady went and stood at the bottom of the stairs, but heard no sound until a door opened and Harold appeared buttoning his jacket on the way down.

'What was all that then?' he demanded. 'Thought the house was falling down.'

'Just my driver on his way out to the car. I think the wind caught the door. Ready to go?'

'Whenever you are.' Harold took down his raincoat and struggled into it as he made for the door. 'Fame and fortune here I come. Who knows, I might be selling my story to the *Sunday News* before I'm finished.'

With an effort of will, Brady managed to stop himself from assisting him down the steps with a boot in the backside. Instead he took a deep breath and closed the door behind him with infinite gentleness. He was beginning to feel sorry for Harold's mother.

It was chance more than anything else that led Miller to The King's Arms after leaving Joanna Hartmann's flat. His quickest route back to Central C.I.D. took him along Lazer Street and the pub stood on the corner. It was the light in the rear window which caused him to brake suddenly. The landlord would have to be interviewed sooner or later to confirm the circumstances of Grace Packard's meeting with Faulkner and Morgan, but there was no reason why that couldn't wait till morning.

The real truth was that Miller was more interested in the disturbance that had taken place, the trouble with the girl's boyfriend which Faulkner had hinted at. 'Nothing I couldn't handle,' he had said. The sort of phrase Miller would have expected from some back street tearaway, indicating a pattern of violence unusual and disturbing in a man of Faulkner's education and background.

He knocked on the back door and after a while it was opened on a chain and Harry Meadows peered out. He grinned his recognition for they were old friends.

'What's this then, a raid?'

Miller went on as Meadows unchained the door. 'A few words of wisdom, Harry, that's all.'

'Nothing stronger?'

'Only if you've got a cup of tea to put it in.'

'Coming up.'

Miller unbuttoned his coat and went across to the fire. The kitchen was large, but cluttered with crates of bottled beer and cases of whisky. It was warm and homely with the remains of the supper still on the table and the old sofa on the other side of the fireplace looked very inviting.

'See you've got another killing on your hands,' Meadows said as he came back into the room with a mug of tea.

'Where did you hear that?'

'Late night news on the radio. Not that they were giving much away. Just said the body of a woman had been found near Jubilee Park.'

'Dob Court to be precise.' Miller swallowed some of his tea, coughing as the whisky in it caught at the back of his throat.

'Dob Court? That's just round the corner from here.' Meadows looked grim. 'Was it anyone I knew?'

'A girl called Grace Packard.'

Meadows stared at him, the skin tightening visibly across his face. Quite suddenly he went to the sideboard, opened a bottle of brandy and poured a large dose into the nearest glass. He swallowed it down and turned, shuddering.

'She was in here earlier tonight.'

'I know, Harry, that's why I'm here. I understand there was some trouble.'

Meadows helped himself to another brandy. 'This is official then?'

'Every word counts so take your time.'

Meadows was looking a lot better as the brandy took effect. He sat down at the table. 'There's a bloke called Faulkner comes in here a lot. Only lives a couple of streets away. He was in here earlier tonight with a friend of his, a solicitor called Morgan. Nice bloke. He handled the lease of this place for me when I decided to buy last year.'

'What time did they come in?'

'Somewhere around half-eight.'

'Who else was here?'

'Nobody. Trade's been so bad in the evenings since this Rainlover business started that I've had to lay off the bar staff.'

'I see. When did the girl arrive?'

'About five minutes after the other two.'

'You knew her name, so presumably she'd been in before?'

'Two or three times a week, usually with a different bloke and she wasn't too particular about their ages either.'

'Was she a Tom?'

'That's the way it looked to me.'

'And what about this boyfriend of hers?'

'You mean Harold?' Meadows shrugged. 'He's met her in here maybe half a dozen times. I don't even know his second name.'

'Was he picking up her earnings?'

'Could be, I suppose. He didn't look so tough to me, but you can never tell these days.'

Miller nodded, 'All right, what happened between Faulkner and the girl?'

'She sat on a stool at one end of the bar and he told me to give her a drink. It seems he and Morgan were going on to some posh do and Faulkner got the idea it might be fun to take the girl. She must have liked the idea because they all left together.'

'And then Harold arrived.'

'That's right and he didn't like what he found. Ended up taking a punch at Faulkner who got very nasty with him. I had to intervene. In fact I told Morgan to tell him he needn't come back. I've had about as much as I can take.'

'He's been mixed up in this sort of trouble before then?'

'Too damned much for my liking. When he loses his temper he's a raving madman, that one. Doesn't know what he's doing. He was in here one Saturday night a couple of months back and a couple of market porters came in. You know what they're like – rough lads – they started taking the mickey out of his posh voice and so on. He took them both out in the alley, gave them a hell of a beating.'

'Did you report it?'

'Come off it, Mr Miller. I've got the reputation of the house to think of. I only put up with him because most of the time he's a real gent and why should I cry over a couple of tearaways like that? They asked for it, they got it.'

'A point of view,' Miller started to button his coat. 'Strange in a man of his background, all this violence.'

Meadows hesitated perceptibly. 'Look, I don't know if this is any use to you, but he was in here on his own one night, not exactly drunk, but well on the way. We were talking about some court case in the evening paper. Three blokes who'd smashed up an old-age pensioner for the three or four quid that was in her purse. I said blokes like that were the lowest form of animal life. He leaned across the bar and took me by the tie. "No, they're not, Harry," he said. "The lowest form of animal life is a screw".'

In other days the man who turned the key in the lock had been called a warder. In more enlightened times he was known as a prison officer, but to anyone who had ever served time he was a screw, hated and despised.

'You think he's been inside?' Miller said.

Meadows shrugged. 'Sounds crazy, I know, but I've reached the stage where I could believe anything about that one.' He opened the door. 'You don't think he killed Grace Packard, do you?'

'I haven't the slightest idea. What happened to Harold after the others left, by the way? You didn't tell me that.'

'I offered him a drink and he told me where to go and went out after them. Funny thing was he turned up again about five minutes afterwards full of apologies. Said he was sorry he'd lost his temper and so on. Then he tried to get Faulkner's address out of me.'

'He knew his name then?'

'Apparently he'd heard me use it during the fuss when I called out to Faulkner to lay off.'

'Did you give him the address?'

'Do I look as if I came over on a banana boat?' Meadows shrugged. 'Mind you, there's always the telephone book.'

'As you say.' Miller punched him lightly in the shoulder.
'See you soon, Harry.'

He went. Crossed the yard through the heavy rain.
Meadows watched him climb into the Cooper, then closed
the door.

Miller went up the steps of the Central Railway Station and
paused to light a cigarette in the porch. The match flared
in his cupped hands briefly illuminating the white face and
dark eyes.

Here and there in the vast concourse a lounger stiffened,
turned and faded briskly into the night which was no more
than Miller had intended, for the railway station of any
great city is the same the world over, a happy hunting
ground for wrongdoers of every description.

He moved across to the buffet by the ticket barrier and
looked in through the window. The young woman he was
searching for was sitting on a stool at one end of the tea
bar. She saw him at once, for there were few things in life
that she missed, and came out.

She was about twenty-five years of age with a pleasant,
open face and her neat tweed suit was in excellent taste. She
might have been a schoolteacher or someone's private secretary. In fact she had appeared before the local bench on no
fewer than five occasions for offences involving prostitution
and had recently served three months in a detention centre.

She nodded familiarly. ''Evening, Mr Miller, or should I
say good morning?'

'Hello, Gilda. You must be hard up to turn out on a night
like this with a bloody maniac hanging around out there
in the rain.'

'I can look after myself.' When she lifted her umbrella
he saw that the ferrule had been sharpened into a wicked
looking steel point. 'Anyone makes a grab at me gets this
through the eyes.'

Miller shook his head. 'You think you can take on the whole world, don't you? I wonder what you'll look like ten years from now.'

'Just older,' she said brightly.

'If you're lucky, only by then you'll be down to a different class of customer. Saturday night drunks at a quid a time for a quickie round the back of the station.'

She wasn't in the least offended. 'We'll see. What was it you wanted?'

'I suppose you heard there was a girl killed earlier tonight?'

'That's right. Other side of the park, wasn't it?'

'Her name was Grace Packard. I've been told she was on the game. Is that true?'

Gilda showed no particular surprise. 'Kinky looking little tart, all plastic mac and knee boots.'

'That's it.'

'She tried working the station about six months ago. Got herself into a lot of trouble.'

'What kind?'

'Pinching other people's regulars, that sort of thing. We moved her on in the end.'

'And how did you manage that?' She hesitated and he said harshly, 'Come on, Gilda, this is murder.'

'All right,' she said reluctantly. 'I asked Lonny Brogan to have a word with her. She took the point.'

'I can imagine she would after hearing what that big ape had to say,' Miller said. 'One other thing, did anyone pimp for her?'

Gilda chuckled contemptuously. 'Little half-baked kid with a face like the underbelly of a fish and black sideboards. Harold something or other. Christ knows what she saw in him.'

'You saw her give him money?'

'Plenty of times – mostly to get rid of him from what I could see.'

He nodded. 'All right, Gilda, I'll be seeing you.'

'Oh, Mr Miller,' she said reprovingly. 'I hope you don't mean that the way it sounds.'

Her laughter echoed mockingly from the vaulted ceiling as he turned and walked away.

11

When Brady and Harold entered the general office at Central C.I.D. it was bustling with activity for no man might reasonably expect to see his bed on a night like this. Brady left Harold on an uncomfortable wooden bench with the Saturday sport's paper and went in to Chief Superintendent Mallory who was using Grant's office.

Mallory was shaving with a battery-operated electric razor and reading a report at the same time. His white shirt was obviously fresh on and he looked crisp and alert in spite of the hour.

'I've got the girl's boyfriend outside,' Brady said. 'Phillips his name is – Harold Phillips.'

'What's your first impression?'

'Oh, there's something there all right. For a start, he's an unpleasant little bastard.'

'You can't hang a man for that.'

'There's a lot more to it than that.'

Brady gave him the gist of his conversation with Harold and when he was finished, Mallory nodded. 'All right, let's have him in.'

When Brady called him, Harold entered with a certain bravado and yet his nervousness was betrayed in the muscle that twitched in his right cheek.

Mallory greeted him with extreme politeness. 'Good of you to come at this hour, Mr Phillips. We appreciate it.'

Harold's confidence received a king-size boost and he sat down in the chair Brady brought forward and gave Mallory a big man-of-the-world smile. 'Anything I can do, Super-intendent. You've only got to say.'

Brady offered him a cigarette. As he was lighting it, there was a knock on the door and Miller glanced in. He was about to withdraw, but Mallory shook his head and beck-oned him inside. Miller closed the door behind him and took up a position by the window without a word.

'Now then sir, just to get the record straight, you are Mr Harold Phillips of 10, Narcia Place?' Mallory began.

'That's me.'

'I'm given to understand that you and Miss Grace Packard were engaged to be married. Is that correct?'

'I suppose you could say that in a way.' Harold shrugged. 'I bought her a ring a couple of months back, but nothing was really official. I mean we hadn't set a date or anything.'

'I understand, sir. Now I wonder if you'd mind going over the events of last night again. I know you've already discussed this with Constable Brady, but it would help me to hear for myself.'

'Well, as I told Mr Brady, I had a date with Grace at half-eight.'

'Just one moment, sir. What happened before that? What time did you get home from work?'

Harold smiled bravely. 'To tell you the truth I'm not actually working at the moment, Superintendent. It's my back you see. I had this accident about a year ago so I have to be very careful.'

Mallory looked sympathetic. 'That must be difficult for you. You were saying that you had an appointment with Miss Packard at eight-thirty?'

'That's right. In The King's Arms, the one near Regent Square on the corner of Lazer Street.'

'And you kept that appointment?'

'I was a couple of minutes late. When I got there she was leaving with two blokes.'

'Who were they?'

'I don't know – never seen 'em before.'

'Did she often do this sort of thing?'

Harold sighed heavily. 'I'm afraid she did. She was sort of restless, if you know what I mean. Always looking for something new.'

It sounded like a line from a bad television play, but Mallory simply nodded and went on, 'What happened when you arrived and found her leaving with these two men?'

'I tried to stop her, tried to reason with her, but she wouldn't listen.' Harold flushed. 'Then one of them got hold of me – great big bloke he was. He twisted my hand in one of these judo locks or something. Put me down on my face. That's when the landlord moved in and told 'em to clear off.'

'And what did you do then, sir?'

Harold frowned as if trying to remember. 'Oh, had a drink with the landlord – on the house.'

'Did you go straight home afterwards?'

'No, like I told Mr Brady, I was too upset. I walked around in the rain for a while, then I had a coffee in the station buffet. Got home about half-nine. Me mum was in bed so I took her a cup of tea and went myself.'

Mallory had been making notes. He added a sentence and as he glanced up, Miller said, 'Excuse me, sir, I've been expecting a message.'

He went out into the main office, picked up the telephone on his desk and rang through to Mallory. 'Miller here, sir. He's lying.'

'That's certainly nice to know,' Mallory said calmly. 'I'll be straight out.'

He put down his phone and smiled brightly at Harold. 'I'll only be a moment.' He got to his feet and said to Brady,

'See that Mr Phillips gets a cup of tea, will you, Constable? There should be some left in the pot.'

He found Miller sitting on the edge of his desk drinking someone else's coffee. Mallory sat down in the chair and started to fill his pipe. 'Nasty little bastard, isn't he?'

'He may have his moments, but they must be few and far between,' Miller said. 'To start with I've seen Harry Meadows, the landlord of The King's Arms. After the fuss, he offered Harold a drink on the house. Harold told him to get stuffed and went off after the others. Five minutes later he returned full of apologies to claim his free glass.'

'Now why would he do that?' Mallory said thoughtfully.

'Apparently he spent the time trying to pump Meadows. Wanted to know where Faulkner lived.'

'You mean he actually knew Faulkner by name?'

'Oh, yes, he made that clear enough. He'd heard Meadows use it during the argument.'

Mallory grinned like the Cheshire cat, the first time Miller had ever seen him smile. 'Well, that's a nice fat juicy lie he's told us for a start.'

'There's more,' Miller said. 'Grace Packard was on the game. Worked the station until the rest of the girls moved her on a month or two back. According to my informant she had a boyfriend who picked up her earnings pretty regularly. The description fits our Harold exactly.'

Mallory got to his feet. 'Let's go back in.'

Harold was half-way through his third cigarette and glanced round nervously when the door opened. 'Sorry about that, Mr Phillips,' Mallory said. He smiled heartily and held out his hand. 'Well, I don't think we need to detain you any longer. You can go back to bed now.'

Harold's mouth gaped. 'You mean you don't need me any more?'

'That's right. The information you've given us will be most helpful. I can't thank you enough for turning out at this hour in the morning. It's that kind of co-operation that helps us beat these things you know.' He turned to Brady who came to attention briskly. 'See that Mr Phillips gets home will you, Constable?'

'See to it myself, sir.' Brady put a hand under Harold's elbow, looking more avuncular than ever. 'Have you home in fifteen minutes, sir.'

Harold grinned. 'Be seeing you, Superintendent,' he said and went out of the room like a turkey-cock.

Mallory sat down and put a match to his pipe. 'No harm in letting him think he's out of the wood for a few hours. When we pull him in again in the morning the shock will just about cripple him.'

'You really think he's got something to hide, sir?' Miller demanded.

'He's lying when he says he doesn't know Faulkner by name – that's for a start. Then there's this business about the girl – the fact that he was pimping for her.'

'It still doesn't add up to murder.'

'It never does to start with, Sergeant. Suppositions, inac-curacies, statements that don't really hold water – that's all we ever have to work with in most cases. For example, Phillips says that he walked the streets for a while after leaving the pub, then had a coffee at the station buffet. How many people would you say use that buffet on a Saturday night?'

'Thousands, sir.'

'Exactly. In other words it would be unreasonable to expect some sort of personal identification by any of the buffet staff. Another thing – as far as we can judge at the moment, 'the girl was killed at around half-ten.'

'And Phillips was home at nine-thirty and in bed ten minutes or so later. What was it he said? That he took his mother a cup of tea?'

'Interesting thing about Mrs Phillips,' Mallory said. 'Brady had to kick on the door for a good five minutes before he could rouse Phillips. There wasn't a bleat from the old girl. In fact Phillips told him she was sleeping like a baby.'

Miller frowned. 'That doesn't make very good sense.'

'Even more interesting was the bottle of Canbutal capsules Brady found on the mantelpiece. A couple of those things and you wouldn't hear a bomb go off in the next street.'

'Might be an idea to check with her doctor in the morning, just to get a complete picture.'

Mallory nodded. 'Brady can handle that.' He got to his feet. 'I'm going over to the Medical School now. We've hauled Professor Murray out of bed. He's going to get cracking on the post-mortem just as soon as the Forensic boys have finished with her. You'd better get a couple of hours' sleep in the rest room. If I want you, I'll phone.'

Miller helped him on with his coat. 'What about Faulkner?'

Mallory shook his head. 'I never had much of a hunch about him, not in the way I do about Phillips.'

'I'm afraid I can't agree with you there, sir.'

For a moment, Mallory poised on the brink of one of those sudden and terrible wraths for which he was famous. With a great effort he managed to control himself and said acidly, 'Don't tell me you're going to solve this thing in a burst of intuitive genius, Miller?'

'Meadows had some very interesting things to say about him, sir,' Miller said patiently. 'There's a pattern of violence there that just doesn't fit in a man of his background. He uses force too easily, if you follow me.'

'So do I when the occasion calls for it,' Mallory said. 'Is that all you have to go on?'

'Not exactly, sir. He had a pretty strange conversation with Meadows one night when he was drunk. Meadows got the impression that he'd been inside.'

Mallory frowned. 'Did he indeed? Right, get on to C.R.O.

in London. Tell them it's for me. Say I want everything they
have on Faulkner by breakfast. I'll discuss it with you then.'

The door banged behind him and Miller grinned softly.
For a moment there, just for a moment, it had looked as
if they were going to clash. That moment would come again
because George Mallory was a stubborn man and Nick Miller
was a sleeping partner in a business so large that he didn't
need to put himself out to anyone for the sake of keeping
his job. Not God or even Chief Superintendents from New
Scotland Yard. An interesting situation. He lit a cigarette,
picked up Mallory's telephone and asked for Information
Room.

12

The small rest room was badly overcrowded and there was
hardly room to move between the camp beds which had
been specially imported. Miller slept badly which was hardly
surprising. There was an almost constant disturbance at
what seemed like five minute intervals throughout the night
as colleagues were sent for and the rain continued to
hammer relentlessly against the window pane above his
head.

At about seven a.m. he gave up the struggle, got a towel
and went along the corridor to the washroom. He stood
under a hot shower for a quarter of an hour, soaking the
tiredness away and then sampled the other end of the scale,
an ice-cold needle spray for precisely thirty seconds just to
give himself an appetite.

He was half-way through a plate of bacon and eggs and
on his third cup of tea in the canteen when Brady found
him. The big Irishman eased himself into the opposite chair
and pushed a flimsy across the table.

'Hanley in Information asked me to give you that. Just come in from C.R.O. in London.'

Miller read it quickly and took a deep breath. 'Quite a lad when he gets going, our Bruno. Where's Mallory?'

'Still at the post-mortem.'

Miller pushed back his chair. 'I'd better get over to the Medical School then. You coming?'

Brady shook his head. 'I still haven't contacted Mrs Phillips' doctor. Mallory told me to wait till after breakfast. Said there was no rush. I'll be across as soon as I've had a word with him.'

'I'll see you then,' Miller said and left quickly.

The mortuary was at the back of the Medical School, a large, ugly building in Victorian Gothic with stained glass windows and the vaguely religious air common to the architecture of the period.

Jack Palmer, the Senior Technician, was sitting in his small glass office at the end of the main corridor and he came to the door as Miller approached.

'Try and arrange your murders at a more convenient hour next time will you,' he said plaintively. 'My first Saturday night out in two months ruined. My wife was hopping mad, I can tell you.'

'My heart bleeds for you, Jack,' Miller said amiably. 'Where's the top brass?'

'Having tea inside. I shouldn't think you rate a cup.'

Miller opened the door on the other side of the office and went into the white-tiled hall outside the theatre. Mallory was there, seated at a small wooden table talking to Henry Wade, the Head of Forensic, and Professor Stephen Murray, the University Professor of Pathology, a tall spare Scot.

Murray knew Miller socially through his brother and greeted him with the familiarity of an old friend. 'You still look as if you've stepped straight out of a whisky advert, Nick, even at eight-fifteen in the morning. How are you?'

'Fine – nothing that a couple of weeks' leave wouldn't cure.' Miller turned to Mallory. 'I've just been handed the report on Faulkner from C.R.O.'

'Anything interesting?'

'I think you could say that, sir. Harry Meadows wasn't wrong – he does have a record. Fined twice for assault and then about two years ago he ran amok at some arty Chelsea party.'

'Anybody hurt?'

'His agent. Three broken ribs and a fractured jaw. Faulkner's a karate expert so when he loses his temper it can have rather nasty results.'

'Did they send him down?'

'Six months and he did the lot. Clocked one of the screws and lost all his remission.'

'Anything known against him since?'

'Not a thing. Apparently some sort of psychiatric investigation was carried out when he was inside so there's quite an interesting medical report. Should be along soon.'

Mallory seemed curiously impatient. 'All right, all right, we'll talk about it later.' He turned to Professor Murray. 'What do you think then, is this another Rainlover thing or isn't it?'

'That's for you to decide,' Murray said. 'I'm the last man to make that kind of prediction – I've been at this game too long. If you mean are there any obvious differences between this murder and the others, all I can say is yes and leave you to form your own conclusions.'

'All right, Professor, fire away.'

Murray lit a cigarette and paced up and down restlessly. 'To start with the features which are similar. As in all the other cases, the neck was broken cleanly with a single powerful blow, probably a blunt instrument with a narrow edge.'

'Or the edge of the hand used by an expert,' Miller suggested.

'You're thinking of karate, I suppose,' Murray smiled faintly. 'Always possible, but beware of trying to make the facts fit your own suppositions, Nick. A great mistake in this game, or so I've found.'

'What other similarities were present, Professor?' Mallory asked, obviously annoyed at Miller's interruption.

'No physical ones. Time, place, weather – that's what I was meaning. Darkness and rain – the lonely street.'

'And the features in this one that don't fit?' Henry Wade said. 'What about those?'

'Recent bruising on the throat, another bruise on the right cheek as if someone had first grabbed her angrily around the neck and then struck her a violent blow, probably with his fist. The death blow came afterwards. Now this is a very real departure. In the other cases, there was no sign of violence except in the death blow itself. Quick, sharp, clean, obviously totally unexpected.'

'And in this case the girl obviously knew what was coming,' Mallory said.

Henry Wade shook his head. 'No, I'm afraid that won't work, sir. If she was attacked by an unknown assailant, she'd have put up some sort of a struggle, even if it was only to get her nails to his face. We didn't find any signs that would indicate that such a struggle took place.'

'Which means that she stood there and let someone knock her about,' Mallory said. 'Someone she knew.'

'I don't see how we can be certain of that, sir.' Miller couldn't help pointing out what seemed an obvious flaw. 'She was on the game after all. Why couldn't she have been up that alley with a potential customer?'

Again the irritation was noticeable in Mallory's voice. 'Would she have stood still while he grabbed her throat, fisted her in the face? Use your intelligence, Sergeant. It's quite obvious that

she took a beating from someone she was perfectly familiar
with and she took it because she was used to it.'

'I think the Superintendent's got a point, Nick,' Henry
Wade said. 'We're all familiar with the sort of relationship
a prostitute has with her minder. Beatings are the order of
the day, especially when the pimp thinks his girl isn't
coughing up all her earnings and the women take their
hidings quietly, too. God knows why. I suppose a psychiatrist would have an answer.'

'True enough,' Miller admitted.

'And there's one important point you're forgetting,' Wade
added. 'In every Rainlover case yet he's always taken some
memento. Either an article of clothing or a personal
belonging. That doesn't seem to have happened here.'

'Anything else, Miller?' Mallory enquired.

'Was there any cash in her handbag, sir?'

'Two or three pounds in notes and silver.'

'Faulkner said he gave her a ten-pound note.'

'Exactly, Sergeant.' Mallory gave him a slight, ironic smile,
'Any suggestions as to what happened to it?'

'No, sir.' Miller sighed. 'So we're back to Harold Phillips?'

'That's right and I want him pulled in now. You can take
Brady with you.'

'And Faulkner, sir?'

'Oh, for God's sake, Sergeant, don't you ever take no for
an answer?'

There was an electric moment and then Murray cut in
smoothly. 'All very interesting, gentlemen, but you didn't
allow me to finish the story. If it's of any use to you, the
girl had intercourse just before her death.'

Mallory frowned. 'No suggestion of rape, is there?'

'None whatsoever. In view of the conditions I would say
the act took place against the wall and definitely with her
consent. Of course one can't judge whether under threat
or not.'

Mallory got to his feet. 'Only another nail in his coffin.' He turned to Miller. 'Go and get Phillips now and bring the clothes he was wearing last night. I'll expect you back within half an hour.'

There was a time to argue and a time to go quietly. Miller went without a word.

Miller met Brady coming down the steps of the main entrance of the Town Hall. 'You look as if you've lost a quid and found a tanner,' he told Miller. 'What's up?'

'We've got to pull Harold Phillips in right away. Mallory thinks he's the mark.'

'Harold – the Rainlover?' Brady said incredulously.

Miller shook his head. 'Could be this wasn't a Rainlover killing, Jack. There were differences – I'll explain on the way.'

'Did you and Mallory have a row or something?' Brady asked as they went down the steps to the Mini-Cooper.

'Not quite. He's got the bit between his teeth about Harold and I just don't see it, that's all.'

'And what about Faulkner?'

'The other side of the coin. Mallory thinks exactly as I do about Harold.'

'He could change his mind,' Brady said as they got in the car. 'I've just seen a report from Dwyer, the beat man who found the body and got slugged.'

'How is he?' Miller said as he switched on the ignition and drove away.

'A bit of concussion, that's all. They're holding him in the Infirmary for observation. There's an interesting titbit for you in his report though. Says that about ten minutes before finding the body, he bumped into a bloke leaving the coffee stall in Regent Square.'

'Did he recognize him?'

'Knows him well – local resident. A Mr Bruno Faulkner.'

The Mini-Cooper swerved slightly as Miller glanced at him involuntarily. 'Now that is interesting.'

He slowed suddenly, turning the car into the next street and Brady said, 'Now where are we going? This isn't the way to Narcia Street.'

'I know that coffee stall,' Miller said. 'Run by an old Rugby pro called Sam Harkness. He usually closes about nine on a Sunday morning after catching the breakfast trade.'

Brady shook his head sadly. 'Mallory is just going to love you for this. Ah well, a short life and a merry one.' He eased back in the seat and started to fill his pipe. '

Rain drifted across Regent Square in a grey curtain and when Miller braked to a halt, there were only two customers at the coffee stall, all-night taxi drivers eating fried egg sandwiches in the shelter of the canopy. Miller and Brady ran through the rain and Harkness turned from the stove, a frying pan in his hand.

'Oh, it's you, Mr Miller. Looking for breakfast?'

'Not this time, Sam,' Miller said. 'Just a little information. You know about last night's murder in Dob Court?'

'Don't I just? Carts around here most of the night. Did all right out of it in tea and wads, I can tell you.'

'I've just been looking at Constable Dwyer's report on what happened. He says he called here about ten past ten.'

'That right.'

'I understand you had a customer who was just leaving – a Mr Bruno Faulkner according to Dwyer.'

Harkness nodded and poured out a couple of teas. 'Artist. Lives round the corner from here. Regular customer of mine. Turns out at any old time in the a.m. when he's run out of fags. You know what they're like, these blokes.'

'And it was cigarettes he wanted last night was it?' Brady asked.

'He bought twenty Crown King-size. As a matter of fact

I'm waiting for him to look in again. He left a pair of gloves
– lady's gloves.

He searched under the counter and produced them. They
were in imitation black leather, heavily decorated with
pieces of white plastic and diamanté, cheap and ostentatious
– the sort of thing that was to be found in any one of a
dozen boutiques which had sprung up in the town of late
to cater for the needs of young people.

'Rather funny really,' Harkness said. 'He pulled them out
of his pocket when he was looking for change. I said they
were hardly his style. He seemed a bit put out to me. Tried
to make out they were his fiancée's, but that was just a
load of cobblers if you ask me. She's been here with him
– his fiancée I mean – Joanna Hartmann. You see her on
the telly all the time. Woman like that wouldn't wear this
sort of rubbish.'

Amazing how much people told you without being asked. Miller
picked up the gloves. 'I'll be seeing Mr Faulkner later this
morning, Sam. I'll drop these in at the same time.'

'Probably still in bed with the bird they belong to,'
Harkness called. 'Bloody artists. I should be so lucky.'

'So Faulkner had Grace Packard's gloves in his pocket,'
Brady said when they got back to the Mini-Cooper. 'So
what? He didn't deny having her at his flat. He'll simply
say she left the gloves by mistake or something.'

Miller handed him the gloves, took out his wallet and
produced a pound note. 'This is on me, Jack. Take a taxi
to the Packard house. I don't suppose the mother's in too
good a state, but see if the father can give you a positive
identification on those gloves. Come straight on to Narcia
Street from there. I'll be waiting for you.'

'Mallory isn't going to like this.'

'That's just too bloody bad. How far did you get with
Mrs Phillips's doctor?'

'He wouldn't discuss it on the phone. It's that Indian

bloke – Lal Das. You know what these buggers are like. Give 'em an inch and they'll take a mile every time.'

'All right, Jack, all right, I'll see him myself,' Miller said, an edge to his voice, for the kind of racial prejudice that seemed to be part of the make-up of so many otherwise decent men like Brady was guaranteed to bring out the worst in him.

'Half an hour then,' Brady said, checking his watch. 'That's all it should take.'

'I'll wait for you outside.' Miller watched him run across to one of the taxis, got into the Mini-Cooper and drove away quickly.

13

Lal Das, to whom Brady had referred so contemptuously, was a tall, cadaverous Indian. A Doctor of Medicine and a Fellow of the Royal College of Physicians, he could have secured a senior post in a major hospital any time he wanted and yet he preferred to run a large general practice in one of the less salubrious parts of the city. He had a national reputation in the field of drug addiction and, in this connection, Miller had frequently sought his advice.

The Indian had just finished breakfast and was working his way through the Sunday supplements when Miller was shown in. Das smiled and waved him to a seat. 'Just in time for coffee.'

'Thanks very much.'

'Business, or did you just happen to be in the neighbourhood?'

Miller took the cup of coffee the Indian handed to him and shook his head. 'You had a call earlier – a query concerning a Mrs Phillips of 10, Narcia Street.'

The Indian nodded. 'That's right. The officer who spoke to me wasn't terribly co-operative. Wouldn't tell me what the whole thing was about, so I simply refused to give him the information he required until I knew more about it. A doctor/patient relationship can only function satisfactorily when there is an atmosphere of complete trust. I would only be prepared to discuss a patient's case history and private affairs in exceptional circumstances.'

'Would murder be extreme enough?' Miller asked.

Lal Das sighed and put down his cup carefully. 'I think you'd better tell me about it. I'll judge for myself.'

'Fair enough. The man at the centre of things is the woman's son – Harold Phillips. Presumably he's a patient of yours also?'

An expression of real distaste crossed the Indian's face. 'For my sins. A particularly repellent specimen of present-day youth.'

'He had a girlfriend called Grace Packard. Ever meet her?'

Das shook his head. 'I notice you use the past tense.'

'She was murdered last night. Naturally Harold was called upon to explain his movements, especially as he'd had some sort of row with her earlier in the evening. His story is that he was home by nine-thirty. He says that his mother was in bed and that he took her a cup of tea and went himself.'

'So his mother is his alibi?'

'That's about the size of it. The murder was committed around ten-fifteen you see.'

Das nodded. 'But what is it you want from me? Surely it's straightforward enough.'

'It might have been if something rather strange hadn't occurred. Two police officers went to Narcia Street just after midnight to bring Harold in for questioning. They had to kick on the door for a good five minutes before he showed any signs of life. His mother failed to put in an appearance at all. He said she was sleeping like a baby and hadn't been very well, but according to the officer in charge, no one could have slept through such a disturbance.'

'Unless drugged of course,' Das said.

'He did find a box of Canbutal capsules on the mantel-piece, which seemed to offer a solution.'

'So what you're really wondering is whether or not Mrs Phillips could have been in bed and asleep when Harold returned home – whenever that was.'

'Naturally – I understand Canbutal is pretty powerful stuff. I also understand that it's not usually prescribed in simple cases of insomnia.'

Das got to his feet, went to the fireplace and selected a black cheroot from a sandalwood box. 'What I tell you now must be treated in the strictest confidence. You're right about Canbutal. It works best in cases where the patient cannot sleep because of extreme pain. It's as close to the old-fashioned knock-out drops as you can get.'

'Mrs Phillips must be pretty ill to need a thing like that.'

'Cancer.'

There was a moment of silence as if darkness had drifted into the room. Miller took a deep breath and went on, 'Does Harold know?'

'She doesn't know herself. She's had bronchial trouble for years. She thinks this is the same thing she gets every winter only a little worse than usual. She'll go very quickly. Any time, any day.'

'What kind of an effect would the Canbutal have – can she be awakened, for example?'

'That would depend on the amount taken. Mrs Phillips is on a dosage of two each night. She visits me once a week and I give her a prescription for a week's supply. As a matter of fact I saw her yesterday morning.'

'But she definitely could be awakened even an hour or two after having taken a couple of these things?'

'Certainly. Mind you, it depends on what you mean by

awakened. What took place might seem like a dream to her afterwards – there might not even be a memory of it.'

Miller got to his feet. 'Very helpful – very helpful indeed.'

They went out into the hall and Das opened the door for him. 'Do you intend to arrest young Phillips? Is there really a case against him?'

'I've been ordered to take him in again for further questioning,' Miller said. 'I can't be more definite than that. I suppose you've heard that Grant's in hospital after a car accident? That means the Scotland Yard man, Chief Superintendent Mallory, is in charge. If you want to go any further with this, he's the man to see.'

'I'm concerned with one thing only,' Das said. 'The welfare of Mrs Phillips. I would hope that you could keep the seriousness of this business from her until the last possible moment. If you intend to question her then I think I should be there.'

'As I said, I'm going round to pick up her son now,' Miller told him. 'And there are obviously certain questions I must put to his mother. You're perfectly at liberty to come with me. In fact I'd welcome it.'

'Very well,' Das said. 'I'll follow in my own car. You'll wait for me before entering?'

'Certainly,' Miller said and he went down the steps to the Mini-Cooper and drove away.

Brady was standing in the doorway of a newsagent's shop just round the corner from Narcia Street and he ran across the road through the heavy rain and scrambled into the Mini-Cooper as Miller slowed.

'Not bad timing,' he said. 'I've only just got here.' He produced the gloves. 'The girl's father recognized these straightaway. He bought them for her as a birthday present. She was with him at the time. He even remembers the shop. That boutique place in Grove Square.'

'Good enough,' Miller said. 'I've seen Das. He tells me you only prescribe Canbutal when a patient can't sleep because of pain.'

'So the old girl's in a bad way?'

'You could say that. Das is following on behind, by the way. He's coming in with us, just in case she gets a funny turn or anything.'

'Good enough,' Brady said.

A horn sounded behind them as Das arrived. Miller moved into gear, drove round the corner into Narcia Street and pulled up outside number ten.

When Harold opened the door there was a momentary expression of dismay on his face that was replaced in an instant by a brave smile.

'Back again then?' he said to Brady.

'This is Detective Sergeant Miller,' Brady said formally, 'He'd like a few words with you.'

'Oh, yes.' Harold glanced at Das curiously. 'What are you doing here?'

'I'm interested in one thing only,' Das said. 'Your mother's welfare. In her present state of health she can't stand shocks so I thought it better to be on hand.'

They all went into the living-room and Miller said, 'I wonder whether you'd mind getting dressed, sir? We'd like you to come down to Central C.I.D. with us.'

'I've already been there once,' Harold said. 'What is this?'

'Nothing to get excited about, son,' Brady said kindly. 'One or two new facts have come up about the girl and Chief Superintendent Mallory thinks you might be able to help him, that's all.'

'All right then,' Harold said. 'Give me five minutes.'

He went out and Brady picked up the box of Canbutal capsules from the mantelpiece. 'These are what she's been taking,' he said, holding them out to Miller.

Das took the box, opened it and spilled the capsules out

on his palm. He frowned. 'I gave her the prescription for these at two-thirty yesterday afternoon. She's taken three since then.' He put the capsules back into the box. 'I think I'd better go up and see her.'

'All right,' Miller said. 'I'll come with you.'

'Is that absolutely necessary?'

Miller nodded. 'I must ask her to confirm Harold's story – can't avoid it. Better with you here surely.'

'I suppose so. It might help for the present if you could handle it other than as a police enquiry though. Is there really any need to upset her at this stage?'

'I'll do what I can.'

Das obviously knew his way. They went up the stairs and he opened the door that stood directly opposite. The curtains were still half-drawn and the room was grey and sombre. The furniture was many years old, mainly heavy Victorian mahogany and the brass bed had now become a collector's item if only its occupant had realized that fact.

She was propped against the pillows, eyes closed, head turned slightly to one side, the flesh drawn and tight across the bones of her face. Someone on the way out. Miller had seen it before and he knew the signs. Death was a tangible presence, waiting over there in the shadows to take her out of her misery like a good friend. Das sat on the bed and gently touched her shoulder. 'Mrs Phillips?'

The eyes fluttered open, gazed at him blindly, closed. She took several deep breaths, opened her eyes again and smiled weakly. 'Doctor Das.'

'How are you today, Mrs Phillips. Little bit better?'

The Indian's slightly sing-song voice was incredibly soothing carrying with it all the compassion and kindness in the world.

'What day is it, Doctor?' She was obviously muddled and bewildered, the effects of the drug, Miller surmised.

'Sunday, my dear. Sunday morning.'

She blinked and focused her eyes on Miller. 'Who – who are you?'

Miller came forward and smiled. 'I'm a friend of Harold's, Mrs Phillips. He was supposed to meet me last night, but he didn't turn up. I thought I'd better call and see if everything was all right.'

'He's about somewhere,' she said in a dead voice. 'A good boy, Harold. He brought me some tea when he came in.'

'When would that be, Mrs Phillips?' Miller said softly.

'When?' She frowned, trying to concentrate. 'Last night, I think. That's right – it was last night when he came in. She shook her head. 'It gets harder to remember.'

'Did Harold tell you that he brought you tea last night, Mrs Phillips?'

'I don't know – I don't remember. He's a good boy.' Her eyes closed. 'A good boy.'

Behind them the door opened and Harold appeared. 'What's going on here?' he demanded angrily.

'Your mother is very ill,' Das said. 'I must make arrangements to have her admitted to hospital at once.' He held up the box of Canbutal capsules. 'Did you know she has been increasing her dosage? Didn't I warn you that the effects could be disastrous?'

Harold had turned very pale. Brady appeared behind him and took his arm. 'Come on, son,' he said. 'Let's go.'

They moved to the head of the stairs and Miller went after them. 'Are those the clothes you were wearing last night?' he asked Harold.

Harold turned, answering in a kind of reflex action, 'Sure.' Then it dawned on him and fear showed in his eyes. 'Here, what is this?'

'Take him down,' Miller said and turned away.

Das closed the bedroom door quietly. 'Things don't look too good for him, do they?'

'He's in for a bad time, that's as much as I can say at the moment. What about her? Anything I can do?'

'Don't worry. They have a telephone next door. I'll ring for an ambulance and stay with her till it comes. You'll keep me posted?'

Miller nodded and they went downstairs. When he opened the door, rain drifted to meet him, pushed across the slimy cobbles by the wind. He looked down towards the Mini-Cooper where Harold sat in the rear with Brady.

'Sunday morning,' he said. 'What a hell of a way to make a living.'

'We all have a choice, Sergeant,' Das told him.

Miller glanced at him sharply, but nothing showed in that brown, enigmatic face. He nodded formally. 'I'll be in touch,' and moved out into the rain.

14

When they reached Central C.I.D. they took Harold to the Interrogation Room where, in spite of his angry protests, he was relieved of his trousers.

'What the hell do you think you're playing at?' he demanded. 'I've got my rights, just like anyone else.'

'Our lab boys just want to run a few tests, son, that's all,' Brady informed him. 'If they come out right, you'll be completely eliminated from the whole enquiry. You'd like that, wouldn't you?'

'You go to hell,' Harold shouted furiously. 'And you can knock off the Father Christmas act.'

There was a knock on the door and a constable entered carrying a pair of police uniform trousers. 'Better get into those and do as you're told,' Miller said, tossing them across. 'You'll make it a lot easier on yourself in the long run.' He turned to Brady. 'I've got things to do. I'll see you later.'

The medical report on Faulkner which C.R.O. had promised was waiting on his desk. He read it through quickly, then again, taking his time. When he was finished, he sat there for a while, staring into space, a frown on his face. He finally got up and crossed to Mallory's office taking the report with him.

The Chief Superintendent was seated at his desk examining a file and glanced up impatiently. 'Took you long enough. What's going on then?'

'Brady's got him in the Interrogation Room now, sir. His trousers have gone over to Forensic for examination. I understand Inspector Wade's got one of the Medical School serologists to come in. You should get a quick result.'

'You saw the mother?'

Miller told him what had taken place at Narcia Street.

'From the looks of her, I wouldn't give her long.'

Mallory nodded. 'So Master Harold could have awakened her at any time with that cup of tea, that seems to be what it comes down to. From what the doctor says she wouldn't know whether it was yesterday or today in her condition.'

'That's about the size of it.'

'Good show.' Mallory rubbed his hands together. 'I'll let him stew for a while then get to work. I don't think he'll last long.'

'You sound pretty certain.'

'You're a smart lad, Miller, so I'm going to tell you something for your own good. You don't know what it's all about up here in the sticks. I've been on more murder investigations than you've had hot dinners. You get an instinct for these things, believe me. Harold Phillips killed that girl – I'd stake my reputation on it.'

'And what about Faulkner? He's still a strong possibility in my book. Have you read Constable Dwyer's report yet on what happened last night?'

'I know what you're going to say,' Mallory said. 'He saw Faulkner at a coffee stall in Regent Square just before the murder took place.'

'Something he conveniently forgot to mention to us when we questioned him.'

'Perfectly understandable in the circumstances.'

Miller produced the gloves and tossed them down on the desk. 'Those belonged to Grace Packard. Faulkner left them at the coffee stall by mistake.'

Mallory picked them up, frowning. 'You mean you've been there this morning?'

'That's right. Brady told me about Dwyer's report. I thought I might as well call at the coffee stall on my way to pick young Phillips up, just to see what the proprietor had to say.'

'I thought I told you I wanted Phillips picked up right away?' Mallory demanded harshly.

'So I wasted ten minutes. Would it interest you to know that when those gloves dropped out of Faulkner's pocket he told the owner of the coffee stall they belonged to his fiancée? Now why would he do that?'

Mallory laughed in his face. 'Because he didn't want him to know he'd been out with another woman or is that too simple for you?'

'But a great many people already knew he'd been in Grace Packard's company that night. Everyone at the party saw him leave with her. Why tell the bloke at the coffee stall such a silly lie at this stage?'

'I think you're placing far too much importance on a very minor incident.'

'But is it minor, sir? Inspector Wade reminded us earlier that in every other incident the Rainlover had taken some item or another from the victim. He said that didn't seem to have happened in this case. Can we be certain of that knowing about these gloves?'

'So we're back to the Rainlover again?' Mallory shook his head. 'It won't fit, Miller. There are too many other differences.'

'All right,' Miller said. 'But I still think Faulkner has a lot of explaining to do. To start with he was in the girl's company and his reasons for taking her back to the flat were eccentric enough to be highly suspect.'

'Not at all,' Mallory countered. 'Typical behaviour according to his friends and past record.'

'He was in the immediate area of the murder only minutes before it took place, we've two witnesses to that. And he lied about the girl's gloves to Harkness.'

'Why did he visit the coffee stall? Did Harkness tell you that?'

'To buy cigarettes.'

'Was this the first time?'

'No, he frequently appeared at odd hours for the same reason.'

'Can you imagine what a good defence counsel would do with that?'

'All right,' Miller said. 'It's circumstantial – all of it, but there are too many contributing factors to ignore. Take this pattern of violence for example. Unusual in a man of his background. I've got the medical report on him here.'

He handed it across and Mallory shook his head. 'I haven't got time. Tell me the facts.'

'It's simple enough. He was involved in a serious car accident about six years ago – racing at Brand's Hatch. His skull was badly fractured, bone fragments in the brain and so on. He was damned lucky to pull through. His extreme aggressiveness has been a development since then. The psychiatrists who examined him at Wandsworth were definitely of the opinion that the behaviour pattern was a direct result of the brain damage, probably made worse by the fragments of bone which the surgeons had been unable to remove. The pattern of violence grew worse during his sentence. He was involved in several fights with prisoners and attacked a prison officer. He was advised to enter an institution for treatment on his discharge, but refused.'

'All right, Miller, all right.' Mallory held up both hands defensively. 'You go and see him – do anything you like. I'll handle Harold.'

'Thank you, sir,' Miller said formally.

He got the door half-open and Mallory added, 'One more thing, Miller. A quid says Harold Phillips murdered Grace Packard.'

'Fair enough, sir.'

'And I'll give you odds of five-to-one against Bruno Faulkner.'

'Well, I don't really like to take the money, but if you must, sir.'

Miller grinned and gently closed the door.

It was at that precise moment in another part of the city that the man known as the Rainlover opened his Sunday newspaper and found Sean Doyle staring out at him from the middle of page two. He recognized him instantly and sat there staring at the picture for a long moment, remembering the girl standing in the lighted doorway and the darkness and the rain falling.

He had unfinished business there, but first it would be necessary to get rid of the man. Of course he could always telephone the police anonymously, give them the address, tell them that Doyle was in hiding there. On the other hand, they would probably arrest the girl also for harbouring him.

The solution, when it came, was so simple that he laughed out loud. He was still laughing when he put on his hat and coat and went out into the rain.

*

Miller got no reply to his persistent knocking at Faulkner's door and finally went down the stairs to the flat below where someone was playing a tenor sax, cool and clear, so pure that it hurt a little.

The instrumentalist turned out to be an amiable West Indian in dark glasses and a neat fringe beard. He took off the glasses and grinned hugely.

'Aint's I seen you play piano at Chuck Lazer's club?'

'Could be,' Miller told him.

'Man, you were the most. Someone told me you was a John.' He shook his head. 'I tell you, man, you get some real crazy cats around these nights. Sick in the head. They'll say anything. You coming in?'

'I'm looking for Bruno Faulkner. Any idea where he might be? I can't get a reply.'

The West Indian chuckled. 'Sunday's his brick smashing day.'

'Come again?'

'Karate, man. He goes to the Kardon Judo Centre every Sunday morning for a workout. Of course if he can't find any bricks to smash he'd just as soon smash people.' He tapped his head. 'Nutty as a fruit cake. He don't need the stuff, man. He's already there.'

'Thanks for the information,' Miller said. 'See you some-time.'

'The original wild man from Borneo,' the West Indian called as he went down the stairs. 'That the best you Western European civilization cats can do? The day is coming, man! The day is coming! '

From the sound of it, he was on the stuff himself, but Miller had other fish to fry and he got into the Mini-Cooper and drove away quickly.

Miller himself had been an ardent student of both judo and karate for several years. A brown belt in both, only the pressure of work had prevented him from progressing further. Although he did most of his own training at the police club, he was familiar with the Kardon Judo Centre and knew Bert King, the senior instructor, well.

There were two dojos and King was in the first supervising free practice with half a dozen young schoolboys. He was a small, shrunken man with a yellowing, parchment-like skin and a head that seemed too large for the rest of him. He was a fourth Dan in both judo and aikido and incredible in action on the mat as Miller knew to his cost.

King came across, all smiles. 'Hello, Sergeant Miller. Not seen you around much lately.'

'Never have the time, Bert,' Miller said. 'I'm looking for a man called Faulkner. Is he here?'

King's smile slipped a little, but he nodded. 'Next door.'

'You don't think much of him?' Miller demanded, quick to seize any opportunity.

'Too rough for my liking. To tell you the truth he's been on the borderline for getting chucked out of the club for some time now. Forgets himself, that's the trouble. Loses his temper.'

'Is he any good?'

'Karate – second Dan and powerful with it. He's good at the showy stuff – smashing bricks, beams of wood and so on. His judo is nowhere. I'll take you in. He's on his own.'

Faulkner wore an old judogi which had obviously been washed many times and looked powerful enough as he worked out in front of the full-length mirrors at one end of the dojo, going through the interminable and ritualistic exercises without which no student can hope to attain any standard at all at karate. His kicks were one of his strongest features, very high and fast.

He paused to wipe the sweat from his face with a towel and noticed his audience. He recognized Miller at once and came forward, a sneer on his face.

'Didn't know you allowed coppers in here, Bert, I'll have to reconsider my membership.'

'Sergeant Miller's welcome here any time,' King said, his face flushed with anger. 'And I'd be careful about going on the mat with him if I were you. You could get a nasty surprise.'

Which was a slight exaggeration judging from what Miller had just seen, but Faulkner chuckled softly. 'And now you're tempting me – you really are.'

King went out and Faulkner rubbed his head briskly. 'I'm beginning to get you for breakfast, dinner and tea. Rather boring.'

'I can't help that,' Miller said and produced Grace Packard's gloves from his pocket. 'Recognize these?'

Faulkner examined them and sighed. 'Don't tell me. I left them at Sam Harkness's coffee stall in Regent Square last night. As I remember, I pulled them out of my pocket when looking for some loose change. He said something about them not being my style.'

'And you told him they belonged to your fiancée.'

'I know, Miller, very naughty of me. They were the Packard girl's. She left them at the flat.'

'Why did you lie about it to Harkness?'

'Be your age – why should I discuss my private affairs with him?'

'You've never seemed to show that kind of reluctance before.'

Faulkner's face went dark. 'Anything else, because if not I'd like to get on with my work-out?'

'You've had that. You've got a lot of explaining to do, Faulkner. A hell of a lot.'

'I see. Am I going to be arrested?'

'That remains to be seen.'

'So I'm still a free agent?' He glanced at his watch. 'I'll be here for another twenty minutes, Miller. After that I'll

shower for five minutes, dress and take a taxi to my flat.
If I have to see you, I'll see you there and nowhere else.
Now good morning to you.'

He turned and stalked across the mat to the mirrors,
positioned himself and started to practice front kicks.
Strangely enough Miller didn't feel angry at all. In any case
the flat would be preferable to the judo centre for the kind
of conversation he envisaged. The important thing was that
there was something there, something to be brought into
the light. He was certain of that now. He turned and went
out quickly, his stomach hollow with excitement.

15

The Gunner came awake slowly, yawned and stretched his
arms. For a moment he stared blankly around him,
wondering where he was and then he remembered.

It was quiet there in the comfortable old living-room – so
quiet that he could hear the clock ticking and the soft patter
of the rain as it drifted against the window.

The blanket with which Jenny Crowther had covered
him had slipped down to his knees. He touched it gently
for a moment, a smile on his mouth, then got to his feet
and stretched again. The fire was almost out. He dropped
to one knee, raked the ashes away and added a little of the
kindling he found in the coal scuttle. He waited until the
flames were dancing and then went into the kitchen.

He filled the kettle, lit the gas stove and helped himself
to a cigarette from a packet he found on the table. He
went to the window and peered out into the rain-swept
yard and behind him, Jenny Crowther said, 'Never stops,
does it?'

She wore an old bathrobe and the black hair hung straight

on either side of a face that was clear and shining and without a line.

'No need to ask you if you slept well,' he said. 'You look as if they've just turned you out at the mint.'

She smiled right down to her toes and crossed to the window, yawning slightly. 'As a matter of fact I slept better than I have done for weeks. I can't understand it.'

'That's because I was here, darlin',' he quipped. 'Guarding the door like some faithful old hound.'

'There could be something in that,' she said soberly.

There was an awkward pause. It was as if neither of them could think of the right thing to say next, as if out of some inner knowledge they both knew that they had walked a little further towards the edge of some quiet place where anything might happen.

She swilled out the teapot and reached for the caddy and the Gunner chuckled. 'Sunday morning – used to be my favourite day of the week. You could smell the bacon frying all the way up to the bedroom.'

'Who was doing the cooking?'

'My Aunt Mary of course.' He tried to look hurt. 'What kind of a bloke do you think I am? The sort that keeps stray birds around the place?'

'I'm glad you put that in the plural. Very honest of you.'

On impulse, he moved in behind her and slid his arms about her waist, pulling her softness against him, aware from the feel of her that beneath the bathrobe she very probably had nothing on.

'Two and a half bleeding years in the nick. I've forgotten what it's like.'

'Well, you needn't think you're going to take it out on me.'

She turned to glance over her shoulder, smiling and then the smile faded and she turned completely, putting a hand up to his face.

'Oh, Gunner, you're a daft devil, aren't you?'

His hands cupped her rear lightly and he dropped his head until his forehead rested against hers. For some reason he felt like crying, all choked up so that he couldn't speak, just like being a kid again, uncertain in a cold world.

'Don't rub it in, lass.'

She tilted his chin and kissed him very gently on the mouth. He pushed her away firmly and held her off, a hand on each shoulder. What he said next surprised even himself.

'None of that now. You don't want to be mixed up with a bloke like me. Nothing but a load of trouble. I'll have a cup of tea and something to eat and then I'll be off. You and the old girl had better forget you ever saw me.'

'Why don't you shut up?' she said. 'Go and sit down by the fire and I'll bring the tea in.'

He sat in the easy chair and watched her arrange the tray with a woman's instinctive neatness and pour tea into two cups. 'What about the old girl?'

'She'll be hard on till noon,' Jenny said. 'Needs plenty of rest at her age.'

He sat there drinking his tea, staring into the fire and she said softly, 'What would you do then if this was an ordinary Sunday?'

'In the nick?' He chuckled grimly. 'Oh, you get quite a choice. You can go to the services in the prison chapel morning and evening – plenty of the lads do that, just to get out of their cells. Otherwise you're locked in all day.'

'What do you do?'

'Read, think. If you're in a cell with someone else you can always play chess, things like that. If you're at the right stage in your sentence they let you out on to the landing for an hour or so in the evening to play table tennis or watch television.'

She shook her head. 'What a waste.'

He grinned and said with a return to his old flippancy,

'Oh, I don't know. What would I be doing Sundays on the outside? Spend the morning in the kip. Get up for three or four pints at the local and back in time for roast beef, Yorkshire pud and two veg. I'd have a snooze after that, work me way through the papers in the afternoon and watch the telly in the evening. What a bloody bore.'

'Depends who you're doing it with,' she suggested.

'You've got a point there. Could put an entirely different complexion on the morning in the kip for a start.'

She put down her cup and leaned forward. 'Why not go back, Gunner? There's nowhere to run to. The longer you leave it, the worse it will be.'

'I could lose all my remission,' he said. 'That would mean another two and a half years.'

'Are you certain you'd lose all of it?'

'I don't know. You have to take your chance on that sort of thing.' He grinned. 'Could have been back now if things had turned out differently last night.'

'What do you mean?' He told her about Doreen and what had happened at her flat. When he finished, Jenny shook her head. 'What am I going to do with you?'

'I could make a suggestion. Two and a half years is a hell of a long time.'

She examined him critically and frowned. 'You know I hadn't realized it before, but you could do with a damned good scrub. You'll find a bathroom at the head of the stairs and there's plenty of hot water. Go on. I'll make you some breakfast while you're in the tub.'

'All right then, all right,' he said good-humouredly as she pulled him to his feet and pushed him through the door.

But he wasn't smiling when he went upstairs and locked himself in the bathroom. *Two and a half years.* The thought of it sent a wave of coldness through him, of sudden, abject despair. If only that stupid screw hadn't decided to sneak off to the canteen. If only he hadn't tried to touch up the staff nurse. But that was the trouble with life, wasn't it? Just one big series of ifs.

He was just finishing dressing when she knocked on the door and said softly, 'Come into my room when you've finished Gunner – it's the next door. I've got clean clothes for you.'

When he went into her room she was standing at the end of the bed bending over a suit which she had laid out. 'My father's,' she said. 'Just about the right fit I should say.'

'I can't take that, darlin',' the Gunner told her. 'If the coppers catch me in gear like that they'll want to know where it came from.'

She stared at him, wide-eyed. 'I hadn't thought of that.'

'If I go back it's got to be just the way I looked when I turned up here last night otherwise they'll want to know where I've been and who's been helping me.'

The room was strangely familiar and he looked around him and grinned. 'You want to get a curtain for that window, darlin'. When I was in the loft last night I could see right in. Quite a view. One I'm not likely to forget in a hurry.' He sighed and said in a whisper, 'I wonder how many times I'll think of that during the next two and a half years.'

'Look at me, Gunner,' she said softly.

When he turned she was standing at the end of the bed. She was quite naked, her bathrobe on the floor at her feet. The Gunner was turned to stone. She was so lovely it hurt. She just stood there looking at him calmly, waiting for him to make a move, the hair like a dark curtain sweeping down until it gently brushed against the tips of the firm breasts.

He went towards her slowly, reaching out to touch like a blind man. Her perfume filled his nostrils and a kind of hoarse sob welled up in his throat.

He held her tightly in his arms, his head buried against

her shoulder and she smoothed his hair and kissed him gently as a mother might a child. 'It's all right, Gunner. Everything's going to be all right.'

Gunner Doyle, the great lover. He was like some kid presented with the real thing for the first time. His hands were shaking so much that she had to unbutton his shirt and trousers for him. But afterwards it was fine, better than he had ever known it before. He melted into her flesh as she pulled him close and carried him away into warm, aching darkness.

Afterwards – a long time afterwards, or so it seemed – the telephone started to ring. 'I'd better see who it is.' She slipped from beneath the sheets, and reached for her bathrobe.

The door closed softly behind her and the Gunner got up and started to dress. He was fastening his belt when the door opened again and she stood there staring at him looking white and for the first time since he had known her, frightened.

He took her by the shoulders. 'What's up?'

'It was a man,' she said in a strained voice. 'A man on the phone. He said to tell you to get out fast. That the police would be here any time.'

'Jesus,' he said. 'who was it?'

'I don't know,' she said and cracked suddenly. 'Oh, Gunner, what are we going to do?'

'You stay put, darlin', and carry on as normal,' he said, going to the bed and pulling on the boots she had given him. 'I'm the only one who has to do anything.'

He yanked the sweater over his head and she grabbed his arm. 'Give yourself up, Gunner.'

'First things first, darlin'. I've got to get out of here and so far away that the coppers don't have a hope of connecting me with you and the old girl.'

She looked up into his face for a moment then turned to the dressing-table and opened her handbag. She took out a handful of loose coins and three pound notes.

When she held the money out to him he tried to protest, but she shook her head. 'Better take it, just in case you decide to keep on running. I'm not holding you to anything.' She went to the wardrobe and produced an old single-breasted raincoat. 'And this. It was my father's. No use to him now.'

Suddenly she was the tough Yorkshire lass again, rough, competent, completely unsentimental. 'Now you'd better get out of here.'

He pulled on the coat and she led the way into the passageway. The Gunner started towards the stairs and she jerked his sleeve.

'I've got a better way.'

He followed her up another flight of stairs, passing several doors which obviously led to upper rooms. At the top, they were confronted by a heavier door bolted on the inside and protected by a sheet of iron against burglars.

She eased back the bolts and the door swung open in the wind giving him a view of a flat roof between two high gables. There was a rail at one end and on the other side of it the roof sloped to the yard below.

'If you scramble over the gable end,' she said, pointing to the left, 'you can slide down the other side to the flat roof of a metalworks next door. Nothing to it for you – I've done it myself when I was a kid. You'll find a fire escape that'll take you all the way down into the next alley.'

He stared at her dumbly, rain blowing in through the open doorway, unable to think of anything to say. She gave him a sudden fierce push that sent him out into the open.

'Go on – get moving, you bloody fool,' she said and slammed the door.

He had never felt so utterly desolate, so completely cut-

off from everything in his life. It was as if he had left
everything worth having back there behind that iron door
and there was nothing he could do about it. Not a damned
thing.

He followed her instructions to the letter and a minute
or so later hurried along the alley on the far side and turned
into the street at the end.

He kept on walking in a kind of daze, his mind elsewhere,
turning from one street into the other in the heavy rain.
About ten minutes later he found himself on the edge of
Jubilee Park. He went in through a corner entrance, past
the enigmatic statue of good Queen Victoria, orb in one
hand and sceptre in the other, and walked aimlessly into
the heart of the park.

He didn't see a living soul which was hardly surprising
considering the weather. Finally he came to an old folks'
pavilion, the kind of place where pensioners congregated
on calmer days to gossip and play dominoes. The door was
locked, but a bench beside it was partially sheltered from
the rain by an overhanging roof. He slumped down, hands
thrust deep into the pockets of the old raincoat and stared
into the grey curtain. He was alone in a dead world.
Completely and finally alone.

16

When Faulkner got out of the taxi there was no sign of
Nick Miller. Faulkner was surprised, but hardly in a mood
to shed tears over the matter. He hurried up to his flat,
unlocked the door and went in. The fire had almost gone
out and he took off his wet raincoat, got down on one knee
and started to replenish it carefully. As the flames started
to flicker into life the door bell sounded.

He opened it, expecting Miller, and found Joanna and Jack Morgan standing there.

'Surprise, surprise,' Faulkner said.

'Cut it out, Bruno,' Morgan told him. 'We had a visit from Nick Miller early this morning and what he told us wasn't funny.'

Faulkner took Joanna's coat. 'This whole thing is beginning to annoy me and there's a nasty hint of worse to come. Visions of a lonely cell with two hard-faced screws, the parson snivelling at my side as I take that last walk along the corridor to the execution room.'

'You should read the papers more often. They aren't hanging murderers this season.'

'What a shame. No romance in anything these days, is there?'

Joanna pulled him round to face her. 'Can't you be serious for once? You're in real trouble. What on earth possessed you to bring that girl back here?'

'So you know about that, do you?'

'Miller told us, but I'd still like to hear about it from you,' Morgan said. 'After all, I am your lawyer.'

'And that's a damned sinister way of putting it for a start.'

The door bell rang sharply. In the silence that followed, Faulkner grinned. 'Someone I've been expecting. Excuse me a moment.'

When Miller left the judo centre he was feeling strangely elated. At the best of times police work is eighty per cent instinct – a special faculty that comes from years of handling every kind of trouble. In this present case his intuition told him that Faulkner had something to hide, whatever Mallory's opinion might be. The real difficulty was going to be in digging it out.

He sat in the car for a while, smoking a cigarette and thinking about it. Faulkner was a highly intelligent man and something of a natural actor. He enjoyed putting on a show and being at the centre of things. His weakness obviously lay in his disposition to sudden, irrational violence, to a complete emotional turnabout during which he lost all control or at least that's what his past history seemed to indicate. If only he could be pushed over the edge . . .

Miller was filled with a kind of restless excitement at the prospect of the encounter to come and that was no good at all. He parked the car beside the corner gate of Jubilee Park, buttoned his trenchcoat up to the chin and went for a walk.

He didn't mind the heavy rain – rather liked it, in fact. It somehow seemed to hold him safe in a small private world in which he was free to think without distraction. He walked aimlessly for twenty minutes or so, turning from one path to another, not really seeing very much, his mind concentrated on one thing.

If he had been a little more alert he would have noticed the figure of a man disappearing fast round the side of the old folks' shelter as he approached, but he didn't and the Gunner watched him go, heart in mouth, from behind a rhododendron bush.

When Miller walked into the flat and found Joanna Hartmann and Morgan standing by the fire he wasn't in the least put out for their presence suited him very well indeed.

He smiled and nodded to the woman as he unbuttoned his damp raincoat. 'We seem to have seen rather a lot of each other during the past twenty-four hours.'

'Is there any reason why I shouldn't be here?' she demanded coldly.

'Good heavens no. I've got one or two loose ends to tie up with Mr Faulkner. Shouldn't take more than five minutes.'

'I understand you've already asked him a great. many questions,' Morgan said, 'and now you intend to ask some more. I think we have a right to know where we stand in this matter.'

'Are you asking me as his legal representative?'

'Naturally.'

'Quite unnecessary, I assure you,' Miller lied smoothly. 'I'm simply asking him to help me with my enquiries, that's all. He isn't the only one involved.'

'I'm happy to hear it.'

'Shut up, Jack, there's a good chap,' Faulkner cut in. 'If you've anything to say to me, then get on with it, Miller. The sooner this damned thing is cleared up, the sooner I can get back to work.'

'Fair enough.' Miller moved towards the statues. 'In a way we have a parallel problem. I understand you started five weeks ago with one figure. In a manner of speaking, so did I.'

'A major difference if I might point it out,' Faulkner said. 'You now have five while I only have four.'

'But you were thinking of adding a fifth, weren't you?'

'Which is why I paid Grace Packard to pose for me, but it didn't work.' Faulkner shook his head. 'No, the damned thing is going to be cast as you see it now for good or ill.'

'I see.' Miller turned from the statues briskly. 'One or two more questions if you don't mind. Perhaps you'd rather I put them to you in private.'

'I've nothing to hide.'

'As you like. I'd just like to go over things again briefly. Mr Morgan called for you about eight?'

'That's right.'

'What were you doing?'

'Sleeping. I'd worked non-stop on the fourth figure in the group for something like thirty hours. When it was finished I took the telephone off the hook and lay on the bed.'

'And you were awakened by Mr Morgan?'

'That's it.'

'And then went to The King's Arms where you met Grace Packard? You're quite positive you hadn't met her previously?'

'What are you trying to suggest?' Joanna interrupted angrily.

'You don't need to answer that, Bruno,' Morgan said.

'What in the hell are you both trying to do . . . hang me? Why shouldn't I answer it? I've got nothing to hide. I should think Harry Meadows, the landlord, would be the best proof of that. As I recall, I had to ask him who she was. If you must know I thought she was on the game. I wasn't looking forward to the party and I thought she might liven things up.'

'And you met her boyfriend on the way out?'

'That's it. He took a swing at me so I had to put him on his back.'

'Rather neatly according to the landlord. What did you use . . . judo?'

'Aikido.'

'I understand there was also some trouble at the party with Mr Marlowe?'

Faulkner shrugged. 'I wouldn't have called it trouble exactly. Frank isn't the physical type.'

'But you are – or so it would seem?'

'What are you trying to prove?' Joanna demanded, moving to Faulkner's side.

'Just trying to get at the facts,' Miller said.

Morgan moved forward a step. 'I'd say you were aiming at rather more than that. You don't have to put up with this, Bruno.'

'Oh, but I do.' Faulkner grinned. 'It's beginning to get rather interesting. All right, Miller, I've an uncontrollable temper, I'm egotistical, aggressive and when people annoy me I tend to hit them. They even sent me to prison for it once. Common assault – the respectable kind, by the way, not the nasty sexual variety.'

'I'm aware of that.'

'Somehow I thought you might be.'

'You brought the girl back here to pose for you and nothing else?'

'You know when she got here, you know when she left. There wasn't time for anything else.'

'Can you remember what you talked about?'

'There wasn't much time for conversation either. I told her to strip and get up on the platform. Then I saw to the fire and poured myself a drink. As soon as she got up there I knew it was no good. I told her to get dressed and gave her a ten-pound note.'

'There was no sign of it in her handbag.'

'She slipped it into her stocking top. Made a crack about it being the safest place.'

'It was nowhere on her person and she's been examined thoroughly.'

'All right, so the murderer took it.'

Miller decided to keep the information that the girl had had intercourse just before her death to himself for a moment.

'There was no question of any sexual assault so how would the murderer have known where it was?'

There was a heavy silence. He allowed it to hang there for a moment and continued, 'You're quite sure that you and the girl didn't have an argument before she left?'

Faulkner laughed harshly. 'If you mean did I blow my top, break her neck with one devastating karate chop and carry her down the back stairs into the night because she refused my wicked way with her, no. If I'd wanted her to stay the night she'd have stayed and not for any ten quid either. She came cheaper than that or I miss my guess.'

'I understand she was found in Dob Court, Sergeant?' Morgan said.

'That's right.'

'And are you seriously suggesting that Mr Faulkner killed the girl here, carted her downstairs and carried her all the way because that's what he would have to have done. I think I should point out that he doesn't own a car.'

'They took my licence away last year,' Faulkner admitted amiably. 'Driving under the influence.'

'But you did go out after the girl left?'

'To the coffee stall in Regent Square.' Faulkner made no attempt to deny it. 'I even said hello to the local bobby. I often do. No class barriers for me.'

'He's already told us that. It was only five or ten minutes later that he found Grace Packard's body. You left Joanna's gloves on the counter. The proprietor asked me to pass them on.'

Miller produced the black and white gloves and handed them to Joanna Hartmann who frowned in puzzlement. 'But these aren't mine.'

'They're Grace Packard's,' Faulkner said. 'I pulled them out of my pocket when I was looking for some change, as you very well know, Miller. I must have left them on the counter.'

'The man at the coffee stall confirms that. Only one difference. Apparently when he commented on them, you said they belonged to Joanna.'

Joanna Hartmann looked shocked, but Faulkner seemed quite unperturbed. 'He knows Joanna well. We've been there together often. I'd hardly be likely to tell him they belonged to another woman, would I? As I told you earlier, it was none of his business, anyway.'

'That seems reasonable enough surely,' Joanna said.

Miller looked at her gravely. 'Does it?'

She seemed genuinely puzzled. 'I don't understand. What are you trying to say?'

Morgan had been listening to everything, a frown of con
centration on his face and now he said quickly, 'Just a
minute. There's something more here, isn't there?'

'There could be.'

For the first time Faulkner seemed to have had enough.
The urbane mask slipped heavily and he said sharply, 'I'm
beginning to get rather bored with all this. Is this or is it
not another Rainlover murder?'

Miller didn't even hesitate. 'It certainly has all the hall-
marks.'

'Then that settles it,' Morgan said. 'You surely can't be
suggesting that Mr Faulkner killed the other four as well?'

'I couldn't have done the previous one for a start,'
Faulkner said. 'I just wasn't available.'

'Can you prove that?'

'Easily. There were three statues up there two days ago.
Now there are four. Believe me, I was occupied. When Jack
called for me last night I hadn't been out of the. flat since
Thursday.'

'You still haven't answered my question, Sergeant,'
Morgan said. 'The gloves . . . you were getting at something
else, weren't you?'

'In killings of this kind there are always certain details
not released to the Press,' Miller said. 'Sometimes because
they are too unpleasant, but more often because public
knowledge of them might prejudice police enquiries.'

He was on a course now which might well lead to disaster.
he knew that, and if anything went wrong there would be
no one to help him, no one to back him up. Mallory would
be the first to reach for the axe, but he had gone too far
to draw back now.

'This type of compulsive killer is a prisoner of his own
sickness. He not only has the compulsion to kill again. He
can no more alter his method than stop breathing and that's
what always proves his undoing.'

'Fascinating,' Faulkner said. 'Let's see now, Jack the Ripper always chose a prostitute and performed a surgical operation. The Boston Strangler raped them first then choked them with a nylon stocking. What about the Rainlover?'

'No pattern where the women themselves are concerned. The eldest was fifty and Grace Packard was the youngest. No sexual assault, no perversions. Everything neat and tidy. Always the neck broken cleanly from the rear. A man who knows what he's doing.'

'Sorry to disappoint you, but you don't need to be a karate expert to break a woman's neck from the rear. One good rabbit punch is all it takes.'

'Possibly, but the Rainlover has one other trademark. He always takes something personal from his victims.'

'A kind of *memento mori*? Now that is interesting.'

'Anything special?' Morgan asked.

'In the first case it was a handbag, then a headscarf, a nylon stocking and a shoe.'

'And in Grace Packard's case a pair of gloves?' Faulkner suggested. 'Then tell me this, Miller? If I was content with one shoe and one stocking previously why should it suddenly be necessary for me to take two gloves? A break in the pattern, surely?'

'A good point,' Miller admitted.

'Here's another,' Joanna said. 'What about the ten-pound note? Doesn't that make two items missing?'

'I'm afraid we only have Mr Faulkner's word that it existed at all.'

There was a heavy silence.

For the first time Faulkner looked serious – really serious. Morgan couldn't think of anything to say and Joanna Hartmann was just plain frightened.

Miller saw it as the psychological moment to withdraw for a little while and smiled pleasantly. 'I'd better get in touch with Headquarters, just to see how things are getting on at that end.'

Faulkner tried to look nonchalant and waved towards the telephone. 'Help yourself.'

'That's all right. I can use the car radio. I'll be back in five minutes. I'm sure you could all use the break.'

He went out quickly, closing the door softly behind him.

Faulkner was the first to break the silence with a short laugh that echoed back to him, hollow and strained. 'well, now, it doesn't look too good, does it?'

17

Harold Phillips was hot and uncomfortable. The Interrogation Room was full of cigarette smoke and it was beginning to make his eyes hurt. He'd already had one lengthy session with Chief Superintendent Mallory and he hadn't liked it. He glanced furtively across the room at the stony-faced constable standing beside the door.

He moistened his lips. 'How much longer then?'

'That's up to Mr Mallory, sir,' the constable replied.

The door opened and Mallory returned, Brady following him. 'Did they get you a cup of tea?' the Superintendent asked.

'No, they didn't,' Harold answered in an aggrieved tone.

'That's not good enough – not good enough at all.' He turned to the constable. 'Fetch a cup of tea from the canteen on the double for Mr Phillips.'

'He turned, smiling amiably and sat at the table. He opened a file and glanced at it quickly as he started to fill his pipe. 'Let's just look at this again.'

In the silence which followed the only sound was the clock ticking on the wall and the dull rumble of thunder somewhere far off in the distance.

'Sounds like more rain then,' Harold commented.

Mallory looked up. His face was like stone, the eyes dark and full of menace. He said sharply and angrily, 'I'm afraid you haven't been telling the truth, young man. You've been wasting my time.'

The contrast between this and his earlier politeness was quite shattering and Harold started to shake involuntarily. 'I don't know what you mean,' he stammered. 'I've told you everything I can remember.'

'Tell him the truth, son,' Brady put in, worried and anxious. 'It'll go better with you in the long run.'

'But I am telling him the bleeding truth,' Harold cried. 'What else does he want – blood? Here, I'm not having any more of this. I want to see a lawyer.'

'Lie number one,' Mallory said remorselessly. 'You told us that you didn't know the name of the man you'd had the argument with at The King's Arms. The man who went off with Grace Packard.'

'That's right.'

'The landlord remembers differently. He says that when you came back to the pub to take him up on his offer of a drink on the house, you already knew the name of the person concerned. What you'd really come back for was his address only the landlord wouldn't play.'

'It's a lie,' Harold said. 'There isn't a word of truth in it.'

'He's ready to repeat his statement under oath in the box,' Brady said.

Mallory carried on as if he hadn't heard. 'You told us that you were home by half-nine, that you took your mother a cup of tea and then went to bed. Do you still stick to that story?'

'You ask her – she'll tell you. Go on, just ask her.'

'We happen to know that your mother is a very sick woman and in severe pain most of the time. The pills the doctor gave to make her sleep needed to be much stronger than usual. Her dosage was two. We can prove she took three yesterday. Medical evidence would indicate that it would be most unlikely that you would have been able to waken her at the time you state.'

'You can't prove that,' Harold sounded genuinely indignant.

'Possibly not,' Mallory admitted candidly, 'but it won't look good, will it?'

'So what. You need evidence in a court of law – real evidence. Everybody knows that.'

'Oh, we can supply some of that as well if you insist. You told us that after leaving The King's Arms you didn't see Grace Packard again, that you walked round the streets for a while, had a coffee at the station buffet and went home, arriving at half-nine.'

'That's right.'

'But you found time for something else, didn't you?'

'What are you talking about?'

'You had intercourse with someone.'

Harold was momentarily stunned. When he spoke again he was obviously badly shaken. 'I don't know what you mean.'

'I wouldn't try lying again if I were you. You asked for evidence, real evidence. I've got some for you. For the past couple of hours your trousers, the trousers you were wearing yesterday have been the subject of chemical tests in our laboratory. They haven't finished yet by any means, but I've just had a preliminary report that indicates beyond any shadow of a doubt that you were with a woman last night.'

'Maybe someone forgot to tell you, son,' Brady put in, 'but Grace Packard had intercourse just before she died.'

'Here, you needn't try that one.' Harold put out a hand defensively. 'All right. I'll tell you the truth. I did go with a woman last night.'

'Who was she?' Mallory asked calmly.

'I don't know. I bumped into her in one of those streets behind the station.'

'Was she on the game?' Brady suggested.

'That's it. Thirty bob for a short time. You know how it goes. We stood against the wall in a back alley.'

'And her name?' Mallory asked.

'Do me a favour, Superintendent. I didn't even get a clear look at her face.'

'Let's hope she hasn't left you something to remember her by,' Brady said grimly. 'Why didn't you tell us about this before?'

Harold had obviously recovered some of his lost confidence. He contrived to look pious. 'It isn't the sort of thing you like to talk about, now is it?'

The constable came in with a cup of tea, placed it on the table and whispered in Mallory's ear. The Chief Superintendent nodded, got to his feet and beckoned to Brady.

'Miller's on the phone,' he said when they got into the corridor.

'What about Harold, sir?'

'Let him stew for a few minutes.'

He spoke to Miller from a booth half-way along the corridor. 'Where are you speaking from?'

'Phone box outside Faulkner's place,' Miller told him. 'He's up there now with his lawyer and Joanna Hartmann.'

'You've spoken to him then?'

'Oh, yes, thought I'd give him a breather, that's all. We've reached an interesting stage. You were right about the gloves, sir. He didn't even attempt to deny having had them. Gave exactly the reason for lying about them at the coffee stall that you said he would.'

Mallory couldn't help feeling slightly complacent. 'There you are then. I don't like to say I told you so, but I honestly think you're wasting your time, Miller.'

'Don't tell me Harold's cracked?'

'Not quite, but he's tying himself up in about fifty-seven different knots. I think he's our man. More certain of it than ever.'

'But not the Rainlover?'

'A different problem, I'm afraid.'

'One interesting point, sir,' Miller said. 'Remember Faulkner told us he gave the girl ten pounds?'

'What about it?'

'What he actually gave her was a ten-pound note. He says she tucked it into her stocking top. Apparently made some crack about it being the safest place.'

'Now that is interesting,' Mallory was aware of a sudden tightness in his chest that interfered with his breathing – an old and infallible sign. 'That might just about clinch things if I use it in the right way. I think you'd better get back here right away, Miller.'

'But what about Faulkner, sir?'

'Oh, to hell with Faulkner, man. Get back here now and that's an order.'

He slammed down the phone and turned to Brady who waited, leaning against the wall. 'Miller's just come up with an interesting tit-bit. Remember Faulkner said he gave the girl ten pounds for posing for him. He's just told Miller it was actually a ten-pound note. Now I wonder what our friend in there would do with it.'

'Always assuming that he's the man we want, sir,' Brady reminded him.

'Now don't you start, Brady,' Mallory said. 'I've got enough on my hands with Miller.'

'All right, sir,' Brady said. 'Put a match to it if he had any sense.'

'Which I doubt,' Mallory chuckled grimly. 'Can you imagine Harold Phillips putting a match to a ten-pound note?' He shook his head. 'Not on your life. He'll have stashed it away somewhere.'

At that moment Henry Wade appeared from the lift at the end of the corridor and came towards them, Harold's trousers over his arm.

'Anything else for me?' Mallory demanded.

wade shook his head.

'I'm afraid not. He was with a woman, that's all I can tell you.'

'Nothing more?'

Wade shrugged. 'No stains we can link with the girl if that's what you mean. Sometimes if you're lucky you can test the semen for its blood group factor. About forty per cent of males secrete their blood group in their body fluids. Of course it won't work if the subject isn't a member of that group. In any case you need a large specimen and it's got to be fresh. Sorry, sir.'

Mallory took a deep breath. 'All right, this is what we do. We're all going back in there. I want you to simply stand with the trousers over your arm and say nothing, Wade. Brady – just look serious. That's all I ask.'

'But what are you going to try, sir?' Brady demanded.

'A king-size bluff,' Mallory said simply. 'I'm simply betting on the fact that I'm a better poker player than Harold Phillips.'

18

Nick Miller replaced the receiver and stepped out of the telephone box into the heavy rain. Mallory's instructions had been quite explicit. He was to drop the Faulkner enquiry and return to Headquarters at once and yet the Scotland Yard man was wrong – Miller still felt certain about that. It was nothing he could really put his finger on, something that couldn't be defined and yet when he thought of Faulkner his stomach went hollow and his flesh crawled.

But orders were orders and to disobey this one was to invite the kind of reaction that might mean the end of his career as a policeman. When it finally came down to it he wasn't prepared to throw away a life that had come to mean everything to him simply because of a private hunch that could well be wrong.

He crossed to the Mini-Cooper, took out his keys and, above his head, the studio window of Faulkner's flat dissolved in a snowstorm of flying glass as a chair soared through in a graceful curve that ended in the middle of the street.

There was a heavy silence after Miller left and Faulkner was the first to break it. He crossed to the bar and poured himself a large gin. 'I can feel the noose tightening already. Distinctly unpleasant.'

'Stop it, Bruno!' Joanna said sharply. 'It just isn't funny any more.'

He paused, the glass half-way to his lips and looked at her in a kind of mild surprise. 'You surely aren't taking this thing seriously?'

'How else can I take it?'

Faulkner turned to Morgan. 'And what about you?'

'It doesn't look too good, Bruno.'

'That's wonderful. That's bloody marvellous.' Faulkner drained his glass and came round from behind the bar. 'How long have you known me, Jack? Fifteen years or is it more? I'd be fascinated to know when you first suspected my homicidal tendencies.'

'Why did you have to bring that wretched girl back with you, Bruno? Why?' Joanna said.

He looked at them both in turn, his cynical smile fading. 'My God, you're both beginning to believe it, aren't you? You're actually beginning to believe it.'

'Don't be ridiculous.' Joanna turned away.

He swung her round to face him. 'No, you're afraid to give it voice, but it's there in your eyes.'

'Please, Bruno . . . you're hurting me.'

He pushed her away and turned on Jack. 'And you?'

'You've a hell of a temper, Bruno, no one knows that better than I do. When you broke Pearson's jaw it took four of us to drag you off him.'

'Thanks for the vote of confidence.'

'Face facts, Bruno. Miller's got a lot to go on. All circumstantial, I'll grant you that, but it wouldn't look good in court.'

'That's your opinion.'

'All right, let's look at the facts as the prosecution would present them to a jury. First of all there's your uncontrollable temper, your convictions for violence. The medical report when you were in Wandsworth said you needed psychiatric treatment, but you refused. That won't look good for a start.'

'Go on – this is fascinating.'

'You bring Grace Packard back here late at night and give her ten pounds to pose for you for two or three minutes.'

'The simple truth.'

'I know that – I believe it because it's typical of you, but if you think there's a jury in England that would swallow such an explanation you're crazy.'

'You're not leaving me with much hope, are you?'

'I'm not finished yet.' Morgan carried on relentlessly. 'No more than a couple of minutes after she left you went out after her. You bought cigarettes at that coffee stall in Regent Square and she was killed not more than two hundred yards away a few minutes later. And you had her gloves – can you imagine what the prosecution would try to make out of that one?'

Faulkner seemed surprisingly calm considering the circumstances. 'And what about the ten-pound note? If it didn't exist why should I bother to mention it in the first place?'

'A further complication . . . all part of the smokescreen.'

'And you believe that?'

'I think a jury might.'

Faulkner went to the bar, reached for the gin bottle and poured himself another drink. He stood with his back to them for a moment. When he finally turned, he looked calm and serious.

'A good case, Jack, but one or two rather obvious flaws. You've laid some stress on the fact that I had Grace Packard's gloves. I think it's worth pointing out that I had them before she was killed. In any case, the gloves are only important if you maintain that Grace Packard was killed by the Rainlover. Have you considered that?'

'Yes, I've considered it,' Morgan said gravely.

'But if I am the Rainlover then I killed the others and you'd have to prove that was possible. What about the woman killed the night before last for example? As I told you when you called for me last night, I'd been working two days non-stop. Hadn't even left the studio.'

'The body was found in Jubilee Park no more than a quarter of a mile from here. You could have left by the back stairs and returned inside an hour and no one the wiser. That's what the prosecution would say.'

'But I didn't know about the murder, did I? You had to tell me. Don't you remember? It was just after you arrived. I was dressing in the bedroom and you spoke to me from in here.'

Morgan nodded. 'That's true. I remember now. I asked if you'd heard about the killing, picked up the paper and discovered it was Friday night's.' He seemed to go rigid and added in a whisper, 'Friday night's.'

He went to the chair by the fire, picked up the newspaper that was still lying there as it had been on his arrival the

previous evening. 'Final edition, Friday 23rd.' He turned to
Faulkner. 'But you don't have a paper delivered.'

'So what?'

'Then how did you get hold of this if you didn't leave
the house for two days?'

Joanna gave a horrified gasp and for the first time
Faulkner really looked put out. He put a hand to his head,
frowning. 'I remember now. I ran out of cigarettes. I was
tired . . . so tired that I couldn't think straight and it was
raining hard, beating against the window.' It was almost as
if he was speaking to himself. 'I thought the air might clear
my head and I needed some cigarettes so I slipped out.'

'And the newspaper?'

'I got it from the old man on the corner of Albany Street.'

'Next to Jubilee Park.'

They stood there in tableau, the three of them, caught
in a web of silence and somewhere in the distance thunder
echoed menacingly. Morgan was white and strained and a
kind of horror showed in Joanna's face. Faulkner shook his
head slowly as if unable to comprehend what was happening.

'You must believe me, Joanna, you must.'

She turned to Morgan. 'Take me home, Jack. Please take
me home.'

Faulkner said angrily, 'I'll be damned if I'll let you go
like this.'

As he grabbed at her arm she moved away sharply, colliding
with the drawing board on its stand, the one at which
Faulkner had been working earlier. The board went over,
papers scattering and his latest sketch fell at her feet, a rough
drawing of the group of four statues with a fifth added.

There was real horror on her face at this final, terrible proof.
As she backed away, Morgan picked up the sketch and held it
out to Faulkner. 'Have you got an explanation for this, too?'

Faulkner brushed him aside and grabbed Joanna by both
arms. 'Listen to me – just listen. That's all I ask.'

She slapped at him in a kind of blind panic and Morgan tried to pull Faulkner away from her. Something snapped inside Faulkner. He turned and hit Morgan back-handed, sending him staggering against the bar.

Joanna ran for the door. Faulkner caught her before she could open it and wrenched her around, clutching at the collar of her sheepskin coat.

'You're not leaving me, do you hear? I'll kill you first!'

Almost of their own volition his hands slid up and around her throat and she sank to her knees choking. Morgan got to his feet, dazed. He staggered forward, grabbed Faulkner by the hair and pulled hard. Faulkner gave a cry of pain, releasing his grip on the woman's throat. As he turned, Morgan picked up the jug of ice water that stood on the bar top and tossed the contents into his face.

The shock seemed to restore Faulkner to his senses. He stood there swaying, an almost vacant look on his face and Morgan went to Joanna and helped her to her feet.

'Are you all right?'

She nodded, without speaking. Morgan turned on Faulkner. 'Was that the way it happened, Bruno? Was that how you killed her?'

Faulkner faced them, dangerously calm. His laughter, when it came, was harsh, completely unexpected.

'All right – that's what you've been waiting to hear, isn't it? Well, let's tell the whole bloody world about it.'

He picked up a chair, lifted it high above his head and hurled it through the studio window.

Miller hammered on the door and it was opened almost immediately by Jack Morgan. Joanna Hartmann was slumped into one of the easy chairs by the fire, sobbing bitterly and Faulkner was standing at the bar pouring himself another drink, his back to the door.

'What happened?' Miller demanded.

Morgan moistened dry lips, but seemed to find difficulty in speaking. 'Why don't you tell him, Jack?' Faulkner called.

He emptied his glass and turned, the old sneer lifting the corner of his mouth. 'Jack and I were at school together, Miller – a very old school. The sort of place that has a code. He's finding it awkward to turn informer.'

'For God's sake, Bruno, let's get it over with,' Morgan said savagely.

'Anything to oblige.' Faulkner turned to Miller. 'I killed Grace Packard.' He held out his wrists. 'Who knows, Miller you might get promoted over this.'

Miller nodded slowly. 'You're aware of the seriousness of what you're saying?'

'He admitted it to Miss Hartmann and myself before you arrived,' Morgan said wearily. He turned to Bruno. 'Don't say anything else at this stage, Bruno. You don't need to.'

'I'll have to ask you to accompany me to Central C.I.D. Headquarters,' Miller said.

He delivered a formal caution, produced his handcuffs and snapped them over Faulkner's wrists. Faulkner smiled. 'You enjoyed doing that, didn't you?'

'Now and then it doesn't exactly make me cry myself to sleep,' Miller took him by the elbow.

'I'll come with you if I may,' Morgan said.

Faulkner smiled briefly, looking just for that single instant like an entirely different person, perhaps that other self he might have been had things been different.

'It's nice to know one's friends. I'd be obliged, Jack.'

'Will Miss Hartmann be all right?' Miller asked.

She looked up, her eyes swollen from weeping and nodded briefly. 'Don't worry about me. Will you come back for me, Jack?'

'I'll leave you my car.' He dropped the keys on top of the bar.

'Nothing to say, Joanna?' Faulkner demanded.

She turned away, her shoulders shaking and he started to laugh. Miller turned him round, gave him a solid push out on to the landing and Morgan closed the door on the sound of that terrible weeping.

19

It was quiet in the Interrogation Room. The constable at the door picked his nose impassively and thunder sounded again in the distance, a little nearer this time. Harold held the mug of tea in both hands and lifted it to his lips. It was almost cold, the surface covered by a kind of unpleasant scum that filled him with disgust. He shuddered and put the mug down on the table.

'How much longer?' he demanded and the door opened.

Mallory moved to the window and stood there staring out into the rain. Wade positioned himself at the other end of the table and waited, the trousers neatly folded over one arm.

Harold was aware of a strange, choking sensation in his throat. He wrenched at his collar and glanced appealingly at Brady who had closed the door after the constable who had discreetly withdrawn. The big Irishman looked troubled. He held Harold's glance for only a moment, then dropped his gaze.

'What did you do with the tenner?' Mallory asked without turning round.

'Tenner? What tenner?' Harold said.

Mallory turned to face him. 'The ten-pound note the girl had in her stocking top – what did you do with it?'

'I've never handled a ten-pound note in my life.'

'If you'd had any sense you'd have destroyed it, but not you.' Mallory carried on as if there had been no interruption.

'Where would you change it at that time of night – a pub? Or what about the station buffet – you said you were there.'

The flesh seemed to shrink visibly on Harold's bones. 'What the hell are you trying to prove?'

Mallory picked up the phone and rang through to the C.I.D. general office. 'Mallory here,' he told the Duty Inspector. 'I want you to get in touch with the manager of the buffet at the Central Station right away. Find out if anyone changed a ten-pound note last night. Yes, that's right – a ten-pound note.'

Harold's eyes burned in a face that was as white as paper. 'You're wasting your time.' He was suddenly belligerent again. 'They could have had half a dozen ten-pound notes through their hands on a Saturday night for all you know, so what does it prove?'

'We'll wait and see shall we?'

Harold seemed to pull himself together. He sat straighter in his chair and took a deep breath. 'All right, I've had enough. If you're charging me, I want a lawyer. If you're not, then I'm not staying here another minute.'

'If you'll extend that to five I'll be more than satisfied,' Mallory said.

Harold stared at him blankly. 'What do you mean?'

'I'm expecting a chap from the lab to arrive any second. We just want to give you a simple blood test.'

'Blood test? What for?'

Mallory nodded to Wade who laid the trousers on the table. 'The tests the lab ran on these trousers proved you were with a woman last night.'

'All right – I admitted that.'

'And the post-mortem on Grace Packard indicated she'd had intercourse with someone just before she died.'

'It wasn't with me, that's all I know.'

'We can prove that one way or the other with the simplest of tests.' It was from that point on that Mallory started to bend the facts. 'I don't know if you're aware of it, but it's possible to test a man's semen for his blood group factor.'

'So what?'

'During the post-mortem on Grace Packard a semen smear was obtained. It's since been tested in the lab and indicates a certain blood group. When the technician gets here from the lab he'll be able to take a small sample of your blood and tell us what your group is within a couple of minutes – or perhaps you know already?'

Harold stared wildly at him and the silence which enveloped them all was so heavy that suddenly it seemed almost impossible to breathe. His head moved slightly from side to side faster and faster. He tried to get up and then collapsed completely, falling across the table.

He hammered his fist up and down like a hysterical child. 'The bitch, the rotten stinking bitch. She shouldn't have laughed at me! She shouldn't have laughed at me!'

He started to cry and Mallory stood there, hands braced against the table, staring down at him. There was a time when this particular moment would have meant something, but not now. In fact, not for some considerable time now.

Quite suddenly the whole thing seemed desperately unreal – a stupid charade that had no substance. It didn't seem to be important any longer and that didn't make sense. Too much in too short a time. Perhaps what he needed was a spot of leave.

He straightened and there was a knock at the door. Brady opened it and a constable handed him a slip of paper. He passed it to Mallory who read it, face impassive. He crumpled it up in one hand and tossed it into the waste bin.

'A message from Dr Das. Mrs Phillips died peacefully in her sleep fifteen minutes ago. Thank God for that anyway.'

'It would be easy to say *I told you so*, Miller, but there it is,' Mallory said.

Miller took a deep breath. 'No possibility of error, sir?'

'None at all. He's given us a full statement. It seems he waited outside Faulkner's flat, saw Faulkner and the girl go in and followed her when she came out. He pulled her into Dob Court where they had some kind of reconciliation because she allowed him to have intercourse with her and she gave him the ten-pound note.'

'What went wrong?'

'God alone knows – I doubt if we'll ever get a clear picture. Apparently there was some sort of argument to do with Faulkner and the money. I get the impression that after the way he had treated him, Phillips objected to the idea that Faulkner might have had his way with the girl. The money seemed to indicate that he had.'

'So he killed her?'

'Apparently she taunted him, there was an argument and he started to hit her. Lost his temper completely. Didn't mean to kill her of course. They never do.'

'Do you think a jury might believe that?'

'With his background? Not in a month of Sundays.' The telephone rang. Mallory picked up the receiver, listened for a moment, then put it down. 'Another nail in the coffin. It seems the manager of the station buffet has turned up the assistant who changed that ten-pound note last night. Seems she can identify Phillips. He was a regular customer. She says he was in there about a quarter to eleven.'

'The bloody fool,' Miller said.

'They usually are, Miller, and a good thing for us, I might add.'

'But what on earth is Faulkner playing at? I don't understand.'

'Let's have him in and find out shall we?'

Mallory sat back and started to fill his pipe. Miller opened the door and called and Faulkner came in followed by Jack Morgan.

Faulkner looked as if he didn't have a care in the world. He stood in front of the desk, trenchcoat draped from his shoulders like a cloak, hands pushed negligently into his pockets.

Mallory busied himself with his pipe. When it was going to his satisfaction, he blew out the match and looked up. 'Mr Faulkner, I have here a full and complete confession to the murder of Grace Packard signed by Harold Phillips. What have you got to say to that?'

'Only that it would appear that I must now add a gift for prophecy to the list of my virtues,' Faulkner said calmly.

Morgan came forward quickly. 'Is this true, Superintendent?'

'It certainly is. We've even managed to turn up the ten-pound note your client gave the girl. Young Phillips changed it at the station buffet before going home.'

Morgan turned on Faulkner, his face white and strained. 'What in the hell have you been playing at, for God's sake? You told us that you killed Grace Packard.'

'Did I?' Faulkner shrugged. 'The other way about as I remember it. You told me.' He turned to Mallory. 'Mr Morgan, like all lawyers, Superintendent, has a tendency to believe his own arguments. Once he'd made up his mind I was the culprit, he couldn't help but find proof everywhere he looked.'

'Are you trying to say you've just been playing the bloody fool as usual?' Morgan pulled him round angrily. 'Don't you realize what you've done to Joanna?'

'She had a choice. She could have believed in me. She took your road.' Faulkner seemed completely unconcerned. 'I'm sure you'll be very happy together. Can I go now, Superintendent?'

'I think that might be advisable,' Mallory said.

Faulkner turned in the doorway, the old sneer lifting the corner of his mouth as he glanced at Miller. 'Sorry about that promotion – better luck next time.'

After he had gone there was something of a silence. Morgan just stood there, staring wildly into space. Quite suddenly he turned and rushed out without a word.

Miller stood at the window for a long moment, staring down into the rain. He saw Faulkner come out of the main entrance and go down the steps. He paused at the bottom to button his trenchcoat, face lifted to the rain, then walked rapidly away. Morgan appeared a moment later. He watched Faulkner go then hailed a taxi from the rank across the street.

Miller took out his wallet, produced a pound note and laid it on Mallory's desk. 'I was wrong,' he said simply.

Mallory nodded. 'You were, but I won't hold that against you. In my opinion Faulkner's probably just about as unbalanced as it's possible to be and still walk free. He'd impair anyone's judgement.'

'Nice of you to put it that way, but I was still wrong.'

'Never mind.' Mallory stood up and reached for his coat. 'If you can think of anywhere decent that will still be open on a Sunday afternoon I'll buy you a late lunch out of my ill-gotten gains.'

'Okay, sir. Just give me ten minutes to clear my desk and I'm your man.'

The rain was falling heavier than ever as they went down the steps of the Town Hall to the Mini-Cooper. Miller knew a restaurant that might fit the bill, an Italian place that had recently opened in one of the northern suburbs of the city and he drove past the Infirmary and took the car through the maze of slum streets behind it towards the new Inner Ring Road.

The streets were deserted, washed clean by the heavy rain and the wipers had difficulty in keeping the screen clear. They didn't speak and Miller drove on mechanically so stunned by what had happened that he was unable to think straight.

They turned a corner and Mallory gripped his arm. 'For God's sake, what's that?'

Miller braked instinctively. About half-way along the street, two men struggled beside a parked motorcycle. One of them was a police patrolman in heavy belted stormcoat and black crash helmet. The other wore only shirt and pants and seemed to be barefooted.

The policeman went down, the other man jumped for the motorcycle and kicked it into life. It roared away from the kerb as the patrolman scrambled to his feet, straight down the middle of the street. Miller swing the wheel, taking the Mini-Cooper across in an attempt to cut him off. The machine skidded wildly as the rider wrenched the wheel, and shaved the bonnet of the Mini-Cooper with a foot to spare, giving Miller a clear view of his wild, determined face. *Gunner Doyle*. Well this was something he *could* handle. He took the Mini-Cooper round in a full circle across the footpath, narrowly missing an old gas lamp, and went after him.

It was at that precise moment that Jack Morgan arrived back at Faulkner's flat. He knocked on the door and it was opened almost at once by Joanna Hartmann. She was very pale, her eyes swollen from weeping, but seemed well in control of herself. She had a couple of dresses over one arm.

'Hello, Jack, I'm just getting a few of my things together.'

That she had lived with Faulkner on occasions was no surprise to him. She moved away and he said quickly, 'He didn't kill Grace Packard, Joanna.'

She turned slowly. 'What did you say?'

'The police had already charged the girl's boyfriend when we got there. They have a full confession and corroborating evidence.'

'But Bruno said . . .'

Her voice trailed away and 'Morgan put a hand on her arm gently. 'I know what he said, Joanna, but it wasn't true. He was trying to teach us some sort of lesson. He seemed to find the whole thing rather funny.'

'He doesn't change, does he?'

'I'm afraid not.'

'Where is he now?'

'He went out ahead of me. Last I saw he was going for a walk in the rain.'

She nodded briefly. 'Let's get out of here then – just give me a moment to get the rest of my things.'

'You don't want to see him?'

'Never again.'

There was a hard finality in her voice and she turned and went into the bedroom. Morgan followed and stood in the entrance watching. She laid her clothes across the bed and added one or two items which she took from a drawer in one of the dressing tables.

There was a fitted wardrobe against the wall, several suit-cases piled on top. She went across and reached up in vain.

'Let me,' Morgan said.

He grabbed the handle of the case which was bottom of the pile and eased it out. He frowned suddenly. 'Feels as if there's something in it.'

He put the case on the bed, flicked the catches and opened the lid. Inside there was a black plastic handbag, a silk headscarf, a nylon stocking and a high-heeled shoe.

Joanna Hartmann started to scream.

20

Strange, but it was so narrowly avoiding Miller in the park which finally made the Gunner's mind up for him, though not straight away. He waited until the detective had disappeared before emerging from the rhododendron bushes, damp and uncomfortable, his stomach hollow and empty.

He moved away in the opposite direction and finally came to another entrance to the park. Beyond the wrought iron gate he noticed some cigarette machines. He found the necessary coins from the money Jenny had given him, extracted a packet of ten cigarettes and a book of matches and went back into the park.

He started to walk again, smoking continuously, one cigarette after the other, thinking about everything that had happened since his dash from the Infirmary, but particularly about Jenny. He remembered the first time he had seen her from the loft, looking just about as good as a woman could. And the other things. Her ironic humour, her courage in a difficult situation, even the rough edge of her tongue. And when they had made love she had given every part of herself, holding nothing back – something he had never experienced in his life before. *And never likely to again* . . .

The thought pulled him up short and he stood there in the rain contemplating an eternity of being on his own for the first time in his life. Always to be running, always to be afraid because that was the cold fact of it. Scratching for a living, bedding with tarts, sinking fast all the time until someone turned him in for whatever it was worth.

The coppers never let go, never closed a case, that was the trouble. He thought of Miller. It was more than an hour since the detective had walked past the shelter and yet at the memory, the Gunner felt the same panic clutching at his guts, the same instinct to run and keep on running. *Well, to hell with that for a game of soldiers.* Better to face what there was to face and get it over than live like this. There was one cigarette left in the packet. He lit it, tossed the packet away and started to walk briskly towards the other side of the park.

A psychologist would have told him that making a definite decision, choosing a course of action, had resolved his conflict situation. The Gunner would have wondered what in the hell he was talking about. All he knew was that for some unaccountable reason he was cheerful again. One thing was certain – he'd give the bastards something to think about.

On the other side of the park he plunged into the maze of back streets in which he had been hunted during the previous night and worked his way towards the Infirmary. It occurred to him that it might be fun to turn up in the very room from which he had disappeared. But there were certain precautions to take first, just to make certain that the police could never link him with Jenny and her grandmother.

A few streets away from the Infirmary he stopped in a back alley at a spot where houses were being demolished as fast as the bulldozers could knock them down. On the other side of a low wall, a beck that was little more than a fast-flowing stream of filth rushed past and plunged into a dark tunnel that took it down into the darkness of the city's sewage system.

He took off the raincoat, sweater, boots and socks and dropped them in. They disappeared into the tunnel and he emptied his pockets. Three pound notes and a handful of change. The notes went fluttering down followed by the coins – all but a sixpenny piece. There was a telephone box at the end of the street . . .

He stood in the box and waited as the bell rang at the other end, shivering slightly as the cold struck into his bare feet and rain dripped down across his face. When she answered he could hardly get the coin into the slot for excitement.

'Jenny? It's the Gunner. Is anyone there?'

'Thank God,' she said, relief in her voice. 'Where are you?'

'A few hundred yards from the Infirmary. I'm turning myself in, Jenny. I thought you might like to know that.'

'Oh, Gunner.' He could have sworn she was crying, but that was impossible. She wasn't the type.

'What about the police?' he asked.

'No one turned up.'

'No one turned up?' he said blankly.

A sudden coldness touched his heart, something elemental, but before he could add anything Jenny said, 'Just a minute, Gunner, there's someone outside in the yard now.'

A moment later the line went dead.

'You fool,' the Gunner said aloud. 'You stupid bloody fool.'

Why on earth hadn't he seen it before? Only one person could possibly have known he was at the house and it certainly wasn't Ogden who hadn't even seen his face. But the other man had, the one who had attacked Jenny outside the door in the yard.

The Gunner left the phone box like a greyhound erupting from the trap and went down the street on the run. He turned the corner and was already some yards along the pavement when he saw the motorcycle parked at the kerb half-way along. The policeman who was standing beside it was making an entry in his book.

The policeman glanced up just before the Gunner arrived and they met breast-to-breast. There was the briefest of struggles before the policeman went down and the Gunner swung a leg over the motorcycle and kicked the starter.

He let out the throttle too fast so that the machine skidded away from the kerb, the front wheel lifting. It was only then that he became aware of the Mini-Cooper at the other end of the street. As he roared towards it, the little car swung broadside on to block his exit. The Gunner threw the bike over so far that the footrest brought sparks from the cobbles, and shaved the bonnet of the Mini-Cooper. For a brief, time-less moment he looked into Miller's face, then he was away.

In the grey afternoon and the heavy rain it was impossible to distinguish the features of the man in the yard at any distance and at first Jenny thought it must be Ogden. Even when the telephone went dead she felt no panic. It was only when she pressed her face to the window and saw Faulkner turn from the wall no more than a yard away, a piece of the telephone line still in his right hand that fear seized her by the throat. She recognized him instantly as her attacker of the previous night and in that moment everything fell neatly into place. The mysterious telephone call, the threat of the police who had never come – all to get rid of the only man who could have protected her.

'Oh, Gunner, God help me now.' The words rose in her throat, almost choking her as she turned and stumbled into the hall.

The outside door was still locked and bolted. The handle turned slowly and there was a soft, discreet knocking. For a moment her own fear left her as she remembered the old woman who still lay in bed, her Sunday habit. Whatever happened she must be protected.

Ma Crowther lay propped against the pillars, a shawl around her shoulders as she read one of her regular half-dozen Sunday newspapers. She glanced up in surprise as the door opened and Jenny appeared.

'You all right, Gran?'

'Yes, love, what is it?'

'Nothing to worry about. I just want you to stay in here for a while, that's all.'

There was a thunderous knocking from below. Jenny quickly extracted the key on the inside of her grandmother's door, slammed it shut and locked it as the old woman called out to her in alarm.

The knocking on the front door had ceased, but as she went down the stairs, there was the sound of breaking glass from the living-room. When she looked in he was smashing the window methodically with an old wooden clothes prop from the yard. She closed the door of the room, locked it on the outside and went up to the landing.

Her intention was quite clear. When he broke through the flimsy interior door, which wouldn't take long, she would give him a sight of her and then run for the roof. If she could climb across to the metalworks and get down the fire escape there might still be a chance. In any case, she would have led him away from her grandmother.

The door suddenly burst outwards with a great splintering crash and Bruno Faulkner came through with it, fetching up against the opposite wall. He looked up at her for a long moment, his face grave, and started to unbutton his raincoat. He tossed it to one side and put his foot on the bottom step. There was an old wooden chair on the landing. Jenny picked it up and hurled it down at him. He ducked and it missed him, bouncing from the wall.

He looked up at her still calm and then howled like an animal, smashing the edge of his left hand hard against the wooden banister rail. The rail snapped in half, a sight so incredible that she screamed for the first time in her life.

She turned and ran along the landing to the second staircase and Faulkner went after her. At the top of the stairs she was delayed for a moment as she wrestled with the bolt on the door that led to the roof. As she got it open, he appeared at the bottom.

She ran out into the heavy rain, kicked off her shoes and started up the sloping roof, her stocking feet slipping on the wet tiles. She was almost at the top when she slipped back to the bottom. Again she tried, clawing desperately towards the ridge tiles as Faulkner appeared from the stairway.

She stuck half-way and stayed here, spread-eagled,

caught like a fly on paper. And he knew it, that terrible
man below. He came forward slowly and stood there looking
up at her. And then he laughed and it was the coldest laugh
she had ever heard in her life.

He started forward and the Gunner came through the door
like a thunderbolt. Faulkner turned, swerved like a ballet
dancer and sent him on his way with a back-handed blow
that caught him across the shoulders. The Gunner lost his
balance, went sprawling, rolled beneath the rail at the far end
and went down the roof that sloped to the yard below.

The Gunner skidded to a halt outside Crowther's yard and
dropped the motorcycle on its side no more than four or
five minutes after leaving the phone box. He went for the
main gate on the run and disappeared through the judas
as the Mini-Cooper turned the corner.

It was Mallory who went after him first, mainly because
he already had his door open when Miller was still braking,
but there was more to it than that. For some reason he felt
alive again in a way he hadn't done for years. It was just
like it used to be in the old days as a young probationer in
Tower Bridge Division working the docks and the Pool of
London. A punch-up most nights and on a Saturday
anything could happen and usually did.

The years slipped away from him as he went through the
judas on the run in time to see the Gunner scrambling
through the front window. Mallory went after him, stumbling
over the wreckage of the door on his way into the hall.

He paused for a brief moment, aware of the Gunner's
progress above him and went up the stairs quickly. By the
time he reached the first landing, his chest was heaving
and his mouth had gone bone dry as he struggled for air,
but nothing on earth was going to stop him now.

As he reached the bottom of the second flight of stairs, the
Gunner went through the open door at the top. A moment

later there was a sudden sharp cry. Mallory was perhaps half-way up the stairs when the girl started to scream.

Faulkner had her by the left ankle and was dragging her down the sloping roof when Mallory appeared. In that single moment the whole thing took on every aspect of some privileged nightmare. His recognition of Faulkner was instantaneous, and at the same moment, a great many facts he had refused to face previously, surfaced. As the girl screamed again, he charged.

In his day George Mallory had been a better than average rugby forward and for one year Metropolitan Police light-heavyweight boxing champion. He grabbed Faulkner by the shoulder, pulled him around and swung the same right cross that had earned him his title twenty-seven years earlier. It never landed. Faulkner blocked the punch, delivered a forward elbow strike that almost paralysed Mallory's breathing system and snapped his left arm like a rotten branch with one devastating blow with the edge of his right hand. Mallory groaned and went down. Faulkner grabbed him by the scruff of the neck and started to drag him along the roof towards the railing.

For Miller it was as if somehow all this had happened before. As he came through the door and paused, thunder split the sky apart overhead and the rain increased into a solid grey curtain that filled the air with a strange, sibilant rushing sound and reduced visibility to a few yards.

He took in everything in a single moment. The girl with her dress half-ripped from her body, crouched at the foot of the sloping roof crying hysterically, and Faulkner who had now turned to look towards the door, still clutching Mallory's coat collar in his right hand.

Faulkner. A strange fierce exhilaration swept through Miller, a kind of release of every tension that had knotted up inside him during the past twenty-four hours. A release that came from knowing that he had been right all along.

He moved in on the run, jumped high in the air and delivered a flying front kick, the devastating mae-tobi-geri, full into Faulkner's face, one of the most crushing of all karate blows. Faulkner staggered back, releasing his hold on Mallory, blood spurting from his mouth and Miller landed awkwardly, slipping in the rain and falling across Mallory.

Before he could scramble to his feet, Faulkner had him by the throat. Miller summoned every effort of will-power and spat full in the other man's face. Faulkner recoiled in a kind of reflex action and Miller stabbed at his exposed throat with stiffened fingers.

Faulkner went back and Miller took his time over getting up, struggling for air. It was a fatal mistake, for a blow which would have demolished any ordinary man had only succeeded in shaking Faulkner's massive strength. As Miller straightened, Faulkner moved in like the wind and delivered a fore-fist punch, knuckles extended, that fractured two ribs like matchwood and sent Miller down on one knee with a cry of agony.

Faulkner drew back his foot and kicked him in the stomach. Miller went down flat on his face. Faulkner lifted his foot to crush the skull and Jenny Crowther staggered forward and clutched at his arm. He brushed her away as one might a fly on a summer's day and turned back to Miller. It was at that precise moment that the Gunner reappeared.

The Gunner's progress down the sloping roof had been checked by the presence of an ancient Victorian cast iron gutter twice the width of the modern variety. He had hung there for some time contemplating the cobbles of the yard thirty feet below. Like Jenny in a similar situation, he had found progress up a steeply sloping bank of Welsh slate in heavy rain a hazardous undertaking. He finally reached for the rusting railings above his head and pulled himself over in time to see Faulkner hurl the girl from him and turn to Miller.

The Gunner, silent on bare feet, delivered a left and a right to Faulkner's kidneys that sent the big man staggering forward with a scream of pain. As he turned, the Gunner stepped over Miller and let Faulkner have his famous left arm screw punch under the ribs followed by a right to the jaw, a combination that had finished no fewer than twelve of his professional fights inside the distance.

Faulkner didn't go down, but he was badly rattled. 'Come on then, you bastard,' the Gunner yelled. 'Let's be having you.'

Miller pushed himself up on one knee and tried to lift Mallory into a sitting position. Jenny Crowther crawled across to help and pillowed Mallory's head against her shoulder. He nodded, face twisted in pain, unable to speak and Miller folded his arms tightly about his chest and coughed as blood rose into his mouth.

There had been a time when people had been glad to pay as much as fifty guineas to see Gunner Doyle in action, but up there on the roof in the rain, Miller, the girl and Mallory had a ringside seat for free at his last and greatest battle.

He went after Faulkner two-handed, crouched like a tiger. Faulkner was hurt – hurt badly, and the Gunner had seen enough to know that his only chance lay in keeping him in that state. He swayed to one side as Faulkner threw a punch and smashed his left into the exposed mouth that was already crushed and bleeding from Miller's efforts. Faulkner cried out in pain and the Gunner gave him a right that connected just below the eye and moved close.

'Keep away from him,' Miller yelled. 'Don't get too close.'

The Gunner heard only the roar of the crowd as he breathed in the stench of the ring – that strange never-to-be-forgotten compound of human sweat, heat, and embrocation.

He let Faulkner have another right to the jaw to straighten him up and stepped in close for a blow to the heart that might finish the job. It was his biggest mistake. Faulkner pivoted, delivering an elbow strike backwards that doubled the Gunner over. In the same moment Faulkner turned again, lifting the Gunner backwards with a knee in the face delivered with such force that he went staggering across the roof and fell heavily against the railing. It sagged, half-breaking and he hung there trying to struggle to his feet, blood pouring from his nose and mouth. Faulkner charged in like a runaway express train, shoulder down and sent him back across the railing. The Gunner rolled over twice on the way down, bounced across the broad iron gutter and fell to the cobbles below.

Faulkner turned slowly, a terrifying sight, eyes glaring, blood from his mouth soaking down into his collar. He snarled at the three of them helpless before him, grabbed at the sagging iron railing and wrenched a four-foot length of it free. He gave a kind of animal-like growl and started forward.

Ma Crowther stepped through the door at the head of the stairs, still in her nightdress, clutching her sawn-off shotgun against her breast. Faulkner didn't see her, so intent was he on the task before him. He poised over his three victims, swinging the iron bar high above his head like an executioner, and she gave him both barrels full in the face.

21

It was almost nine o'clock in the evening when Miller and Jenny Crowther walked along the second-floor corridor of the Marsden Wing of the General Infirmary towards the room in which they had put Gunner Doyle.

They walked slowly because Miller wasn't in any fit state to do anything else. His body seemed to be bruised all over and he was strapped up so tightly because of his broken ribs, that he found breathing difficult. He was tired. A hell of a lot had happened since that final terrible scene on the roof and with Mallory on his back, he had been the only person capable of handling what needed to be done. A series of pain-killing injections weren't helping any and he was beginning to find difficulty in thinking straight any more.

The constable on the chair outside the door stood up and Miller nodded familiarly. 'Look after Miss Crowther for a few minutes will you, Harry? I want a word with the Gunner.'

The policeman nodded, Miller opened the door and went in. There was a screen on the other side of the door and beyond it the Gunner lay propped against the pillows, his nose broken for the fourth time in his life, his right leg in traction, fractured in three places.

Jack Brady sat in a chair on the far side of the bed reading his notebook. He got up quickly. 'I've got a statement from him. He insists that he forced his way into the house last night; that Miss Crowther and her grandmother only allowed him to stay under duress.'

'Is that a fact?' Miller looked down at the Gunner and shook his head. 'You're a poor liar, Gunner. The girl's already given us a statement that clarifies the entire situation. She says that when you saved her from Faulkner in the yard, she and her grandmother felt that they owed you something. She seems to think that's a good enough defence even in open court.'

'What do you think?' the Gunner said weakly.

'I don't think it will come to court so my views don't count. You put up the fight of your life back there on the roof. Probably saved our lives.'

'Oh, get stuffed,' the Gunner said. 'I want to go to sleep.'

'Not just yet. I've got a visitor for you.'

'Jenny?' The Gunner shook his head. 'I don't want to see her.'

'She's been waiting for hours.'

'What in the hell does she want to see me for? There's nothing to bleeding well say, is there? I'll lose all my remission over this little lot. I'm going back to the nick for another two and a half years plus anything else the beak likes to throw at me for the things I've done while I've been out. On top of that I'll be dragging this leg around behind me like a log of wood for the rest of my life when I get out.'

'And a bloody good thing as well,' Brady said brutally. 'No more climbing for you, my lad.'

'I'll get her now,' Miller said. 'You can see her alone. We'll wait outside.'

The Gunner shrugged. 'Suit yourself.'

Miller and Brady went out and a second later, the girl came round the screen and stood at the end of the bed. Her face was very pale and there was a nasty bruise on her forehead, but she was still about fifty times better in every possible way than any other woman he'd ever met. There was that strange choking feeling in his throat again. He was tired and in great pain. He was going back to gaol for what seemed like forever and for the first time he was afraid of the prospect. He felt just like a kid who had been hurt. He wanted to have her come round the bed and kiss him, smooth back his hair, pillow his head on her shoulder.

But that was no good – no good at all. What he did now was the most courageous thing he had ever done in his entire life, braver by far than his conduct on the roof when facing Faulkner.

He smiled brightly. 'Surprise, surprise. What's all this?'

'I've been waiting for hours. They wouldn't let me in before. Gran sends her regards.'

'How is she?' The Gunner couldn't resist the question.

'They tell me she finished him off good and proper up there. How's she taken it? Flat on her back?'

'Not her – says she'd do it again any day. They've told you who he was?' The Gunner nodded and she went on, 'I was in such a panic when he started smashing his way in that I locked her in the bedroom and forgot all about the shotgun. She keeps it in the wardrobe. She had to shoot the lock off to get out.'

'Good job she arrived when she did from what they tell me.'

There was a slight silence and she frowned. 'Is anything wrong, Gunner?'

'No – should there be?'

'You seem funny, that's all.'

'That's me all over, darlin'. To tell you the truth I was just going to get some shut-eye when you turned up.'

Her face had gone very pale now. 'What is it, Gunner? what are you trying to say?'

'What in the hell am I supposed to say?' He snapped back at her, genuinely angry. 'Here I am flat on my back like a good little lad. In about another month they'll stick me in a big black van and take me back where I came from. That's what you wanted, isn't it?'

She had gone very still. 'I thought it was what *you* wanted – really wanted.'

'And how in the hell would you know what I want?'

'I've been about as close to you as any woman could get and . . .'

He cut in sharply with a laugh that carried just the right cutting edge to it. 'Do me a favour, darlin'. No bird gets close to me. Just because I've had you between the sheets doesn't mean I've sold you the rights to the story of my life for the Sunday papers. It was very nice – don't get me wrong. You certainly know what to do with it, but I've got other fish to fry now.'

She swayed. For a moment it seemed as if she might fall and then she turned and went out. The Gunner closed his eyes. He should have felt noble. He didn't. He felt sick and afraid and more alone than he had ever done in his life before.

The girl was crying when she came out of the room. She kept on going, head-down and Miller went after her. He caught her, swung her round and shoved her against the wall.

'What happened in there?'

'He made it pretty clear what he really thinks about me, that's all,' she said. 'Can I go now?'

'Funny how stupid intelligent people can be sometimes,' Miller shook his head wearily. 'Use your head, Jenny. When he left your house he was wearing shoes and a raincoat, had money in his pocket – money you'd given him. Why did he telephone you?'

'To say he was giving himself up.'

'Why was he barefooted again? Why had he got rid of the clothes you gave him? Why did he come running like a bat out of hell when you were in danger?'

She stared at him, eyes wide and shook her head. 'But he was rotten in there – he couldn't have done more if he'd spat on me.'

'Exactly the result he was hoping for, can't you see that?' Miller said gently. 'The biggest proof of how much he thinks of you is the way he's just treated you.' He took her arm. 'Let's go back inside. You stay behind the screen and keep your mouth shut and I'll prove it to you.'

The Gunner was aware of the click of the door opening, there was a soft footfall and he opened his eyes and looked up at Miller. 'What do you want now, copper?'

'Congratulations,' Miller said. 'You did a good job – on the girl, I mean. Stupid little tart like that deserves all she gets.'

It was all it took. The Gunner tried to sit up, actually

tried to get at him. 'You dirty bastard. She's worth ten of you – any day of the week. In my book you aren't fit to clean her shoes.'

'Neither are you.'

'The only difference between us is I know it. Now get to hell out of here and leave me alone.'

He closed his eyes as Miller turned on her and limped out. The door clicked and there was only the silence. He heard no sound and yet something seemed to move and then there was the perfume very close.

He opened his eyes and found her bending over him. 'Oh, Gunner,' she said. 'Whatever am I going to do with you?'

Miller sat on the end of Mallory's bed to make his report. The Chief Superintendent had a room to himself in the private wing as befitted his station. There were already flowers in the corner and his wife was due to arrive within the hour.

'So you've left them together?' Mallory said.

Miller nodded. 'He isn't going to run anywhere.'

'What about the leg? How bad is it?'

'Not too good, according to the consultant in charge. He'll be lame for the rest of his life. It could have been worse, mind you.'

'No more second-storey work at any rate,' Mallory commented.

'Which could make this injury a blessing in disguise,' Miller pointed out.

Mallory shook his head. 'I hardly think so. Once a thief always a thief and Doyle's a good one – up there with the best. Clever, resourceful, highly intelligent. When you think of it, he hasn't done anything like the time he should have considering what he's got away with in the past. He'll find something else that's just as crooked, mark my words.'

Which was probably true, but Miller wasn't going down without a fight. 'On the other hand if he hadn't been around last night Jenny Crowther would have been number five on Faulkner's list and we'd have been no further forward. I'd also like to point out that we'd have been in a damn bad way without him up there on the roof.'

'Which is exactly how the newspapers and the great British public will see it, Miller,' Mallory said. 'You needn't flog it to death. As a matter of interest I've already dictated a report for the Home Secretary in which I state that in my opinion Doyle had earned any break we can give him.'

Miller's tiredness dropped away like an old cloak. 'What do you think that could mean – a pardon?'

Mallory laughed out loud. 'Good God, no. If he's lucky, they'll release him in ten months on probation as they would have done anyway if he hadn't run for it.'

'Fair enough, sir.'

'No, it isn't, Miller. He'll be back. You'll see.'

'I'm putting my money on Jenny Crowther.' Miller got to his feet. 'I'd better go now, sir. You look as if you could do with some sleep.'

'And you look as if you might fall down at any moment.' Miller turned, a hand on the door and Mallory called, 'Miller?'

'Yes, sir?'

'Regarding that little wager of ours. I was right about Phillips – he killed Grace Packard just as I said, but taking everything else into consideration I've decided to give you your pound back, and no arguments.'

He switched off the light with his good hand and Miller went out, closing the door softly behind him.

He took the lift down to the entrance hall and found Jack Brady standing outside the night sister's small glass office talking to her. They turned as Miller came forward and the sister frowned.

'You look awful. You should be in your bed, really you should.'

'Is that an invitation, Sister?' Miller demanded and kissed her on the cheek.

Brady tapped out his pipe and slipped a hand under Miller's arm. 'Come on, Nick, let's go.'

'Go where?'

'The nearest pub. I'd like to see What a large whisky does for you, then I'll take you home.'

'You're an Irish gentleman, Jack. God bless you for the kind thought.'

They went out through the glass doors. The rain had stopped and Miller took a deep breath of fresh, damp air. 'Hell is always today, Jack, never tomorrow. Have you ever noticed that?'

'It's all that keeps a good copper going,' Brady said and they went down the steps together.

ABOUT THE AUTHOR

Jack Higgins lived in Belfast till the age of twelve. Leaving school at fifteen, he spent three years with the Royal Horse Guards, serving on the East German border during the Cold War. His subsequent employment included occupations as diverse as circus roustabout, truck driver, clerk and, after taking an honours degree specializing in Psychology and Criminology, was a teacher and university lecturer.

His thirty-sixth novel, *The Eagle Has Landed* (1975), turned him into an international bestselling author, and his novels have since sold over 250 million copies and have been translated into sixty languages. In addition to *The Eagle Has Landed*, ten of them have been made into successful films. His more recent bestselling novels include *A Devil is Waiting*, *The Death Trade*, *Rain on the Dead* and *The Midnight Bell*, all of which were *Sunday Times* bestsellers.

In 1995 Jack Higgins was awarded an honorary doctorate by Leeds Metropolitan University. He is a fellow of the Royal Society of Arts and an expert scuba diver and marksman. In 2014 he was awarded an honorary degree by the University of London. He died in 2022, at his home in Jersey, surrounded by his family.